Burn Me From the Inside

Scorched Memories
Book 1

Laci Mae Wyld

Laci Mae Wyld
AUTHOR

This novel contains material that may be distressing for some readers. Themes and scenes include strong language, explicit sexual content, corruption and abuse of power, references to the death of a parent, arson, and threats of violence.

Reader discretion is advised.

I want to dedicate this book to the most inspirational person I have ever met, Matty. The happiest and most beautiful person in the world, who, no matter what challenges life throws your way, never lets it bring you down. You are a beacon of love and light, and everyone who has the privilege of meeting you loves you.

Love you, Matty.

Contents

1

Ashes in Her Wake

Sophie

The "Welcome to Willow Creek" sign still stands at the town limits, its cheerful paint job only slightly faded after all these years, but I catch the new layer of rust clinging to the bolts. It wasn't there a decade ago, when I'd last sped beneath its arch with the windows down, a mixtape playing over the wind's howl, and a future that felt heartbreaking. Now, ten years and one ruined career later, my knuckles blanch against the steering wheel as I crawl past it at the posted speed limit, windows up, AC humming, the trunk packed to the hinges with everything I couldn't stand to leave in storage.

There's that antique store—now a vape shop—and the mural on Main Street, the one of the blue herons, a little less blue and a little more washed out. I drag my gaze over the storefronts, clocking each change: the new awnings on O'Connell's Pharmacy, the double-stacked. "Help Wanted" sign taped to the bakery window. Everything's the same, and nothing is. A decade telescopes in and out, sometimes it feels like ten minutes, sometimes like a hundred years, depending on what corner I turn.

I try to convince myself I'm invisible behind the windshield, but the eyes are always there. At the first red light, a pair of teenagers in logo hoodies gives my beat-up Toyota a once-over. I clock a woman outside a salon, phone to her ear, squinting like she's trying to summon a name from my face. For a second, I consider driving straight through town and not stopping until I hit a coast or a city that never heard of me. But I hear my aunt's voice, "Handle my estate with your head held high, Sophia." She only called me Sophia when she meant business.

The lot outside Wilson's Grocery is half-full. I steer between a Subaru with flower decals and a work van sporting the fire department's logo, which I pointedly ignore. If I time my shopping right, I might not have to see anyone who remembers me. I might even make it to the house before dark, where the keys to the house and whatever's left of my childhood await.

Inside, the place smells exactly as I remember: the slightly stale chill, the undercurrent of detergent and bruised fruit. I dodge the endcap displays, keeping my eyes on the floor tiles and my head angled low. It's amazing how little muscle memory you lose, within thirty seconds, I'm two aisles deep, already plotting the shortest route through perishables and snacks before escape.

I was determined to buy something with color to prove I ate like a grown-up.

I'm halfway down the bread aisle when I catch movement at the endcap, and for a split second, my body goes rigid. A tall man in a navy t-shirt with the store logo stenciled over the breast pocket, khakis just a hair too fitted for a stock boy. He's pulling flats of bagels from a rolling cart, arms straining under the weight. I relax. I don't know him. I ease the cart past the open boxes, grab a loaf of whole wheat, and move on.

Only when I round the corner do I spot the next threat: a flash of red hair, a boom of laughter, a mother I once babysat for whose daughter got suspended for smoking in the teachers' lounge, my senior year. She's older now, more lined around the eyes, but her stare still lands like a thumbtack in the heel. I pivot sharply into the canned goods section, nearly colliding with a pyramid of off-brand soup.

I THINK I'M SAFE, AT LEAST UNTIL CHECK-OUT, BUT AS IT turns out, fate is a fucking asshole.

BECAUSE THEN, IN THE ANTISEPTIC FLUORESCENCE OF Aisle 6, I see him, Lucas Hayes.

HE'S A DIFFERENT ANIMAL THAN THE BOY I KNEW: broader shoulders, tighter in the jaw, blue eyes hyper-focused on the shelf in front of him. There's a paleness to his skin now, the kind that comes from too many overnight shifts and not enough real food, and his hair is cut close to the scalp, the way he wore it after the fire academy. He's not in uniform, but he doesn't need it. You could throw him into any city in the world, and he'd still read as a firefighter: the way he scans a room, the way he sets his feet for quick movement, the way the veins pop along his forearms even at rest.

I try to reverse course, but the cart betrays me. Its janky

wheel rattles against a box of pancake mix, and he looks up—right at me.

For a long, unblinking second, we just stare. My hands go clammy on the plastic handle. I feel my pulse spike, hot and reckless, beneath my skin.

"Sophie," he says, first. He doesn't even try for the small talk smile.

"Lucas." I match his lack of inflection, my voice miraculously even.

He looks me over, eyes flicking to the groceries in my cart, then back to my face. "Back for long?"

"Just enough to close out my aunt's place. I'm not a glutton for punishment." My words come out crisp, polished, and sharp by a thousand imaginary versions of this conversation.

His mouth twitches. Not quite a smile, more like an aborted attempt at one. "If you need help, moving furniture, or whatever, I'm around. I was sorry to hear about your Aunt, she was a good person." His tone is businesslike, the same one he probably uses when offering to rescue cats from trees. I have no idea if he expects gratitude or a fight.

I give him a tight nod. "Thanks," I wasn't prepared for condolences. "I'll keep that in mind."

He steps to the side, like he's going to let me pass, but he doesn't really move. I have to edge my cart around him, and in doing so, my bare elbow grazes his t-shirt. It's nothing, a stupid accidental touch, but every nerve in my arm lights up with it. I don't look back.

At the end of the aisle, I can feel his stare like a pressure point between my shoulder blades.

The rest of the trip goes mercifully fast. I pay cash,

BAG MY OWN GROCERIES, AND BOLT FOR THE EXIT. THE sunlight is so bright outside, I actually flinch.

Only once I'm in the safety of my car, bags dumped onto the passenger seat, do I let myself breathe. My hands are still shaking, but I force them to be steady. There is no reason to feel rattled. I'm a grown-ass woman. I have lived through far worse than this, than him, in this town.

In the rearview mirror, I see Lucas exit the store, a single bag in hand. He doesn't look for me, but he stands by the curb for a long minute, his silhouette clean and unyielding against the town I tried to leave behind.

I peel out of the lot, feeling more seen than I have in years.

The second time I see Lucas, he's screaming at a rookie while a six-foot geyser of water hisses over the wreckage of my aunt's backyard shed.

I'M STILL IN JEANS AND A TANK TOP, HANDS SMUDGED with newsprint from digging through boxes that smell like ancient lavender and mothballs. The only thing more exhausting than sorting the possessions of the dead is fielding the constant mental landmines—every chipped mug, every battered paperback, a new opportunity to remember. I'm going elbow-deep in a bin of old photo albums when the smoke alarm chirps.

At first, I think it's a battery thing. The house is full of that sad, sour scent unique to homes nobody's lived in for a while, and the alarms look older than me. But then a second alarm goes off, somewhere near the back door, and I catch the unmistakable whiff of something burning.

Adrenaline is a strange thing—it makes everything both slower and louder. I drop the album, run barefoot through the kitchen, and slam into the mudroom door so hard it rattles on its hinges. The backyard is soaked in late-day sun, all warm gold and green, except for the furious black column rising behind the shed.

The old shed, the one with the painted blue door where I used to play house with dolls and imaginary friends, is half-eclipsed by the smoke. Flames snarl along the roofline, eating it from the top down. For a wild second, I can hear my dad's voice, "No, no, always call the professionals, don't be a hero, Soph", but all I can think is I don't want this fire touching the main house, not after everything else.

I fumble my phone out of my pocket, then dial 911 with hands that won't stay still. The operator is calm, practiced, a series of yes ma'am's and what's your address, but I'm already backing out of the kitchen door, barefoot in dry grass, looking for a hose, a bucket, anything.

THE GARDEN HOSE IS KINKED AND TANGLED LIKE NOBODY'S touched it since before my aunt got sick. I manage to wrestle it halfway across the lawn and turn the nozzle at the shed. The water pressure is pitiful, and that blast only makes the smoke billow faster, swirling with an acrid, oily tang that makes my lungs seize. I cough, stumble back, feel the heat roll off the structure in slow, hungry pulses. Useless. I am so goddamn useless.

By the time I hear the sirens, I'm half-sitting, half-crouched behind the withered rhododendrons, hose forgotten at my feet, watching my childhood in flames.

The firetruck tears down the drive, tires biting into the gravel so hard I think they might break through the bedrock. A pair of uniformed men leap out, already dragging hoses and barking orders before the engine is even off. And then, of course, there's Lucas.

He's in turnout gear, the jacket unzipped and hanging off his hips, helmet in one hand. For the second time today, I get the full effect of him—the way he's grown into his own gravity, the kind of man who could walk into a burning building and expect the building to apologize. He's shouting over the wind and the pop of splintering wood, and for a second, his eyes rake the yard like he's searching. When he finds me, crouched in the weeds, he holds my gaze for just long enough that I feel pinned in place. Then he's all motion—directing the crew, flanking the blaze, setting up a perimeter in the neat choreography of someone who's done this a hundred times.

It takes less than ten minutes. The crew punches holes in the shed walls, sending dense smoke pouring out the sides. The fire gutters, then goes out with a petulant hiss, like it's being robbed of its purpose. Lucas circles the remains, boots crunching on soaked ash, then walks up to me with a posture so squared-off I almost laugh.

"Are you hurt?" he asks bluntly.

I shake my head. My voice is a scratchy mess. "Fine. Just inhaled half a lung's worth."

"Ambulance is on the way. Get checked out." He doesn't ask; it's an order.

I want to protest—tell him to mind his own business, that

I'm not the one on fire—but the look in his eyes makes it clear there's no point. He stares at the ruined shed for a moment, jaw working in that way that always made me swoon, then says, "You try the garden hose?"

I look at my feet, at the limp, leaking line snaking across the lawn. "Not my finest moment."

He shrugs. "It's what most people do. Usually just spreads the fire."

"You'd think I'd know better. My dad lectured me about this crap every summer."

He glances at me, something unreadable in his expression. "It's different when you're standing in front of it."

THE ROOKIE—PROBABLY BARELY OUT OF HIGH SCHOOL—shuffles over with a clipboard and starts asking questions about insurance, combustibles, and when I noticed the smoke. I answer on autopilot, numbly ticking through the details. Lucas hovers nearby, listening but not interrupting. When the questions are done, the rookie hands me a business card and jogs back to the engine.

For a minute, the only sounds are the groan of cooling wood and the far-off drone of some traffic. The smell is pure nostalgia: wet ash, charred wood, the metallic aftertaste of adrenaline.

Lucas stands with his hand on his hips, eyes fixed on the wreckage. I know the shape of this silence. It's the same one that fell between us the last night we spoke, years ago, when neither of us could think of the right thing to say, so we just let everything burn down.

"DO YOU WANT TO KNOW WHAT I THINK?" HE SAYS, finally.

I cross my arms. "You're going to tell me anyway."

He lets out a short, humorless laugh. "Probably." He turns to face me, blue eyes sharper than they have any right to be after a day like this. "That wasn't accidental. The way it took off? The speed, the smoke color? Somebody started it. I'd bet on it."

I feel my mouth go dry. "You think it was arson. Out here?"

He shrugs, but it's a hard, angry motion. "Could be a prank, could be something else. But it wasn't an accident. Not unless your aunt was stockpiling lighter fluid in there."

I TRY TO REMEMBER WHAT WAS EVEN IN THAT SHED. OLD bikes, paint cans, garden tools. My aunt was a lot of things, but a firebug and careless wasn't one of them.

Lucas studies me for a long second. "I'll come by tomorrow. Walk the property, see if anything looks off."

I bristle. "I can handle it. I'm not a helpless—"

He cuts me off, voice low but edged. "Never said you were. But this is what I do, Sophie. Let me help."

The last word lands heavy between us, more like a plea than an offer. I force myself to look away, at the ruin of the shed, the soggy mess where so many half-formed childhood memories used to live. I remember the way my aunt would say, in that voice that brokered no argument, "You can ask for help and still be strong." I hated that then. I hate it now.

"Fine," I say, softly. "Tomorrow."

He nods, and for the briefest second, there's a flicker of something in his face—a relief, a regret, or just the ghost of an old feeling neither of us has the vocabulary for anymore. Then the moment snaps, and he's back to business.

He tells me to stay inside, that he'll file the report, and that the crew will be gone soon. I watch as he strides away, calling out orders with a voice that could peel paint, moving with the kind of certainty I can only fake.

I don't realize how cold my feet are until I step back into the kitchen. I leave ash prints on the linoleum all the way to the sink.

For a long time, I just stand there, trying to remember what I was unpacking before the fire started. But all I can see is the way Lucas looked at me through the smoke, like there was something left to salvage.

Lucas comes by just after noon, right on time, not that I was watching the clock.

I've managed to transform my aunt's kitchen from a catastrophic hoarder's den to a functional war zone overnight. The sink is piled with old cutlery, and the counter is a graveyard for appliance manuals and the kind of mismatched mugs that only exist in homes predating running water. I'm sorting legal pads into 'useful' and 'psychotic scrawlings' when the screen door rattles.

He doesn't knock. He just walks in like he belongs here, like it's still his job to save me from burning houses and small-town politics and my own worst ideas. There's a dusting of soot on his work boots, but otherwise, he's so clean and precise he might as well have stepped off a recruitment poster.

"Morning," he says, his eyes are different in daylight, less stormy, more focused.

"Coffee?" I say, because I'm not actually a monster, and also because I need the excuse to turn my back.

"I'm good." He stands in the center of the room, refusing

the invitation to sit, hands deep in his pockets, eyes tracing every movement I make.

I finish pouring my cup and lean against the counter. "Find anything?"

He tilts his head, and for a second, I remember every summer we spent on the high school debate team, arguing each other's points so fiercely that the teacher had to separate us. "Accelerant. On the north side of the wall. Looks like gasoline."

A flicker of fear, then irritation, passes through me. "Kids screwing around, or are you expecting an old family nemesis to pop out of the hydrangeas?"

He shrugs. "Maybe just kids. But the fire's too clean for amateurs.

I laugh, a brittle sound. "If you're angling for a security system referral, I'll save you the pitch. I don't know how long I'm staying, I could be out of here in a week."

He moves in closer, dropping the sarcasm. "That's the thing, Sophie. It doesn't make sense. Nobody lights a fire for no reason, not on a property like this."

I stare him down, refusing to give ground. "Unless they're bored. Or trying to send a message. Which would be a waste, because there's nothing here to fight over anymore."

He holds my gaze. "You sure about that?"

Something ugly bubbles up. "You think I'm being targeted? For what? Being the last Grant standing? News flash, Lucas, I peaked at seventeen, and I'm not interesting enough for conspiracy theories."

He sighs, but then he steps so close I can count the flecks of green in his blue eyes. "You never give yourself enough credit," he says, voice dropping, "and you always downplay danger until it's too late."

"And you always pretend you're not enjoying the hero routine." The words are out before I can snatch them back.

He smiles, but it's a knife-edge. "It's not about being a hero."

"No?" I snort, crossing my arms. "Then what is it?"

He looks at me, really looks, and for a second, all the fight goes out of him. "It's about you. It always has been."

I'm thrown so hard I almost spill my coffee.

"Bullshit," I manage, but my voice comes out thin. "You don't get to disappear for a decade and then act like you still know me."

He leans in, hands braced on either side of my shoulders, trapping me against the wall. His breath is warm, laced with the aftertaste of coffee and something sharper.

"I never stopped knowing you. Never stopped caring."

I can't breathe. Not with him this close, not with the echo of everything we never said.

"Let me go," I say, but my hands stay frozen at my sides.

He doesn't move, just stares at my mouth like he's memorizing it for a test he'll never have to take. "You want me to leave?"

I do. I don't. I hate that he can still short-circuit my brain with a single look.

"Lucas." It comes out as a warning, but also as a plea.

He leans in, lips just a hair from mine. "Yeah?"

I hate myself for it, but I don't turn away.

Then, as suddenly as he closed the distance, he pushes off the wall and takes two full steps back, as if he's afraid of what might happen next.

"We're not kids anymore," he says, roughly. "I can't—"

I find my voice, shaky but alive. "You can't what?"

He laughs, but it's a sound made of splinters. "I can't keep doing this to myself."

There's nothing left to say, so I watch him leave, footsteps heavy on the floorboards, the screen door banging behind him; it's the period at the end of a bad sentence.

For a long time after, I stay pressed against the wall, heart jackhammering, fingertips tingling with the memory of how close he got. I want to be furious at him, at myself, at the universe for orchestrating this rerun of our least graceful moments. Instead, I sip cold coffee and try to remember how to inhale without shaking.

That night, after I've made a meal out of microwaved soup and resentment, I walk out to the mailbox. The air smells like wet leaves and char. Somewhere far off, a dog is barking, mournful and relentless. The box is empty except for a single envelope, curled and brown along the edges like it spent too long over a flame.

No stamp, no address. Inside, a single scrap of paper:

Leave while you still can.

The handwriting is sharp, insistent. Ash falls away as I unfold it.

For a moment, I just stand there, the note smoldering between my fingers, while the sound of the woods and the echo of Lucas's voice fight for space in my head.

This was supposed to be a brief detour, a week's worth of paperwork and a thousand petty irritations, then freedom. But tonight, it feels like I'm in for the full burn.

2

Sparks and Silence

Lucas

The overhead lights in the Willow Creek firehouse are the kind that hum even when they're off, always a faint afterburn of energy stuck in the linoleum and cinderblock. I'm alone in the briefing room, where the only illumination is a crooked beam of late-afternoon sun and the greenish glow of my laptop's screen saver. It's not enough to read by, but I don't bother fixing it. Makes it easier to ignore the stacks of paperwork, the fire scene diagrams, and the printouts of blackened wood all scattered across the desk in front of me.

I stare down at the photos of what used to be Sophie Grant's shed, flipping one over to catch the fluorescent post-it I'd scribbled at three this morning: Unnatural V-pattern, north wall, traces indicate fuel source. I take a red pen and circle the burn lines, drawing them tighter and tighter until the paper gives out and the felt tip leaks through. It's the third time today I've done it, but the gesture never gets old—like if I squeeze the pen hard enough, I'll wring the answer straight out of the ink.

The room smells like instant coffee and fireman's sweat. My own hands still carry the tang of smoke, no matter how many times I scrub. Each time I look at the evidence, the whole incident replays behind my eyes: the quick bloom of flame, the metallic taste in my throat, Sophie in the yard with her hair yanked into a crooked bun and her arms crossed tight, as if she could keep her entire history from burning down by sheer force of will.

The radio crackles behind me. Some dispatcher is halfway through a weather update before cutting out, the signal garbled. It's all white noise, but it fills the space enough to keep my thoughts from getting too loud.

I shuffle the papers and hit the report again: Burn source low to the ground. Accelerant present. Substrate: aged wood and paint. There's a pattern here, but it's one I don't want to see. I stare at the pixelated chemical analysis on the screen and feel a knot go hard and sour just below my sternum.

The station's chief—just a few years from retirement, and already acting like he's dead to the world—sticks his head into the room. "Anything jump out at you, Hayes?"

I keep my posture neutral, but my voice turns cold. "Classic pour pattern, probably gas. Not an accident."

He gives a noncommittal grunt and tips his chin at my laptop. "Any suspects?"

I shake my head. "Not yet. I'll know more after I talk to the insurance guy." I don't mention that Sophie's the only one on the property, or that I think she is the target.

The chief watches me for a beat, then leaves without a word. I listen to his footsteps fade, then exhale for the first time in minutes.

The next photo is a close-up of the shed's entry point. I lean in until my nose nearly grazes the print, studying the way the paint blistered along the jamb. I can see the scaling of the paint, the old childhood carving into the wood of spirals and scratches. There's no mistaking it, the kind of fire that moves like this is personal. Someone wanted to see it catch. I can almost picture the bastard, hunched in the shadow of the garden fence, lighter in one hand and the other tight on the red plastic canister.

I'm so caught up in the geometry of destruction that the phone's buzz nearly tips my coffee. I slap at it, half-expecting another department update, but the screen lights with a name I can't ignore:

Sophie Grant: We need to talk.

I stare at it, thumb hovering, the blood in my ears so loud I'm surprised the radio can compete. For a second, I don't move. Ten years ago, a message from her would've had me sprinting out of my own skin. Now, it feels like a dare, or maybe a warning.

She texts again, before I even decide how to answer: Did you find something you're not telling me?

A small, involuntary smile twitches at the corner of my mouth. Even now, she knows how to get under my armor. I flick the phone face down and watch the screen pulse with unread alerts until it goes black. Instead of answering, I pick up the pen and set to work on the next photograph, my hand moving fast, angry. I mark up the floorboards, tracing the spill like a cartographer mapping out the last stand of a dying city.

A rookie wanders past the open door, a pizza box in hand. He stops, looks at the forensic tornado on my desk, and makes a half-hearted attempt at humor. "Late night, Lieutenant?"

"Not if I can help it," I say, eyes never leaving the desk. "You need something?"

He backs up, muttering, "Didn't mean to interrupt."

The place empties out again. I can feel the shift as the station changes guards, one crew winding down and another arriving, their chatter carrying just enough to let me know I'm not completely alone. But in here, it's just me and the ruins of an old shed, and the echo of Sophie's voice in my head—dry, cutting, always two steps ahead.

I try to focus on the facts. Standard procedure: establish timelines, gather witness statements, and run the labs. But I already know I'm not operating by the book. The accelerant pattern is wrong for an amateur prank; the ignition points are too precise, the aftermath almost surgical. It reeks of someone with a grudge, or maybe someone who wanted a message sent loud and clear.

I scroll through the incident log, my jaw clenching when I see Sophie's name next to mine in the response roster. It's not the first time our paths have crossed in a blaze, but it's the first time in years that the fire feels like an afterthought.

THE PHONE VIBRATES AGAIN. THIS TIME, I LET IT ring out.

I LEAN BACK IN THE CHAIR, RUNNING BOTH HANDS OVER my face until my vision goes swimmy with afterimages. If I close my eyes, I can still see the way she looked at me through the haze of smoke and regret—like she expected me to fix something I broke a decade ago, and maybe she's right.

The pen hovers over the next printout, but my hand won't move. I stare at the jagged edges of the burn, the black streaks spiderwebbing out from the origin point, and I see my own failure mapped out in negative space.

Outside, the sky goes from gray to black without warning. It'll be a long night, and I'll probably still be here when the sun comes up, pretending I'm just doing my job. But I know the real reason I can't let this go, and it has nothing to do with gasoline or accelerant patterns.

I grab the phone, scroll up to the last message, and type out a reply that isn't nearly enough:

Come by the station in the morning. We'll talk then.

I hit send, and the ache in my chest eases, just a little. I tell myself I'll sleep tonight. I tell myself a lot of things that don't happen.

I sit alone in the dark, waiting for the next fire.

The early morning cold creeps in through the seams of the firehouse, settling in the bones like a dare. I managed to get home for a shower and a quick kip, but I am back in before dawn, before the day shift clogs the lot with pickups and the first pot of coffee goes from burnt to black sludge. I have the place to myself, but it's not a luxury; it's a necessity. The only way I can stay ahead of the memories is by burying them under paperwork, and the shed fire's incident file is already as thick as a cinder block.

I'm at the conference table, sleeves rolled past the elbows, scanning through last night's raw data when the outer door slams. The sound ricochets down the hallway, too sharp to be the wind or the cleaning crew. There's a rhythm to the footsteps; they are deliberate, too quick for someone with nowhere to be at this hour. I look up, already knowing.

Sophie rounds the corner in jeans and a windbreaker, hair twisted up in a savage knot, eyes glassy but focused. Her mouth is tight, and there's residue of old mascara under her eyes, the way it always clung after a rough night. She carries a single manila envelope, burned at one end.

She doesn't waste a hello. "Did you get it?"

I have to fight the urge to stand. "Get what?"

Her hand shakes just a little as she slides the envelope across the table. The smell hits before it lands, a chemical, sooty tang that brings the shed fire right back to my sinuses. She waits, arms folded, daring me to dismiss it.

I pull out the note. The handwriting is crude, the words gouged into the page like someone hated the pen almost as much as the recipient:

LEAVE WHILE YOU STILL CAN

Even the letters look singed at the edges. Classic intimidation play, but the way her jaw locks, I know it's working. I look up. "When?"

"Last night late or early this morning. It was in the mailbox. No return address." She swallows, audibly. "I'm guessing it's related."

I nod, running my thumb along the charred paper. I don't say what I'm thinking: That it's too soon, too calculated. I can't help noticing the similarity in the small doodle of a spiral on the page and the carving at the shed fire. That this isn't the first time I've seen something like this, but it's the first time I've cared so much about the target.

Sophie stands there, rigid, as if she's braced for me to laugh it off. "Do you think it's the same person who lit the shed?"

"I'd bet on it," I say. "But arsonists don't usually escalate to threats unless the threat was the purpose of the fire or unless they want attention."

She lets out a short, brittle sound. "Congratulations. They have it."

The room goes silent except for the drone of the overheads and the tick of the wall clock. She breaks first, crossing to the coffee machine and slamming in a new filter. "You said you'd walk the property. Find anything?"

"Just confirmation. Someone poured gas along the north wall. Ignition was simple, possibly lighter or matches, but nothing was left behind." I hesitate, then add: "They knew what they were doing. This wasn't random."

She processes that, staring into the carafe like it might reveal a secret. "Why me, Lucas? I haven't lived here in ten years. I'm not even planning on staying."

I want to tell her I've been asking myself the same thing since the first time I saw her name pop up on a report again. Instead, I stick to facts. "You're the only Grant left. Some people don't like loose ends."

She turns, her face open but her gaze hard as granite. "Are you talking about my family, or yours?"

The question lands harder than she intends. Maybe. Maybe not. I know she means the firehouse when she talks about my family.

She pours coffee, but her hands are steady now, the adrenaline kicking in. She leans over the table, her voice pitched low so it doesn't echo off the tile. "What are you not telling me?"

I look at her, for a second, it's high school again, the two of us in an empty gymnasium, arguing rules and consequences like there's nothing else at stake. Only now, the stakes are everything.

"Whoever did this wants you gone. That's clear."

"But why?

I exhale, staring at the walls, at the closed doors of all the things I don't want to let out. "Small towns have long memories. Sometimes people get off on revenge for things that never even happened."

She narrows her eyes. "You sound like you know who it is."

I shake my head, but it's not denial; it's fatigue. "No. But I know how they think."

She stares me down, all the old stubbornness packed into that tiny frame. "And you're still avoiding the real answer."

I push the note back to her, careful not to touch her hand. "I'm not. I just don't have it yet."

She takes the envelope and tucks it under her arm, movements clipped. "Fine. I'll keep watching my back. Thanks for nothing, Lieutenant."

She starts for the door, but something in me refuses to let her walk out angry. Not again. I follow, my boots thumping on the floor, and catch up to her in the hallway.

"Sophie."

She stops, back rigid, and I lower my voice. "If you need protection—"

She spins, eyes blazing. "If I need protection, I'll call the sheriff. You made it clear you're not interested in that a long time ago."

The words slice straight to the bone. I can't help myself. "You think I wanted to leave? You think I liked what happened?"

She closes the gap, fury so bright it's almost a relief. "I think you got scared. I think you ran."

I clench my fists to keep from grabbing her shoulders. "You don't know everything that happened that night."

"Then tell me," she says, quiet, but savage.

But I can't. Not here, not with the whole day shift about to spill in and watch us rip each other apart. Instead, I step back, breaking the line of sight, and point her toward the exit.

She walks away, head high, never looking back.

I stand there, spine pressed to the cinderblock, and wait for the room to stop spinning. It doesn't.

I know I'll see her again. That's the problem.

The note still burns in my mind, its message as clear as the one she just delivered: leave, or everything goes up in smoke.

I NEED AIR, AND NOT THE STALE, CHEMICAL-LACED variety that pools in the squad room. I duck out the back, into the narrow hallway that runs behind the main engine bay. The corridor always reminds me of a loading dock at a hospital, functional and antiseptic, a place designed for moving bodies fast and with no audience. I pace once, twice, trying to burn off the static in my muscles, but the conversation with Sophie keeps playing on a loop: her voice, her accusations, the raw pulse of old anger.

A clatter down the far end of the hall makes me stop. For a second, I think I'm alone, but then I see a shadow flick past the storage closet. Sophie, hair wild, coat slung over her shoulder, walking like she just remembered an appointment she never wanted to keep. I catch her by the elbow without thinking, the way you'd stop someone from stepping in front of a train.

She whips around, ready for a fight. "What?"

I should say something measured, something that will settle her, but all that comes out is, "You shouldn't leave alone."

She twists free. "Is that an order, Lieutenant?"

The rank lands between us like a thrown punch. I see her breathing hard, cheeks flushed, fingers digging into the strap of her bag. It's not the fear I expected, but something sharper.

She moves to brush past, but I step into her path. The space between us shrinks to nothing—her back to the cinderblock wall, my hands braced to either side, palms pressed flat against the paint-spattered concrete. I'm aware of the heat bleeding off me, and the heat bleeding off her.

Her eyes flick from my face to my chest to the floor, then up again. She's defiant, always was, her chin is tipped, but I see the tremor in her throat.

For a second, neither of us talks. It's all in the breathing, the way her chest rises with each tight inhale, the way my own heart refuses to slow down.

She says, "You gonna tell me the truth now, or is this just for show?"

I KNOW I SHOULD BACK OFF. WE'RE STANDING IN THE open, any rookie could wander by and see the two of us locked in this silent standoff, but I can't move. I lean in, close enough to smell the coffee on her breath and the faint trace of shampoo.

Her voice goes low. "Lucas. Let me go."

"I can't," I say, before I even register it as truth.

Her face remains stone. "You need to decide which one of us you're actually trying to protect."

It hits, somewhere between the ribs and the heart. I stare at her, see all the years stacked up in the lines around her eyes, the tired bravado, the refusal to break.

I drop my head, just enough to bring our foreheads within a hair of touching. For a wild second, I think about kissing her—just once, to see if it's still there, if all that unfinished business could be solved with a single, reckless move.

But I don't. Instead, I slam both hands against the wall and step back, the echo ringing down the corridor. She closes her eyes, just for a heartbeat, then opens them again, steady as glass.

"I have work to do," she says, voice level.

I nod, but it's more of a bow, and then I turn and walk away before she can see what's left of my composure slip out from under me. The hallway stretches in front of me, long and empty, but I feel her presence behind me like a live wire.

I don't stop until I'm outside, sucking in lungfuls of real, bitter cold, hands shaking like a rookie's first call. I wonder if she's still standing there, staring after me, or if she's already left me behind for good.

Either way, the fire hasn't gone out. Not by a long shot.

It's after dark when I finally step out of the station, I head to the grocery store, the lot nearly empty except for a couple of battered pickups and Sophie's hatchback under a crooked streetlamp. I tell myself I'm just heading to the store for a six-pack and some bad dinner, but I know better. I know she's out here somewhere, and that neither of us is going to sleep until this thing is over.

I catch her in the corner of my eye as I cross the lot, moving fast and head down, a paper bag of groceries tucked against her ribs. The sodium lights overhead flicker in and out, casting her shadow long and then snapping it short with each pulse. She's not watching for trouble; she's watching for ghosts.

I think about calling out, but my voice sticks. I hover by the curb, pretending to check my phone, tracking her steps. She fumbles for her keys at the driver's side door, groceries shifting, one can rolling out and skittering across the asphalt. For a second, she sags against the door, all the fight from earlier bleeding out into the cold.

Then she looks up and stops. Dead still.

At first, I don't see what's wrong. Then I do.

Somebody's smeared a message across her windshield, letters spelled out in powdery black, ash, maybe, or fine soot from a chimney. The words slant up, big enough to read from the next county over:

YOU'RE NEXT

The phrase hits like a slap. Sophie doesn't move, keys in hand, just staring at the words. The lights overhead strobe in time with her breathing, turning the letters into shadows that stretch and shudder across the car hood.

She goes to wipe the message off, but her fingers hover just above the glass. I see them shaking, even from this far.

I can't hang back anymore. I cross the lot, shoes loud on the frostbitten pavement. She hears me, but doesn't look away from the windshield.

I say, "Apparently, the note wasn't clear enough."

She winces, then forces a laugh. "Guess they thought I needed a visual aid."

I scan the surrounding lot, looking for a lingering presence —a figure in the shadows, the glow of a cigarette—but there's nothing. Just us and the words. And another spiral.

She finally scrapes her sleeve across the windshield, smearing the message into a black, oily cloud. "You think it's a joke?"

I shake my head. "This isn't how jokers operate. They'd have slashed your tires or egged the paint. This is...calculated."

She looks at me, and for the first time all day, there's no sarcasm left. "Do you think they're watching us right now?"

I want to say no, to give her some kind of comfort, but lying to her never did either of us any good. "I don't know," I say. "But I'm not going to let them scare you off."

A muscle jumps in her jaw. "What if I want to be scared off? What if that's the smartest move?"

I step in close, close enough that the ghost of the message is still visible over her shoulder, faint but stubborn. "You're not leaving," I say. "Not like this."

She looks away, and I catch the glint of tears, but she blinks them down hard.

I want to reach out to touch her shoulder or her hair, but I don't; I open the car door for her and load the groceries in, a clumsy gesture that makes us both smile in spite of everything.

When she gets in, she pauses, one foot still on the ground. "You coming with me, Lieutenant, or am I on my own from here?"

There's no heat to it, no challenge—just a need. It's enough to crack me right down the middle.

"I'm with you," I say.

She starts the car, and I watch the taillights drift away, red haze dissolving in the dark. I wait until the parking lot is empty before I head home, pulse pounding, adrenaline burn riding just under the skin.

It's not over. Not even close.

But for the first time, I know I'm not fighting it alone.

3

Burned Bridges

Sophie

It's not far. That's the sick part, how close it all is, the graveyard of my former life, barely a mile from the house I'm supposed to be sorting, selling, and eventually forgetting. Every time I drive past the turnoff on Sycamore, I can feel it lurking beyond the line of trees, that cleared rectangle of land, the outline of home still faintly stamped on the earth like a phantom limb. My therapist in the city used to call it "exposure therapy." She said, "If you walk the old ground enough times, it'll lose its power." She never said how many times that took.

The road is worse than I remember. Deep ruts from winter plows, a slop slick with moss, the trees above knitting into a canopy that dims the already sullen daylight. I park at the break in the fence, angle the car so that I can make a fast getaway if needed, and kill the engine. For a second, I just sit, keys gripped so hard the fob leaves a dent in my palm, then force myself out.

There's no house, not anymore. Just the twisted suggestion of where it once squatted, the bones picked clean by salvage crews years ago. The only things left are the foundation—cracked, sunken, tattooed with the initials of kids who came here to drink or fuck or both—and the wild riot of plants that have claimed it. Goldenrod and thistle, burdock taller than my head, and everywhere, little white flowers that refuse to care about history. The ruins have been scrubbed free of warning tape of "No Trespassing signs; it's as if the town finally decided even the memory was bad luck.

The air smells of rain, though none has fallen yet. I tell myself this is an ordinary walk, a data-gathering mission. I don't notice my hands shaking until I'm halfway up the drive.

I step over the old threshold, the cracked rectangle where the front door once hung. I used to think it was the best part of the house, the way it opened to the world with a sound like a summer storm, the way the hinges squealed if you pushed hard enough. Now it's a border between two universes: the normal one, and this, a bubble of suspended time.

The first memory hits hard and out of nowhere. The sound of a dog barking, echoing over the yard. I see the yard as it was: green, uneven, the grass always longer than my mother wanted, the maple tree's lower branches raw from where I stripped the bark. Then I blink and the yard is gone, replaced by the upthrust stalks of milkweed and bindweed, the branches stripped bare by winter and wind.

I move through the ruins as if casing a crime scene. Step, pause, scan the ground. I spot the warped outline of the old kitchen slab, a few rusted pipes jutting up where the sink used to be. I remember the way the faucet ran rusty for a full minute before settling, the way the morning light would hit that wall, butter yellow, enough to make even cold cereal taste warm.

Another step, and the ground under me shifts. For a second, the air is thick with smoke—the real kind, not the polite memory version. It's in my mouth and nose, in my eyes, until I nearly stagger sideways. I press a hand to my throat and will it away, but the echo is insistent: the screaming, the heat, the taste of melting plastic and burning insulation. My head buzzes with it.

I force myself forward, following the plan, tracing the path from the front door to what used to be my bedroom. It's just dirt and weeds now, a rectangle shape leveled by the fire crew, but I can still see the shape of it: the pink rug, the dresser with the cracked mirror, the window I used to crawl through on summer nights when I was desperate for air.

I kneel, though the ground is muddy and half-frozen. The sky's gotten heavier, gray on gray, the kind of weather that makes you think twice about going out at all. I dig my fingers into the earth, expecting to find only stones and roots, but there's a shock of something hard and flat. I scrape the soil away and uncover a chunk of charred wood, black as onyx but still showing the grain where my father's hand had sanded it smooth. The remains of my old bedframe. The last time I saw it, it was on fire.

The shaking comes back. I tell myself I'm just cold, but the tremors run deeper. I press the blackened wood to my chest, ignoring the smear it leaves on my jacket.

I let the memory play out, because I know I have to. The way the night tasted—like an electric storm and panic. The way my mother's arms felt, rough with fear, dragging me down the stairs. The way I looked back just in time to see Lucas—ten years younger, so cocky he barely seemed real—charging through the flames, his face raw and set, eyes locked on me like he could will me to safety.

And then the way he vanished, a wall of smoke swallowing him whole.

I was the first one out of the house, but the last one to stop screaming.

When I finally let go of the wood, my hands are black and raw. I wipe them on my jeans, then stand, vision flickering with black spots. The rain hasn't started, but the sky promises it's coming.

I walk the perimeter one last time, checking for ghosts. I half-expect to see Lucas's shadow behind the trees, or maybe my own reflection ten years gone, running wild and unscarred through the weeds.

When I leave, I don't look back. But I can feel the site watching me, holding on to every molecule of smoke I ever breathed.

I slam the car door, shove the keys into the ignition, and sit until the ache in my hands dulls. The engine turns over on the second try.

As I pull away, the first drops of rain hit the windshield, erasing the view behind me one watery line at a time.

Lucas

THE FIREHOUSE AT SHIFT CHANGE IS PURE ENTROPY. Boots thud the length of the hallway, some jackass has left a puddle at the bay entrance, and the air vibrates with the smell of diesel and floor polish. All of it hums at the edge of my hearing, just enough to keep me from going completely feral from staring at computer screens for six straight hours.

I'm in the back office with my own personal archive of nightmares: the department's digital incident logs, stretching back further than I care to count. Most guys prefer the hands-on work—tool checks, hose drills, the satisfying thunk of loading gear—but I've always been the one idiot who gets high off database access. The logic, the order. It's supposed to make sense. Except it doesn't.

I have three windows open on my laptop, each one a different layer of the same problem. Window One: the official report of the Grant house fire, May 17, ten years ago. Window Two: the backup logs, time-stamped and cold as a coroner's toe tag, but not matching the version I just pulled from the main system. Window Three: a log of every access to that file in the past month.

Someone's been poking around. Repeatedly. And not from my desk.

I write it down: 4/7, 4/10, 4/14, 4/18, always after midnight, always from a remote login. I don't recognize the username, but the IP pings back to a county library branch on the other side of town. I'm not paranoid enough to believe in hackers, but I've seen enough inside jobs to know a diversion when I spot one.

I scribble a note on a Post-It, then crumple it and start over. My hand is steadier now than it was ten years ago—less adrenaline, more cold math.

The rest of the station is gearing up for a response drill, but I keep my ass planted and eyes on the prize. I highlight the critical lines in the fire report:

- "Origin: first floor, northeast quadrant."

- "Accelerant traces: negative."

-"Occupants escaped, one responder injured during search."

A liar's matrix, if you know what you're looking for.

I compare it to the version from the backup, and there it is: a sentence missing from the new copy. I print both, grab a red pen, and draw a box around the line:

"Unidentified secondary accelerant odor noted upon entry, source indeterminate."

I stare at the two sheets, side by side. The difference is small, but it's enough to make the hair on my forearms rise. Someone went to the trouble of cleaning the file. Recently.

A shadow falls across the desk. The Chief, his shirt is untucked, face red from too much coffee, he approaches and leans over my shoulder.

"You tracking the pizza receipts, Hayes, or you actually working?"

I flip the printouts over. "Just reconciling last month's fire logs. There's a few inconsistencies."

He snorts. "That time of year, huh? We get the prank calls, you get the paper cuts."

I tap the laptop. "Actually, it's not a prank. Old files keep getting opened from outside the department. At night."

He shrugs, unconcerned. "Probably just IT doing backups. Or the insurance people. Nothing worth losing sleep over."

I don't buy it, and he knows it, but the Chief has his own brand of protocol. "If you have a minute, you can help with inventory," he says, and he's already moving on, leaving the smell of burnt coffee in his wake.

I wait until he's out of sight, then bring the laptop closer. I search the username again, now looking for similar logins on recent fires. And damned if it doesn't show up on the shed fire last week—the same one that put Sophie in danger.

I log the information in my notebook. Someone wants to rewrite the story, and they're not subtle.

A rookie stumbles past the office, helmet clutched under his arm like a toddler's stuffed animal. He gives me a nervous look, as if he's heard I am digging in places I shouldn't. I ignore him.

For the next hour, I cross-reference every incident connected to the Grant family, every suspicious note, every threatening message. The pattern is too clean, the targeting too specific. Whoever it is, they're not just lighting fires—they're erasing footprints, too.

By the time the drill kicks off in the bay, I've lost all sense of time. I keep coming back to the same lines in the report, the red-inked boxes, the words that aren't supposed to be there. It gnaws at me, the possibility that we missed something the first time around, or worse, that someone made sure we did.

I sit back in the chair, stare at the computer, and let the noise of the station wrap around me like insulation. I can feel the pull in my gut—the old need to chase the problem until it's cornered and begging for air.

I'm not done. Not by a long shot.

I flip the page in my notebook, label it: GRANT CASE, and start making a list of the people who might want to set history on fire.

Sophie

It happens fast, the way all disasters do. One minute I'm scrolling through emails in the living room, the next I'm transfixed by the siren song of fire engines screaming down the road in front of my house. There are more of them than I've heard at once—an entire convoy, lights strobing so hard they paint the ceiling red through double-paned glass. I stand and watch, numb, then they veer off toward the border of my old house.

If I were a better person, I'd call someone to ask what's happening, or wait until it was on the country town grapevine tomorrow. But I just grab a hoodie, slip on my boots, and head into the night drawn forward as if by gravity.

There's a crowd forming at the fence line, the usual gathering of Lookie-Loos, phones aimed at the sky, faces lit up with the kind of hunger you only see in people who want something to break up the boredom. I recognize half the faces, but none of them recognize me, at least not until I edge closer and someone mutters my name, the syllables stretched thin with disbelief.

I ignore them, push past, and see the scene: the old Linder barn, fully engulfed, the top story already collapsed in on itself, flames churning upward like a vision of hell. The grass around it is lit up like an alien landing. It should be impossible to see this much fire without the heat, but the wind is high, carrying it away from the crowd, the smoke trailing off in a lazy banner across the fields.

I can't see Lucas right away, but I know he's here. He'd never pass up a show like this. Sure enough, I spot him on the edge of the chaos, helmet on, bunker gear zipped up, barking orders at his crew. He moves like a chess player, sees every angle, every possible move, and adjusts in real time. It's terrifying how much better he is in crisis than anywhere else.

A paramedic tries to herd the onlookers back, but I slide around her, eyes on the barn. I'm not close enough to feel the heat, but I taste it: the dry, chemical tang of burning insulation and old hay, the memory of my own house fire detonating in my chest.

I keep watching, hands in pockets to keep from shaking, until the entire upper wall slumps outward with a wet groan and the crowd lets out a collective gasp. The fire crew is right there, laying down foam, keeping the edges from spreading to the pasture. In ten minutes, the whole barn is little more than a pile of hissing, half-molten wood.

Lucas finally turns, scans the perimeter, and sees me. He's stripped off his helmet, and the sweat in his hair makes him look younger, almost breakable. He waves me over, and the crowd parts in front of me, whispering like I'm bad luck. Maybe I am.

He meets me at the fire line, the reflective tape on his jacket catching every stray light. "You okay?" he asks, voice hoarse from shouting.

I nod, but it's a lie. "Did anyone get hurt?"

He shakes his head, then glances back at the barn, jaw tight. "We got lucky. Wind shifted just in time."

The glow from the barn flickers across his face, making his eyes look almost silver. He's doing the math, already thinking ahead to the next emergency, but he won't say it out loud in front of me. Not yet.

I look at the skeleton of the barn, the way the fire is already losing interest, and say, "This isn't random, is it?"

He doesn't even blink. "No. Three in two weeks, all near the old property line. There's a pattern, if anyone's paying attention."

I stare at the grass, then at the crowd, then back at the barn. "Someone wants me gone."

He exhales sharply, and I can smell the smoke in it. "I won't let that happen."

It's not a promise, but it's the closest thing he's capable of.

The wind shifts, blowing a gust of embers over the line. I brace myself, even though I know they can't hurt me from here. For a second, I can feel the old panic coming back—lungs closing up, vision tunneling to a pinprick. I grab onto the fence post, grounding myself in splinters and cold.

Lucas moves closer and puts a hand over mine. His gloves are off, his palm warm and dry.

"You should go inside," he says, softer now. "It's only going to get worse."

I look up at him, and for a moment neither of us moves. The air is full of ash, falling like black snow. I want to say something comforting, something adult, but all I manage is, "Why me?"

His hand slides up my wrist, thumb steady on my pulse. "I don't know. But I'll figure it out."

THE OTHER FIREFIGHTERS ARE STARTING TO WRAP UP, hosing down hot spots, laughing as the adrenaline burns off. The crowd disperses, bored now that the flames are down to embers. We're the only ones left at the line.

My knees go weak, and it's not just the cold or exhaustion. I'm shaking, full-body, the crash after so much held tension. Lucas catches me, arms around my waist, holding me close against the reflective armor of his gear.

I rest my head on his shoulder, breathing in the bitter, familiar stink of burnt wood and sweat. For a long minute, we stand there, holding each other, and I let myself remember how it used to feel, how simple it was to trust him to keep me alive.

His lips find my temple. He doesn't say anything; he doesn't have to. It's a moment outside of language, a promise that's older than both of us.

Eventually, the cold gets through the layers, and I pull away. He lets me go, but only far enough to keep his hand at my back.

We walk away from the fire together, the barn still smoldering behind us, the world gone quiet except for the hiss of steam and the distant sound of trucks packing up for the night.

I know it's not over. I know whoever's doing this is still out there.

But for now, I'm not alone in the dark.

After the fire, after Lucas has left, I don't sleep. I just sit at the kitchen table and watch the clock stutter through every hour, the numbers burning blue on the old stove display. My phone buzzes with messages, but I leave them unread. If anyone really needs to find me, they'll come in person.

Outside, the world is charcoal and silence. I can still see the afterimage of the flames on my eyelids, the way the barn folded in on itself, the way Lucas's hands shook only after the fire was dead. I replay the night in reverse, trying to find a seam, a logic, but all I get are splinters.

I'm not scared anymore. That's the dangerous part.

Instead of pacing, I make a list. Everything I know, everything I can guess. Who would want me gone? Who even remembers me well enough to care? The usual suspects, old classmates, distant cousins, they don't fit. This is more than a grudge; it's precision. It's a pattern.

I start another list, but halfway through, something clicks—a memory, sharp and sudden as an electric shock. My father's voice, low and urgent: "If anything ever happens, you look for the box. You remember that, Sophie."

I do. I remember the box. I know exactly where it is.

The small garden shed, thankfully not the one that went up in smoke, crammed to the rafters with my aunt's spare lawn chairs and warped Tupperware, but I find the fireproof lockbox behind the stack of dead extension cords. It's heavy as regret, the kind of black steel you only buy if you expect to be found by arson investigators. I haul it inside, cracking my knuckles against the freezing metal, and drop it on the table.

The combination is a birthday. Mine, not his. Original Dad.

Inside: a battered composition notebook, a handful of receipts, a plastic baggie with an extra house key. I go for the notebook first, flipping pages with my thumb like a deck of cards. The ink is faded, the paper yellowed and soft, but the handwriting is still a match for every report card, every Post-it left on the fridge.

The first few pages are nothing—shopping lists, repair notes, Dad's endless war with the water heater. But then the entries turn, getting weirder, more frantic.

- SOMETHING'S NOT RIGHT WITH THE NEW NEIGHBOR
    - He watches at night. Why?
    - Two cars in the drive, only ever see one person
    - They know about the thing in the shed
    - Do not let Sophie go alone at night

I KEEP READING, HEART IN MY THROAT. THERE ARE DATES, names; some I recognize from the old neighborhood, some I don't. In the margins, Dad's pen has made heavy, looping spirals; it pops up everywhere, sometimes filling half a page.

I flip ahead, searching for a pattern. The spirals repeat, always near notes about fires: "Garage fire on Hawthorn. Ruled accidental...was it?" ot "Shed burned at night, only ashes left. No footprints, but a spiral carved in the dirt."

A chill slides down my back. It's the same shape Lucas found near the shed last week, the same spiral on my note, and that someone drew in ash on my windshield.

My hands go cold, even though the kitchen is warm from the old radiators. I trace one of the spirals, and for a second, I swear I can feel the paper pulse under my fingertip.

The rest of the journal is a mess of theory and panic. Dad trying to fit the facts together, fighting to see the outline of something bigger, something nobody else would believe. He writes about 'watchers' and 'test runs' and 'the fire isn't for the house, it's for the story.' In the final entry, the pen bites so deep it tears the page:

- If I can't stop it, maybe she can.

I close the notebook, the words echoing in the stillness. My father was not a conspiracy nut. He was careful, methodical, the kind of man who triple-checked the oven before leaving for work. If he wrote it down, it mattered.

I pull the receipts from the box, expecting the usual nothing. But one of them jumps out: a purchase for four gallons of fire accelerant, dated two weeks before our house burned down. The signature isn't his.

I sit back, letting the facts realign. Someone's been running this playbook for a decade, and it's not about me or Lucas or even the barn. It's about control. It's about erasing every trace.

I look at the spiral again, inked into the paper like a warning. The shape means something, maybe not to anyone else, but to the person who left it, it's a signature, a challenge.

I snap a photo of the notebook and send it to Lucas, no words attached. He'll know what it means. Or he'll come over to ask, and I'll have to see him again, and neither of us will be able to pretend this is just a coincidence.

I leave the journal open on the table, the last page up, the spiral staring back at me. The fire outside may be out, but the one in my chest is just getting started.

When the wind rattles the window, I don't react. I sit there, hands flat on the table, and I wait for the next move.

4

Smoke in the Walls

Sophie

The second time it happens, I'm so wound up that I almost miss it entirely.

I'M RUNNING ON FOUR HOURS' SLEEP AND HALF A PROTEIN bar, keys jabbing my palm as I cross the municipal lot. The sunset is all red smear and cloud crust, and I'm rehearsing a speech for the lawyer I'm about to meet, something about irregularities in my aunt's estate, the kind of adult shit I should be used to be now. My brain is so preoccupied that when I spot my car at the far end, I don't notice the windshield right away. Not until I'm a dozen steps away and the words come into focus, raw and perfect, stretching across the glass in uneven strokes of black.

YOU SHOULD HAVE DIED

For a long second, I think it's just the afterimage from the burned barn, the optical hangover you get from staring at fire too long. But the message is real, gritty, scrawled in what looks like soot or fine ash. The letters streak down onto the hood, as if written by a finger pressed too hard, the trails blooming out like veins.

I stand there, numb, for at least ten seconds. Then the world speeds back up: I glance around, half expecting to catch the culprit ducking behind the trash enclosure, but the lot is empty except for an old Camry and a landscaping truck parked crooked in two spaces.

There's a sharp, chemical tang in the air, almost metallic. I taste it at the back of my throat.

I reach out, hand trembling, and drag a knuckle over the word DIED. The ash comes away in a smear, leaving gray streaks on the glass. The particles stick to my skin, and for a sick moment, I think about the way bodies turn to dust in a fire. I have to press the heel of my hand to my stomach to keep from gagging.

By the time I fumble my phone out to take a picture, my hands are shaking so hard that the screen blurs. I can't even bring myself to open the car door.

I call Lucas. There's no preamble, just the sound of my own breathing as I wait for him to pick up.

"Yeah?" His voice is lower than usual, rough like he's just gotten off a call or a nap or both.

"It's me," I say, and my tone must carry the right weight because he skips the banter.

"Where are you?"

"Library lot. By the trailhead."

He doesn't ask what's wrong. "I'll be there in five."

I watch the horizon, waiting for his truck to crest the hill, and in the meantime, I scan every shadow, every movement at the edge of my vision. The world feels suddenly porous, like anything could reach through and grab me.

Lucas arrives in three minutes. He must've been closer than I thought, or maybe he just drove like he was responding to a five-alarm. His arrival is kinetic—engine idling, door not even shut before he's at my side.

He clocks the message instantly, and for a moment, he stands with his arms at his sides, fists bunched, eyes narrowing in a way that makes him look even bigger than usual.

"Again?" he sighs, "Did you touch it?"

"Just...here." I show him the back of my hand. My knuckles are a bad watercolor of gray.

He leans close, examining the windshield. His breath steams the glass, fogging the last letter of the message. He takes a step back, turns, and scans the perimeter of the lot with a slow, methodical sweep. I know he's cataloging every detail—the tire marks in the gravel, the angle of the streetlight, the path from the sidewalk.

He takes his own phone out, snaps photos from three different angles, then sets the camera to flash and zooms in on the edge of the ash trail.

He says, "It's not from a cigarette. There's too much." Then, almost to himself, "Could be fireplace. Could be from one of the burn sites."

I manage, "Maybe it's just someone who watched too many true crime shows."

He doesn't smile. "They'd need gloves to do this without leaving prints."

I feel the urge to laugh, just to cut through the horror-movie silence, but the sound dies in my throat.

Lucas checks the parking lot again, then steps so that his body is angled between me and the open lot; it's almost like he thinks he can shield me from whoever sent this message. "You're not going home alone. I'll follow you," he says.

"I'm not five years old," I say, but my voice is too thin, and I know I've already lost this argument.

He ignores me. "Tonight you stay at my place, or you let me sweep the house first. No negotiation."

I run a hand over my face. "This is overkill."

He points at the windshield. "That's an escalation, Sophie. Three messages? Whoever this is, they're not just lighting up buildings anymore."

I want to argue. I want to tell him that it's just some loser with a grudge and a can of lighter fluid. But all I can think about is the chemical reek of the fine gray dust still clinging to my palm.

He must see something in my face, because his voice softens. "Look, it's one night. I'll set up the security cameras and run the tapes from last week. You can play watchdog all you want, but let me do my job."

I let out a shudder of breath. "Fine. One night. But only because I don't want my aunt's house to end up a headline."

He smiles, just barely. "It'll be the safest house in Willow Creek by morning."

He grabs a roll of paper towels from the back of his truck and hands it to me. "Don't use your sleeve," he says, and I realize I've been unconsciously wiping my hands on the hem of my jacket.

I take the towels, but my hands still shake as I ball one up and scrub at the windshield. The ash doesn't come away clean —it smears, and the words ghost across the glass, growing fuzzier and more grotesque with every swipe. By the time I'm done, my hands are raw, and the air smells like a campfire in hell.

Lucas watches, then opens the car door for me. His free hand hovers at my back, never quite touching. "Ready?"

I nod.

As I turn the ignition, the radio blares to life, and for a second, the sudden noise nearly makes me jump out of my skin. I kill it and drive slowly out of the lot, and watch Lucas's headlights lock onto my rear bumper.

We drive like that the whole way home, his truck pacing me with the perfection of a bodyguard, or a predator. I try to pretend it's normal, that I'm in control, but the message stays burned into my memory, even after the windshield was clean.

At the next stoplight, I glance in the rearview and see Lucas watching the world, eyes flicking from side to side, mouth set in a hard line.

For once, I'm glad he's here.

By the time we pull into the driveway, night has taken over. The porch light casts a sickly yellow pool on the steps. Lucas parks on the street, then walks the perimeter of the property before he even sets foot on the porch.

I unlock the door, step inside, and feel the tightness in my shoulders finally start to ease. Lucas enters after me, his presence so solid that it shifts the air in the room.

He sets the security kit on the counter. "You want to help, or just supervise?"

"Supervise," I say, but I'm already rolling up my sleeves.

We work side by side, unpacking motion sensors and small black cameras. He explains every placement, every angle, and when I make a suggestion, he actually listens. It's all business until he finishes the last camera and turns to face me, just a little too close.

"If you see anything, anything at all, you call me," he says.

He holds my gaze for a second too long. I nod, but it feels like there's something else he's not saying.

When he leaves, it's with one last sweep of the street, his eyes burning holes in the darkness. I lock the door behind him, then stand in the entryway, hands still dusted with gray.

I don't sleep that night. Every time I close my eyes, the words swim back into view, bold and absolute.

YOU SHOULD'VE DIED

I can almost hear my father's voice: Always call the professionals. Don't be a hero.

I'm not planning on being a hero.

But I'm not backing down, either.

For three nights running, Lucas shows up at my door after shift, uniform still creased, smelling faintly of pine soap and wet wool. At first, it's just about the cameras; he needs to check the angles, reset the Wi-Fi, make sure the footage is uploading to his off-site storage, just in case. But by the second night, it's clear he's using the excuse to stay. I don't call him on it. I even start to look forward to the sound of his truck in the drive, the way he knocks exactly twice before letting himself in, the way he always pauses in the entryway to scan for new threats.

We establish a rhythm: he brings takeout, I supply coffee. We sit at the kitchen table, shoulders hunched over two laptops, watching the same five minutes of driveway footage on endless repeat. At first, we keep a full chair's worth of space between us. By the third night, we're so close that my bare arm occasionally grazes his as we both reach for the mouse.

The kitchen transforms into a trench. Takeout containers pile up on the counter, and coffee mugs multiply on every surface. The only light comes from the laptop screens and the old under-cabinet fixture, which flickers at random intervals. There's a blanket draped across the back of my chair, originally for me, but it migrates to our shared laps whenever the wind cuts through the aging windows.

We don't talk about anything real, not at first. The first night is all business—camera placement, power outages, what to do if the system goes down. The second night is banter: Lucas trying to convince me that Thai food is a crime against taste buds, me countering with a monologue about the superiority of green curry. But underneath, something else is happening. Every time our hands brush, there's a static charge, a pause that lingers just half a second too long.

By the third night, the surveillance is almost an afterthought. I catch him watching me in the reflection of the laptop, his eyes softer than I remember, his mouth fixed in that half-smirk he used to wear when he thought nobody was looking.

I call him on it. "You're not even watching the footage anymore."

He shrugs, mouth quirked. "It hasn't changed in the last five loops."

"Maybe you're hoping it will," I say, trying to keep the edge out of my voice.

He looks at me, and for a second, the kitchen is so quiet I can hear the hum of the fridge in the next room.

"Do you want me to leave?" he asks.

I start to say yes, but the lie won't come. "No," I admit. "But you probably should."

He laughs, not unkindly. "Stubborn," he says, like it's a compliment.

I change the subject. "Did you ever figure out who keeps hacking the incident reports?"

He sighs, shoulders slumping a little. "Still working on it. Whoever it is, they're good. It's like trying to catch smoke."

I glance at him sideways. "Maybe you're just used to the old ways. It seems that these days, fires are digital, too."

He nods, acknowledging the point. "Doesn't mean I like it."

We fall silent, eyes on the screen, but our knees are touching under the table now, and neither of us moves away.

I can't stand the silence, so I reach for a file, a printout of the latest camera logs, highlighted in yellow, and our hands collide. For a second, we both freeze. His hands are warm, his fingers calloused, and I feel my own pulse thrum in the tips of my fingers.

He pulls back first, but not far. "Sorry," he mutters.

"Don't be," I say, because I mean it.

He sets his hand flat on the table, open, palm up. An invitation. I stare at it, then at his face, and see the question there, the same one he never asked a decade ago.

I almost answer. I almost reach for his hand.

But I chicken out and go for my coffee instead, taking a long, scalding sip. The mug rattles against my teeth.

Lucas doesn't press. He just sits, breathing slow and steady, like he's willing to wait forever.

It's after midnight when the footage finally shows something new. A shape—a blur of movement at the far edge of the backyard. Not a person, not exactly, but not an animal, either. The shadow moves with purpose, then disappears into the hedgerow.

Lucas leans forward, all business again. "Reverse it. Play it at half speed."

I do, and the shape resolves into a tall, thin figure, arms tight to the body, a hood pulled low over the face. No visible features, but the way it moves is familiar: the gait, the hunched shoulders, the way it pauses to look back before vanishing.

"That's not a stranger. That's someone who knows this house," he says.

"Do you think it's the same person who left the message?"

"Could be," he says, but he doesn't sound convinced. "Or it could be someone sending a warning. Either way, we need to be ready."

I nod, but the sight of the shadow has me rattled. I pull the blanket higher, suddenly cold.

Lucas notices. "You want me to stay the night?" he asks, voice gentle.

For a second, pride wars with the very real need not to be alone. I finally say, "Maybe just until the sun comes up."

He smiles, not in victory, but in solidarity. "I'll take the couch."

We shut down the laptops and clean up the table, but the tension lingers, thick and sweet as syrup. I catch him looking at me as I rinse out the mugs, and I realize I want to tell him everything, the things I remember, and even the things I'm afraid to remember.

Instead, I say, "Why did you really leave, Lucas? After the fire?"

He doesn't answer right away. He walks to the window, pulls the curtain aside, and stares into the darkness. His silhouette is big, but there's a vulnerability to it, a slouch in the shoulders that makes him seem younger, and maybe a bit lost.

Finally, he speaks, voice barely above a whisper. "I blamed myself. For not getting you out sooner. For losing control. I was a fucking idiot. I was angry, I was confused, your Dad just ... I didn't get him out in time, you were hurting, I thought I was making it worse." He turns, and his eyes are wet, shining in the low light. "I thought if I left, the guilt would burn off. But it just followed me."

I grip the counter to keep from shaking. "I never blamed you."

He nods, but he doesn't believe it. "I did, enough for both of us."

We stand there, the silence between us a living thing.

He takes a step closer. "I'm sorry I left you alone."

The words land heavy, but they don't hurt the way I thought they would. I want to say it's okay, that I forgive him, but I'm not sure I do. Or maybe I do, but I'm not ready to let go of the anger that's kept me alive all these years.

I settle for, "You're here now."

He moves so close I can see the stubble on his jaw, and those amazing flecks of green in his eyes. For a second, I think he's going to kiss me. He reaches forward and brushes a strand of hair from my cheek, gentle, like he's afraid I'll break.

"I'm not going anywhere," he says.

I believe him.

He sleeps on the couch that night, but I can hear him shifting, awake, every time the old house settles. I lie in bed, staring at the ceiling, and think about how much can change in three nights. How much can heal. How much can still burn.

In the morning, I find him already at the kitchen table, reviewing the footage again, a new pot of coffee brewing. He looks up and offers me a mug.

We watch the sunrise together, neither of us saying a word.

But the space between us is smaller than ever.

On Friday afternoon, I come home from errands and know, with absolute certainty, that someone's been inside my house.

It's not dramatic—no shattered glass, no alarms. The mailbox is unmolested, the porch exactly as I left it. But the second I step up, I see the door is off by a hair, the latch not quite flush. I tell myself it's nothing, that maybe the old wood has warped in the humidity, but my gut knots so hard I have to lean against the railing and breathe through it.

Inside, the air is stale and metallic. I stop on the threshold and listen. There's no sound, but every sense is screaming. My shopping bag swings from my hand, bumping the doorframe, the dull thud impossibly loud. I set it down and take inventory: nothing missing from the entry, no muddy footprints, the throw rug still crooked from where I kicked it aside this morning.

I move slow and quiet, the way I used to when checking the house for monsters after a nightmare. I sweep through the kitchen, the living room, then up the narrow stairs to the bedrooms. It's all the same, almost aggressively so, until I walk into my room and see what's waiting for me.

On my bed, propped against the faded blue pillow, is a photograph. It's a Polaroid, edges singed, the image warped from heat. I recognize it instantly, me at maybe six, face smeared with cake and pride, perched on my father's lap in front of the old Willow Creek fire engine. The same photo that used to live on the fridge, the same one I thought got lost when my family's home burned down. Only now, the bottom third is charred black, a chemical burn curling the plastic like a tongue.

For a long time, I just stand there, throat closing up. My hands shake so badly I have to put them behind my back.

I call Lucas. There's no preamble.

"Someone broke in," I say, voice thin. "They left a message."

He's at the house in under five minutes, this time in a civilian jacket, eyes scanning every angle of the street as he approaches. He doesn't touch me, but stands close enough that I can feel the heat from his body, a wall against whatever the world is trying to throw at me.

He goes room by room, methodical, eyes raking the surfaces for prints or clues or signs of forced entry. Nothing, except the photo.

He holds it up by the corner, careful not to smudge. "Where did this come from?"

"It was on the fridge," I say, "Until the fire."

He turns it over, inspects the burn. "A lighter, probably. Something hot, but fast, controlled. This was deliberate; it wasn't just plucked out of the debris."

I nod, because I already know. "What are they trying to say?"

He shakes his head, jaw tight. "That they can get close. That they're in control."

We stand there, the photo between us, the silence thick as glue. I feel like if I speak, I'll start crying and never stop.

He sets the photo on the desk, careful, like it might explode. "We need to lock this down," he says. "Tonight I stay."

I want to argue, to tell him that I don't need a babysitter, but the image of the burned Polaroid is still stamped on the backs of my eyes. "Fine," I say, and it's almost a relief.

He's in full protection mode: checks every window, moves a chair under the front knob, resets the security cams. He tells me to go about my night, but I can't. I hover in the kitchen, hands clutching a mug that's gone cold. I hear him moving downstairs, the weight of his boots, the measured way he opens and closes each door.

After an hour, he sits on the living room couch, phone in one hand, the other resting flat on his thigh. He's not pretending to relax; he's holding a vigil.

I try to sleep, but the house is alive with sound. Every floorboard pop is a threat, every wind gust against the siding a warning. I lie in bed and stare at the ceiling, counting the seconds between creaks, waiting for the next thing to go wrong.

At 2:17 a.m., I give up and pad downstairs. The lights are low, but Lucas is awake, head bowed, reading something on his phone. He looks up when I enter, eyes instantly alert.

"Can't sleep?" he asks.

I shrug. "Never could, after."

He nods, he understands exactly what 'after' means.

I sit on the edge of the couch, folding my legs under me. For a while, we just listen to the silence, the house breathing around us.

Finally, he says, "You remember the night of the fire?"

I look at him, surprised. "Every second."

"I saw you in the window," he says, voice flat. "I was supposed to stay outside, but I didn't. I ran in, because—"

He stops, shakes his head. "I never told anyone this, but I thought if I could just get to you, nothing else would matter."

I stare at the floor. "You did get to me."

He exhales, a shaky sound. "Yeah. But not in time to save anything else."

I reach out, without thinking, and put my hand on his. His skin is rough, scarred. The hand of a man who's spent his life fighting things he can't control.

He doesn't move, but the muscles in his jaw relax a little.

"I hated you for leaving," I say. "But I hated myself more for needing you."

He nods, and we sit like that, hands barely touching, until the fridge kicks on and breaks the spell.

He stands, paces to the window, checks the street again. I want to follow, to press up against him and say something true, but the moment's gone, replaced by the cold weight of reality.

He turns back, softer this time. "Go get some sleep, Soph. I'll be here."

I hesitate, then go. The climb up the stairs feels harder, heavier.

Back in bed, I stare at the ceiling and listen to the house. Every sound is different now, every creak a note in the song of being watched. But underneath, there's a new hum—a quiet sense of being protected, even if it's only temporary.

I don't sleep. But I don't panic, either.

Downstairs, I hear Lucas shifting on the couch, the sound of his breathing anchoring me to the present. The photo is on my nightstand, edge still singed, face smiling out from a place that doesn't exist anymore.

The threat is real. So is the fear.

But for the first time since coming home, I'm not alone in it.

The sun creeps up over the horizon, pale and exhausted, and I lie there in the dim, listening to the world rebuild itself.

In another hour, I'll have to get up and face whatever comes next.

For now, I let myself rest.

5

Flashpoint

Sophie

The only place in Willow Creek where you can be invisible and under a microscope at the same time is the public library. I take the corner table furthest from the entrance, the one under the humming light that flickers every eleven seconds. The chair is engineered to be uncomfortable after ten minutes, but I've been here for nearly three hours, spine braced straight, elbows planted hard enough on the tabletop to leave matching red crescents in my skin.

The digital catalog would be faster, but I don't trust the gaps in small-town digitization. There are always pages that go missing—sometimes by accident, sometimes by design. I want the real thing: the papery stench of old microfilm, the texture of newsprint brittle from too many years and too few hands. If there's anything left to find about my father's death, it won't be on the internet.

The local history stacks run along the far wall, right beneath the bank of glass-brick windows that have never once let in enough light. I alternate between the microfilm reader and a cardboard box labeled "Obits, 1989–2004." The box coughs up a pale drift of dust every time I reach inside. With each handful, I get a sense of turning someone else's bones.

I'm on my sixth spiral-bound notebook of the day. My notes start off meticulous—date, headline, byline, any names that recur more than twice—but after the first hour the handwriting devolves into a kind of angry, upright shorthand. Frank Grant. House fire. Financial audit. Community hero, then not. The scandal outlasted his actual life by a good two years, eating up every spare inch of copy in the "Pulse" section. The details are exactly as I remember, and also not.

I scrawl the headline in all caps: EX-FIRE CHIEF GRANT CLEARED OF ARSON, FOUND DEAD. The photo underneath is the one every paper used—my father on the steps of Town Hall, mouth half open, hand outstretched as if shielding his eyes from a future he didn't want to see.

The archive table wobbles whenever I lean too far, which is every time I find another hole in the story. The official narrative was a neat spiral: Dad was accused of setting a fire a month before the fire that gutted our house; the investigation turned up nothing. Dad reinstated, just in time to be felled by a 'sudden cardiac event' during the house fire that destroyed my home. But the clippings are sloppier, edged with rumors and letters to the editor. There's a recurring name in the letters: A concerned citizen, sometimes signed 'An Old Friend.' The handwriting on these is always the same. I jot it down and circle it, hard enough to nearly rip the page.

The librarian stalks the edges of the stacks with the silent conviction of a housecat. She's lived here forever; she used to hand out juice boxes to our third-grade reading group, back when the shelves barely came up to our chins. Her hair is steel-gray now, but she recognizes me instantly. I catch her watching from the reference desk, her gaze swinging between me and the box of obits, as if waiting for the moment I'll snap and scatter the pages across the tile.

I ignore her and keep reading. Somewhere around page 43 of the "Pulse" microfilm, I find a buried item: "WCFD whistle-blower claims missing incident logs." It's one paragraph, sandwiched between a bake sale blurb and an ad for discount propane. The whistleblower is unnamed, but the quote rings a bell: "Records don't just burn themselves." I run the sentence in my head three times before I remember the phrase from my dad's own lips, muttered after too many bourbons, always when he thought I was already asleep.

I photograph the clipping with my phone, careful to get the date stamp, then scroll back to compare it with the day the fire report vanished from the county server. The match is exact. My pulse thrums so hard I nearly drop the phone.

The next envelope is labeled "Grant, F. — Editorials & Features." I open it and out pours a blizzard of yellowed cuttings, edges curling like dried leaves. I fan them out in a nervous, even grid across the table. There's a rhythm to it: stack, read, reject, annotate. Halfway through, I find what I've been looking for—a letter to the editor, unsigned, but the phrasing is my father's, all sharp angles and clipped sarcasm. The ink is faint but legible:

"It is the height of irony that the men trusted to protect our town are the same ones destroying it from the inside. Ask the right questions, and you'll see what's burning isn't just wood and drywall."

Below it, a sticky note in unfamiliar handwriting: "Soph—if you're reading this, stop digging. For your own sake. —L."

I stare at the note, a twist of cold in my gut. L could be Lillian, but it's not her script. Lucas? The possibility needles at me, but I file it away for later.

I photograph everything. My hands are shaking now, enough that I have to brace the phone with both palms. The ash motif carries—by the end, my fingerprints are so blackened with newsprint they leave smudges on the glass.

After another hour, the words start to blur. I squeeze my eyes shut, rub the bridge of my nose, and try to reconstruct the logic. My father wasn't an arsonist, but he was investigating someone. He left a trail, maybe on purpose, maybe out of desperation. The people who wanted him gone were still out there, or else their proteges had inherited the grudge.

I'm re-packing the envelopes when the librarian materializes at my shoulder, voice a gentle creak. "We close at six on the dot, Sophie."

I blink at the clock on the wall—fifteen minutes left. "I'll be quick."

She nods, but doesn't leave. Instead, she hovers, shuffling and re-shuffling the return cart, eyes never quite leaving the stack of clippings I've made. "Your father was a good man," she says, barely above a whisper.

I don't look up. "You were here the night of the fire, weren't you?"

She hesitates, then: "They called me to open the building. For the evacuation. Your father insisted on double-checking every room before leaving. That's the only reason the janitor survived."

"Did anyone else come back after? To look around, or...?"

Her lips press into a line. "The police chief. And the fire captain. They said it was routine."

I nod, pretending to jot down a reminder, but really I'm just anchoring myself to the table. The world feels like it's tilting, the lines between memory and motive blurring.

When she finally leaves, I slip the stickiest clippings and the note into the pocket of my father's battered notebook, the one I found in the lockbox. It fits so snugly that it feels like it always belonged there.

At five fifty-nine, I shoulder my bag and walk out. The librarian is at the desk, lights already dimmed, face pinched with something between pity and fear. She says nothing, just lifts a hand in the most careful, deliberate wave I've ever seen.

Outside, the daylight is bruised and cold. I unlock the car and sit for a second, just breathing. The clippings, the notebook, the sticky residue of every page—these things weigh more than the groceries or the change cup or the sadness that never quite leaves the passenger seat.

I put the keys in the ignition, but I don't turn them. Instead, I pull out my phone and scroll through the photos, one by one, each new headline a match dropped onto the gasoline of my memory.

They wanted me to stop digging.

Too bad.

Lucas

Chain of command is a joke. It's a leash, at best, and tonight it's wound so tight around my neck that every breath tastes like cheap vinyl and sweat of men who think 'tradition' is an excuse for not dying first.

The captain's office is smaller than the janitor's closet. Half the wall is taken up by a display case full of generic commendations—some real, most inherited from the last guy. There's a flag in a triangular frame, a dust-free row of retired pagers, and a photo of the department softball team that's been sun-bleached to the color of nicotine. The captain himself sits behind a desk so cluttered with forms and legal pads that you'd need a front-end loader just to find the monitor.

He's not looking at the paperwork. He's looking at me, the way you look at a raccoon that's just wandered into your kitchen and might start shitting in the silverware drawer at any second.

I clench my jaw so hard it buzzes, hands locked behind my

back. “I need the full incident reports for the Grant house fire,” I say, again, this time slow and even.

He doesn’t blink. “And I already told you, I have already sent you the digital copies. Should be in your inbox, Hayes.”

“I need the originals. The logbooks, the hard copies. There’s a discrepancy in the ignition point, and it’s not reflected in the database.”

He lifts a single eyebrow, which is supposed to communicate world-weary patience but mostly just looks like a worm fighting to free itself. “What’s past is past, son. Department’s got more urgent fires to put out these days.”

“It’s an active investigation,” I say, putting every inch of rank into it. “If arson’s using old tactics, I need to know the baseline.”

He steeples his fingers, breathing out hard through his nose. “You been up all night again?

He wants to laugh it off, make me look unstable. I let the silence fill the room. It’s an old trick, but I’m better at it than he is.

“I’m telling you,” I say, “the same patterns are repeating. The old fires—Grant, Linder, three more, including the library —they’re all connected. I just need the damn records.”

He leans forward, lowering his voice. “Let me be clear. There’s no budget for witch hunts or midnight research expeditions. You want to play detective, you do it on your own time. If you’re asking for sealed files, you need a warrant, not a hunch.”

I see the glint in his eyes: this is the part where I’m supposed to fold. Instead, I plant my boots wider and let my hands uncurl at my sides.

“Why are the files sealed, Captain? Who signed off on that?”

The temperature drops a full ten degrees. He’s done pretending now.

"It's departmental policy. Keeps things tidy, keeps the press from making trouble. Besides, nobody wants to revisit the worst day this fire department had; they cannot help it."

I force my voice flat. "With all due respect, sir, covering up mistakes doesn't make them go away. It just means they're waiting to burn you down later."

The smile he gives me is all teeth. "You're a good firefighter, Hayes. Don't let old ghosts drag you under. This town's got enough problems without you turning molehills into mountains."

The urge to upend his desk is so strong I almost black out for a second.

Instead, I turn on my heel, pausing with my hand on the door. "I'm not letting this go," I say. "If someone's making history repeat itself, I'll find them. With or without your help."

His answer is the soft thunk of a pen dropping onto paper. "Dismissed, Lieutenant."

The hallway outside the office is arctic-bright and smells like Pine-Sol and scorched rubber. I make it ten feet before I put my fist into the side of the file cabinet, just enough to dent it. The sound is loud enough to rattle the glass in the trophy case, but nobody comes to check. Either nobody heard, or nobody wants to get in my way.

I check my phone. No messages. I thumb through my call log, but there's nothing from Sophie. I almost dial her number, just to hear her voice, but I don't want ot sound as shaken as I am. I open the 'Evidence' album and scroll through the photos she sent earlier—yellowed headlines, her father's name circled in red, a sticky note with handwriting I could pick out even half asleep.

There's a pattern here. There has to be. But every time I get close to it, the department slaps my hands and tells me it's nothing.

I grab my jacket and stalk out to the parking lot. The sun's already gone, replaced by the kind of late-winter dusk that makes everything look like it's been dipped in old grease. My truck starts on the second try, headlights stuttering to life as if reluctant to illuminate anything.

I sit there for a full minute, knuckles pale on the wheel, fighting the urge to just drive until the engine quits. Then I see the time—6:17 p.m.—and remember that Sophie hates being alone after the streetlights come on. Not that she'd ever admit it.

I tap out a text: "You home?"

No answer.

I try again, this time just: "Safe?"

Still nothing.

The feeling in my gut is part dread, part adrenaline. I gun the engine and head toward her house, the needle on the dash edging toward the red even though I'm barely doing forty. Every block I pass, I check the rearview, expecting to see flames.

Tonight, I'm not waiting for permission. Tonight, I'll break every rule they've got, and maybe a few of my own.

This time, I won't be too late.

Sophie

The walk from the car to the front porch is maybe thirty yards, but it stretches out like a century when your nerves are set to vibrate at the frequency of disaster. The night is glassy and sharp, every sound carried for miles by the cold. My boots crunch the gravel with a careful hesitation: step, pause, scan, repeat. There's nothing out of place except the porch light, which flickers like it's getting instructions in Morse Code.

I hit the bottom step and freeze. The air tastes wrong. There's a sweetness underneath the damp and mulch, a tang of gasoline so faint it might be my own imagination. The house is in full shadow, windows blank, the only movement is the slow pendulum of the porch swing.

Except: there's no wind tonight.

The swing drifts, creaking at the apex, then reverses. No animal in sight, nothing that could push it. I edge forward, pulse in my ears, hand already in my bag where my pepper spray lives. The door's only a few feet away now, but every instinct says to back the hell up.

That's when the headlights hit. High beams, full force, cut across the yard and trap me in the spotlight. For a second, I think it's a cop, or worse, the person who's been leaving me notes. I shield my eyes and step back, and the porch swing erupts.

It's not subtle: the whole seat and chains go up in a single, savage whoosh, the flame traveling up the cord like a fuse on a cartoon bomb. The swing is instantly engulfed, fire licking at the wood, heat pushing against my face even from ten feet out.

Behind me, tires scream against the curb. A truck door

slams, and then a body slams harder—Lucas, coming in low and fast, driving his shoulder into my ribs and knocking me off my feet. We hit the grass, the wind knocked out of me, his weight all that keeps the blast of heat from rolling over.

The fire is brighter than any memory. It flares upward, devouring the swing, casting everything in orange and black. Then suddenly an explosion, its controlled, but I would have been directly in the firing line if I was trying to put the fire out. The front windows reflect it, turning the house into a burning cathedral, even though the flames are still outside.

We stay on the ground, bodies tangled, his arm hooked over my head to shield me from the debris raining down in little burning chips. Our faces are close enough that I can feel every shudder of his breath.

He's the first to move. "You could've died," he says, voice all gravel and panic.

I taste blood in my mouth. "You already killed me once," I say, and it's not meant to be a joke, but it comes out that way.

He laughs, one bark, then nothing. He pushes himself up, checks my arms, my face, every inch, as if I might still be on fire.

"Are you burned?" he says, hands going up and down my sides, professional but not.

"No," I say, "You didn't have to tackle me."

He looks at the swing, which is now a skeleton, burning itself clean. "Yeah," he says, "I did."

For a second, neither of us moves. We just lie there, adrenaline making everything sharper and looser at the same time.

I push at his chest. "You're crushing me."

He doesn't move right away. His hand goes to the grass beside my face, fingers digging in. "You got a death wish, or did you not smell the fuel?"

I want to tell him that I did, but I didn't care. It's easier to walk into danger than to wait for it to come to you. I just shake my head, though, and he sees through it.

He sits back, hauls me up with him. The side of my face is wet, tears or sweat or melted frost, I don't know. He wipes it with his sleeve, his own hand shaking.

"You good?" he asks.

I nod, but my neck won't work right.

He stands pulling me with him and keeping one hand on my shoulder. The fire is already dying down, but the explosion has woken every house on the block. Lights flicker on, shadows move in windows. Someone will call 911 in a minute, if they haven't already.

Lucas stares at the porch and the remnants of the ruined swing. "That was meant for you," he says. "Not the house. You."

I look at him. His face is raw in the firelight, older and more wrecked than I have seen him before.

"They want me to run," I say.

He grins, but it's all teeth. "Or to finish what they started."

He won't let go of my arm. The smell of gasoline is stronger now, mixed with singed hair and sweat. We're both breathing hard, so close our foreheads nearly touch.

I'm the one who breaks eye contact. "You going to ask if I'm okay again?"

He shakes his head. "I already know you're not."

We stand there, the orange glow painting us into a version of our younger selves: reckless, doomed, unwilling to quit even when the world tells you to lie down and die.

"You're coming with me," he says, breaking the silence.

I start to protest, but he leans in, voice so quiet it's almost lost under the hiss of the fire. "I'm not letting them get to you."

He waits, eyes searching my face.

I want to believe him. I want to believe that there's a safe place somewhere in this town.

But I can't yet. I look at the burning porch, then at him. "You can't protect me from history, Lucas. You never could."

He opens his mouth, but nothing comes out.

The fire is down to embers now, smoke curling around us like a second skin. We're frozen in place, stuck in the moment between disaster and aftermath, waiting for the world to catch up to what's already happened.

Our faces are only inches apart. We stay like that, breathing each other in, until the sirens finally arrive.

The first thing I do when I get inside is check the locks. Lucas does the same, moving room to room with the aggression of someone who expects every shadow to spit out a threat. The windows are already shut, but he double-checks anyway, rattling each pane like he's testing for a weak spot.

I watch him from the kitchen, arms wrapped tight around myself, not for warmth but for structure. The porch is a blackened mess outside, the glass in the front door spider-webbed from the heat. The house still smells of gasoline and melted plastic, and now, us—our sweat, the burnt hair, the fear.

He sweeps through the hallway, checks the utility closet, then the back patio. His voice is a rough bark: "Stay where I can see you."

I'm not a child, but I obey. I lean against the sink, watching the clock's second hand stutter forward. It's been sixty minutes since the flames. That's all. Sixty minutes and already the town is moving on, sirens gone, the neighbors shuttered behind their curtains. The only sign that anything happened is the thin spiral of smoke still curling up from the ruined swing.

Lucas returns and stands in the doorway, arms braced on

either side. "No one in the yard. No one on the street." He won't look at me directly, but I see his eyes, wide and rimmed red.

I cross the kitchen in three strides. "What aren't you telling me?"

He shakes his head. "Not now."

"Don't—" My voice cracks. I take a breath, steady it. "Don't you dare keep me in the dark. You think I'm not used to this? You think I can't handle a little fire?"

That gets him. He turns, jaw flexing, every tendon in his neck standing out like rebar.

"You don't get it, Soph. Someone is making you a target, and I can't—" He stops, breathes out through his teeth. "I can't keep you safe if you won't listen."

"I never asked you to." My voice comes out colder than I want. "I just want to know what's going on. What happened the night my dad died? What do you know that I don't? Why did you run away?"

He drops his head, lets the words hang between us. The old kitchen clock ticks away the silence, louder and louder.

"You want the truth?" he finally says, voice stripped raw. "I saw him. The night of the fire. He wasn't trying to get out—he was looking for someone. He said your name, over and over. He begged me to get you out before him." His hands clench, knuckles bone-white. "I failed him. I got you, but he—" He slams a fist into the wall, just hard enough to rattle the cabinets. "He didn't want to be saved if it meant leaving you behind. I should have made him; I would have had time to get you both."

I let it sink in, the words colder than the air outside.

"You think that's your fault?" I say, incredulous.

He laughs, hollow. "Yeah. Every fucking day."

I don't know if I want to scream at him or hold him, but

before I can decide, we're nose to nose, both of us shaking with the effort of not falling apart.

He grabs my arms, gentle but not gentle. "You're the strongest person I've ever met. But you don't have to carry this alone," he whispers.

There's a wild energy crackling between us, a tension that's not all anger. I feel myself leaning into it, drawn like a moth to the only light left in the world.

It happens fast: he pulls me in, mouth crashing mine, hands in my hair and at my waist. I kiss him back, teeth and tongue and heat, all the rage and loss and years of wanting. I bite his lip, hard, and he grins against my mouth, like he expected nothing less.

For a second, there's no fire, no threats, no history, just us, locked together, burning hotter than anything outside.

I shove him away, both palms to his chest. He stumbles back, startled but not angry.

"I can't," I say, breathless, "not like this. Not when the world's on fire."

He steadies himself, nods. "You don't have to explain."

But I do. "Every time I get close to something good, it goes up in smoke. I can't watch that happen again. Lucas. Not to you. Not to me."

He's quiet. He runs a hand through his hair. "I'm not going anywhere," he says, voice steadier than before. "Not unless you tell me to."

I want to believe him, but trust is a dry well tonight.

I turn, pacing the kitchen, feeling the old anger resurface—at my dad, at the town, at Lucas for carrying my ghosts when I never asked him to.

He watches me. "We'll get through this. But you have to let me in."

I stop and spin on him. "Only if you promise to stop trying to be the hero."

He smirks, but it's sad. "You always did hate white knights."

We lock eyes, the moment stretching out. The smoke smell is everywhere, suffocating, but it's better than the silence.

I go to the counter, pull out the folder of clippings from the library, and toss them onto the table between us. "My dad was onto something. He was tracking the fires, the cover-ups, before the house burned down."

He flips through the pages, skimming faster than he probably should. "Whoever did this—they're still out there."

"I know," I say. "And I want to find them."

He closes the file, looks up at me, and for the first time tonight, there's a glimmer of the old Lucas; the stubborn, smart, impossible bastard I fell for in the first place.

He takes a step closer, stops just shy of touching.

"I'm with you, Sophie. All the way."

My heart kicks, hard. "Even if it means burning everything else down?"

He grins, fierce and proud. "Especially then."

The porch is covered in ash, the front yard a ruin, but the house is still standing. So are we.

Whatever's coming next, we'll face it together. And for the first time in years, I truly feel him by my side.

6

Embers and Echoes

Sophie

THE NIGHT IS SILVER AND RESTLESS. I PACE THE LENGTH of the living room, barefoot, pretending I'm organizing receipts for the insurance company but really just circling the same block of memory, over and over. Every so often, I pull the curtain an inch to the left and check if the truck is still out there.

It is. Lucas, ever the sentry, has stationed his Ford across the street. Engine off now, but the outline of his frame is unmistakable behind the wheel, illuminated at intervals by the slow blink of the streetlamp and the faint blue glow of a phone screen.

It's the third night in a row. The first night, I'd brushed it off as a coincidence, maybe he had a call on this side of town, maybe he needed to make sure the fire was really out. By the second, it felt like a stakeout. Now, it's become the new normal: Lucas posted up in his makeshift foxhole, watching my windows as if expecting a sniper to take me out from the rhododendrons.

I'd be lying if I said it wasn't comforting, in some animal way. But mostly, it makes me want to march out there, rap on the driver's side glass, and tell him to get a hobby that isn't monitoring my existence.

I don't, I just kill the lights and move to the window seat, drawing my knees up and resting my forehead against the cold glass. There's condensation here from where the old storm window leaks. A single moth is trapped between panes, beating itself to death with slow, futile taps. I know the feeling.

I go to bed eventually. I leave the lamp on, though, because this is how I win: I sleep in my own damn house, in my own bed, unafraid.

THE MORNING IS A CLICHE OF SMALL-TOWN SERENITY: birdsong, golden sunlight, the neighbor's dog lifting its leg on the same patch of grass as always. I watch the dew bead up on the mailbox; the street looks like it has been freshly scrubbed by last night's storm. I make coffee with the French press and then step out onto the porch in pajama bottoms and an ancient college sweatshirt.

The Ford is still there. Lucas has migrated to the tailgate, boots on the curb, mug in hand. He's shed the bunker gear in favor of jeans and a thermal, but he still wears the look of a man expecting to be called to action any second.

I take a long, petty sip of coffee, then march down the walk, chin up. He sees me coming and tries for a smile, but it's not his best work.

More of a grimace. There are hollows beneath his eyes, the skin taut and colorless.

I stop at the end of the driveway, fold my arms across my chest, and let the silence build.

"Morning," he says, eventually.

"Is it?"

He doesn't take the bait. He tips his head toward the house, then back to me. "Couldn't sleep."

"Seems contagious."

He sets his mug on the tailgate. "You should be at my place."

I snort. "What, so we can both lie awake staring at the ceiling in shifts? I'd rather risk the arsonist."

He pushes off the tailgate and takes a few steps toward me, careful, as if I'm a deer that might bolt. "I'm serious, Sophie. There's a pattern to this. Whoever's doing it isn't going to stop just because you locked the doors."

I can feel the familiar surge—equal parts pride and irritation—rise through my chest. "This is my home. I'm not leaving it just because someone's got a grudge and a book of matches."

He sighs, a sound so deep it rattles his ribcage. "You're making it easy for them."

"Funny, I thought I was making it easy for you." The words snap out before I can leash them.

He stares at me, expression flat, but his hands are fisted tight. "You don't have to make this hard."

"Believe me, it comes naturally."

The neighbor's dog barks, breaking the tension for a microsecond. I take another sip of coffee, savoring the bitterness, the heat.

He tries again, softer this time. "Let me protect you."

I drop my arms, set the mug down on the sidewalk with a click. "Protect me from what, Lucas? The same thing that got my dad? The same thing that burned us down to the foundation?"

He doesn't answer. He can't.

I let the silence hang, then: "If you want to be useful, you can help me board up the window on the back porch. Otherwise, you're just in the way."

He shakes his head, but there's a flicker of admiration there, like he's proud of my stubbornness even as it drives him insane.

"I'll get my toolbox," he says.

"Good."

I head back up the walk, the grass wet against my ankles. The morning light glances off the water, scattering little diamonds across the lawn. I leave the door open behind me, half invitation, half challenge.

HE SHOWS UP ON THE PORCH A FEW MINUTES LATER, toolbox in hand, sleeves rolled up. I stand at the kitchen sink, watching him through the window as he appraises the busted frame, calculating the best angle of attack. He's methodical and efficient, but I can see the edge of exhaustion in his movements. He's running on caffeine and rage.

I bring out a second mug and set it on the railing. "You didn't have to stay out here all night."

He gives a one-shouldered shrug and pulls a tape measure from his belt. "Couldn't help it."

I lean against the post, arms folded again. "You can't fix this, you know. Whatever's broken here, it's bigger than a couple of boards and a deadbolt."

He doesn't look at me. "I don't have to fix everything. I just have to keep you alive."

For a second, I let the words hang between us, heavier than the humidity.

I nod at the mug. "You want more coffee?"

He glances over, and there's a real smile this time, small and sheepish. "Yeah. Black, if you don't mind."

I go inside, fill it up, and watch the way the morning sun catches in the glass, illuminating every fingerprint, every smudge. When I bring it out, he takes it from my hand, the brush of his fingers deliberate and lingering.

We stand in silence, side by side, watching the lawn steam as the sun burns off the last of the dew.

He says, "I'm not going anywhere."

I say, "Neither am I."

And for a minute, maybe longer, the world feels bearable.

Then the neighbor's sprinkler kicks on, and the moment dissolves, both of us blinking against the spray.

We go inside, close the door, and face whatever comes next.

It's not like the movies. There's no yellow tape or bored patrolman keeping me out, just the wind and the smell. I park on the old shoulder, my tires half sinking into the mud, and step out into the cold morning like it's a dare.

My family home, or the Old Grant House as it's now known to the town, is gone, but the land remembers. The way the dirt slopes downward, the outlines of flower beds that never quite took, the stubborn patch of clover near where the porch used to be. If I squint, I can see the shape of my childhood overlaid on the ruin, one world burning through the other like a double exposure.

I slip the gate. The grass is slick, and the air is heavy with last night's fog. Every step is a crunch of glass and cinder under my boots. I pick my way to the slab, the old foundation still ringed by footings, some toppled sideways like broken teeth. I kneel and run my hands through the debris, what was once ash and shards of drywall, turning my skin gray.

At first, it feels aimless, just another ritual, something to do with my hands while the brain gnaws at itself. But the closer I look, the more I see. There's a logic to the ruins, a hierarchy: heavy char on the north end, softer, sooty residue toward what was once my bedroom. I run my palm along the side of a support beam, half buried in blackened insulation. The surface is glossy in spots, but here and there the wood is scorched deep, cratered with blisters.

That's when I find it. The spiral.

It's not big, maybe three inches across, but it's deliberate. Burned in with something precise. The lines are clean, the pattern tight. I freeze, heart going pinprick-cold, because I've seen this before—not just on my windshield or the mailbox, but in the battered composition notebook my dad left behind.

The same spiral. A warning. Or a signature.

I wipe a patch of ash from my jeans, hand shaking, and reach for my phone. I have to prop my wrist against the slab to get a clear shot; it takes three tries before I manage it. The image on the screen looks surreal, almost staged. For a second, I want to laugh at the melodrama of it, but there's nothing funny about the way my stomach twists.

I stand too fast, the world tilts. The air tastes like old fear.

The urge to call Lucas is immediate and overwhelming, but I make myself stop. There's something about this I want to keep for myself, at least for now. I text the image to my own email, label it "Spiral Beam, NE Corner," and tuck the phone away.

I walk the perimeter of the lot, scanning for other marks on trees, rocks, and any surface that might hold a message. I find nothing, but the feeling of being watched never quite fades.

By the time I make it back to my car, my hands are raw and the morning has lost its shine. I drive with the heat up, trying to thaw the ache from my fingers, but it doesn't help. I spend the next half hour in the parking lot of the old Denny's, staring at the photo and reading it like an obituary. I write a list in my notebook: names, dates, possible suspects, every theory I can conjure. Halfway down the page, I add Lucas's name, then immediately scribble it out. Then I rewrite it, just in case.

I get another coffee at the drive-through, just for something to do, and sit in the car until the sun climbs higher and the engine ticks cool.

Lucas

I am already sitting at the table in the diner when Dalton arrives. We take the back booth, the one near the service station where the waitresses can pretend not to listen but absolutely do. I ordered a black coffee, and nothing else; I don't have the stomach for food right now. Dalton waves off the menu and folds his hands on the table, skin gone papery and pink at the knuckles.

The old Chief looks at me the way a battered prizefighter sizes up his own reflection, resentful and a little amazed to still be standing. The silence stretches so long that even the waitress gets uncomfortable and drops off our coffees with a muttered, "Shout if you need pie."

Dalton breaks first. "You've been looking into old business."

I nod, no denial. "There's a connection. Grant, the Linder fire, a string of arson cases in the late 90's. Same M.O., same spiral mark."

Dalton sips his coffee, winces, and sets it aside. "You think your girl's in danger?"

I don't blink. "I know she is."

Dalton's eyes go soft, then hard again. "That house fire wasn't an accident. Not that the town ever wanted to admit it. Your girl's father—he was a pain in the ass, but he knew how to follow a thread. He was looking into budget irregularities. Safety violations, some of them buried deep."

"Who stood to lose if he went public?" I ask, leaning in.

Dalton pulls a napkin from the dispenser, turns it over, and writes a single name in block capitals. He slides it across the table. "He came to me with this name a week before he died. Said if anything happened, to look here first."

I look at the name and feel the muscles in my jaw tighten like a vice.

Dalton holds up both hands, palms out. "Don't drag me back into this, son. I'm two years from the grave, and I'd like to make it on my own terms."

I pocket the napkin, "Thanks for the coffee, Chief." I say softly.

Dalton's smile is thin, but not unkind. "You're welcome. Tell her to keep her head down."

Sophie

My phone rings, it's Lucas, I consider answering it, but I let it go to voicemail instead. I stare at my phone and he sends me a text. "Something new. Will explain tonight. Don't go anywhere."

I smile in spite of myself, and type back: "Wouldn't dream of it."

But I don't go home, not yet. I drive the long way around the lake, letting the memory of the spiral burn itself onto the backs of my eyelids, and head to the grocery store.

There are answers out there, if I can survive long enough to find them.

I CATCH HIM AT THE EDGE OF THE PARKING LOT, HUNCHED low beside my rear tire, one hand braced on the undercarriage. The way he moves is too careful for a flat or a routine check; he's looking for something, and he's hoping nobody sees him do it. In a town this size, that means trouble, or at least an open invitation for rumors.

I'm halfway between two bags of groceries and the safety of the car before he even looks up. When he does, the expression on his face is stripped of every defense: not the cool blue of the investigator, not the practiced, unbothered scowl. This is raw panic. For a second, I freeze, paper bag sagging in my arms.

He wipes his hand on his jeans, stands, and waits for me to reach him. The sun is bright enough to make him squint, and his hair looks darker with the sweat beading at his temples.

"You okay?" I ask because there's something about his stance that says he's not.

He doesn't answer right away. Instead, he grabs my elbow, hard but not bruising, and pulls me to the other side of the car, away from the view of the street.

"Look," he says, voice low.

I squint at the spot where his thumb presses. There's a small, dark rectangle affixed to the frame, almost invisible unless you know what to look for. He slides a pocketknife from somewhere in his jacket and pries it loose in one clean motion.

He hands it to me. It's lighter than I expected, no bigger than a pack of gum, but the weight of it is in the intent. I turn it over in my palm, the casing smooth and cold. There are no markings, just the faint magnetic bite along one edge.

"Tracker?" I ask.

"Professional grade," he says. "Not a toy."

I close my hand around it, not trusting myself to look at him. I'm scared, but I don't want him to see it in my eyes.

"Someone's keeping tabs on you," he says. "Not just here. Wherever you go."

My mouth goes dry. I want to make a joke, but nothing comes out.

He leans in, crowding me against the car. "You need to come with me. Right now. We'll pack, we'll go—"

"No," I say, too loud, too fast.

He steps back, startled.

"I'm not running, Lucas."

He closes his eyes for a beat and pinches the bridge of his nose. "This isn't about pride—"

"It's about not letting them win." I jab a finger at the tracker. "You think they want me scared? You think they want me to disappear?"

He opens his mouth, then closes it. The tension in his jaw could cut glass.

"I'm going home," I say. "If you want to play bodyguard, be my guest. But I'm not leaving."

We ride in silence, my groceries between us on the seat, the tracker sitting atop the eggs like a curse. He doesn't even try to argue. He just drives with both hands on the wheel, the line of his mouth drawn tight.

At the house, he checks every window and door before he'll even let me inside. The kitchen feels too small, the air electric with unsaid things.

He sets the tracker on the counter, next to the phone. It sits there, black and inert, soaking up all the light in the room.

I unpack the groceries—half as a distraction, half as a performance. Cereal, milk, bread, and a single pint of ice cream, I don't even remember picking up. I arrange them in the fridge, methodical as a surgeon, refusing to look up.

He just stands there, arms folded, watching.

Finally, I turn to face him. "You going to say something, or just glare at me until I combust?"

He doesn't move. "Do you even understand what this means?"

"Sure," I say, stacking soup cans in neat rows. "It means I've got an audience."

He laughs, but it's not a pleasant sound. "It means someone knows where you are every minute. It means they could be outside right now, waiting."

I slam a can down, harder than I mean to. "And what? You think you can keep me safe by locking me up? By making me hide?"

"I think it's a hell of a lot better than the alternative."

"Which is what? Letting them chase me until I run out of road?"

He steps closer, palms flat on the counter. The space between us is a live wire. "You don't get it. You can't just muscle your way through this."

I meet his eyes, steady. "Maybe not. But I'm sure as hell not letting you muscle me out of my own life."

He grits his teeth. "You're impossible."

"Good. Because I'm not my father."

He recoils a little. The hurt flickers, but then it's gone, buried under something else.

He grabs the tracker, holds it up like proof. "They're escalating. Next time, it won't be a warning."

I snatch it from his hand. "Then let them come."

He slams the counter with his fist; the sound is loud enough to make me jump.

"Goddamit, Sophie. I can't lose you. Not like this."

The words hang heavy and hot.

I take a breath, exhale slowly. "You don't own me, Lucas."

He's across the kitchen in one stride, hands braced on either side of my face, not quite touching. His voice drops, almost a whisper. "But I want to."

My throat closes. For a second, I can't breathe at all.

He presses his forehead to mine, breathing hard. "Let me do this. Let me protect you."

I shake my head, but I'm not sure if it's no, yes, or just survival.

He kisses me. Not gentle, not tentative, just full, relentless, years of wanting collapsed into a single, bone-deep need. I taste the salt of his skin, the smoke in his hair, and all the arguments dissolve.

My hands are in his hair, on his shoulders, pulling him closer. The groceries scatter to the floor. The tracker spins across the linoleum and comes to rest in the dust beneath the stove.

He picks me up, hauls me onto the counter, and pushes my knees apart with his thighs. The denim of his jeans grinds against bare skin, friction so good it hurts. I gasp into his mouth, bite his lower lip, and he laughs, low and wrecked.

He tears at the hem of my shirt, yanking it over my head. My hair goes wild, static-charged. He runs his hands down my sides, finding every bruise, every mark, every place this world has tried to leave its print on me. He memorizes it, hungry.

I fumble with his belt, fingers clumsy. He helps, one-handed, never breaking the kiss. When his jeans hit the floor, I slide my palm down, find him hard and throbbing.

He kisses down my jaw, my neck, tongue tasting the salt, the edge of the vulnerability I never let anyone else see. His hands are everywhere, at my hips, cupping my ass, guiding me onto him.

He thrusts hard. The jolt rips a sound from my throat I don't recognize. He sets a rhythm, relentless, the counter thudding in time. My head falls back, eyes closed, nothing in the world but him and me and the heat building between us.

He whispers my name, once, twice, a prayer or a warning. I answer with my body, locking my ankles around his waist, pulling him deeper.

It's rough and raw, neither of us pretending to be gentle. He slams into me, again and again, and the pleasure comes fast, violent. I break around him, shuddering, nails digging into his back. He keeps going, chasing the high until he groans my name, burying his face in my shoulder.

After, we stay like that, tangled, sweat-slicked, and shaking. The world outside is quiet for once, the only sound our breathing and the cooling click of the stove.

He pulls out, softens, but doesn't let go. His hands stay on my hips, anchoring me.

I rest my forehead on his, heart still racing.

"I'm not leaving," I say, softly.

"I know," he says, softer.

We don't move for a long time.

Eventually, I slide off the counter, knees wobbly. He steadies me, pulls my shirt back over my head. We laugh, as my face is covered by my hair.

He picks up the tracker off the floor and turns it over in his palm. "I'm going to find them."

I nod, dizzy and breathless. "Together."

He kisses me again, slower this time.

WE LEAVE THE KITCHEN WRECKED, THE GROCERIES forgotten, the counter marked with handprints, and the air charged.

Outside, the world is still waiting, but inside, we've drawn our line.

Let them come.

7

Smoke Signals

Sophie

The morning after is always uglier than you think. I make a show of being up and moving before Lucas, even though I know he's a light sleeper and that he's probably been listening to my every move since I creaked out of bed. There's a tension in my neck so sharp I half-expect to find a wire running from skull to collarbone. The air in the kitchen is thick with the scorched smell of last night's coffee and something else; old smoke, maybe, or just the afterburn of two people trying to unsee what they did to each other on a laminate countertop.

Lucas doesn't so much enter the room as occupy it, broad-shouldered and freshly showered, his hair still wet at the temples. He's changed into clean jeans and a t-shirt that would have looked like a threat on any man with less bone structure. There's a cut above his left eyebrow, faint but angry, that I don't remember from the night before. I stare at it, and then at the sink, and then at the eggs in their cracked plastic carton. Anything but his face.

He clears his throat. "You want breakfast?"

I don't look up. "Not hungry."

He moves past me to the coffee pot, and for a second, our hands almost brush; my pulse jumps, hot and electric, but he yanks his away as if the touch would scald him. He pours himself a mug, black, and stands by the window, mug hovering near his mouth, but he never drinks. His gaze is fixed outside, jaw flexing in little microspasms like he's fighting with himself.

I DUMP GROUNDS INTO THE FRENCH PRESS WITH MORE force than necessary. "You don't have to stay, you know."

Lucas sets his coffee down so hard it sloshes. "And you don't have to act like last night didn't happen."

I slam the spoon into the sink. "I'm not acting. I just have things to do."

He makes a noise in the back of his throat, equal parts frustration and—I don't know—hurt? I refuse to look at him directly, so I can't confirm. He retreats to the kitchen table, where he's already spread out half a dozen folders and a battered spiral notebook, the one he always used for notes even after the department went digital. He flips through pages without reading, fingers tracing the same line over and over.

I open the fridge, pull out a jar of peanut butter, and stare into its hollow, like the right answer might be written in oily brown along the bottom. There's no script for this. We've had sex before, years ago, when it was messy but easier; back seats and motel rooms, the world ending at dawn, but this is different. This is older, more desperate, with the kind of consequences neither of us wants to name.

"We should talk about it," he says.

I spread peanut butter on a slice of stale bread. "What's there to say? We had a bad night. We fucked. It's not news."

He exhales, long and slow, but doesn't argue. I admire him for that; his ability to let things rot in silence until they grow their own legs and run away.

We exist in the same room, but on separate planets. He keeps to his paperwork, occasionally making marks with a pen, but the scratch is barely audible. I chew my bread like it's a dare, swallowing fast to keep from gagging on the memory of last night. I could say it was adrenaline, or fear, or the way the world has been closing in, but it would be a lie. I wanted it. I wanted him. I still do.

He finally breaks the stalemate. "I have to go to the station. Bennett called. Something about the fire report."

I nod, even though he's not looking.

He pushes back from the table, his chair scraping the floor in a way that makes me freeze. "You're not safe here alone, Soph."

I bristle at the old nickname, but I don't give him the satisfaction of a reaction. "I'll be fine. There are cameras, remember? and you set the alarm."

He moves toward the door, pauses. "Just...text if you see anything weird. Or if you leave."

"Sure," I say, and I mean to sound flippant, but it comes out brittle as glass.

He hesitates, then leaves without another word. The door clicks shut, and I count the seconds it takes for his footsteps to vanish down the walk. Only then do I let myself breathe.

I'm still at the window when he gets in his truck. He sits there, engine running, staring straight ahead like he's waiting for permission to move. Eventually, he pulls away, tires crunching on gravel, and the house goes quiet. I pour myself another cup of coffee and watch the empty street.

There's work to do. I have a plan, even if I'm not sure it's a good one.

I text Lucas: "Running errands. Will update."

No reply. I almost smile.

By the time I leave the house, the sun is full up, and the birds have gone silent, as if they know what's coming.

In the rearview, I see Lucas's truck two blocks down, just out of sight but exactly where he thinks I won't notice. For all his talk of protection, he's not subtle.

I drive anyway, the roads familiar and alien all at once, every turn a reminder that the world I grew up in isn't the one I'm living in now.

As I merge onto the highway, I check the mirror. He's still there, two cars back.

For once, I don't mind.

The Willow Creek Fire Station's records office hasn't changed since I was a kid, except that now the paint is more faded and the coffee pot on the front counter looks older than most of the volunteers. The inside smells like bleach, stale toast, and that sticky undertone of burnt plastic that never quite leaves a firehouse, no matter how many air fresheners you hang from the alarm panel.

I park in the municipal lot, angle the car so I can see the door, and kill the engine. No sign of Lucas's truck; he must have taken the main highway into the city. I pull my jacket tight and do a slow count to ten before heading in. His absence allows me a head start I don't want to waste.

The clerk behind the glass doesn't look up at first; he's mid-scroll on a fantasy football app, the blue light washing out what's left of his summer tan. I tap the glass with two fingers, gentle at first, then with more intent.

He looks up, "Help you?"

"I'm hoping to look up some fire incident logs from a few years ago." I keep my voice soft, put just enough quaver in it to suggest genuine curiosity, not obsession.

"Which years?" he asks, already sounding bored.

I pull a sticky note from my purse and hold it up to the glass. "Ninety-four, ninety-seven, and two-thousand-one, if you have them."

He frowns, does a slow mental math, then sighs. "That's gonna be in the archives, ma'am. You renovating a property or something?"

I smile. "Yeah, family home. Want to know if the real estate told me the truth."

He grunts, disappears through a side door, and the only sound is the hum of ancient fluorescent bulbs and the echo of my pulse in my ears. A few minutes later, he returns with a battered file box, sets it in the gap under the glass.

"Don't take 'em out of the lobby," he says. "If you need copies, flag 'em for me. Black and white's a dime a page."

"Thanks," I say sincerely. He could have made this harder.

The lobby isn't built for privacy, but there's a bench by the exit where the sun sneaks through and lights the dust motes up like fireflies. I haul the box over and settle in, careful to keep my back to the rest of the room. I pop the lid and am immediately hit with a wall of dust.

The files are in no particular order; some are loose, some clipped, some in manila folders scrawled with dates and blocky handwriting. I work methodically: Pull a stack, check the year, flip through the pages for anything interesting, then re-stack. My fingers get gray fast, the tips smudged with years of other people's work.

I find the first anomaly twenty minutes in. The incident log for the Grant house is there, my family home, but the page is a

Frankenstein, halves taped together, some sections redacted with thick black marker, others whited out so aggressively the paper is thin as tissue. The report itself is terse: "Source undetermined, possible accelerant, investigation ongoing." The signature line at the bottom is blank.

My hands go slick. I dig deeper, cross-referencing the other two years. Same pattern: a lot of fires around the neighborhood, each file more gutted than the last, as if someone came through with a chainsaw to the public record. The Linder barn, the Hawthorn garage, three more I'd never heard of. All redacted, all missing the origin story.

I slide the Grant log onto my lap, raise my phone inside my jacket, and snap a series of quick photos, one per page. I angle for no flash, keeping the movement tight and close. I repeat for the Linder file, and again for the Hawthorn.

The more I flip, the less the files look like history and the more they look like a cover-up. There's a pattern to what's missing: names, ignition points, chemical findings. Whoever did this, they weren't subtle, but they were thorough.

Halfway through the second box, I hear the distinct thunk of boots on linoleum. Someone else is in the lobby, maybe a volunteer or a paramedic on break. My breath stalls. I force myself to keep turning pages, pretending I'm too lost in what I am doing to care about an audience.

The voice that comes next is a gravelled baritone, slow and suspicious. "You need help with anything, ma'am?"

I look up, paste on the city-girl smile. "No, thank you. Just doing some research."

The man—a senior firefighter, judging by the uniform—leans on the counter and eyes me over the top of his glasses. "Not a lot of people interested in that kind of research."

I shrug. "I'm not most people."

He smiles at that, but it doesn't reach his eyes.

"Just don't take the files home, okay?" He straightens, looks to the clerk, who gives a lazy salute from behind the glass.

I nod, and he leaves.

I wait until the door swings shut, then go back to work. The redactions are even heavier in the last batch; someone has used a razor or scissors to slice out entire sections. I find a fragment of a note, hand-written in blue ink: "Initial suspect cleared. Motive unknown." The rest of the note is gone.

My phone is nearly full from all the images. I delete a couple of old voicemails to make space. The nerves are gone now, replaced by a cold curiosity. If someone was willing to butcher public records, it means there's something worth hiding.

I finish the last stack, re-align the files exactly as I found them, and close the lid. My hands are streaked with black, a visible record of my own trespass.

I walk the boxes back to the counter. The clerk glances at my hands, but doesn't comment on them. "Find what you needed?"

I give him the same smile as before. "I always do."

Outside, the air is clean and cold, a million miles from the burned-out stink of the archives. I get in the car, lock the doors, and pull up the photos, scrolling one by one, each new blacked-out line a fuse waiting to burn down what's left of my memory.

I should call Lucas. I should tell him what I found. I send the photos to my encrypted folder and start my engine. I need to print these.

There's one more place to check before I go see him.

THE HALLWAY OUTSIDE LUCAS'S OFFICE IS PAINTED THE same institutional gray as every other municipal building in Willow Creek, but it feels colder, like the color could leach warmth straight from your bones. The door is propped with a battered stopper; inside, the overhead fluorescents strobe against the battered linoleum. I step through and catch him mid-phone call, one hand covering the receiver, eyes already rolling before he even sees me.

He gestures for me to sit, but I shake my head. I'm not staying enough to warm the seat.

He wraps up the call with a series of grunts and half-sentences, then drops the phone onto its cradle and leans back in his chair, arms folded. "Let me guess," he says, voice thin with fatigue. "You found something."

I pull the manila envelope from my bag and slap it down on the desk, hard enough that the papers fan out, revealing the uneven, redacted pages.

Lucas regards the mess, expression unreadable. "Nice haul."

I stare him down. "Why are these sealed, Lucas? Why is half the story missing?"

He looks up at me, eyes sharp as broken glass. "That's what you came to ask?"

I lean over the desk, hands braced on the edge. "Don't bullshit me. The files for my dad's case, my entire neighborhood, are more blacked out than a CIA op. Did you even look at them before you let the department bury them?"

He rubs the bridge of his nose, a muscle ticking in his jaw. "I tried, Soph. I really did. The order came down from above. Way above."

I snap. "Who?"

He glances over his shoulder, lowers his voice as if the walls could rat us out. "Bennett. The Chief. Maybe even higher, but Bennett signed off."

I let that settle. "So, what, you're just a good little soldier now? You take orders from the same guy who fucked up my father's case?"

He bristles at that, shoulders squaring up. "It's not that simple."

"Then make it simple."

He stands, comes around the desk, hands in his pockets. "Bennett was my mentor. He taught me everything I know about fire, about people, about how not to get burned twice by the same mistake. I owed him. Maybe I still do."

I shake my head. "That's not loyalty, Lucas. That's cowardice."

He winces, but I don't let up.

I pull the last page from the envelope, a copy of the incident map, annotated in blue pen. I toss it at his chest. "You see this? It's a pattern. Every fire, every accident, it spirals in. My house, my father, the barn, everything. Someone wanted it covered up. Someone still does."

He lets the paper drift to the floor, then picks it up slowly. "You think Bennett's behind this?"

I don't answer right away. Instead, I fix him with the kind of stare that used to make him laugh, back when he was the only person I trusted. "I think you're protecting someone who doesn't give a damn about you, or me, or what really happened."

He paces, agitated. "Bennett's a hardass, but he's not dirty. He's not an arsonist."

I arch an eyebrow. "You sure about that?"

He looks like he wants to throw something, but instead, he opens a desk drawer and pulls out a massive rolled-up map, the kind that belongs in a war room, not a shitty municipal office.

He unrolls it on the desk, pins the corners with a coffee mug and his cell phone.

"Look," he says, and points with a chewed-off pencil. "Every major fire in the last decade, plotted to the block. You're right, it's a spiral. But it's not just yours. It's half the damn town."

I take in the map, the red pen crisscrossing points, the careful arcs tracking the inferno's progress through Willow Creek. At the dead center is a black star—my address.

He traces the line, then taps his finger at the periphery. "Whoever's doing this, they're not just random. They're methodical. They're pushing us, herding us, until—" He stops.

"Until what?" I prompt.

He hesitates. "Until you're back in the center. Until you're home again."

The room goes very quiet.

He leans back, hands braced behind him. "I didn't want to believe it. But then the threats, the porch, the tracker on your car. It all adds up."

I want to scream, but I make myself stay calm. "Why not tell me any of this? Why keep pretending you didn't know anything?"

He shrugs, eyes locked on mine. "You were never going to let me protect you, Soph. So I did what I could from here. I tracked the fires, I cross-checked every report, every rumor. I tried to get ahead of it."

I cross my arms, the anger cooling into something sharper. "So you're either an idiot, or you think I am. You don't get to run this investigation without me."

He opens his hands, palms up. "I'm not trying to—"

"Yes, you are," I cut in. "You always have. Even now, you're standing there like you're the last sane man in a room full of smoke, and I'm just another victim waiting for rescue."

He starts to protest, but I shake my head. "I'm not the kid you pulled out of a burning house, Lucas. I'm not even the girl you left behind."

He goes quiet, but his jaw works like he's chewing through a mouthful of regret.

For a moment, neither of us moves.

I break the standoff. "So what's the plan? Wait for another fire? Or do we go to Bennett and force him to admit what he did?"

Lucas exhales, glances at the map. "First, we go over the footage. The security cams from your place. There's a good chance we'll see our guy. Or at least where he went."

I nod, but I can't help one last shot. "And if Bennett shows up in that footage?"

He finally manages a smile, small and bitter. "Then I'll have him arrested myself."

I start gathering my papers, but he puts a hand over mine, stopping me.

"Let's do this together, Soph," he says. There's no arrogance in it. Just the kind of plea I used to dream about.

I swallow hard. "Fine. But if you try to shield me from the truth again, I'll burn your entire office down."

He laughs, and for a second, the world doesn't feel like it's closing in.

Lucas's living room is barely furnished: a battered couch, a scarred coffee table, and a flat-screen mounted with visible drywall screws. The only illumination is the blue glow of the monitor and the slant of dusk bleeding in through the cheap blinds. I sit on the edge of the couch, knees locked, while Lucas boots up his laptop, a tangle of cables connecting it to a DVR box and the new security cams he installed at my place last week.

He logs in, clicks through folder names with dates and abbreviations, each one a neat little tombstone of uneventful nights. He's precise with the mouse, but his hands shake just enough to make the pointer jitter. I keep mine clenched in my lap, as if that will keep them from shaking too.

The video loads: four quadrants, each showing a different slice of my house and the perimeter. Black and white, resolution garbage, but the time stamps tick forward. We sit in silence, watching nothing. A possum trundles past the shed. Wind jostles the hedges. A pair of headlights sweeps the street at 2:11 AM and vanishes again.

He fast-forwards, then rewinds, then slows to quarter-speed. "Here," he says, pausing on a frame where something—a blur—moves along the tree line at the back edge of the property. He clicks forward, frame by frame. The blue resolves: a figure, tall, hooded, arms held close to the body. The face is a smear, but the posture is unmistakably human.

Lucas leans in, the muscles in his jaw flexing. "That's not just some punk."

He zooms in, pixelating the image further, but it's clear enough to show the way the figure moves, deliberate, like a surveyor or a predator. It stops at the back corner of the yard, crouches, and seems to look directly into the lens. My breath catches. I know that stance. I know it in my bones.

He scrolls through the other angles, hoping for a better shot, but the figure stays in the shadows, never crossing the threshold of the motion sensor's hot zone. It's like he knows the limits of the system.

Lucas plays the clip again, this time letting the footage run.

The figure lingers for a full five minutes, then turns and slips back into the woods.

He pauses on the last frame, the figure's head tilted just enough that for a split second, I think I see a sliver of jawline, the barest crescent of a cheekbone in the ambient light.

"Does he look familiar to you?" he asks.

I can't speak, so I nod.

He leans back, arms crossed over his chest. "You're not safe there. Not alone."

"I never said I was," I snap, voice sharper than intended.

He runs a hand over his face, then looks at me with something between exasperation and fear. "Then why the hell do you keep running toward the danger?"

"Because I can't stand sitting around, waiting for something else to burn down," I spit back.

He stares at me, and the silence is a taut wire between us.

Finally, he says, "Stay here tonight. We'll set up more cameras, maybe double up the perimeter."

I shake my head. "I need to check something at the house. I think I know who it is."

He slams the laptop shut, the sound echoing off the barren drywall. "No. You're not going back out there."

I square my shoulders, glaring him down. "You can't stop me."

He stands, and for a second, I think he might actually try to block the door. "Jesus, Soph, you're going to get yourself killed."

I grab my bag, keys already in my hand. "That's my problem, not yours."

He follows me to the door, boots thudding on bare floor. "You want to tell me what you saw? What you recognized?"

I pause in the entryway, half in shadow. How do I tell him I still don't know who, I just know that I know them. "It's not a stranger. That's the part that scares me."

He goes quiet then: "At least let me follow you."

I don't answer, just let the screen door slap behind me as I jog to the car.

In the rearview, I see him watching from the porch, face a mask of frustration and fear, or maybe just the helplessness of a man who's always been able to pull people out of burning buildings, but never learned how to keep them from running in.

I drive the back roads, the sun already bleeding out of the sky, and aim the headlights at the wooded edge behind my property.

I park, kill the engine, and sit with my heart beating so loud it drowns out the chirp of summer insects. I check my phone: one missed call, then a single text from Lucas.

"Don't go alone. Please."

I step out, lock the car, and head for the woods.

Somewhere in the dark, I know, someone is waiting.

The woods are thicker than I remember, the undergrowth clawing at my jeans, dead leaves clinging to my boots like they don't want to let go. Above, the branches tangle into a canopy that sifts out the last of the evening light, turning the world blue and black and barely navigable. Every step forward is a negotiation, roots and rocks, mud slick from yesterday's rain, and the persistent sting of nettles against my skin.

I don't bother with a flashlight. I don't want whoever's out here to see me coming.

I move slow at first, counting off ten paces at a time. My breath comes shallow, the air wet and sour with rot. There's a path, sort of, but it's long since gone to seed; the only clearings are those made by deer, or by people who don't care about footprints.

I pause, scan the darkness. Nothing but the throb of insect song and the faint, far-off drone of a generator back toward the road.

I push deeper. The silence sharpens. Each step is a crunch, a pop, a warning to anything in earshot that I'm here, and I'm not scared.

Liar.

A hundred yards in, I stop to listen. The birds have gone quiet, and my pulse is so loud it's like I swallowed a drum kit. I glance back: the gap I came through is already gone, stitched up by shadow.

I keep going, legs trembling from effort and something else —anticipation, maybe, or the memory of the last time I ran through these trees, a child with fire at my back.

The crunch of my steps is joined by something else. Softer, but matched to my rhythm. I freeze, hold my breath, and the sound dies too. For three heartbeats, there's nothing.

Then: a twig snaps. Close.

I spin, squint into the dark, and see only the blur of movement, then gone. A flicker of black against a darker black.

I try to steady my breathing, but it won't come. My hands are cold, fingers numb and stiff.

I move again, faster this time, but so do the steps behind me. I break into a jog, dodging around trees, my boots slipping on the mossy ground. I look back—just a glance, but enough to catch the hint of a figure, maybe fifty feet back, keeping pace but not closing.

My heel catches on a root and I go down hard, both palms scraping open on gravel and bark. I grit my teeth against the pain and scramble upright, but the crash has given the pursuer ground. The footsteps come faster, less cautious now.

I run. Really run. The woods blur to nothing, branches whip at my arms, hair tangles in my mouth. I hear the other set of footsteps, relentless, and my own ragged breathing drowning out everything else.

Another root, another stumble, and I'm back on the ground, this time tasting blood where I bit my tongue. I push up, legs screaming, and see the figure closer now, just at the edge of vision. Too big for a woman, moving like he's done this before.

I cut left, off the path, crashing through saplings and brush, desperate for any advantage. The ground slopes down, steep and slippery, and I almost lose my footing again, arms pinwheeling for balance.

Through a break in the trees, I see the pale shape of my aunt's truck, the metal catching what little light remains. I lunge for it, putting everything into a last sprint, lungs on fire.

Behind me, the footsteps break into a run too. Closer. Closer.

I clear the last few feet and yank the door handle, praying it isn't jammed. It opens, and I throw myself inside, slam it shut, thumb the lock just as a fist hits the glass—hard, but not enough to break it.

I scream, more from shock than fear, and the face behind the glass is nothing but a shadow, a blur of hood and eyes and—God, is that a smile? No. Just the play of light, the trick of adrenaline.

I fumble for the keys, drop them once, twice, then jam them into the ignition. I start the engine, headlights blasting the woods in a wash of white. The figure backs away, hands up in a mock surrender.

I lock the doors again, just to be sure, and watch as the figure melts into the trees, gone as suddenly as he appeared.

I sit in the dark, hands shaking so bad I can barely keep them on the wheel. I breathe, count to ten, and breathe again.

I check my phone. Nothing from Lucas. Nothing from anyone.

I watch the tree line, waiting to see if the shadow will return.

It doesn't.

I peel out, mud and gravel spraying behind me, and don't stop until I'm a mile down the road, the woods a blur in my rearview.

For the first time, I believe it:

They're not trying to scare me.

They're hunting me.

I sit in the truck, hands gripping the wheel so tight the bones ache. My chest heaves with every breath, adrenaline burning through my veins in caustic little pulses. I replay the chase again and again, the faceless figure, the impact of the fist on the glass, the electric jolt of knowing I am not just being watched—I am being hunted.

Headlights flare behind me, turning the inside of the cab into a fishbowl. For a second I think it's the shadow come back for round two, but then I recognize the shape of the truck: Lucas's, barreling down the dirt road with the high beams on.

He screeches to a stop a few yards behind me, slamming his door so hard I hear the frame protest. The distance between us collapses in seconds. He stalks up to my window, face a thundercloud, lips white with fury.

He raps on the glass, and I only hesitate a second before cranking it down just enough for air to pass.

"What the fuck are you doing?" he spits, voice low and ragged.

I keep my face neutral. "Isn't it obvious? I'm setting a trap."

He shakes his head, disgusted. "You could have been killed."

I lift my chin. "So could you."

He opens the door, arms braced on the roof and window frame, the muscle in his jaw twitching. "You can't outrun this, Soph."

"I'm not trying to outrun it," I snap. "I'm bait, remember? You said it yourself."

He opens his mouth like he's about to lecture, but the words get tangled. His eyes flick up and down my body, taking in the dirt, the blood, the wild hair. "You're bleeding."

"It's nothing," I say, but my hands shake as I try to find a tissue in the glove compartment. He snatches it away, his hand enveloping mine for a second—a flash of heat, then gone.

He drags his sleeve over the cut on my cheek, not gentle but not cruel, either. "You're a fucking idiot," he says, but his voice has gone soft. "You could have called me."

I look him straight in the eye. "And you would have stopped me."

He doesn't deny it. Instead, he drops his hand, shoulders caving in just a fraction. "You're not expendable, Soph. Not to me."

There's a silence, a hollow between us so wide I could fall into it and never hit bottom. He steps back, runs both hands through his hair, pacing a short, angry line along the side of the truck.

"Lucas—" I start.

He cuts me off, voice barely above a whisper. "I can't do this if you won't let me help."

I step out, dirt and dead leaves tumbling out with me. I stand toe-to-toe with him, the hood of the truck at our backs, the woods at our feet.

"I don't need saving," I say. "I need a partner."

He closes the gap, his chest brushing mine, the heat off his skin radiating like a second sun. "I can do that," he says, but there's a tremor to it—like the words cost him something.

I don't know who moves first, but then we're on each other, all hands and teeth and the salt of old wounds. He grabs my waist, lifts me against the door, mouth crushing mine so hard I feel the crack of teeth. It's not a kiss, not really—it's a collision, two people desperate to prove they're still alive, that the world can't burn them out entirely.

My hands find his shoulders, then his hair, tugging hard enough to make him growl. His lips are rough, his beard scraping raw across my jaw. He tastes like sweat and rage and something sweeter, something I can't name.

He pulls back just enough to breathe, forehead pressed to mine. "You drive me insane," he says, voice wrecked.

"Right back at you," I whisper.

He kisses me again, softer this time but no less urgent,

hands roaming under my shirt, skin to skin. I arch against him, wanting more, needing it, needing him.

But then I remember the shadow in the woods, the fist on the glass, and I shove him back, both palms flat on his chest.

"Not here," I say, voice hoarse. "Not when someone's still out there."

He lets me go, breathing hard, hands up in surrender. "Fine."

I step back, smoothing my hair, trying to catch my breath. We stare at each other, both of us vibrating with something that isn't quite anger, isn't quite lust, isn't quite fear.

The woods are dead silent. The figure is gone, but its memory is stamped behind my eyelids, a negative space where safety should be.

Lucas breaks first. "I'll follow you home."

I nod, not trusting myself to speak.

I get back in the truck, engine idling, the sweat on my back already turning cold. I watch him in the mirror as he returns to his truck, the set of his shoulders daring the world to try again.

We drive home in tandem, two vehicles in lockstep, neither willing to let the other out of sight.

When we get to my house, he parks right behind me, headlights painting the whole driveway in harsh yellow. I sit for a while, watching the empty yard, the windows blank and black.

He walks me to the door, stands behind me while I unlock it. For a second, I think he'll follow me inside, but he stops on the threshold.

"If you need me," he says, "just call."

I look at him, really look, and see the rawness there, the fear under the bravado. "I will," I say.

He waits until I close the door behind me before turning away.

Inside, I lean against the wood, slide to the floor, and press my hands to my face.

I should be scared. I should be angry.

But all I feel is the heat of his mouth on mine, and the wild certainty that whatever is coming next, it's going to set the whole world on fire.

Let it.

8

Kindling

Lucas

The first thing you notice is the smell. It never leaves, not really, not even a decade later with the foundation picked clean and the grass re-growing in wild green clumps through the old cinders. I stand at the center of the old slab, hands jammed in my jacket pockets, staring at the ghost footprint of the Grant house and trying not to count the number of times I've done exactly this.

It's early. Dew beads up on the weeds, and my boots leave dark prints wherever I step. Every few yards, the white sun catches on something ugly: a nail, a curl of melted wire, the bite mark of a shovel where they scraped the ground for evidence the night after. Somewhere out in the trees, a chainsaw starts up and then chokes out, leaving the world even quieter than before.

I come here when I need to remember why I left, or why I came back. It's a habit with teeth.

The slab's not big. I can cross it in six steps, slow, heel to toe. At the far end is a chunk of scorched two-by-four, propped up like a headstone. That's where I first kissed her, if you want to call it that. Sixteen, both of us, and still smelling like the fire that ate her living room. She'd come back from a volunteer shift at the station, hair in a mess, overalls stiff with sweat and ancient soot. I was supposed to be boarding up the windows, but instead I let her talk me into stealing Cokes from the squad's breakroom fridge.

I remember how she laughed—loud, but with a hitch like she wasn't used to the sound. She handed me the can, opened hers, and then turned her mouth up in a dare: "Bet you can't chug it in five seconds."

I lost, obviously. She wiped foam off her chin and said, "Try again next time, city boy." Then, before I could think about it, she was kissing me. Not soft. Not careful. Her lips tasted like copper and sugar and the burnt lining of the house. Her hand slid into my hair, gripping hard, and the whole world vanished.

It didn't last. It never does. Not in a place like this.

I snap back to the present and the cold, my fingers numb inside the gloves. The slab is cracked now, splintered by freeze and thaw, but the shape is still the same. Sometimes I think if I stand here long enough, the air will rehydrate the memory, the house will spring up around me, the windows sweating, and the siding still hot to the touch.

I wonder if she comes back here, too, when she thinks nobody's looking.

My phone buzzes, but I don't check it. Instead, I crouch by the headstone two-by-four, kneading my knuckles into my thigh. The beam is old but not gone; the edges still black, the grain warped and peeled. I remember the night I pulled it out of the mess. There was a note stapled to the bottom, scorched so bad that half the words were almost unreadable.

I close my eyes and recite what I remember: "If you stay, she dies. Go." The rest was just smoke and threat, but I got the message. I always do.

I still don't know if it was for me or for her. Doesn't matter. I left.

The next time I see her is back at the station, mid-morning, the world already too bright for the kind of talk we're about to have. She's at the side door, one foot braced against the cinderblock, arms crossed, the exact posture I hated on her old man. There's sweat on her brow and a rawness around the eyes that means she's running on two hours, max.

She doesn't wait for me to close the distance. "I hear you've been hanging around my dad's house," she says, like it's an accusation. Maybe it is.

I shrug. "Just checking for new burn patterns."

"Don't lie, Lucas. You're a shit liar." Her lips go tight, the jaw working side to side, a tic she gets when she's angry or about to cry.

I want to say something—about the slab, about the memory, about the note that I never told her existed. But the words stick, and I just stand there, shuffling my boots, wishing I could be someone who knew what to say.

"There was a note that night." I blurt out.

She moves first. "You could have told me," she says. "All these years, and you just...what, ghost me?"

I look at her. Really look. She's older, yeah, but in the way steel is older after a few thousand pounds of pressure. The lines on her face are from laughter, but also from clenching her teeth through things nobody should have to survive. She's beautiful, but not in the way people mean when they say it. Beautiful like a warning flare.

"I thought it'd be better for you if I left," I say, and immediately regret the softness of it.

She makes a noise, ugly and sharp. "That's bullshit, and you know it."

I feel the old anger start to boil—the anger I used to keep from feeling everything else. "You want the truth? Fine. I got a note. Threatening you. If I stayed, you'd burn too. So I left. I figured you'd rather be pissed off than dead."

She goes still, every muscle in her body going wire-tense. "Show me."

I shake my head. "I don't have it anymore. The fire—"

She cuts me off. "You're still lying. If you cared, you'd have told me then."

I laugh, short and bitter. "Yeah? What was I supposed to say? 'Hey Soph, someone's coming for you, and if I don't vanish, you're next'?"

She doesn't flinch. "Yes. That's exactly what you should have said."

We're standing so close now that I can see the flecks of gold in her eyes, the way her pupils go wide when she's about to swing at someone. I brace for it, but she just stares, letting the silence do what fists can't.

"Why now?" she asks, softer.

I pull in a lungful of air, taste the old coffee, the new dust, the memory of her mouth on mine. "Because this time, I can't run from you."

It hangs there between us, the unspoken fact of our lives: history's got us by the throats, and the more we struggle, the tighter it squeezes.

She finally moves, stepping back just enough to break the

charge. "Next time you keep something from me, I'll torch your truck," she says, but there's no venom in it.

"Deal," I say, and my hands unclench for the first time all day.

She turns to leave, but glances back. "You're a shit liar, Lucas," she repeats. "But you're the only one I trust to tell me the truth, even if it hurts."

I nod, throat too tight to talk.

When she's gone, I stand in the sun and let the warmth wash over me, the memory of her kiss chasing out the cold, just for a minute.

But when I look at my hands, they're still shaking.

Sophie

The shed is exactly as I remember it, choked with blackberry vines, roof sagging, the door hanging on a single hinge like a broken jaw. Nobody's been out here since I was a kid, unless you count the local possum population or the brief appearance of a flashlight-wielding arson investigator the week after the house burned down. I'm pretty sure the same mold spores are floating in the air, breeding in the damp and dark.

I stand at the edge of the weed line, take a breath, and shoulder through. The branches snag my hair, and one of the thorns nicks my forearm, leaving a bright red line in its wake. This is the easy part.

Inside, the shed smells like rot, like wet cardboard and rust, like the earth is trying to reclaim everything all at once. There's an old lawnmower under a tarp, a stack of plastic planters, and a coiled extension cord that looks more like a snake than anything useful. I sweep my gaze across the warped shelves, the upended paint cans, the rat droppings, and then zero in on the far corner, where the floorboards don't quite meet the wall.

When I was seven, Dad let me keep a 'treasure box' out here. He pretended not to know about the gum wrappers and lost buttons I hid inside, but once, when he was sure I wasn't looking, I saw him lift the lid, smile, and close it again, like the most precious thing in the world was a box full of junk.

I kneel, the denim of my jeans soaking up a chill from the damp earth, and tug at the loose board. It creaks but doesn't budge. I pry at it with my keys, and finally the thing pops up with a sound like a wet snap. Beneath is exactly what I'd hoped for, and also what I'd dreaded: a blackened, rusted rectangle of metal, heavy as a brick.

I pull it free, brushing off decades of dust and spiderwebs. The lock is a rusted joke, but I wedge the key in, wiggle, and the latch gives with a reluctant click.

I open it, expecting to find my years of collecting kids' junk, but that small voice in the back of my mind, which told me to check if this box was still here, knows there will be something else. The voice was right.

I find another notebook, the edges curled from old water damage, and some news clippings in a plastic bag. My hands shake as I lift the notebook, and for a second I'm a child again, waiting for the world to catch fire.

I flip through the first few pages, expecting nothing, or hoping, but immediately my heart jumps. Dad's handwriting, tight and tidy, the script of a man who never wasted a word.

There are lists: dates, names, cross-references to city contracts, and budget numbers. Some entries are underlined in red, others circled, annotated with things like "ask L" and "possible repeat." Dad must have known he was in danger to hide something in this box, somewhere only I would find. Why didn't I look here sooner?

I page ahead, the light from the filthy window barely enough to read by, and the entries shift: more personal, more frantic. Warnings. Paranoia. There are drawings in the margins, looping spirals like fingerprints, the same spiral I've been seeing everywhere, including the first notebook and now here on the page in black ink.

I run my finger over one of the spirals, and my nail comes away smudged. For a second, I think I might be losing my mind.

But the more I read, the more it makes sense. Dad wasn't just a casualty; he was a witness. He saw something, started tracking it, and then someone made sure he stopped. Did Dad get the same warning as Lucas, or did Lucas get the threat against me, because Dad didn't take a threat against him seriously?

My hands are trembling now, but I force myself to keep reading. There are names I recognize—old neighbors, town officials, even the captain from the fire station. There are cryptic references to a 'Circle' and to incidents that never made the local paper. Near the back, Dad's handwriting unravels, the last entries jagged, almost illegible: "It's not fire for insurance. It's the spiral. The story. Don't let her forget."

I close the notebook, pressing the cover so hard my knuckles go white.

Outside, the light is shifting to late afternoon, the sun a thin orange disc barely clearing the treetops. I sit back on my heels, clutch the notebook to my chest, and let myself feel the gravity of it. Dad tried to warn me. Maybe even tried to protect me, in his own convoluted way. Was our house fire meant to kill me?

I stand, legs stiff, and let the shed door bang shut behind me. The words are heavier now; they hold the certainty that someone burned my family home to the ground because they were afraid of what we'd find.

I step into the dying light, brush the mud from my jeans, and walk back toward where our house used to be. Each step feels different, like the ground is less willing to swallow me.

When I hit the edge of the yard, I glance back at the shed. The window catches the last of the sun, the dirty glass glinting. For a second, I swear I see the spiral reflected there, a black mark burned into the world.

I turn away, clutch the notebook tighter, and keep walking. I know what I have to do next.

Lucas

THE CALL COMES IN AT 17:34, JUST AS I'M FINISHING THE last of the incident paperwork at the station. Nothing special: "Smoke visible at Willow Diner. All units respond." But the dispatcher's voice has that tight, clipped edge, the one that means it's already out of hand.

We're in the engine and rolling within sixty seconds. The new guy, Morgan, is at the wheel, driving like he's got nothing left to lose. I barely remember buckling in before the world blurs by in sirens and sodium-yellow streetlights. As we pull onto Main, the column of smoke is already visible, a thick, angry plum, black as a busted vein.

"Shit," I mutter. "We're behind the clock."

The diner's windows are full of faces, pale and flickering in the strobe of flames licking up from the kitchen line. Most of the crowd is outside, but a few stubborn holdouts are trapped at the back, banging on the glass or screaming into their phones. I clock Sophie's car in the lot, still parked but empty. I try not to think about it.

"Establish perimeter," I bark to Morgan. "Hose on the main, axes to the rear. Go, go, go!"

The world telescopes: smoke in my lungs, sweat in my eyes, every sense narrowed to the calculus of heat and oxygen and the shifting soundscape of disaster. My boots hit the asphalt, and I'm already through the entry, using my shoulder to break the door. It swings wide and dumps a lungful of hell into my face. The fire's already at flashover in the kitchen—grease fire, maybe, or somebody poured water on the wrong pan—but it's moving too fast, which means accelerant.

I don't have time to be angry about that. The sound of screaming cuts through the roar of the flame. "Help! Somebody, please." The voice is high, raw, desperate. I pull the mask down and plunge in.

Visibility is zero. I go by sound, crouch low, and sweep left, hand trailing the wall until I slam into a booth. I can feel the heat through the bunker gear; my skin is already prickling. "Call out!" I shout, and the answer is a whimper, maybe ten feet ahead.

I move fast, leapfrogging overturned chairs and shattered glass, and there she is: a waitress, maybe twenty, crammed under the lip of the counter, apron pulled over her nose, eyes wild and rolling. "Help me! I can't move my leg!"

A beam has come down, pinning her at the shin. I check the load, quick calculation: heavy, but not full collapse. I wedge my Halligan under the board, use the counter for leverage, and grunt until the thing shifts just enough to free her. She howls as

I haul her out, but it's pain, not panic. I scoop her up in a fireman's carry and make for the exit.

The world behind us is collapsing. The ceiling is a waterfall of burning tile and insulation, each step a negotiation with gravity and entropy. Something gives, a joist, maybe, and the back half of the kitchen drops in a boiling rush of light and noise. I shield her with my body, duck and cover, and pray the gear holds.

It does. Barely. I stumble through the front door and out onto the grass, where Morgan is ready with a hose and a grin. "Got her?" he asks, voice muffled by the mask.

"Yeah," I gasp. "But I think there's still somebody in the back office."

"Shit," Morgan says, but he's already turning to the others, barking orders. "You want me on the line?"

"Keep the flames off the left wall. I'm going around." I set the waitress down, check her for major bleeds, and hand her to the EMTs just arriving on scene. Then I take off, sprinting full around the side of the building.

The office window is lit up orange from within, fire already chewing through the wall. I can see a shadow, moving slowly, like someone's crawling. I grab the axe, smash the glass, and climb in.

The air inside is molten, unbreathable. I clamp my glove on the figure's shoulder and drag them toward the opening. It's the owner, Mr. Santos, half-conscious and coughing blood. "You good?" I shout, but he just gurgles. I yank him out and onto the grass, rolling him to the EMTs, who swarm instantly.

Then it's just me, the engine, and the fire.

For the next fifteen minutes, time runs in reverse. We knock down the front line, then pivot to the roof, hacking at hot spots and venting heat until the smoke thins and the world comes back into focus. When it's over, I stand in the wreckage, helmet off, hair plastered to my head with sweat and soot.

It's only then that I notice the pattern.

The fire didn't start in the kitchen. Not exactly. It started outside the office, accelerant poured in a perfect spiral, soaking the old shag carpet, igniting from a timer or a chemical fuse. The kitchen burn was just for show, a distraction from the real work.

I kneel, squint at the char pattern, and my gut goes cold. The spiral is the same as the one at the Grant house. Same as the Linder barn. Same as the mark left on Sophie's windshield.

I check my hands, just to make sure I'm not imagining things.

Morgan walks up, cradling his arm. "You see this?" he says, nodding at the spiral. "Looks like art, almost."

"Not art," I say, jaw tight. "Message."

He stares at me, waiting for more, but I don't give it. I just stand, wipe the sweat from my face, and let the pieces rearrange in my head.

They're targeting Sophie. Everywhere she goes, everything she touches is a goddamn bullseye. This isn't about money, or revenge, or any of the usual motives. This is a hunt, and she's the prey.

I text her: "Call me. Now."

No answer.

I think of the slab, the way her hair looked lit up by firelight, the taste of copper and sugar and fear.

Then I think of the spiral, burned so deep into the world that I'm not sure anything will ever scrub it out.

I grab my helmet, look one last time at the smoldering ruin, and make a promise: whoever's doing this, I will put them out myself.

With or without backup.

Sophie

Night makes the world smaller. The drive to Lucas's place is a strobe of headlights and empty black, every bump in the road an extra warning shot straight to my nervous system. By the time I reach his block, my hands are so tight on the wheel I have to peel them off finger by finger.

His porch light is the only thing awake on the street. The house is dark, but I can see the outline of him through the living room window, pacing. I watch for a second, let the rhythm of his movement calm me down, then grab the notebook and head up the steps.

He answers the door before I can knock, and for a half-beat we just stand there, both of us waiting for the other to say something first.

His voice is wrecked—smoke, whiskey, and maybe something broken further down. "If you're here to argue, stay outside."

I step past him, boots leaving wet on his mat. "I'm not here to argue," I say. "I found something."

He closes the door, leans against it, arms folded. "I figured you would. You always do."

The inside of his house is chaos: a couch with springs showing, papers everywhere, a row of empty coffee cups on the counter. I take the only clear surface—the kitchen table—and drop the notebook onto it with a sound that rings louder than it should. The table wobbles. The lamp above it flickers.

Lucas doesn't move closer. He just watches, eyes rimmed red, skin gone sallow from the diner fire and whatever else he's been dragging through. "What is it?"

"Journal," I say. "Dad's. He kept records. Of everything."

Lucas's eyes land on the notebook, but he doesn't reach for it. "You read it?"

"Twice. Some of the entries are in code, but the pattern is there. Names. Places. The spiral. He was onto something, and they killed him for it."

Lucas nods, slow. He doesn't ask who 'they' is. Maybe he already knows.

For a few seconds, neither of us speaks. The only sound is the clock on the wall and the wet, wheeze-breath he tries to hide when he's hurt.

I open the notebook to the middle and slide it across. The page is a mess of spiral drawings, some perfect, some frantic, a few trailing off the line as if Dad's hand was shaking. Next to it: "Do not let Sophie go alone at night."

I wait for him to react, to crack a joke, but he just rests his fingers on the paper and looks up at me. "I saw it," he says, and his voice is so soft I almost don't catch it. "At the diner. On the floor, right where the burn started."

I stand behind my chair, braced, the adrenaline from the

drive replaced by a different current—fear, or relief, or both. "It's not random. None of it."

He shakes his head. "He's escalating. Or she is. Whoever's doing this, they're playing a game. And we're the only ones still on the board."

We don't talk about the last time we were in a kitchen together. The silence is thick with everything we've said and all the things we never did.

I reach into my coat, pull out the sandwich bag with the old receipts, and toss it next to the journal. "This is proof, at least of the old stuff. If we can figure out the next target, maybe we can stop them."

Lucas picks up the bag, thumbs through the slips, then sets them down. His hands tremble, just a little. He folds his arms again and sets his jaw.

"Did you ever think," he says, "that maybe your dad left all this so you'd not make the same moves he did, so you would protect yourself?"

I don't answer. The thought has been chewing at me since the shed. I stare at the spiral on the page, let it pull my eyes to the center.

"It doesn't matter," I say. "I'm finishing it."

He laughs, short and bitter. "That's what I always liked about you."

We're both standing, facing the table, the journal between us. If we were any other version of ourselves, this would be the part where he reached across and touched my hand, or I let myself lean into him just long enough to remember what it felt like to be safe.

Instead, I draw a line in the dust with my finger. "We're running out of time."

Lucas nods, looks up. "We can use the notebook as bait. Leak the story. Make them come to us."

I don't disagree. For the first time, I think maybe we have a shot.

He grabs a chair, sits, and winces as the motion catches his ribs. He pulls another chair for me. "You hungry?"

I almost smile. "I haven't eaten since noon."

"Me either," he says, and there's a ghost of the old Lucas in the way he says it.

I sit, take a breath, and for a while we just listen to the clock and the world going quiet outside.

The notebook lies open, the spiral on the page like a beacon. We watch it, together, and I know we're both thinking the same thing: Whoever set this firestorm in motion, we're going to drag them out into the light.

Lucas reaches out and grabs my jacket, pulling me close. He cups my face and whispers, "I won't let anything happen to you." I clutch his shirt, anchoring myself in the moment as I realize how much I miss him, his touch, and the heat between us. softly, I say, "You are the only one allowed to ruin me." His hands slide down to grab my hips, lifting me against him, his lips crashing into mine. He carries me to his room, whispering, "Let's ruin each other."

9

False Alarms

Sophie

In the morning, the world comes back in pieces. The smell of scorched sugar and sweat; the hush of a town that hasn't quite decided if it wants to wake. I'm somewhere between sleep and story, half-aware of the weight of Lucas's arm curled around my ribs, the heat of his body still radiating even though the room is cool. I don't remember when we finally gave up and passed out—just a blur of hands and mouths and old anger transmuted into something else entirely. But the evidence is everywhere: my hip pressed into his, my face buried in the crook of his arm, the sheets a riot of creases.

I don't want to move, but I know I have to. The urge is ancient and cellular; fight-or-flight hardwired straight into my marrow. I shift a little, careful not to wake him. His hand slides from my stomach, fingertips grazing the hem of the tank top I put back on sometime in the night. He mutters something—my name, maybe, or just the syllables that mean me—and then goes slack again.

The light coming through the blinds is surgical, slicing the bed in uneven stripes. Every surface in Lucas's room is scrubbed clean, but the corners still remember their share of shadows. The only evidence of life—of his life—is the alarm clock, military-precise and blinking an hour ahead of schedule, and the gear bag half-zipped under the dresser. The rest is all bare floor, pale blue walls, the kind of tidiness that comes from years of living in barracks and firehouses.

I prop myself up on one elbow, studying him. He looks older in sleep, the lines on his forehead deeper, the jaw less stubborn, lips parted just enough to remind me that he used to be beautiful in a way I never got tired of memorizing. His chest rises and falls, every inhale a gentle claim on the space we're sharing. There's a scar at the edge of his hairline, newer than the last time I saw him bare, and for a second I want to trace it with my tongue and ask for the story. Instead, I slide out from under his arm, holding my breath as I do.

I stand, legs unsteady, and scan the room for my jeans. They're halfway across the floor, one leg inside-out, belt still looped. I tiptoe, more out of habit than necessity, and wriggle into them while keeping an eye on the bed. Lucas doesn't stir. I almost wish he would—say something dumb and self-effacing, give me a reason to stay—but the only sound is the shush of my own breath and the slow, low hum of the street outside.

His apartment is exactly how I imagined it would be, which is to say: not really an apartment at all, but an extension of him. The living room is a grid of discipline: two identical armchairs, a coffee table with exactly three magazines (two fire science, one psychology), the remote squared to the edge of the couch like a threat. The kitchen is a gallery of stainless and glass, everything nested and wiped and put away, except for the French press on the counter and the sugar canister left open, like a crime scene from the night before. The fridge has more beer than food, and the freezer is full of nothing but ice packs and cheap burritos.

On the far wall, a bookcase—his only real indulgence. There's a shelf of fire investigation manuals, another for true crime, a battered row of sci-fi paperbacks that look like they've been through a flood. And then, tucked between a field guide to arson chemistry and a photo atlas of major burn sites, a small collection of framed photos: Lucas in bunker gear, Lucas in high school, Lucas with his arm slung around a younger version of me, both of us filthy and beaming in the aftermath of the town's worst Fourth of July disaster.

I stare at that last one. I must be sixteen—hair too long, teeth still crooked, eyes so bright it's embarrassing. Lucas is the same but not; he wears his old face like a mask, the one before life started strip-mining his softness. I remember the day perfectly: we'd been caught lighting bottle rockets off the old train bridge, and when the sheriff dragged us back to the station, Dad didn't say a word—just pointed at the mop and made us clean until our arms shook. When we finally finished, Lucas stole the camera from the front desk and snapped the photo, daring me to smile even though I was still furious.

I reach out, fingertips resting on the glass. There's a fingerprint there, too—his, smudged at the bottom right, maybe from last night or maybe from all the times he's moved it but never packed it away. I feel the twist in my gut, the old ache of wanting something I can't name.

I find a notepad near the phone, a stubby pencil stabbed through the spiral. I scribble a quick note: "Gone for errands. Don't call—will be back before you have time to miss me." I hesitate, then add a dumb little smiley face, because I want to, and because it will annoy him.

I prop the note on the coffeemaker, then take one last look at the sleeping shape in the bedroom. I want to crawl back in, let him anchor me for another hour, but I know if I do, I'll never leave. And I can't—not when there's a lead burning a hole in my brain, not when every instinct is screaming that the clock is running out.

I close the door behind me, careful not to let it slam. The hallway is cold and echoing, the only sound my boots against the waxed tile. I stand, head against the cool plaster, letting my pulse settle. There's a weight in my pocket—the key to my dad's lockbox, sharp and insistent—and I curl my fingers around it, feeling the edges bite.

It's a long walk to the car. The air outside is brighter than I expected, the sky a blown-out white, the kind of morning that feels like a dare.

I start the engine, and for a second, I just sit there, watching the sun crawl up over the roofs of Willow Creek. The houses are all the same, neat and stubborn and quietly rotting from the inside out. I wonder if anyone else is awake, if anyone else is standing in their kitchen, wondering where the next fire is going to start.

I think about Lucas, about the warmth of his skin and the way he said my name in the dark, like a secret. I think about the notebook, and the spiral, and the way every step I take seems to circle right back to where it all began.

I put the car in gear and pull away, the morning snapping shut behind me like a mousetrap.

If he wakes and finds the note, I hope he understands. Some things you have to do alone, even if you don't want to.

Some things you have to burn all the way through.

The drive out to Martin Reeves's house is longer than I remember. The roads are washed clean by last night's rain, but the ditches are rimmed with black ice, the kind that sneaks up and yanks the steering wheel if you let your guard down for even a second. I keep both hands tight at ten and two, eyes flicking between the gray stripe of pavement and the world hunched on either side: old ranch houses, battered mailboxes, thatched lawns gone brown for the winter. There's a radio, but I keep it off. Silence feels safer, like I might actually be able to hear the past coming for me if I just listen hard enough.

Martin lived out in one of the "good" subdivisions, the kind that got built just before the housing market fell off a cliff and left half the driveways empty and the rest occupied by people who never quite fit the homeowner's association brochures. Dad always called it "Disneyland for the recently divorced," and I see now what he meant: every house identical except for the tiny, desperate attempts at self-expression—pink flamingos, a ceramic gnome with a hat missing, a flag that's been up so long the stars have faded.

I park on the street, kill the engine, and let the heater run until my hands thaw enough to uncurl from the wheel. The house is easy to spot, even before the GPS says I'm here: the front door is webbed with yellow police tape, and a white inspection sticker glares from the center pane like a hex. The grass is flattened and gray, the flowerbeds a ruin of last season's perennials. There's a car in the driveway, covered in a dusting of frost, and for a second I picture Martin stepping out, shivering in his parka, waving me in with a cup of coffee and a thousand-yard stare.

Instead, the only sign of life is a woman in the yard next door, bent over a patch of mulch and jabbing at it with a trowel. She's dressed for the cold—scarf, gloves, a hat with a pom-pom so bright it almost hurts to look at—but her cheeks are flushed, either from the wind or the effort of pretending everything's fine. She doesn't look up when I get out of the car, but I know she's clocked me; nobody spends time in the dirt at 9 AM on a weekday unless they're hiding from something.

I walk up the drive, the soles of my boots crunching on the grit left over from the last snowstorm. The closer I get, the more wrong the house looks. It's not just the tape, or the windows still fogged from the inside; it's the way the mailbox is jammed shut with a fistful of junk mail, the way the curtains hang crooked in the front window, the way the whole place seems to be holding its breath, waiting for something bad to finish happening.

I stop at the porch, squint at the sticker. "PROPERTY OF COUNTY CORONER. ENTRY BY AUTHORIZED PERSONNEL ONLY." Underneath, in smaller type:

"Pending hazardous materials assessment." The door itself is splintered around the lock, like someone forced it after the fire was already out.

"Can I help you?" The voice comes from behind, sharp enough to make me jump. I turn to see the neighbor standing at the edge of the lawn, gloves off, hands planted on hips.

"Hi," I say, and then immediately regret how out-of-place my own voice sounds. "I'm just...here about Martin. Is he—"

She gives me the kind of once-over reserved for salespeople and the rare breed of Girl Scout who still goes door to door. "You a reporter?"

"No. Just a friend. I grew up with him."

She softens, just a little. "You heard, then?"

I try to look surprised, but she doesn't buy it. "He's really gone?"

She nods, a sad smile leaking out. "Happened two weeks ago. They say it was a gas leak, but..." She lets the sentence dangle, the way people do when they want you to finish it for them.

"But you don't believe that," I say.

The neighbor comes up the walk, trowel dangling from one hand. "He was careful. Paranoid, even. Checked his own detectors, always sniffing around the basement after storms. He would've smelled it."

I shift my weight, trying to look at the door instead of her. "Do you know if he had any...visitors? Someone who might have been here the night before?"

She tilts her head, eyes narrowing. "You're not a friend. Are you a cop?"

I hold up both hands, palms out. "No, really. My dad and Martin were in the department together, back in the day. I just want to know what happened."

That unlocks something. She steps closer, voice dropping to a near-whisper. "He'd been acting weird, the last month or so. Kept talking about old business, things from when he was still with the fire department. Said someone was watching him, but wouldn't say who. He got these letters, sometimes, but he'd just burn them in the fireplace without reading."

A cold finger traces the inside of my throat. "Did you see who brought them?"

She shakes her head. "Nope. Mailman, maybe, but I think he was more afraid of who was already here. He told me not to open the door after dark, not even for the pizza guy. Said the whole town was getting stranger."

I force a smile. "Sounds like he'd fit right in with the rest of us."

She laughs, but it's a weak sound, too hollow to stand up on its own. "I'm not sure anyone fits in here anymore."

We stand in silence, both of us watching the house, waiting for the ghost of Martin to open the door and let us in on the punchline.

"Thank you," I say, and mean it.

She nods, eyes lingering on me. "If you hear anything—if you find out what really happened—let me know, okay? He didn't have much family. Not since the divorce."

I nod, and she turns back to her yard, scraping at the mulch as if she can bury the last month's worth of dread in the dirt.

I linger a few minutes longer, then circle the house, looking for any sign of what the official story missed. The side windows are all locked from the inside, curtains drawn tight, but there's a single patch of soot above the vent in the garage door—a spiral, uneven but deliberate, burned just deep enough to show it was made by someone who wanted it to last.

My hands go cold. I take a photo, the flash quick and surgical in the gray morning light. The image on the phone matches what's in my head exactly: the spiral, the signature, the message.

I pace the perimeter again, slower this time, letting myself remember what Dad used to say about crime scenes: "It's not about what's here, it's about what's not." No firemen. No security cams. No signs of a struggle. Just the aftermath, scrubbed and sanitized, as if the house is daring me to find something out of place.

I head back to the car, feeling the neighbor's eyes tracking me the whole way. I slide behind the wheel and just sit there, watching my own breath fog up the windshield. I check the mirrors, then check again, certain that at any second a shadow will slip from between the houses and make a beeline for the car.

I wonder if I should call Lucas. Tell him what I found, or what I think I found. But there's a pulse of something sour in my chest, something that says this is still my job, my hunt.

I watch the neighbor, still hunched in her garden, and for a second I think about asking her in for coffee, or at least warning her to lock the doors twice before she sleeps tonight. But instead, I turn the key, let the engine cough to life, and pull away, the spiral on the garage door shrinking in the rearview until it's nothing but a smudge.

The drive back feels shorter, but colder. I keep checking the mirror, convinced that any second, a pair of headlights will appear and chase me all the way home.

When I get to the apartment, I sit in the lot for a full five minutes before I can make myself go inside. The notebook is still in my bag, but it feels heavier than ever.

I run my thumb over the edge of the pages and tell myself I'm ready.

Even if I'm not, it's too late to turn back.

When I finally drag myself up the stairs and unlock the door, I know Lucas is inside before I see him. There's a heat in the apartment that doesn't belong to the old radiator, a static charge that tells me I'm about to walk into a firefight.

He's in the kitchen, perched on the edge of the counter like he's afraid the ground will collapse under him. His arms are folded tight across his chest, shoulders hunched, jaw clenched so hard I can see the pulse tick in his neck. The second the door closes behind me, he's on his feet, moving with the slow, predatory calm of someone who's rehearsed this confrontation a hundred times.

"Where the hell were you?" The words are flat, but the edge is diamond-sharp.

I shrug off my jacket, toss it onto the chair, and pretend not to hear. "Nice to see you, too."

He closes the distance in three strides, stops just short of grabbing my arm. "Don't do that, Soph. Don't act like you didn't know I was going to notice."

I drop my bag on the table, the journal landing with a thud. "I left a note."

He laughs, hollow. "Yeah, you did. 'Gone for errands. Don't call—will be back before you have time to miss me.'" He recites it in a mocking sing-song, then lets it hang in the air. "I called the station. I called the library. I called the goddamn hospital. Nobody saw you."

I busy my hands unpacking the bag, stacking the notebook and a handful of receipts in a neat pile, just to have something to do besides punch him. "I was careful."

"You don't get to protect me and doubt me at the same time," I snap, my own voice rising before I can leash it.

He slams a fist into the wall—not hard enough to break anything, just hard enough to make the cabinets rattle and the space between us shrink to nothing. "You're not the only one with skin in this game, Sophie. If you disappear—"

I cut him off. "I won't."

He closes his eyes, breathes out slow. "It's not about faith, okay? It's about not wanting to lose you again."

For a second, I want to laugh in his face—at the idea that I could ever belong to anyone, even him—but the look in his eyes gives me pause. It's not just anger. It's terror, the kind that leaves you wide open and shaking.

I cross my arms, plant my feet. "You don't get to make the rules. Not anymore."

He leans in, voice low. "And you don't get to walk into danger like you're immortal. You think I don't know what it's like to be helpless?"

My voice cracks, just a little. "That's not what this is about."

"Isn't it?" He's closer now, so close I can feel the heat coming off his skin, the tremor in his hands where they're clenched at his sides.

We stand there, locked in a contest of who will blink first. The air between us vibrates with every argument we never finished, every time we left each other hanging over an abyss with nothing but good intentions and bad timing to keep us from falling in.

"I can't just sit here," I say, the words thin and desperate.

He softens, barely, and I see the weight of all the years he spent learning how to be strong for everyone but himself. "I know," he says. "But you could at least let me help."

I look at the kitchen table, at the mess of notes and memories. "You want to help? Read these." I shove the receipts toward him, flip open the notebook to the page with Martin's name scrawled at the top.

He skims it, lips moving as he reads. The change is immediate—his posture drops, the tension bleeding out of his shoulders as the facts sink in. "Martin's dead?"

I nod. "Neighbor says it was a gas leak. But there's no way he missed that. He was obsessively careful. There's more—he burned letters, said he was being watched, told her not to answer the door after dark."

Lucas rubs a hand over his face, the anger draining into something closer to grief. "Jesus. I hadn't heard about that. Why wouldn't he tell someone?"

I shake my head. "I guess news doesn't travel upstream anymore."

He sits, hard, in the kitchen chair. The table creaks under the weight of his elbows. He reads through the next few pages, piecing together the pattern.

"We're not dealing with a random psycho," he says, almost to himself. "This is targeted. Generational."

I don't answer. Instead, I watch the way his hands loosen, the way his fingers spread out on the Formica like he's trying to anchor himself to the present. I realize, for the first time, how much of his anger is just terror, how much of his need to control is just a desperate attempt to keep from losing again.

I cross the room, standing behind him, resting my hands on his shoulders. He's solid, but the tension in his neck tells a different story.

"I need you with me," I say, voice so low I barely recognize it.

He reaches up, covers my hand with his. The fight is gone now, replaced by the old alliance, the one that used to carry us through every disaster Willow Creek could throw at us.

We stay like that for a long time, the only sound the hum of the fridge and the wind ticking at the window. Eventually, he stands, turns, and pulls me in, his arms wrapping around me like armor.

"I'm scared," he admits, mouth pressed to my hair.

"Me too," I say, and let myself believe it.

For the first time since Dad's death, I don't feel alone.

I feel watched, yeah—but not by the thing that's hunting us.

By the man who still knows how to catch me, even when I'm burning at both ends.

We turn the kitchen into a war room. Every inch of Formica is covered in paper: my dad's journal, Martin's reccipts, printouts of fire reports from the last twenty years, even the faded spiral-bound calendar that Lucas hauls out from the bottom of a filing box. There's not a clean coffee cup left, so we drink from mismatched mugs, swapping sips and trading bites of limp Thai takeout until the noodles congeal and the curry stains our fingers yellow.

The rhythm of collaboration comes back quick—better than it ever was in high school, when we'd pull all-nighters and cheat off each other's biology notes. This is urgent and physical; we sit hip-to-hip at the table, passing the journal back and forth, talking over each other in bursts. The silence between us is comfortable, sometimes even companionable, and the only time it gets tense is when we both reach for the same sticky note and our hands bump, fingers tangling for a second before pulling away.

Lucas lays out the timeline with the precision of a demolition charge. "Your dad started writing the journal in March of '91, right after the Linder fire. From then until he..." Lucas hesitates, "until he died, he logged every incident. Look—see how the entries cluster?"

I squint at the page he's pointing to. The handwriting is familiar and foreign at the same time: blocky, meticulous, the script of a man who never wanted to be misunderstood. "He circles some dates. Red pen, always. And look here—every time he uses the spiral, it's next to a name, or a property address. Like he's marking them for later."

Lucas nods, jots a note on a yellow square and slaps it onto the wall, joining the growing swarm of reminders and half-finished theories. "The spiral isn't just a signature, it's a warning. Or a link."

I tap the table, remembering the neighbor's words. "Martin burned his letters before he'd even open them. Dad must've done the same. They were both scared, but not of fire—they were scared of the person behind it."

Lucas leans back, fingers laced behind his head, gaze fixed on the ceiling. "Whoever it is, they want you to find the pattern. Otherwise, why leave the spiral at every scene? Why not just vanish, like everyone else in this town?"

I reach for the next batch of printouts, flipping through until my eyes catch on a date circled three times in heavy black. "Look—this one. January fourteenth. Dad notes it every year. 'Anniversary: Watch the mailbox.'"

Lucas's brow furrows. "That's this weekend. Three days from now."

We both go still. I chew the inside of my cheek, tasting the ghost of Sriracha and regret. "You think it's going to happen again?"

He boots up his laptop, fingers flying across the trackpad, and pulls up a fire department roster. "If I were them, I'd use the date. It's ritual. Whoever survived last time—maybe they're on the list. Maybe they're next."

I close my eyes, try to picture what Dad would have wanted me to do. Not just survive, but finish it. Drag the truth out into daylight, even if it burned everyone along the way.

Lucas nudges my shoulder, softer this time. "You okay?"

I force a smile. "I never am. But I'm close."

We pore over the records, matching names to incidents, mapping each address on the back of a napkin. The more we see, the more the spiral tightens. Every fire, every 'accidental' death, every missing person—they all pinwheel back to a core group. The circle.

"We have to warn them," I say, the words out before I know what they mean.

Lucas shakes his head. "Won't work. Anyone left already knows. They're either too scared to talk, or too close to the center to leave."

I feel the urge to run, to get in the car and drive until the world stops spinning, but I know it won't help. I'm tired of running. I want to fight.

"We have three days," I say. "Let's make them count."

He grins, a flash of the old Lucas, the one who used to dare me to jump off bridges or climb water towers at midnight. "That's my girl."

I snort, but the warmth lingers. We keep working, building a case from fragments and coffee stains, each clue another fuse burning toward the inevitable.

At some point, we end up on the same side of the table, both leaning over the calendar, shoulders pressed together. The fatigue is thick and sticky, but I can feel our brains sparking, refusing to quit. When Lucas's hand finds mine, I let it stay. It feels right, or at least less wrong than anything else we've done tonight.

The hours pass in a blur. Outside, the town falls asleep, but inside, we're wide awake, fueled by equal parts caffeine and pure, raw panic.

When we finally look up, the sky is bleeding blue at the edges, and the spiral on the wall is bigger than ever.

"We're close," Lucas says, voice hoarse.

I nod. "I can feel it."

He stands, stretches, and pulls me up with him. For a second, we just breathe, letting the adrenaline bleed off.

Then he kisses me, slow and careful, like he's afraid I might break.

I kiss him back, harder, because I know I won't.

When we part, I press my forehead to his. "We will finish this."

He smiles, eyes bright despite the exhaustion. "Together."

We leave the evidence where it is, scattered like breadcrumbs across the kitchen, and stumble to the couch, collapsing in a heap of tangled limbs and borrowed courage.

The spiral can wait until morning.

But I know it won't.

Sometime after midnight, I can't breathe anymore. The apartment is heavy with sleep and the ghost of old takeout, and the evidence wall in the kitchen pulses in my peripheral vision like a warning light. I slip off the couch, careful not to wake Lucas, and let myself out onto the stoop.

The world is silent, a negative of the day's chaos. The air is so cold it makes my teeth ache, and the only sign of life is the dull orange streetlight pooling at the far end of the block. The wind stirs the trash cans, sets a neighbor's wind chimes jangling, but otherwise the night is a perfect vacuum—no sirens, no dogs, not even the distant hum of the highway.

I close my eyes, lean my forehead against the metal railing, and try to empty my head. I think about my dad, about the way he used to sit out on our old porch after a double shift, just watching the town roll past until the cigarette was down to the filter. Sometimes he'd call me out, let me curl into the space under his arm, and we'd watch the stars together, silent. No lessons, no advice. Just the knowledge that the world was still out there, and that we were in it.

Now, the world feels smaller and meaner. I hug my arms around my body and pace the length of the stoop, boots crunching on the grit. I'm about to go back in when something glints at the edge of the top step, just outside the puddle of porch light.

I crouch, all senses on high alert. There, against the concrete, is a small metal ring. For a second, I think it's just a washer or a piece of hardware dropped by a repairman, but when I pick it up, the weight is unmistakable. Gold, plain, engraved on the inside. My hands start to shake.

It's my father's wedding ring.

I run my thumb over the inscription. "F.G. + L.R. 1975." The inside is scored and pitted, but I'd know it anywhere. I remember how he used to spin it on the kitchen table, how he'd tap it against his coffee cup when he was thinking. After the fire, I thought it was gone for good.

I stand, blood rushing in my ears, and scan the street. Every parked car, every shadow, every half-lit window. I can't see a damn thing, but the sense of being watched is a physical pressure, a hand squeezing the back of my neck.

The door opens behind me. Lucas stands in the frame, backlit, sleep-ruffled and blinking. "You okay?"

I swallow, the taste of metal on my tongue. "Look."

He crosses to me in three steps, reads the ring in my palm. His expression goes flat and cold. "Where did you find it?"

"Right here." I point to the step, my finger unsteady.

He looks up and down the street, his firefighter's brain scanning for threat vectors, safe exits, the things you can and can't control. "Stay inside," he says. "Now."

I don't move. "It's a message."

Lucas grabs my wrist, not gently. "It's a warning."

I want to argue, to say that I'm not scared, that I'm beyond scaring. But the lie gets stuck behind my teeth.

He pulls me toward the door, glancing back at the shadows, the half-lit slice of night that's suddenly become enemy territory. He's got one hand on my elbow, the other on his phone, thumb ready to dial 911 if anything moves.

We stand just inside the threshold, both of us silent, the ring burning a hole in my palm.

"They know I'm close," I whisper, the words dry and small.

Lucas's jaw sets. "Or they're getting closer."

For a moment, we just stand there, shoulder to shoulder, watching the darkness press up against the glass.

"I'm not going to let anything happen to you," he says, and this time there's no anger, just the pure, bright heat of certainty.
I want to believe him. I want to believe that anything in this world can be protected, even for a second.

But I know better.

We close the door, double-lock it, and lean our backs against the wood. Lucas wraps his arms around me from behind, strong and shaking. I press the ring to my chest, anchoring myself to the past even as it tries to kill me.

The night feels longer now, every minute stretching out until dawn.

But if it's a fight, I'm not running.

Not anymore.

Lucas double-checks the locks, then pulls the blackout curtains tight across every window. He moves with the controlled fury of a man who's spent his life preparing for the kind of disaster you hope never comes. He checks the peephole twice, then leans his whole weight against the door as if he could hold back the universe just by refusing to move.

I'm still holding the ring. It feels radioactive in my hand. I turn it over and over, letting the words inside gouge themselves deeper into my palm, until I can't tell if the sting is from the cold or the metal or just the fact that my father's ghost is never going to let me go.

Lucas returns from his circuit of the apartment, stops two feet away, and just looks at me. The air vibrates with a new tension—not the brittle, explosive kind we're used to, but something thicker, a slow-burn that turns your insides to syrup and sand.

"Are you okay?" he asks, low.

I want to say yes. I want to say no. Instead, I slide the ring onto my thumb and close the distance, pressing my forehead to his chest. He stands absolutely still, then wraps his arms around me, sealing me in, his body a wall against the world outside.

For a moment we don't move. We just breathe, in and out, the same rhythm, the same pulse. My heart slows down, and then speeds up again, but for a new reason.

He kisses the top of my head—so gentle it makes my eyes sting. "You're safe," he says, but I hear the tremor in his voice.

"No, I'm not," I whisper. "But I want to feel like it."

I reach up, hook a finger into his belt loop, pull him closer. The need is so sharp, so immediate, that I can't remember what it felt like to be scared just five minutes ago. Only the urge to erase the world, if only for right now.

He gets it. He always does.

His hands are at my back, sliding under my shirt, skin to skin. They're rough, calloused, but the way he touches me is almost reverent. I let my head tilt back, and his lips find my throat, my jaw, the corner of my mouth. His stubble scrapes, the good kind, the kind that makes you want to lean into it and take whatever comes next.

I press him against the wall, hard enough to feel the dent in the drywall behind us. My hands go to his shoulders, then his hair, then down his chest, flattening against the heat of his skin.

His shirt is gone in a second—he tears it off one-handed, not breaking the kiss—and then my own shirt follows, up and over, tangling my arms for a second before I get free.

The difference between last night and this is night and day: this is not gentle, not cautious, not about remembering the old days. This is about taking something back, about being alive and present and real, even if just for the length of a heartbeat.

He pins my wrists above my head, his body pressed all along mine. I hook my legs around his hips, arch into him, feel the weight and the heat and the promise of what's about to happen.

He bites my lip, not enough to hurt but enough to make me gasp. "No more fear," I say, and it comes out broken.

He answers with his mouth, hard and hungry. His hands roam everywhere—my arms, my ribs, the small of my back—memorizing every inch as if it might be the last time.

There's no finesse to this. We knock a lamp off the side table, send a stack of mail skidding to the floor, and the sound echoes in the dark. My back slams the wall, and I want more of it, want to leave a mark that will still be there tomorrow.

He gets my jeans unbuttoned, yanks them down, and lifts me up, braced on the curve of his forearm. I feel the press of him, hard and insistent, and it's all I can do not to claw at his skin until he gives me what I want.

"Please," I say, and it's not a plea. It's a demand.

He obliges. His hands on my ass, my thighs, every part of me claimed and anchored. When he enters me, it's a shock of sensation—raw, perfect, a line of fire all the way up my spine. I dig my nails into his shoulders, and he groans, a real sound, unguarded.

We move together, finding a rhythm that drowns out everything else. The fear, the spiral, the ring on my thumb—they all fade to static. There's just us, bodies colliding, heat and friction and the sweet, animal certainty that nothing can touch us if we just burn hot enough.

He thrusts, again and again, and my world narrows to the ragged edges of sensation. I come first, sharp and sudden, nails drawing blood, and he follows, bracing against the wall, jaw clenched in a soundless shout.

After, we slide to the floor, tangled and breathless, sweat cooling in the still air. He wraps both arms around me, holds me close, and for now I believe him: that I'm safe, that we're safe, that nothing out there can reach us.

But when the silence creeps back in, I know it's not true. The world is still waiting, and the spiral is still spinning, tighter and tighter.

He kisses my shoulder, soft this time. "I'm not going anywhere," he says, voice wrecked.

"Good," I whisper. "Because I don't want to be alone when it happens."

We sit like that, floor cold, bodies warm, staring into the darkness.

Outside, the night is quiet. But inside, we're still burning.

And we're not going out without a fight.

10

Fire Line

Sophie

THE WILLOW CREEK FIRE STATION IS A PARADOX—BOTH the safest place in town and the only building I've ever watched deliberately burn. I stand at the edge of the parking lot, keys cold in my pocket, and try to remember the way my father used to walk this same stretch of concrete: shoulders square, head up, as if he could muscle through the world's inertia by sheer force of posture. I copy the pose, take one breath, then cross to the entrance.

The glass doors are locked at this hour, but the buzzer still works. A tired man's voice rasps through the speaker: "Business or emergency?"

I aim for the middle. "Records request. I called ahead."

A staticky click, then the door buzzes open. The interior is a time capsule of public funding neglect: vending machines with nothing left but mummified jerky, a trophy case coated in a layer of dust that could pass for topsoil, and, at the far end of the hall, the dispatch window, manned by a clerk in a high-viz vest. He doesn't look up from his crossword. The overhead fluorescents stutter and catch, tinting everything in a colorless, morgue-blue wash.

I wait at the window until the clerk glances up. He's got a face like a retriever: good-natured, but bred for obedience. "You said you called ahead?"

I nod, sliding a slip of paper across the counter. "Sophie Grant. Requesting incident logs and hazardous materials reports for the Grant residence, plus cross-references for Linder, Hawthorn, and any other structure fires between ninety-four and oh-five."

He squints at the list, then at me, then back at the list. "That's, uh, a lot of files. You got clearance?"

"I'm cleared through Dalton," I say, which is only half a lie. I left three voicemails for the captain and one email marked 'urgent,' which, in this department, counts as formal approval.

He shrugs, shuffles off. I watch the hallway, counting ceiling tiles, until I hear the tap of boots coming up from the far end. Captain Dalton in the flesh—still built like a linebacker, but the decades have put a stoop in his shoulders and a salmon-pink hue in his face that wasn't there when I was a kid. He wears the rank insignia like a shield. I almost salute, then remember I have a spine.

"Grant," he says, voice a broken bottle dragged over asphalt. "Didn't expect to see you here."

I keep my face blank. "Just tying up some loose ends. Appreciate you making time."

He gestures down the hall, not waiting for me to follow. His office is barely an office—just a room with a battered desk, a wall calendar stuck on the wrong month, and a window that looks straight into the engine bay. Dalton plants himself behind the desk and folds his arms.

"Fire logs are public record," he says. "But you're not the public, and these files aren't normal. They're sealed for a reason."

"Because someone keeps redacting them," I say. "And because there's a two-year gap in the incident timeline for my block. You think I don't know how to read between lines?"

Dalton's eyes narrow. "You want the raw reports, you'll need a subpoena."

"I'm not interested in the raw. I want the versions Dad saw before they were cut to pieces."

He leans forward, the desk groaning under the shift. "You're here to dig up ghosts, you go ahead. But you should know: Bennett put your father's files on the restricted list after the Hawthorn incident. Said it was for your own good."

I let that sit a beat. "Is that your opinion, too, Captain?"

His mouth works, but nothing comes out. He stands, walks to the door, and holds it open. "You can look. But I'll be watching."

He doesn't say 'for your own good,' but it's hanging in the air, toxic and inert.

The archive room is a bunker of old fire, paper, and mildew. The HVAC vent is clogged with a bird's nest of charred insulation, and the light is the kind that makes your retinas throb. Three file cabinets line the back wall, their drawers labeled in marker and reinforced with evidence tape. I circle the room, not touching anything, until Dalton leans in.

"Fifteen minutes," he says. "Then I need you gone."

I give him a tight nod, wait until his boots fade down the hall, then count to sixty before moving. I pace to the cabinets, run a finger along the edge of each drawer, then fish a scrap of notepaper from my pocket. The numbers are Dad's old badge and his city ID; I punch them into the digital lock on the 'ARCHIVE' drawer.

It clicks open. The drawer's packed so tight the folders are warped, color-coded tabs mashed together like ribs in a chest. I tug out the ones I asked for, plus two extra: 'INTERNAL AFFAIRS—96' and 'FATALITIES—CLASSIFIED.' Each folder is stamped with a date and a rubber-stamped signature. The oldest are brittle, the edges yellowed and curling.

I set up my phone camera—silent mode, no flash—and start flipping pages, one hand steady, the other scrolling and clicking. The smell is familiar, a mix of bleach and wet wood and a sweet, metallic rot I remember from the night Dad brought home his turnout gear for the last time.

The first report is a write-up of the Grant house fire. It's more detailed than the one I remember, with extra pages stapled to the back: chemical analysis, a list of first responders, the notation 'ACCELERANT–ORIGIN UNKNOWN' circled in blue pen. The next file covers the Linder barn. Similar story, but the entire second page is blacked out, redacted so heavily the marker bled through to the next sheet.

I keep going, working faster now. Every file has the same pattern—first page normal, second page a block of redactions. Some of the names are visible in the margins: Dad's, Bennett's, and a third I can't place but that recurs often: 'H. Malik.' I snap pictures of everything, camera held flat against the paper, as if being closer could make it safer.

About ten minutes in, my hands start to shake. Not from fear, but from the certainty that I'm getting closer to something big, something that explains the gap between what I lived and what I've been told. I dig into the 'INTERNAL AFFAIRS' folder, expecting stonewalling, but the file is only a few pages. The first is a complaint, unsigned, accusing my father of 'evidence tampering' and 'impeding investigation.' The second is a memo from Chief Bennett: "No further action. Matter closed."

My gut flips. I switch to the 'FATALITIES–CLASSIFIED' folder, the one I wasn't supposed to touch. The first entry is a summary, written in a clipped, impersonal style:

"Subject: Grant, Frederick. Status: Deceased. Cause of death: Asphyxiation, secondary to smoke inhalation. Noted:

presence at scene of unauthorized access to fire evidence storage."

I stare at the last line. 'Unauthorized access to fire evidence storage.' He died at the house, not the station. This doesn't make sense.

The door to the archive room creaks. I drop the folder back into the drawer, spin to face the entrance. I'm expecting Dalton, but it's the clerk from the front desk, hands jammed into his vest pockets, eyes wide.

"You okay in here?" he asks.

I nod, tucking my phone into my waistband. "Just finishing up."

He hovers at the threshold, glancing from me to the cabinets. "Captain says you got five minutes."

"Thanks. I'll be quick."

He lingers, but eventually backs out, the door snicking shut behind him. I use the last seconds to grab a random sample of reports, focusing on the years Dad was most obsessed with. The spiral mark is everywhere, like a hidden language: in the fire logs, in the notes, even in the internal memos.

I close the drawer, wipe my hands on my jeans, and check the phone screen. 143 photos. My thumb hurts from the speed.

As I shoulder out of the archive room, I nearly collide with Dalton in the hall. He's waiting, arms folded, face set in a line that says 'I'm still the boss, no matter what you think you found.'

I walk past him, not looking back.

The sky outside is a bleached white, the kind that pretends it's going to snow but never delivers. I lean against the hood of my car, breathing hard, eyes stinging from the sting of cheap disinfectant and the knowledge that thc world is about to change.

On the phone screen, the images line up in neat, rectangular proof. Every spiral, every redacted line, every name that someone tried to erase.

Let them try, I think.

I'll burn their secrets to the ground.

Lucas

You don't learn about the politics of a fire station from the textbooks, or even from the guys with forty years in and a beer gut to prove it. You learn it from the way the records room always smells faintly of burnt plastic, from the endless paper cuts, from the way the Chief's office light stays on long after the engines are parked and the radios go quiet.

I'm supposed to be on medical leave, but nobody tells the paperwork, and nobody tells the paperwork that I'm the only one who gives a shit about the files no one wants to touch.

I'm at my desk before sunrise, picking through the backlog like a raccoon rooting for the good trash. Today's project is a manila envelope labeled "INTERNAL–PERSONNEL–RETENTION." The words are block-stamped in red, but the corners are chewed up and the paper's gone limp from humidity.

My inbox is full of flagged emails, most of them from Captain Dalton: subtle reminders to let things drop, to stick to protocol, to "let sleeping dogs lie." I hit delete without reading, then run my tongue along the rim of my coffee mug, hoping the bitter will cut through the haze in my head. It doesn't.

The report I'm looking for is about a firefighter named Malik. He'd been on the job less than a year when he went AWOL—officially, a leave of absence, but everyone knew he wasn't coming back. He'd made noise about the budget, about discrepancies in equipment orders and payroll. Two weeks after his last shift, the department's accountant was found dead in his garage. The file is thin, and most of the notes are vague: "personal issues," "unstable temperament," "possibly a flight risk." I know how these euphemisms work. I've written a few myself.

But this file has a sticky residue on the back, like it used to be stapled to something thicker. I fish around in the drawer and find a second envelope, this one labeled "CONFIDENTIAL–BENNETT ONLY." The handwriting is different: blockier, more rushed, but the "B" matches the Chief's scrawl on every discipline report I've ever signed.

I try the computer system, but it's a joke—everything digital ends in a dead link or a "restricted" popup. The only way to get the real story is the old-fashioned way: digging until someone tells you to stop, or until you find the thing that can't be explained away.

The morning passes in fits and starts. I jot notes on a legal pad, cross-reference badge numbers, look for patterns in the weekly fuel orders. The numbers don't make sense: there's too much fuel going out, but not enough training burns or fieldwork to justify it. There are overlapping orders for equipment that never seems to arrive—thermal cameras, radios, even entire sets of turnout gear. If it was just one quarter, I could blame it on clerical error, but it's every quarter, for as long as Bennett's been in charge.

There's a locked file drawer under my desk that I've never bothered to open. The key is taped to the bottom of the drawer, classic rookie mistake. I fish it out, turn it in the lock, and feel the mechanism catch before it finally gives.

Inside is a single folder: "OPERATION PHOENIX." The cover sheet is a printout, but the rest is carbon copy, the kind that smears ink on your hands and smells faintly of ammonia. I flip through the first few pages and feel my skin go cold.

At the top of every page: "CONFIDENTIAL. NOT FOR DISTRIBUTION."

Half the pages are redacted with black marker, but enough is left to piece together the shape of it. There's mention of a controlled burn, but not for training—something about "civilian containment" and "legacy threats." There's a list of names, every one of them familiar: old-timers who retired early, a few who died in "accidents," a handful who just faded out of the picture.

On the last page is a memo, hand-signed in blue ink: "All anomalies to be reported directly to Chief Bennett. No exceptions." Beneath it, a second note, added later: "Grant family is off-limits. Monitor, but do not engage unless protocol is breached."

I stare at the signature for a long time. I've seen Bennett's handwriting on every sick note, every time-off request, every disciplinary action in the last decade. But this is different. The pressure on the pen, the heavy slant of the letters—it's not official. It's personal. The kind of mark you leave when you want someone to know you mean business.

My phone buzzes, a tiny vibration that jolts me out of the trance. It's a text from Sophie: "Got something. Need to meet. Urgent."

I close the file, wipe my hands on my pants, and shove the folder into my jacket. The world feels smaller now, the walls of the office crowding in. I take one last look at the computer screen, then kill the monitor, plunging the room into gray half-light.

On my way out, I pass the Chief's office. The door is open a crack, and I can see the glow of his desk lamp, the neat stacks of paper, the single photo of his family on the shelf behind him. For a second, I wonder if he ever looks at it, or if it's just for show.

I don't linger. I take the back stairs, two at a time, heart pounding. Outside, the air is damp and electric, a storm threatening to break.

I text Sophie back: "On my way. Don't go alone."

The old loyalty is gone. What's left is something harder, more elemental.

I think about the folder, the names, the way the Chief's signature cut through the layers of secrecy.

Then I think about Sophie, and the look in her eyes last night—fearless, but haunted.

I put the truck in gear, floor it out of the lot, and let the adrenaline carry me wherever the hell we're headed.

This time, I'm not playing by anyone's rules.

Sophie

I BUILD MY CASE THE WAY DAD TAUGHT ME: NOT BY collecting evidence, but by assembling it until it refuses to be ignored. By the time I'm through, the living room is a crime scene of its own—papers layered over the carpet like new snow, my father's battered journal cracked open to a page of spirals so dense they blot out the margin. The phone is propped against a mug, its camera roll a stuttering timeline of every redacted page, every blacked-out name, every notation they didn't want me to find.

I sit cross-legged in the center, knees pressed to my chest, using sticky notes as tabs and highlighters as scalpels. The air smells like dust and printer toner, with a persistent undercurrent of the cinnamon candle I light whenever I need to pretend I'm still in control of my own space. I talk to myself—low, barely audible—repeating names, dates, intersections. The rhythm helps, like a spell or a prayer.

I'm piecing together a pattern, something even the men who thought they could erase the past weren't careful enough to break. Every fire, every accident, every mysterious death—it all runs on a schedule, every incident happening in waves, never less than six months apart, always clustered around key dates. At the center of every cluster is a name I almost missed the first time through: Bennett.

Detective Marshall Troy Bennett, the man who ran Dad's case and a dozen more like it. The same Bennett who signs off on every redacted report, every dead-end internal investigation. The same Bennett who, according to a note I find clipped to the back of the fireproof box, visited Dad the night before he died.

The words on the note are clipped, frantic: "If Bennett calls, DO NOT ANSWER. Trust no one."

I don't realize I'm holding my breath until I see the edges of the world start to gray out. I force myself to inhale, then press a palm to the carpet, grounding myself. The highlighter in my hand snaps in two, spraying neon yellow across the timeline I've been drawing on the back of an old pizza box. For a second, I just stare at the mess. Then I laugh—quick, sharp, not quite sane.

The alarm is an air-raid siren that launches me upright. It's so loud I feel it in my teeth. I'm halfway to the front door before I remember to grab the heavy flashlight from the toolbox under the couch. The beams from the porch lamps cut through the early evening dusk, throwing long, predatory shadows across the windows.

I flip the locks in sequence—deadbolt, chain, latch—then crack the door and scan the street. Nothing. Not a car, not a neighbor, not even the stray dogs that usually treat my block like a territory dispute. I check the window, the mailbox, the edge of the porch for any sign of a watcher, but the world is empty except for the howl of the alarm.

I'm debating whether to call Lucas or just drive to the station when the second alarm goes off—this one internal, a tripwire in the back of my head that's always been better at survival than the rest of me. I freeze, then pivot, sweeping the flashlight in a slow arc across the living room. There's a window open in the kitchen, the one above the sink. I'd left it cracked to air out the place after last night's marathon of redacted files, but now it's wide, the curtain sucked in and out by the wind like a lung.

I kill the alarm, every muscle in my body screaming at me to run, but I force myself to check the kitchen anyway. The flashlight beam lands on the sink, where something glows electric red in the center of the stainless basin.

A flare, burning hot and steady, the magnesium light so bright it's nearly white. Next to it, propped against the faucet, is a folded scrap of legal paper. The edges are already starting to blacken, the heat from the flare warping the ink on the page.

I cross the kitchen in three steps and snatch the note, the ends already curling from the heat. It reads:

"Back off, or next time we don't miss."

No signature, but I know the handwriting. It's the same blocky print from the firehouse archives, the same penmanship that spelled out "OPERATION PHOENIX" in the folder Lucas found this morning.

My hands shake so hard I drop the paper, then fumble to pick it up again. The adrenaline makes everything vivid—the way the smoke from the flare curls and splits in the air, the way the smell of burning chemicals slams into my sinuses, the way the edge of the counter leaves a mark on the back of my thighs where I brace myself against it.

The back door rattles open and Lucas is there, face wet with rain, eyes bright and furious. He doesn't even stop to say hello; just scans the room, then barrels straight for the sink.

"Shit," he says, voice gone thin. He yanks a fire blanket from under the counter and drops it over the flare, smothering the light in a single motion. The room dims, but the afterimage pulses behind my eyelids. Lucas's hands move fast, practiced, but I see the tremor in his fingers as he shakes out the blanket and checks the sink for damage.

"You okay?" he says, not looking at me.

I nod, then realize I haven't breathed in thirty seconds. "Yeah. Just...wasn't expecting visitors."

He scans me up and down, eyes pausing at my hands, my face, my hair. "They touch you?"

I shake my head. "Just left a message."

He picks up the paper, reads it, then balls it up and pockets it. For a second, he looks like he might put his fist through the wall. Instead, he paces the length of the kitchen, then circles back to me. "We have to call Bennett."

I let out a short, bitter laugh. "That's not going to help."

He narrows his eyes. "What do you mean?"

I reach for the stack of files on the kitchen table, flipping to the page with Bennett's name circled in red. "He's in on it. All of it."

Lucas takes the page, reads it, then sets it down with a controlled, deliberate motion. "You're sure?"

I point to the photo roll on my phone, scroll to the signature line on the "OPERATION PHOENIX" memo. "Same handwriting. Same pattern of cover-ups. He's been cleaning up after himself for decades."

Lucas's face goes flat, all emotion shoved underground. "So he's not just a bystander. He's the point man."

"Yeah," I say, my own voice shaky. "And he's still watching. Still trying to scare me off."

The smoke in the kitchen is thick now, the smell settling into the wallpaper, the clothes, the skin. I see the edges of panic crowding in on Lucas, but he grabs my hand—hard, anchoring.

“We’re not backing off,” he says, each word iron. “They want us scared. We hit back harder.”

I squeeze his hand, the pressure grounding me, forcing the world to come back into focus. “How?”

He lets go, only to flip open his phone and start dialing. “First, we call the station. Get them on record. Then we take this to the press. Full exposure.”

For a second, I want to argue—say that it’s too dangerous, that we’ll just end up on someone’s list. But I look around at the ruin of my kitchen, the note still smoldering in the sink, and realize the list was written before I was born.

I start packing the files into a box, hands steadier now. Lucas moves with me, his every motion purposeful, like if he stops moving he might fall apart. We don’t talk about what comes next. We just do.

As we work, I feel the burn of old fear recede, replaced by something new: a low, pulsing fury. I remember the way my father’s hands shook when he thought no one was looking, the way he’d stare into the flame of a match and let it burn to his fingers before snuffing it out. I think about what he’d want me to do.

Lucas is at my side, shoulder to shoulder, every once in a while glancing at me with a look that’s half-worried, half-awed.

“You ever scared?” I ask, voice barely above a whisper.

He doesn’t look up. “Only when I’m not with you.”

I let the words hang, then nod.

"Same."

The kitchen is a black smudge, but it's ours. The world outside can burn, but for now, we're alive, and we're together, and we have a plan.

Let them try again.

We're ready.

The world doesn't come back all at once. At first, it's just the slow, staticky return of breath and heartbeat, the way the walls of the kitchen resolve from white-out into their real dimensions. I'm still perched on the edge of the counter, hands wrapped tight around my own wrists like if I let go, I'll shatter. The smoke is thinning, but the sting in my lungs lingers. My hands ache with a deep, raw burn, and for a second I can't move them at all.

Lucas is there, as if he never left the room. He squats in front of me, hands steady, his face set in the expression of a man who's seen too many emergencies and is determined to fix just one. He pries my fingers apart, gentle but insistent, and when I try to pull away, he just shakes his head.

"Don't fight me," he says. The words are low and almost tender.

He disappears down the hall and comes back with the first

aid kit—red plastic, battered, labeled with a faded marker: "KITCHEN/VEHICLE." He opens it with one hand, then kneels, balanced so our eyes are level.

"Give me your hands," he says, and I do, more because I can't imagine saying no than any real trust.

The antiseptic stings, and I can't help but make a sound. He doesn't apologize, just dabs the cotton more gently, moving from knuckle to knuckle. The skin is split in a few places, mostly where I grabbed the burning note. The rest is just red, angry, and going to hurt like hell tomorrow.

He works in silence for a while. I study the top of his head, the way his hair is darker near the roots, the line of sweat at his temple. When he looks up, his eyes are sharp, clear, and for the first time I see no fear in them. Just something that could almost be called hope.

"Why are you so calm?" I ask, my voice thick.

He shakes his head, wraps a strip of gauze around my right hand. "Not calm. Just good at pretending."

"Always?"

"Always," he says, and when he smiles, it's sad. "Except with you."

He finishes the bandage, tapes it off, then takes my left hand and starts over. The cotton swab traces a path over my skin, cleaning away ash, blood, and whatever else got left behind. His fingers are warm and careful. When he finishes, he lifts my hand and kisses it—first the palm, then the back, then each knuckle in turn.

I don't know whether to laugh or cry, so I just let myself exist in the space, the sensation of his lips on my ruined hands anchoring me to the here and now.

He looks up, eyes searching mine. "I mean it. I'm not leaving you again."

I let the words hang, heavy as oxygen tanks. I want to ask what that means, if it's a promise, a threat, or something worse. Instead, I lean forward and press my forehead to his. Our noses bump, awkward and perfect.

"I'm scared," I say.

He closes his eyes, and I feel his breath shudder out. "Me too."

For a long minute, we just stay like that—foreheads touching, the hum of the refrigerator the only sound in the world. His arms wrap around my waist, careful of my hands, and he holds me close. I bury my face in the space between his neck and shoulder, and let myself breathe him in: sweat, smoke, and the faintest trace of detergent.

Eventually, he pulls away just enough to look at me. "We should go public. Now. Get out in front of it before they can stop us."

I nod, but I don't move. "What if we're wrong?"

He laughs, soft and dark. "We're not wrong."

He picks up my hands, studies them like they're an artifact. "These'll heal," he says. "But we need to be careful. No more lone-wolf bullshit. We do this together, or not at all."

I want to argue, but my mouth can't find the words. Instead, I say, "Promise?"

He smiles, for real this time. "Promise."

We sit together at the kitchen table, the world outside distant and irrelevant. The files are piled between us, the evidence of a lifetime of secrets ready to go. The air tastes of smoke and something else—anticipation, maybe, or the last vestiges of fear finally being burned away.

Lucas traçes a finger over the bandage on my hand, then threads his own fingers through mine, careful not to squeeze too tight.

"We're really doing this," I say.

He squeezes my hand, just once. "Yeah. We are."

The kitchen is a mess, my hands are wrecked, and the future is a red-lit warning sign. But for now, there's just the two of us, facing the fire together.

And I wouldn't have it any other way.

11

Fireproof Lies

Lucas

THE CAPTAIN'S OFFICE IS AT THE FAR END OF THE BUNKER, past a warren of drop ceilings and linoleum that never stops squeaking under your boots. I could find it blindfolded, which is good, because that's basically how I'm moving—tunnel-visioned, red-edged, all my focus on the folder in my hand and the forty-eight hours of sleep debt crowding the edges of my vision.

I don't bother to knock. I just push in, catching Captain Dalton mid-sentence on a phone call. He sees the manila folder, and his face clicks through three expressions—annoyance, calculation, and then something blanker, as if his skin can't quite decide which side of the fight it wants to land on. He waves me in with two fingers, tells whoever's on the line, "I'll call you back," and hangs up.

The overhead fluorescents buzz with a high-pitched whine,

the kind that only gets worse the longer you sit with it. The light turns the captain's skin waxy and sick, accentuating the bristle of his mustache and the twin knots of tension at his temples.

"Hayes," he says, like my name is a request for aspirin. "You got a minute?"

I close the door behind me. "You got a couple more than that."

I drop the Operation Phoenix folder on his desk, let the impact echo. It's not dramatic—just enough to shake the ceramic firefighter mug that never leaves his left hand. The mug says 'World's Best Boss.' The way he clutches it, you'd think it was a piece of evidence.

He glances at the folder, then at me. "Is this supposed to mean something?"

I sit. The chair's too low, making him loom above me by at least six inches. He loves that; it's a power move I've seen a thousand times, mostly aimed at rookies and the kind of visitor who doesn't know to keep their knees from knocking.

"It means," I say, "that somebody's running a shadow budget through the station, buying fuel and gear that never show up in training or in the field. It means that every report from the Hawthorn and Grant fires is redacted to hell, and the person doing the blacking-out is signing your initials on the margin. It means—" I lean in, elbows on the desk, "—that this station has a cancer, and it started under your watch."

He doesn't blink. "You think you're the first to come in here with a folder and a bad attitude?"

I let him talk. He always gets more dangerous when he's silent for too long, so I figure if I keep him talking, I'll get a sense of where the land mines are.

He props the mug on his chest, steeples his fingers. "You want to know how a place like this stays open, year after year, when the county keeps slashing our funding to ribbons? I'll tell you: creative accounting, off-books deals, and a lot of shit you'd rather not know about. That's what keeps the trucks fueled and the paychecks from bouncing. Not your little crusade."

I keep my voice flat. "You falsified reports. You buried arson investigations that would have put half this town under a microscope. And now you're threatening me, what, with a pay cut?"

He smirks, the corners of his mouth folding up like origami. "No, Hayes. I'm threatening you with reality. You want to keep this job, you learn the same lesson as everyone else: some things are better left alone."

I push the folder closer, making the edges gouge the scuffed wood of his desk. "That's the second time I've heard that line this week. Starting to sound like a religion."

He snorts. "You think you're a hero, but all you're doing is pissing on a house fire and thinking you saved the day. You dig any deeper, you're going to set off a three-alarm shitstorm that nobody in this town is ready to handle."

I want to tell him about the ring, about the note in Sophie's kitchen, about the way the whole department is sitting on a powder keg, but I see the way his hands tighten on the mug and I know that's what he wants. He's hoping I'll overplay, say too much, give him a reason to shut this down before anyone else hears about it.

I switch gears. "You ever wonder why nobody stays here more than five years? Why everyone either burns out or transfers to the city?"

He shrugs, all big-shouldered indifference. "It's a small town. Small towns eat their own."

I give him a slow smile, teeth clenched. "You're right. But you're running out of people to eat."

He lets the silence balloon, then pops it with a sigh. "I'm going to forget this conversation happened, Hayes. I'm going to pretend you're not walking around with classified personnel files in your backpack. But you keep poking at this, and you'll find yourself working traffic duty on the far side of the county. Or worse."

I stand. The chair squeaks in protest, metal scraping linoleum. "You can threaten me all you want, Captain. But the truth is out. And it's going to get louder."

He sits back, folding his arms over his chest. "You're treading dangerous ground. Think about your future here."

I take the folder and tuck it under my arm. "I already have."

Out in the hall, the lights are brighter, the air thinner, the voices of the new shift drifting down from the day room. I walk the length of the corridor, pulse hammering, ears still ringing with the threat disguised as advice. When I hit the exit, I throw the door open so hard the safety latch shrieks in protest.

Outside, the world is cold, sharp, alive. I look at the folder, then at my own hands, the knuckles white from gripping it too tight.

This isn't a job anymore. It's a war.

And I just made myself the enemy.

Sophie

The newsroom smells like old toner and new regret. Every surface not covered in vintage hardware is buried under the detritus of a dead tree industry: sticky notes, stacks of weeklies, ad proofs yellowed to nicotine, coffee mugs bred by mitosis and never once washed. The only thing holding the office together is the tensile strength of anxiety and Meredith Holloway's refusal to acknowledge entropy as a law of nature.

She sees me coming and flags me in with a fistful of pens. "Five minutes, tops," she says, even as she's clearing space at her desk. "Editor's on my ass about a school levy, but that can wait. You brought the stuff?"

I produce the folder from my bag, the one with my dad's name on half the pages and enough redactions to make a conspiracy theorist out of a golden retriever. Meredith eyes it like it's contraband and yanks me into the back corner, away from the glassed-in boss's office.

"Jesus, Soph," she says. "You look like hell."

"Mutual," I shoot back, but there's no real bite. I drop into the chair opposite her, the legs uneven, so I have to balance my knee against the wall to keep from sliding off.

We get right into it. The next hour is a knife fight with records: school-district laptops, my annotated printouts, Meredith's own stash of bootleg city memos. She's the only person alive who can outpace my research habits; I grew up shadowing her in the public library, long before she had a byline, back when she was just the smartest person in any room and didn't need a press pass to prove it.

"This one," I say, tapping the corner of an incident report from 2001. "See the signature? Captain Bennett. Here's the same on my father's termination paperwork, and again on the supplemental budget request from the summer before. You know what that means?"

She grins, wolfish. "Means our boy likes to sign things. What are you betting?"

"That he's the cutout for every cover-up between '96 and '05." I flip the sheet over, exposing a trio of typewritten lines that should not, by any reasonable logic, exist on an arson report: 'Budget constraints; minimal follow-up authorized. Evidence disposal approved by Chief Bennett.' "They killed the investigation before it started, Mer. Every single time."

She hums, a low, satisfied sound. "What about the Linder case?"

"Same. Chain of command: Bennett. Original notes, all gone." I show her the next page, my own scribbles in blue. "But look here—Bennett's name pops again on the personnel reviews, even when he wasn't on the clock. It's like he had his own calendar, his own set of rules."

She's already reaching for her own pile. "And you said there was an insurance angle?"

"Dad flagged it. There's always a policy uptick right before something torches. And then a settlement, off the books."

Meredith pulls a battered file folder from under the monitor, waggling it. "You need to see this."

She spreads the file on the desk, and it's like someone detonated a memory grenade: clippings from the first days after my dad's death, grainy headshots, a tearful me at age ten frozen behind my mom's elbow, and then, at the bottom, a printout of the original coroner's report. The edges are burned, the ink blistered, but I can still read the last line: "Victim was discovered with second-degree burns inconsistent with reported time-of-death."

I run my finger over the charred edge, feeling the sick heat under my skin. "They torched him to make sure. The fire was just a smokescreen."

Meredith meets my eye. "He knew, and they silenced him for it."

Neither of us says anything. The office noise recedes: the tap of keys, the distant shout of the editor, the brittle laughter of the ad girls. I feel my hands start to shake, but I clamp them together and breathe through it.

Meredith is still moving, always moving. She scribbles something on the back of her hand, then pulls her phone and starts scrolling through ancient texts. "You want to know what's really weird, Soph?"

I nod, numb.

"Every time a firefighter or police officer died under Bennett's watch, the city settled with the families. NDA, hush money, whatever. But in your case, nothing. They just let it hang."

"Because he thought nobody would care. Because he thought—" I choke on the rest. "Because he thought I'd never come back."

Meredith's face softens. "But you did."

"Yeah," I say. "And I'm not leaving until I finish it."

We go through another stack, this one financials from the city's own archives. It's all there: payroll anomalies, hardware that never showed up, 'fuel surpluses' so obvious it's a wonder the auditors didn't riot. The same names repeat, always with Bennett at the hub. The man is a spider, and the town is his web.

Finally, Meredith slides a battered envelope across the desk. "Found this in the courthouse basement last winter. It's addressed to you, but it came two weeks after your dad died."

The return address is the fire station. No stamp, no sender.

I tear it open. Inside is a single sheet, half-burned, the writing jagged and panicked:

"If you stay, she dies. Go."

I can't breathe. The words run into each other, bleeding in black and brown. The handwriting is my father's.

I look up, and Meredith is watching, all the bravado gone.

"I think he meant you," she says, barely audible.

"I know he did."

I fold the letter, slow, and tuck it into my pocket. It's proof of nothing, but it feels like a fuse—one I plan to light as soon as I get back to my car.

"Thank you," I say.

Meredith smiles, tired and lopsided. "Don't thank me yet. You're about to ruin a lot of people's week."

"Good," I say. "That's the plan."

I leave the newsroom with the city's secrets crammed into my bag, the burned letter warm against my thigh, and a new purpose coiling up from my gut.

This is what he died for, I think.

And I'm going to finish what he started.

The sun is gone before I notice. One minute I'm hunched over the laptop, chasing the cursor through a maze of PDFs, the next it's full dark outside, the windows pitch and the corners of the room gone flat as ink. I've had the same song on repeat for an hour; I couldn't tell you the title if you paid me.

On the table: half-eaten takeout, three pens, six legal pads bristling with tabs. On the wall, the evidence board—a fantasy of yarn and thumbtacks, as if pretending at TV detective work will save me from the real thing. The only light is a desk lamp, its bulb humming with the threat of imminent death.

I'm elbow-deep in an old city council budget when the house alarm detonates. It's an animal sound, wild and insistent, the siren pulsing red through every window. The system is new; Lucas put it in last week, muttering about perimeter weaknesses and "target hardening." I'd called him a worrywart. Now, I'm not so sure.

My first move is muscle memory: phone, keys, flashlight. I keep the phone live in one hand as I creep through the kitchen, bare feet ghosting over the tile. The red strobes cast everything in murder scene colors, and the shadows are thick enough to choke on.

The back door rattles. Not the wind—this is deliberate, mechanical. I freeze behind the kitchen island, hear the delicate whine of metal on metal, the unmistakable sound of someone working the lock with tools.

I dial Lucas, press the speaker hard to my ear. He answers on the first ring, breathless, like he was waiting for it.

"Lucas—someone's here," I hiss. "Back door."

"Stay put," he snaps. "I'm four minutes out. Do not engage. Cops on the way."

Four minutes is an eternity. I scan the kitchen for a weapon, settle on the lamp—heavy base, cord already halfway chewed by the cat. I clutch it to my chest and duck low, just as the door gives a groan and the deadbolt shudders.

The glass pane cracks but doesn't shatter. A shape resolves beyond the curtain: dark jacket, hood up, hands gloved. The figure's movements are quick, practiced. A tap at the hinge, a wedge at the frame, and the latch buckles.

The door swings in. I suck in a breath, the lamp raised over my shoulder like a cartoon housewife. The figure steps inside, ducking the alarm's strobe. We lock eyes, or we would if I could see his eyes through the black half-mask. He's taller than me by a head, built like he's spent time in a gym or in prison.

He spots me, hesitates. It's just enough time for the fear to break and let the anger through.

“Get out,” I snarl, voice gone raw.

He doesn’t. He takes a single step my way.

I launch the lamp. It flies low and wild, taking him in the thigh. He grunts, stumbles, recovers fast—too fast—and closes the gap. I backpedal, catch my hip on the fridge, and slam my elbow into the emergency panic button Lucas had installed just above the water dispenser.

The sound that follows is worse than the alarm, a high-frequency screech that seems to slice right through bone. The man recoils, both hands to his ears, and for a second I think I’ve won.

Then he’s on me, one hand clamping my wrist, the other pushing my shoulder against the cabinet. He’s strong, but not as strong as panic and three years of Krav Maga. I twist, stomp the top of his foot, and wrench my arm free. He snarls, a wet, angry sound, and I see the glint of something in his hand—metal, short, not a gun but not good news.

I duck, roll past him, and sprint for the front door. He’s right behind me, breathing hard, the sound hot and primal. I fumble with the chain, my hands shaking so bad I can’t get it to slide. He closes in, grabs the hood of my sweatshirt, yanking me back.

The chain finally gives. I tear free, hit the door at speed, and tumble onto the porch. I scramble to my feet, the world spinning, just as Lucas barrels into the yard from the street, voice already shouting.

"Down!" Lucas's voice bellows, and I drop, more out of instinct than compliance.

Lucas hits the man mid-stride, both of them slamming to the ground in a tangle of limbs. The fight is fast and vicious—no style, no technique, just elbows and fists and the single-minded fury of people who refuse to be victims. They roll once, twice, crushing a line of my mother's geraniums, and then the man gets a knee up, driving it into Lucas's side.

Lucas grunts, but doesn't let go. He wraps both arms around the man's waist and heaves, slamming him into the gravel with a force that would make a linebacker jealous. There's a sickening crunch, a half-second of stillness, and then the man rakes a gloved hand down Lucas's face, catching him just above the cheek.

They break apart. The man is up first, breathing ragged, eyes wide and wild above the mask. He glances over his shoulder, sees the blue of police lights in the distance, and bolts for the side fence. Lucas lurches to his feet, staggering, but doesn't give chase.

He turns to me, bleeding from the cheek, breathing like he just ran a marathon.

"You good?" he manages.

I nod, every muscle shivering.

The police arrive seconds later—two cars, sirens off, both officers stepping out with hands on their holsters. They check on us, radio in a perimeter, and then sweep the block for the intruder. It takes less than five minutes for them to call it: suspect gone, no trace.

I sit on the stoop, head in my hands, the aftershocks still rattling my bones.

Lucas squats beside me, gingerly touching his cut. "You did good," he says.

"Didn't feel like it."

He almost laughs, but it comes out as a wince. "You're alive. That's what matters."

One of the officers comes over, asks for a description. I give him what I can: tall, athletic, dark clothes, face masked. He writes it down, not even pretending to think they'll catch the guy.

When the cop leaves, Lucas leans close, voice low.

"He knew exactly how to disable your alarm," he says. "The timing, the technique—hell, even the way he held the wedge. Who the fuck was that, because it wasn't Bennett."

I swallow, tasting the sour twist of adrenaline and defeat. "You think it's someone from the department?"

"I think," he says, "we're up against people who know exactly what they're doing."

The wind picks up, cold and sharp. I look at my scraped

palms, at the blood on Lucas's face, at the distant swirl of blue and red at the end of the block.

"I'm not scared," I say, and I almost believe it.

He nods, proud and broken at once.

"Neither am I."

We sit there, side by side on the stoop, waiting for the next move.

Because now, it's our turn.

After the cops leave and the yard quiets down, Lucas and I take stock of the damage. The kitchen looks like a war zone: glass everywhere, the fridge dented, one chair snapped clean through the middle. There's a print of my palm in blood on the wall where I braced myself. I want to clean up, but Lucas insists on preserving everything for the private investigator he's already texting, two blocks away and paid in cash.

We end up in the living room, both of us still in the clothes we nearly died in, our faces pinched and raw. I make coffee mostly for the ritual, but the act of pouring it into mismatched mugs calms my hands a little.

On the coffee table, my laptop is already running the home security app. The feed is split in four, each square a different angle of the back door. I click through the timeline, fast-forwarding past hours of nothing: a possum, a wind gust, the neighbor kid sneaking a smoke. Then, at 21:14, the screen jitters with motion.

"There," I say, voice barely above a whisper.

Lucas leans in, his arm warm against my shoulder. The blue from the screen etches shadows on his jaw, making him look older, more tired. He hits pause, then backs up a frame at a time, slow and methodical.

The attacker comes into view. Hoodie up, face half-masked, but the build matches what I remember. He moves quick, knees bent, favoring his left leg. Lucas grunts, pointing. "He's been trained. Not just breaking in—he's clearing corners."

I shiver, more at the implication than the memory.

We watch as the figure disables the exterior motion light, then works the lock in under fifteen seconds. "Shit," Lucas mutters. "He didn't even react at the alarm. That's military or... fire service."

I keep my eyes on the screen, willing the pixels to resolve into something useful. The attacker enters, then freezes in the kitchen, glancing up at the sensor. The security cam catches a slice of his forearm where the sleeve rides up. I squint, but it's just a shadow, a blur.

Lucas replays the moment, this time zooming in. The app pixelates, but the shape becomes clearer: a tattoo, black ink against pale skin, barely an inch of it before the sleeve falls back down.

My breath sticks in my throat. "Pause it. Right there."

He does. Together, we stare at the blue-lit patch of skin.

"It's a flame," I say, heart pounding. "Department issue?"

Lucas's jaw tightens. "Yeah. We get it after five years on the job. It's a rite of passage. But the design—it's the variant from our station. Only active firefighters have it."

I try to process. "You're telling me—"

"I know that arm." His voice is flat, dead. "I've worked beside it for years."

The shock sits between us, heavy and absolute. I think of every shift change, every back-slap in the engine bay, every time Lucas covered for a colleague on a double.

He looks at me, eyes wide and wet. "I trusted them."

I squeeze his hand. "You still can. But only the ones who pass your test."

He nods, but his gaze is far away, doing math I can't see.

On the screen, the attacker's frozen in place, his tattoo like a fingerprint, a signature of betrayal.

"This goes deeper than we thought," I say. "Way deeper."

Lucas closes his eyes, lets out a long, rattled breath. "We can't go to Internal. Not with Bennett still pulling the strings."

"We don't have to," I say, feeling a new fire kindle in my gut. "We burn it all down ourselves."

He almost smiles at that.

"Together?"

"Together."

We let the footage run again, frame by frame, hunting for any scrap we can use. The plan is forming already, sharper by the second, and I know we won't stop until every secret is ash and every badge is accounted for.

The house feels less haunted now.

It just feels ready.

I spend the night with the lights on and every curtain drawn tight. The alarm system is reset, the new code programmed by Lucas himself—six digits, a sequence nobody but us could guess. I sleep maybe an hour, curled on the couch under a blanket that smells like smoke and rain. Lucas doesn't leave, though he spends most of the dark pacing from window to window, checking sightlines, making notes on a pad in a code I don't bother trying to break.

At sunrise, the world looks ordinary again. The street is empty. The kitchen is still a mess, but the air tastes less of panic and more of stale coffee.

I shower, then circle the living room, restless. My arms are crossed so tight it feels like they might fuse to my ribs.

"We need to expose all of it," I say, for the third time in as many minutes.

Lucas stands by the front window, mug in hand, staring into the middle distance. "If it's someone inside, they have access to everything—records, equipment, alibis. There's no way to run it up the chain without them seeing it first."

"Good," I shoot back. "Let them sweat. I'm not going to get scared off because some asshole knows how to pick a lock."

He sets the mug down, turns to me, and his eyes are the calm before the kind of storm that makes national news. "You know how many fires I've run into, Soph? How many times I've bet my life on the guy next to me?"

I nod. "You're the most loyal person I know. But your loyalty got you lied to."

He takes it on the chin. "And now?"

I stop pacing and stand in front of him, head high. "Now we go nuclear. Every name, every file. We take it to the press, to the feds, to whoever will listen."

He considers, jaw tight. "You could end up in the crosshairs. You're already a target."

I shrug. "I've been a target since the night my house burned down. If it ends here, fine. But I won't let them bury me like they buried my father's case."

Lucas's hands flex, then relax. He steps closer, closes the last inch of distance between us. "Whatever it takes, we find the truth. Even if it costs me my badge."

I nod, letting the promise settle. It's not romantic; it's something harder, heavier, the kind of trust you only build with blood and shared secrets.

We spend the next hour plotting our moves: who to trust (no one), how to leak the right files without tipping our hand, which back doors in the system Lucas can still access before they lock him out. I fire off a warning text to Meredith Holloway, then start scanning every last scrap of paper we have.

Every so often, Lucas glances my way, like he's trying to memorize my face in case it's the last time he sees it.

"We're really doing this," he says, more to himself than to me.

"Yeah," I answer, steady and sure. "We are."

Lucas is pulling down the blackout curtains when it hits me: the air in the house is too tight, too loud with our mutual stubbornness. He's about to say something comforting, I can see it, but the words choke off as I cross the room and fist both hands in his shirt, yanking him forward.

The first kiss is savage. Not gentle, not seeking, just a collision. I want to bite him, bruise him, leave marks he'll feel in the morning. He grunts, more shocked than hurt, but a second later his hands are on my hips, hard, possessive, like he's trying to anchor both of us in a world that's spinning too fast.

We break for air, faces inches apart, breath mixing in short, violent clouds. He tries to speak, but I'm already at his jaw, the line of stubble scraping my lips, his pulse jumping under my tongue. I push him until his back hits the counter, crowding him there, pinning him with my whole body.

He fights for control—always, always. One hand catches my wrist, the other finds my lower back, pulling me in until I can feel every frantic beat of his heart through the layers of our clothes. His mouth slants over mine, rough and hungry, tasting like blood and coffee and the last three years of regret.

I thread my fingers into his hair, tug just hard enough to make him growl. My shirt is gone before I realize he's unbuttoned it, the sleeves peeling away as his hands map every new inch of skin. I laugh—half-dare, half-dare-you-back—and kick his feet apart, pressing one thigh between his.

He lifts me, easy as breathing, and sets me on the kitchen table, sweeping aside the evidence files with a forearm. My ass hits the wood hard enough to rattle the mug and knock a stack of sticky notes to the floor. Papers scatter everywhere: photos, printouts, the burned letter. I don't care.

He stands between my knees, breathing hard, looking at me like he's starving. His hands find my waist, my ribs, my breasts, pinching and kneading with the controlled violence of someone who's spent too many nights holding back. I arch into him, greedy for every spark.

"Is this how you want it?" he says, voice wrecked.

I nod, too far gone for words. "Want you somewhere you'll remember," I say, and he shivers.

He strips me down, fast and efficient. Jeans undone, underwear shucked, all of it bunched around my ankles. He doesn't wait for permission, just sinks to his knees and drags his tongue up the inside of my thigh, slow and deliberate. I shove a hand in his hair and guide him where I need him most. He laughs against my skin, a deep, wicked sound, then goes to work.

He's good. Better than he should be, better than I remembered. He licks and sucks and nips, one arm locked around my leg to keep me from squirming away. I clench the edge of the table, white-knuckled, and let the sensation burn away every other thought.

When I come, it's with a sound I don't recognize—half-sob, half-battle cry. He rides it out, then rises, mouth shiny, pupils blown wide. He wipes his chin, then leans in for another kiss, forcing me to taste myself on his tongue.

I pull at his belt, clumsy with urgency, and he lets me. His cock is thick and hot, leaking, already flushed dark at the head. He rubs it against me, up and down, coating himself in my slickness, then pushes in slow. He's too big, too much, but I take him anyway, wanting to split open, wanting to be ruined.

He fucks me like he's afraid of being gentle. The table creaks, the evidence slides around under my ass, and I dig my heels into his back to make him go deeper. Every thrust shoves me up the wood another inch, until my shoulders bang the stack of legal pads and I laugh again, wild and mean.

He buries his face in my neck, biting hard enough to mark me, hands gripping my hips so tight I'll bruise. I want it. I want all of it. I wrap my arms around his shoulders and rake my nails down his spine, leaving red trails he won't see until tomorrow.

He gets close, then pulls out just long enough to flip me over, bending me over the table so my tits mash against the cool wood, my face in the mess of papers. He enters me from behind, deeper this time, the new angle perfect. I brace myself, arch my back, and take everything he gives.

"Don't stop," I say, voice low and ruined.

He doesn't. He grabs my hair, yanks my head back, and comes with a groan, hips slamming against my ass, cock pulsing inside me. I clench around him, milking every last drop, then go limp, the world narrowing to the drumbeat of my heart and the sweat cooling on my skin.

We stay like that: me bent over, him pressed against my back, both of us gasping like we just ran a marathon.

Eventually, he pulls out, tucks himself away, then scoops me up and sets me on the edge of the table. I don't bother covering myself; I just grab his shirt and wipe my face, then toss it at him.

He laughs, a real one this time, and pulls me in for a softer kiss.

We collapse together on the floor, tangled in the mess, breathing hard.

After a while, he props himself up on one elbow, looks at me with a softness I haven't seen since before everything went to shit.

"The lies they're hiding," he says, voice thick, "are more dangerous than any fire."

I nod, feeling the rawness in my throat, the ache between my legs, the bruises forming already. "Then let's torch every secret they've got."

He grins, teeth sharp, eyes bright. "Together?"

I roll on top of him, straddling his hips, and kiss him again—slower now, but no less fierce.

"Always," I whisper.

The world outside can burn. Inside, we're already on fire.

12

Ashes and Oaths

In the morning, the only thing left of the fire is the afterglow. I wake up in Lucas's bed, every muscle sore, skin mapped with heat and fresh marks, the air in the room heavy with the layered scents of sweat, sex, and yesterday's adrenaline. I don't move at first. It's a luxury I rarely allow myself. I just lie there, sheets pooled at my hips, Lucas's arm a dead weight across my stomach—possessive, even in sleep. There's a stubborn patch of stubble chafing my shoulder, his chin jammed at an awkward angle, mouth half-open, breath stirring the hair near my ear with every exhale.

The blinds cut the sunlight into slats, stripes of gold and blue painting the naked geometry of our bodies. I watch dust motes hang and drift, take inventory of every bruise and scrape, the half-healed burns that form a grid across Lucas's left forearm. His hand twitches, maybe dreaming of rescue or running, but the fingers don't let go.

I let myself imagine, for exactly one minute, that this is

what peace feels like. That the war is over, that the world outside can burn but the world inside this room is safe. In the silence, I count the ticks of the old wall clock, the hum of a neighbor's lawn mower starting up across the street, the distant bark of a dog. I measure how long it takes my heart to slow from fight-or-flight to something approaching normal. I note, with clinical detachment, that I like the way our legs tangle under the covers. That I don't hate the vulnerability.

Lucas shifts in his sleep, mouth closing to a thin, hard line, arm tightening around my waist. The hand slides lower, fingers grazing the tender skin at my hip, then curling in. If I didn't know him, I'd call it sweet. I do know him, so I call it survival—staking a claim, marking territory even when he's off duty. I could hate him for it, but I don't.

I twist carefully, propping myself on one elbow. The nightstand is a battlefield of empty water glasses, spent phone chargers, two sets of keys, and the black rectangle of Lucas's phone, screen-down and quiet. My own phone is wedged under the tangle of last night's jeans, the battery probably dead. I let the moment linger another thirty seconds, then slide my arm free and reach for it.

As I do, Lucas stirs, grumbles something that might be my name or just a scrap of last night's argument. His eyelids flutter, and for a second I wonder if he'll wake, see me, and pull me back down with some half-assed apology and a hand on the back of my neck. I want that, maybe, but I want answers more.

His phone buzzes. Not a ring, just a vibration—a cat's-paw tap on the wood. I freeze, hand suspended, and watch as the screen lights up with a text. No password; Lucas is a caveman like that. The preview glows in the blue of morning.

From: T. Bennett

"Keep her out of this."

My stomach flips so hard it might as well be a backdraft. Every inch of my skin goes cold, the afterglow snuffed like a candle in an airless room.

I know, instantly, what it means. Not because I'm paranoid, but because I'm right. Bennett has been the black hole at the center of this shitstorm from the start—chief, puppet master, the one who buried Dad's case and erased everyone who got too close. And Lucas... Lucas has been talking to him, keeping me in the dark, probably since day one.

My whole body locks up. I want to punch the wall, throw the phone, wake Lucas by grabbing him by the throat and demanding he explain himself. Instead, I slip out from under his arm with a practiced, surgical efficiency, moving in slow increments so I don't even disturb the blanket. I dress with the same precision, sliding into jeans and t-shirt, not even bothering to check for last night's underwear. The phone is still buzzing, more insistent now, but I ignore it.

I leave the room on bare feet, snagging my boots and jacket from the hallway. I don't look back. If I did, I might scream.

The front door closes behind me with a click that sounds like a gunshot in the quiet of the cul-de-sac. I stand on the porch, breathing through my teeth, waiting for the rage to hit full force. It does, but not the way I expect. There's no outburst, no ugly-cry meltdown. Just a numb, animal urgency: get away, put distance between me and whatever betrayal is brewing in that house.

My hands are shaking as I jam the key into the ignition. The engine growls, the dashboard lights up, and I drive. No destination in mind, just the need to move. I don't even check the rearview to see if Lucas is following.

At the first red light, I lay my forehead against the steering wheel and let the tremors run their course. I want to be furious. I want to hate Lucas, to hate myself for believing in anything he said or did, even for a second. But the anger is too old, too worn down by years of disappointment to sustain itself. What's left is the slow, sinking ache of betrayal—the kind that burrows under the ribs and stays there forever.

My phone, wedged in the center console, buzzes. It's an unfamiliar number, but I know who it is before I pick up.

"Leave me alone," I say, no hello, no preamble.

Lucas's voice is a rasp, soft but urgent. "Sophie—wait. Just listen. I can explain."

I hang up. Toss the phone onto the passenger seat, where it bounces and lands face-down, like a body.

I drive. Out of habit more than intention, I take the old highway west, following the stretch of asphalt that used to be my escape route as a teenager. Every curve and dip is a memory: the time Dad taught me to drive stick, the spot where

I ditched my first shitty boyfriend, the overlook where I once sat for hours, waiting for the fire trucks to scream past on their way to someone else's disaster.

The cemetery is on the edge of town, a quarter mile past the last strip mall and the rusted-out playground. The gates are always open—no one in Willow Creek is brave enough to steal from the dead, and the caretaker is more likely to offer you coffee than a citation. I park by the fence, engine ticking as it cools, and walk the gravel path to Dad's grave.

The cemetery is more crowded than I remember, but the only witnesses are the dead. I walk the lines between the headstones, each name a bump in my peripheral vision, each date a reminder that every secret in this town eventually makes its way here. The sun is out now, dragging shadows across the patchy grass, turning the mausoleums into slabs of white glare.

Dad's grave is at the back, past the rows of civic heroes and war dead, tucked under a sycamore with bark like peeling paint. The caretakers haven't bothered to clear the winter's debris, so I kick aside a drift of brittle leaves and squat in front of the stone.

"GRANT, FREDERICK A." Plain as always. No medal, no frills, just the line he never let Mom change: "Truth is what you salvage from the fire."

I touch the letters, cold and rough, then fold my hands in my lap like a kid at confession. The words in my throat won't line up, so I just breathe for a while, staring at the lichen and the veins in the granite.

Something smells off.

Not the sweet rot of cut flowers left too long, or the ozone tang that clings to every stone after rain, but a sharp, chemical sting, as if someone lit a match and let it gutter out just beneath my nose. I look down, and see it: a bouquet, black-stemmed, petals scorched and curling, cradled in a paper cone slicked with soot.

Charred lilies. The tips of the flowers are scorched to the color of old blood, and if I squint I can see that some petals are melted together, fused by a heat so precise it feels surgical. No card, no note. Just the stink of a warning, left exactly where I would find it.

I scan the path behind me, half-expecting to catch a shape hiding behind a monument, but the grounds are empty. Only the distant drone of a weed whacker and the soft click of my own pulse.

This isn't a memorial. It's a message.

I crouch, pick up the bouquet, and hold it to my nose. The ash stains my fingers, gritty and dark. The smell drags me back to every fire I ever saw up close: the taste of burnt plastic, the singed-hair flavor that lingers in your mouth for days. I think of the spiral, the signature, the endless cycle of threats that always end in someone's grave.

I set the lilies down with deliberate care, then stand, jaw clenched so tight my teeth might crack. I want to scream, but what's the point? Whoever left this knows I'd find it, and knows exactly what I'd do.

A sound—tires grinding against gravel—echoes off the far fence. I look up in time to see a pickup tear down the access road, dust blooming in its wake. Lucas's truck. He cuts the engine at the gate, jumps out, and starts toward me at a dead run, boots pounding the path.

He's in uniform, the dark blue of duty, not the soft cotton of home. His face is flushed, hair a mess, eyes locked on me like I'm the only thing in the world that matters. He slows just enough not to spook me, then stops at the edge of the plot, hands raised like a cop at a standoff.

"Sophie," he says, voice hoarse from the sprint, or maybe from shouting my name all the way up the drive.

I don't answer. I just wait.

He tries again, softer. "I didn't want you to find out like this."

"You mean find out you've been lying to me?" My voice doesn't break, not yet, but it feels like it might at any second.

He takes a shaky breath. "Bennett—he's got leverage, Soph. He always has. He threatened everything. If I didn't play ball, I'd lose it all."

"That's the story you're going with?"

He pulls back, hands dropping. "I never wanted to hurt you. You have to believe that."

I point at the scorched bouquet. "Was this your idea, or did you just deliver the package?"

He looks down, then back at me, raw panic in his eyes. "I came to warn you. I didn't know about the flowers, I swear—Bennett said he was sending a message, but—"

I cut him off. "But you did nothing to stop it."

He comes closer, desperate now, words tumbling. "You know what he's capable of. If he thinks you're getting too close, he'll finish what he started with your dad. Please. Just let me help. I can get you out."

I step back, the grass slick under my boots. "I'm not running. Not from you, not from him, not from any of it."

He reaches for my hand, and I let him. His palm is warm, rough, the same hand that mapped every inch of me last night. Now it just feels foreign.

"I need you to trust me," he whispers.

I pull my hand free. "You had a hundred chances to be honest. You chose him every time."

His jaw trembles, but he doesn't look away. "I'm choosing you now. That's why I'm here. And I chose you before, too! Why do you think I have been helping you? Why do you think I have been looking into the past? This thing isn't just Bennett! But I was too obvious, and he noticed me snooping."

I want to believe him. I really do.

But the stench of burnt lilies is still in the air, and all I can think about is every promise he broke, every secret he kept until it was too late to matter.

I gather my jacket tight around me, the cold finally getting through. "Go home, Lucas."

He stays rooted, misery etched in every line of his face.

"I trusted you," I say, and it comes out so quiet I'm not sure he hears.

But he does. He nods, slow, then turns and walks back to his truck, shoulders hunched, hands shoved deep in his pockets.

I wait until I can't see him anymore, then kneel again at the grave.

I arrange the lilies on the stone, careful not to smudge the name, and let my hands get dirty.

For a long time, I don't say anything. Just let the silence fill up the space, let the old anger and fresh betrayal settle like silt in a flooded basement.

"I don't know what to do," I say, finally. My voice cracks, but I don't care. "I thought I had it figured out. I thought if I just burned through all the lies, the truth would still be there. But it's just more smoke."

A breeze stirs the dead leaves, sends a plastic wreath skittering across the path. I look at the other headstones, the rows and rows of names, and wonder how many of them are secrets, how many of them are casualties of someone else's agenda.

"I don't know who to trust," I say, softer. "Maybe I never did."

I trace the letters of Dad's name with my fingertip. The granite is cold, and my hands are still trembling, but I force myself to hold steady.

"I miss you," I say, and for the first time in years, I mean it.

My phone buzzes again, but this time I don't answer. I just stay there, kneeling in the mud, until the sun climbs high enough to burn the mist off the grass.

When I finally stand, my knees are wet and my palms are raw from gripping the edge of the stone. I feel lighter, or maybe just empty.

I brush the dirt from my jeans, take a last look at the grave, and turn back toward the car.

I have a plan now.

If the world wants to burn, let it.

I'll be the last one standing in the ashes.

If it's a fight they want, it's a fight they'll get.

The world always feels thinner at midnight, like the walls of the house are just a suggestion, like the dark outside could seep in if you exhale too hard. I sit cross-legged in the center of my living room, Dad's journal balanced on my knees, the desk lamp casting shadows that skitter over the walls every time I flip a page.

I tell myself I'm looking for comfort, but I know better. I'm looking for something I missed—some cipher, some warning, some clue that says, "Here, this is how you survive." The pages are soft with age, corners dog-eared, the ink faded in places but always legible, always urgent. I run my finger along the margin, tracing the spirals, the underlined words, the frantic block capitals that grow more desperate with every entry.

A clock ticks somewhere in the kitchen, the only sound besides my own heartbeat. Outside, the rain starts, slow at first, then building to a steady rattle on the windows. I try to tune it out, but the sound finds every crack in my concentration and pries it open.

I turn another page. Near the middle, a passage I've read a hundred times but never understood. This time, I see it: "THE FINAL IGNITION," circled in red, three times, as if Dad was trying to burn the phrase into the paper. Below it, a string of numbers, dates, and an address I don't recognize. In the margin, a single word—"WARNING"—in blocky, terrified script.

My mouth goes dry. I read it again, slower, letting the meaning settle in like smoke. Dad knew something big was coming, something that would make every fire before it look like a birthday candle. He wasn't just afraid for himself. He was afraid for me.

I close the journal, press the cover so hard my knuckles go

white, then set it on the floor and curl my arms around my knees. I just breathe, in and out, counting each inhale like it might be my last.

There's a flicker of movement outside, a shadow thrown by the porch light. I kill the lamp and crawl to the window, careful not to let my silhouette show. The rain warps everything—streetlamps into comets, houses into melting wax—but I see the figure, standing in the middle of the road, head bowed against the downpour.

It's Lucas. His jacket is soaked through, hair plastered to his skull, hands shoved deep in his pockets. He's looking straight at my window, the light behind him turning his outline to glass. I don't know how long he's been there. Maybe since sunset, maybe since I told him to go.

He doesn't move. Doesn't call my name, doesn't pound on the door, just stands there like a lightning rod waiting for the next strike.

I should look away. I should turn off the world and disappear into the dark, but I can't. I press my palm to the window, the cold biting through the glass, and watch as his hand comes up, mirroring mine from a hundred feet away.

We stay like that, suspended in the downpour, two ghosts in a town that never forgives.

Eventually, I pull the curtain closed and sit back in the dark. The rain keeps falling, steady as a heartbeat. I rest my head against the window and let the cold numb my face.

I want to let him in. I want to believe in the promise of rescue, in the comfort of another body, another heartbeat. But I know better. I know that the world is waiting for me to crack, that every weakness is just another kindling for the fire.

So I stay where I am, safe behind the glass, reading Dad's last words over and over until the letters blur and run together.

When the final ignition comes, I'll be ready.

Even if it means standing alone in the ashes.

13

Fuel to the Flame

Lucas

The Willow Creek firehouse at shift change is an ecosystem—predators, scavengers, the big-dog alpha always somewhere in the haze of burnt coffee and brake cleaner. You could eat off the engine bays, but the common room is pure entropy: stained couches, a television dating back to the first Gulf War, a fridge with more science experiments than food. It's a second home for guys like me, so I notice when the ambient temperature drops two degrees as soon as Troy Bennett walks in.

I catch him in profile, framed by the door like a news photo. He wears the same clothes he always did—department blue, windbreaker zipped to the collar, even in July. There's no badge on the chest, but nobody doubts who's in charge. The detectives age differently; they go from fresh-faced to cinder in five years flat. Bennett's already fossilized. His hair's gone stone gray, but the eyes are pure obsidian, and they never blink unless it's to make a point.

He's not alone. Two rookies clear the hallway as soon as they see him. The shift supervisor, a guy who once ran a marathon with a hairline fracture, gives me a micro-nod and evacuates to the kitchen. That's all the warning I get before Bennett makes a beeline for the breakroom, department mug in hand.

He pours his own coffee, black, then stirs it with a tongue depressor swiped from the med bag. He takes a sip and waits for me to come to him. I oblige, planting myself at the Formica table. The lights overhead flicker, a chronic short in the ballast that nobody ever bothers to fix.

"Detective," I say, fighting the urge to salute.

He doesn't look up. "Hayes. Sit."

I'm already sitting, but I recognize the script. Bennett doesn't do small talk, and he doesn't do it twice. I lean in, hands splayed on the table so he can see them—habit from a dozen IA interrogations, or maybe just my way of showing I'm not armed. Bennett's face is unreadable. He could be about to hand out a commendation or put me on a watchlist. Maybe both.

He finally speaks, voice flat and steady. "You want to tell me what the hell you think you're doing?"

I want to match his tone, but adrenaline makes my hands shake, so I clench them into fists. "I want to know what Operation Phoenix is. I want to know why my chief is signing black-budget requests for equipment that never comes in the front door. I want to know how every arson case for the last twenty years has your name on it, and I want to know what happened to the men who tried to talk about it."

He nods, like he's making a mental note to add my name to that last list. The mug hovers half an inch from his lip, then lands on the table with a thunk.

"You ever think maybe you're out of your depth, Lucas?" he says, eyes never leaving mine.

I don't blink. "Depth's not the problem. It's the shit in the water."

He almost smiles, but the effort dies halfway up his cheek. "Phoenix was before your time. Ancient history. The town needed problems solved, and we solved them. Sometimes that means doing things you can't put on a whiteboard for the city council. You want to be a hero? Fine. But there's a reason you never see heroes with a pension."

I feel my jaw lock. "You set fires to save the town, is that it?"

He shrugs, a motion so casual it could be mistaken for laziness. "You're a firefighter. You know about backburns. Sometimes the only way to stop a bigger disaster is to burn out the fuel before it reaches the houses."

The silence stretches. The overhead lights flicker again, making his eyes flash, predator-bright. The smell of wet turnout gear lingers from the last run, mingling with the hot-metal tang of the coffee burner left on since dawn.

"You killed Sophie's father," I say, the words landing like bricks.

He doesn't react, doesn't even blink. "Grant was a good man. But good men get in the way. He started looking where he shouldn't, same as you. That's what got him killed."

There's a rustle from the hallway—a junior guy, probably waiting for a chance to microwave his dinner, but he's smart enough not to make a sound. The pressure in my temples is like a hydraulic press. I want to leap over the table, smash the mug into Bennett's perfect teeth, but I don't.

Instead, I slide the Operation Phoenix folder across the laminate, making sure my fingerprints are all over it. "You want to explain this, or should I go to the state fire marshal?"

He looks at the folder but doesn't touch it. "You won't. Because you know what happens next. I'm not your enemy, Hayes. I'm just the last guy between you and the people who really run things around here."

His voice drops a register, cold as dry ice. "Some things are better left burned."

It's not a threat. It's a fact.

He stands, draining the last of his coffee, then tosses the mug in the sink, glass on porcelain. The sound echoes. He brushes past me, shoulders squared, and I catch the faintest scent of smoke on his jacket—smoke that doesn't come from any fire I've fought.

When he's gone, I flex my fists until the blood comes back.

The table wobbles. My heart is still jackhammering, but my hands are steady now.

Out in the hallway, the rookies move fast, heads down, pretending not to see me.

I look at the folder, then at the mug in the sink, the dregs already gone cold.

Better left burned. I file it away, but I know I'm not going to let this go.

The next move is mine, and the whole goddamn station knows it.

Sophie

My late aunt's attic is a biome of its own, frozen in a permafrost of dust and bad insulation. The entrance is through a closet: you pop a panel, grope for the string, and pull yourself up by the same splintered rung that's tried to snap under your weight since you were eight. I climb the ladder slow, each step a creak and a complaint. The house breathes around me—timbers groaning, wind sneaking through the soffits, the occasional scuttle of a mouse or squirrel that never made it back out.

It's midafternoon but already the attic feels like twilight. The single window—a disc of glass streaked with moss and bird shit—lets in more haze than light. The rest is illuminated by dust, which swirls around every movement I make. Each time I open a box or shift a stack, a galaxy of gold floats up and then settles, like ash after a burn.

I'm here for a reason. I tell myself that a dozen times as I kneel on the plywood and start pulling banker's boxes from the wall. I'm hunting for evidence, not nostalgia, but every object is a hand on my sleeve, trying to drag me back to the life I left behind. Here's a stack of programs from county fairs, a plastic trophy with a broken baseball player on top, a shoebox of letters my mom never had the nerve to mail. In a Rubbermaid bin labeled "XMAS," I find the angel I made in kindergarten, its hair still crisp with Elmer's glue and glitter. I set it aside, try not to let it guilt me into tears.

The air up here is so dry it mummifies everything. Every photograph is yellowed at the edges, every envelope brittle enough to tear if you breathe too hard. But my fingers are good at this, better than I want to admit. I move quick, scanning for anything that looks official. I skip the boxes that still have price tags, ignore the bags of clothes, and focus on the battered banker's box marked "FAMILY–ARCHIVE." I drag it into the patch of light and pop the lid.

There's an immediate stink of old smoke, not the fresh-tar kind that sticks to your hair after a house fire, but the stale, sour note of cigarettes smoked in cars with the windows up. I almost gag, but it helps, keeps me focused. Inside is a mess of file folders, dog-eared and rubber-banded. A scrapbook with warped pages. A stack of yearbooks bound by a belt, like someone was afraid they'd run off in the night.

I work through the folders first. There are birth certificates, Army discharge papers, a marriage license dated 1973. Nothing useful. Next, I open the scrapbook. The glue is losing its grip; Polaroids fall into my lap as soon as I touch them. I sift, one by one, through pictures of people I barely remember: an uncle with a handlebar mustache, a cousin who died before I was born, my own parents at a Halloween party, Dad in a skeleton mask and Mom in a witch's hat, both grinning like idiots.

I almost miss it. The album has a fold-out plastic sleeve stuck to the back cover, one of those add-on pages you buy at the craft store. It's clouded with static, holding a single 8x10. The first thing I see is the red of the fire engine, polished to a mirror shine. Then the men—seven of them, all in dress blues, all standing in front of the old station house. Dad is on the far left, straight-backed, his face set in the semi-smile he used for cameras and public appearances. Two slots down is Troy Bennett, younger, almost handsome, but the eyes are exactly the same: black as stone, unblinking. Next to him is a guy whose name I should know but can't recall. The fourth man in the row—the one I really notice—has a face that still lives in the missing persons bulletin tacked to the wall at the QuikStop.

I pull the photo out, careful not to smudge it. The back is blank except for a year, 1997, and a set of initials, written in Dad's blocky hand. The air gets thin. I flip back to the front and stare. I scan the faces again, and a cold line of sweat crawls down my spine. Every guy in this picture, except for Bennett, is dead, retired under circumstances labeled "medical," or in the case of the missing man, "disappeared." They're all young in the photo, fit and full of optimism. Now every one is a ghost.

My fingers tingle. I put the photo down and go through the album again. This time I'm surgical, hunting for context. There's another group shot—picnic, this time, everyone out of uniform. Mom is there, laughing at something just off-camera.

There's Bennett, now with a wife I never met, his hand on her shoulder like she might float away if he let go.

In the margins, written in the same spiky script as before, are notations. Dates, initials, sometimes a single word in all caps: "PROMOTED," "RETIRED," "TRANSFERRED." Next to the missing man's name is just one word: "ERASED."

It's not enough, not really, but it feels like evidence. I thumb the photo between my fingers, the emulsion slick and cold. I know what I have to do. I slip it out of the sleeve, tucking it into a legal envelope I found in the bottom of the bin. My hands shake as I write the date and the names on the front, as if I'm signing an affidavit.

A shaft of light slices through the window, catching the dust and the edge of the envelope in a perfect golden line. For a second I see my own reflection, superimposed over the faces in the photo. I look nothing like them. Maybe I never will.

I gather my stuff, make sure the attic looks untouched, and close the panel behind me. The envelope is a weight in my pocket, solid and real. I know what I have to do, but it feels bigger than me. Maybe bigger than anyone.

On the way down the ladder, I nearly slip. My palms are slick, and my heart is hammering like I just ran a four-minute mile.

Let them try to erase me, I think.

I've got proof now. And I won't go quiet.

Willow Creek's only real coffee shop is the kind of place where the air buzzes with secrets and cheap single-origin beans. It's always cold inside, even in August, and the furniture is a thrift store's afterthought—none of the chairs match, the tables all wobble, the floor a disaster of cracked tile and peeling linoleum. I like it because nobody pays attention to you, unless you're new or worth watching. Today I am both.

Meredith Holloway is already there when I arrive, installed in the back corner, one hand curled around a mug, the other furiously scribbling in a battered reporter's notebook. She looks up when I walk in, her stare so direct it's almost a dare. I make my way past a herd of college kids trying to out-ironic each other with mustaches and bad hats, then slide into the seat opposite her.

She doesn't offer small talk, or a handshake, or even a smile. She just taps her pen and says, "What have you got?"

I slide the envelope across the scarred tabletop. The photo inside feels radioactive. Meredith opens it, fingers barely brushing the edges. She's careful, but not gentle. Her eyes flick to the back, scan the handwritten names, then back to the front. She makes a noise—a low whistle, more air than sound.

"Damn," she says, and that's it. She starts taking notes, her writing sharp and fast, like she's afraid the words will escape if she doesn't pin them down.

I keep my voice low, but in here, every word is a risk. "My

father is the leftmost. Second is Bennett—Troy, now Chief. The fourth guy? Disappeared. Never found a body. The rest? Dead, or forced out. Except for Bennett, who gets promoted every time someone else dies."

Meredith's pen never stops. "You think he killed them?"

"I think he arranged it. Or covered for whoever did. There's a pattern—every time a firefighter starts asking questions, something happens. Accidents, 'medical retirements,' staged suicides."

She tilts her head, fixes me with a look I've only seen in predatory animals and children about to do something illegal. "Why you, Grant? Why now?"

"Because I was next," I say. "They tried to scare me off. Failed."

She scribbles a few lines, then folds her hands over the notebook. "I'll need to corroborate this. You got anything else?"

I hand her a printout of the insurance records I pulled from the archives, fingers shaking despite myself. She looks at the spreadsheet, then at me. "You were always the smart one."

I almost laugh. "No. Just the most stubborn."

The barista drops off a refill at our table, giving me a long, sideways glance. The espresso machine hisses, loud enough to mask a conversation but not enough to muffle the tension. Meredith ignores the cup, leans in.

"I can write the story," she says, "but you know what happens next, right?"

"I do."

She nods. "They're going to come after you. Maybe me. You ready for that?"

I glance at the window, half-expecting to see Bennett pacing outside in a trench coat, or Lucas's truck idling at the curb. "I don't have a choice."

She accepts that, no pity, just professional curiosity. "How do you want to play it?"

I tap the envelope. "Tell it slant. Don't say arson, don't say murder. Just run the pattern. Ask the questions."

Her mouth curls into something that could almost be a smile. "You trust me?"

"No." I mean it. "But I trust your appetite for a story."

She barks a single laugh, then stands, shouldering her messenger bag. She tucks the envelope inside, careful not to crease it. "I'll call you before it goes to print," she says.

"Be careful, Mer."

She gives me a salute with the coffee mug, then disappears into the crowd, her stride quick and even.

I sit, watching the swirl of strangers and the jittery energy of a town on the edge. I keep checking the door, waiting for something bad to happen. It doesn't, not yet.

But I know it's coming.

When I finally leave, the barista watches me all the way to the door, like she knows I just started a fire nobody's ever going to put out.

THE CALL COMES IN AT 2:17 A.M. THE NUMBER'S NOT IN my contacts, but I know immediately—before I even swipe right, before the voice says anything—that it's bad.

On the first ring I'm wide awake, up from the couch with the blanket twisted around my knees, journal still open on my lap. The living room is a jigsaw of darkness, pieced together by streetlight and the soft glow of my laptop. The second ring is enough to send my pulse sideways.

"Grant," I answer, and there's so much static I almost miss the voice: "There's been a fire. Holloway's house. They're pulling her out now—"

The phone slips, crashes to the floor. I'm already out the door before I even think to put on shoes. I drive barefoot, barely remembering the turns, the headlights rattling on the frost-heaved road. The world is empty and hollow except for the blue pulse of cop cars and the distant, predatory glow above the trees.

I hit the brakes a block away. You can't get closer—the street's sealed off, hoses everywhere, the air so thick with smoke it's like breathing through a wet towel. Neighbors cluster on the sidewalks, faces lit up orange and blue, each person replaying the disaster in their own private theater. I'm not special. Just another rubbernecker until I see the fire.

Meredith's bungalow is old, cheap, the kind of place where the insulation is newspaper and the windows rattle in their frames all winter. Now it's a bonfire, roof already caved in, flames spearing up like they're hunting the moon. The heat is a wall. I get within thirty feet and have to stagger back, blinking away tears that aren't all from the smoke.

They've got the trucks on it already—three, maybe four engines, men in turnout gear moving with the slow, deliberate choreography of long experience. I scan for Lucas, but it's hard to tell one firefighter from another when they're suited up, faces streaked black, visors down. I watch for the way he moves, the broad-shouldered posture, the way he runs to the fight instead of away. I find him at the side of the house, bracing a ladder while another guy scrambles up. His arms and neck are striped with soot, the helmet's reflective tape a garish smudge in the firelight.

I want to scream, but my voice has locked up. I pace the perimeter, ducking under police tape, every sense turned up to twelve. Paramedics are prepping the sidewalk for casualties—stretchers lined up, oxygen tanks ready. I'm not the only one waiting.

A crunch of gravel behind me and the shift supervisor—

Dalton, still in sweatpants and a reflective vest—grabs my arm. "Sophie, you can't be here."

"I need to see her."

He glances at the house, then at me, and his eyes soften just a millimeter. "We're doing everything we can."

The wind shifts. A burst of flame takes out the front window, the sound like a gunshot. Embers snow onto the street, hissing when they hit the wet pavement. Inside the house, the beams groan, threatening to bring down what's left of the roof. I spot movement in the doorway—a body, hunched, helmeted, arms full. The person stumbles, rights themselves, and crosses the threshold.

Lucas. Even from here I know it's him. He's dragging someone, a dead weight in his arms, legs trailing. The paramedics run to meet them, and for a second the scene is pure chaos—voices yelling, hoses whipping, people crowding around the body on the grass.

I sprint. The ground is freezing, pebbles gouging my feet, but I don't feel it. I elbow through the cordon just in time to see Meredith's face, streaked with black, eyes open and wild. She's coughing, spasms so hard her whole body jerks off the stretcher. Someone's holding an oxygen mask to her face, but she's fighting it, trying to talk.

I kneel, my hands shaking. "Mer. It's me."

She coughs again, then clamps my wrist with a grip like a vise. "Not... accident," she rasps. "Smelled it. Before it started.

Like... gasoline." Her voice is so ragged I can barely piece it together, but the word "gasoline" comes out perfect.

One of the medics tries to push me back, but Meredith won't let go. "Did you see who?" I ask.

She nods, then winces, tears streaming sideways through the soot. "Tall. Heavy. Masked. Knew where to go."

Dalton pulls me away, gentler this time. "Let them work," he says, and I don't argue. I stand, legs rubbery, and watch as they load her into the ambulance. The doors close, the siren kicks in, and she's gone.

Lucas is standing by the truck, helmet off, hair glued to his head with sweat and grime. He looks like hell. He's talking to the incident commander, but his eyes are on me. Always. I push through the knots of people and don't stop until I'm right in front of him.

"You saved her," I say, and I mean it.

He nods, once, then leans in, his voice barely above the crackle of the still-burning house. "This was a warning. For both of us."

"I know."

He glances at the crowd, then back at me. "You need to go. Now. Before they decide you're next."

I want to argue, but I see the fear in his eyes. Not for himself. For me.

"I'm not running," I say, and my voice is steadier than I feel. "Neither are you."

He almost smiles. "What's the plan, then?"

I wipe my nose on my sleeve. "Same as always. We fight."

He puts a hand on my shoulder, fingers leaving a print of ash and sweat. "You're going to get us killed."

"Maybe," I say. "But at least we'll know why."

The fire is still burning when I walk away, my bare feet raw and bleeding. I don't look back. I don't need to.

I already know what happens to people who dig too deep.

But I'm not stopping.

By midnight, I've been up for forty hours straight. My nerves vibrate like a taut cable, and every time a car passes the house, I expect glass to shatter, the front door to splinter, the world to end in a burst of flame. I cycle through news alerts, texts, Meredith's status updates. She's alive—barely. Her skin is bandaged, her lungs full of smoke, but she's still typing, still angry, still alive. There's a kind of relief in that, though it makes the fear sharper.

I clean the cuts on my feet and wrap them in duct tape. I try to eat, but the soup tastes like cardboard and the salt from my own sweat. I keep looking at the clock. I keep expecting a knock at the door, or worse, the sound of my name coming through the scanner.

The knock, when it finally comes, is so gentle I almost miss it.

I open the door to find Lucas standing on the porch, helmet tucked under one arm, coat slung over his shoulder. He's still in uniform, but it's a ruin: black with ash, streaked with blood, the patches scorched to the point of illegibility. His eyes are bloodshot, his jaw cut and swollen, but his body radiates heat. He smells like fire, like everything I ever loved and everything I should have run from.

He doesn't say a word. Neither do I.

I step aside and he walks in, leaving a trail of black footprints on the hardwood. The house contracts around him, like it's remembering a time before ghosts and fear. He puts the helmet down on the entryway table, the clang of it echoing through the silence.

He looks at me, not pleading, not apologetic, just waiting for a verdict.

Instead of giving him one, I reach for his hand. The skin is rough, fingers split and trembling. I pull him down the hall, past the sleeping windows, into the tiny bathroom that still smells like the lavender soap my mother used to buy in bulk.

I run the water hot, as hot as I can stand it, and the pipes clatter a protest. Lucas stands there, shoulders caving, his face a battlefield of cuts and exhaustion. I undo the first button on his shirt, then the second, the third, each one a little harder with the tremor in my hands. He tries to say something, but I shut him up with a finger to his lips.

The shirt is a lost cause, but I peel it off anyway. The skin underneath is raw—soot embedded in every crease, bruises blooming on the ribs. I scrub him with a washcloth, first gentle, then harder, until the gray gives way to pink, to real, to alive. The water in the sink turns black, then gray, then finally clear.

When I finish, he wraps his arms around me, pulling me in so tight my bones creak. His breath rasps in my ear, hot and shallow. I press my face into his chest and let the heat burn away the last of my fear.

He lifts me—just like that, like I'm nothing, like I weigh less than all the fire and blood he's carried tonight—and sets me on the edge of the tub. He kneels in front of me, his forehead to my knee, both hands gripping my calf. I stroke the back of his neck, fingers tracing the line of the burn that snakes down from his hairline. The intimacy is terrifying.

He looks up, face wet with something I don't want to name. "You okay?" he whispers.

"Not even close," I whisper back.

He nods. We understand each other.

I stand, kicking off my ruined sweatpants, and step into the shower. I turn on the tap, water pounding my shoulders, steam filling the room until it's impossible to see the mirror, impossible to see the past. Lucas follows, crowding me into the corner, arms braced against the tile. The heat is unbearable, but I don't want to turn it down.

He kisses me. It's not gentle. It's the kind of kiss that erases the before and after, that says this is the last time, even if it isn't. His hands are everywhere—my shoulders, my waist, the curve of my hip, the place at the back of my skull that still aches from the panic attack three nights ago.

I bite his lower lip. He tastes like blood and ozone, like adrenaline and the aftermath of fear. I grab the hem of his undershirt and pull it over his head. It rips at the collar, exposing a line of pink flesh that I want to lick, to mark, to heal.

He pins me against the wall, mouths my neck, my collarbone, his teeth sharp enough to leave a record. His hands travel down, hooking under my ass, lifting me so my feet don't touch the ground. I wrap my legs around his hips and drag him closer. The edge of the tile digs into my shoulder blades, but I welcome it. I want to feel every scrape, every bruise, every proof that we're still alive.

He enters me all at once, no warning, and the stretch is perfect, painful, necessary. I lock my ankles at his back, dig my nails into his shoulders. He moves fast, desperate, like he's trying to fuck away every bad thing that ever happened to either of us. I meet him, thrust for thrust, breath for breath. The water pours over us, washes the soot and the salt away, makes us slick and slippery and new.

He slows, then stills, forehead to mine. "I'm sorry," he says, voice shredded.

I shake my head. "Not your fault."

"None of this is fair."

"I know." I kiss the scar on his jaw, the one that wasn't there last year. "But we're here."

He shudders, once, then comes—jaw clenched, eyes squeezed shut, hands shaking with the force of it. I hold him through it, then collapse against the wall, the world gone silent except for the hiss of the water and our mingled gasps.

When it's over, we slide down together, bodies tangled, the tile cold under our asses. I curl into his lap and let him stroke my hair. The water is still running, but it's running clear now.

We stay like that for a long time, not talking, not thinking, just breathing. The steam fogs the window, erases the world outside. There's nothing left but the heat and the heartbeat and the promise that, for at least this moment, we're safe.

I kiss his hand, the one with the burn scars, and he squeezes mine in return.

Tomorrow, we'll burn for real.

Tonight, we just survive.

By the time the sun rises, every surface in the kitchen is slick with condensation. I dry my hair with a ratty towel, then wring it out over the sink, drops hitting the steel like a countdown. Lucas sits at the table, shirtless, another towel knotted at his waist. The morning light makes his bruises look like war paint, and the hand that holds the mug is stained blue from old tattoo ink, red from new blood.

Neither of us has slept. I pull up a chair, legs sticking to the vinyl, and pour myself a cup. The coffee is burnt, the taste a kind of punishment, but it keeps my hands from shaking.

We don't talk at first. It's the best kind of silence—companionable, but charged, like the air before a storm. I let it linger until the caffeine gives me enough courage.

"We need to go back to the source," I say. "The old station. The files Bennett didn't think I'd find, the logs Dad kept—maybe there's more."

Lucas shakes his head, slow. "You know it's a trap, right? They want you to come. They want you to walk in and never walk out."

I meet his eyes, let the full weight of my resolve show. "If we stop now, they win. And my father died for nothing."

He reacts to that, but only a little. He reaches across the table, takes my hand in his. His palm is rough, the thumb tracing soft circles against the bruise on my wrist.

"Promise me something," he says, voice hoarse. "If it gets bad, if you have to run—you run. You don't stay for me."

I squeeze his hand until the bones grind. "I'm not leaving you behind. Not again."

He smiles, but it's a sad thing. "I know."

We map it out on legal pads, drawing timelines, piecing together every rumor and record, every name and date, every fire that started or stopped a career. We cross-reference everything—Lucas's station logs, the patterns in Dad's journal, the insurance records that keep surfacing like bodies after a flood.

The evidence builds, slow but steady. We find a common thread: every "accident" lines up with a payout, a promotion, or a sudden transfer. Bennett's signature is everywhere, ghosting in the margins, always just one step from the flames.

I pull out the old photo, the one from the attic, and set it in the center of the table. Seven men, all in blue, all smiling like they know something I don't. My father's eyes are sharper than I remember, the smile just a line. I stare at the image until it burns itself onto my retinas.

Lucas watches me, his gaze softening. "You really are your father's kid, you know that?"

I shrug, a half-laugh. "Someone has to be."

He stands, stretches, and winces at the pain. The towel slips, but he catches it. "You ready?"

"Always."

We dress in silence, Lucas finding an old hoodie in my closet, me in jeans and a t-shirt with the logo of a pizza place that closed ten years ago. We arm ourselves with phones, flashlights, legal pads. The photo goes in my pocket.

Before we leave, I linger at the window, watching the world come alive outside. A jogger passes, oblivious to the carnage that happened blocks away. The newsstand hasn't stocked today's paper yet. The day looks ordinary, but it isn't.

Lucas steps up behind me, his arms a shield around my shoulders. "Last chance to change your mind," he says.

I shake my head. "If we don't do it, nobody will."

He kisses the top of my head, then grabs the keys.

I take one last look at the photo, the faces frozen in time. I promise them, and myself, that I'll see this through.

Even if it means I end up with the rest of them—another ghost in the photo, another line in the logbook.

We head out together, into the blue hour, ready to finish what was started.

For Dad. For the truth.

For both of us.

14

Controlled Burn

Sophie

The kitchen table is buried under evidence, like we're building a pyre out of Dad's paranoia. There's no room for actual food; the closest thing is the crust of a sandwich I left untouched when I realized I could not, in good conscience, eat mayonnaise while reviewing fatality logs. Lucas is at the opposite end, arms folded, watching me connect the dots with highlighter and the practiced aggression of someone who is used to winning arguments by force of personality.

We have three maps spread out, each one overlaid with acetate and the web of lines I drew last night. Every intersection, every old structure fire, every death that didn't belong. There's a pattern, Dad always said, and if you can see it, you can predict the next move. The phrase is so burned into my cortex that it overlays everything I see, like a ghost transparency.

I trace a finger along the spiral, a slow, deliberate arc that tightens with each turn, the epicenter shifting block by block, year by year. At the core: a spot marked "o" with red ink. A date is written next to it—five days from now. The same day as the Willow Creek Founders Festival, a town tradition that is equal parts nostalgia and tactical nightmare.

Lucas clocks it before I can say a word. "No."

I look up, hand hovering over the date. "No what?"

He pushes back from the table, the legs of the chair grinding on linoleum. "No way in hell are you going to that festival."

"I'm not giving them the shot at a soft target." I don't raise my voice, but there's an edge. "If this is the next ignition point, I need to be there."

He stands, runs both hands over his face, then leans against the counter. "You realize this is what they want, right? You out in the open, easy to follow, easy to pick off—"

"You think hiding makes me less of a target?" I cut in. "You think the guy who's been one step ahead of us all year is going to say, 'Oh well, I guess she's not at the festival, I'll just stay home and watch the game'?"

The silence vibrates. The clock on the microwave counts up, minute by minute, the green digits taunting us with the speed of the countdown.

I shuffle through Dad's journal pages, most of them

scorched at the corners, the paper warped and brittle. On one sheet, a circled reference: "'99, Main Street, test run for something bigger." There's an address, and underneath it: "Repeat at scale? Watch for spiral completion." Dad wrote in pen, but he circled with a red marker—the kind that leaves a shadow of color on the page beneath. The ink bled right through.

I slide the sheet across the table. Lucas stares at it, jaw flexing. "They're treating this like a ritual," he mutters.

"Not just a ritual. A demonstration. They want everyone to see it." I jab a finger at the date. "This is the finish line."

He paces the perimeter of the kitchen, restless, animal. I can see him calculating—exit routes, crowd density, the number of off-duty cops that would be at a town festival versus the number of civilians. I let him run through it. It's how he copes.

When he circles back, he's calmer, but his hands are fists. "We go together. But we do it my way. You don't go anywhere without me. We set up redundancy—burner phones, a prearranged meet point, and I'll tap the guys I trust for extra eyes in the crowd. You do not improvise, Sophie."

I let the silence hang a second, just to make it clear who is actually in charge of my body. "Fine. But if you see a guy in a mascot suit with a suspicious limp, you tackle first, apologize later."

A corner of his mouth lifts. "That's the plan."

We get to work, our voices overlapping, every suggestion another layer of insulation between us and the fear. I pull up festival maps on my laptop, marking every entry and exit, every bottleneck. Lucas sketches the block perimeters, makes a list of who will be working security, and cross-references it against the list of fire department personnel who, according to the logs, have an uncanny knack for being present at the last three "accidents." We build a timeline—when the floats arrive, when the fireworks are prepped, when the crowd peaks.

Somewhere in the middle, Lucas brews a new pot of coffee. He pours mine first, and I catch his hand on the lip of the mug —a calloused, bandaged hand, with a faint tremor. He holds the cup steady, but the edge of the saucer clinks against the table.

"Don't do anything reckless," he says, not quite a whisper, not quite a command.

I don't answer right away. Instead, I fold the journal page, crease it until the red circle forms a perfect target. "If we can't stop the fire," I say, "maybe we can contain it."

He looks at me with something like respect, or maybe resignation. "You're not bait, Soph."

I lean forward, elbows on the table, hands wrapped around the mug for warmth. "I'm whatever gets us to the end of this."

His hand covers mine. Just for a second, but enough to make the message clear: it's not protection. It's partnership.

We work until the maps blur, until my eyes burn from staring at the screen and the air tastes like cold caffeine and old tension. By the time we finish, it's past three in the morning and the only light in the house is the glow of my laptop and the flicker of the streetlamp through the blinds.

Lucas checks the locks—twice—then comes back to the table, where I'm still copying the spiral pattern onto a fresh sheet of paper.

He watches me, silent, then says, "You're not your father, Sophie."

I put down the pen. "No. But I'm the only one who remembers him the right way."

We don't sleep, not really. Just stare at the ceiling in separate beds, listening for footsteps or the crackle of a match.

The plan is set. The fuse is burning.

All we have to do is wait.

Main Street hasn't looked this good in decades. Every storefront is draped in bunting, every utility pole a totem pole of "Welcome Founders!" signs and red-white-blue streamers. There's a cordon of volunteers in matching T-shirts shooing cars and rerouting foot traffic, but it's the kind of cheerful martial law you only get in small towns. The air tastes like powdered sugar, propane, and the burnt ozone of early summer. Somewhere, a bratwurst vendor is doing brisk business; every three minutes, a kid with blue-stained lips shrieks and runs past with a sparker, arcing gold fire like a warning to the gods.

I hate it, but I also kind of love it.

Lucas and I make a show of casualness. We hold hands, weaving through crowds, the perfect image of coupledom—never mind the way our eyes tick over every stranger, every service entrance, every alley that could double as a kill box. I wear sunglasses, not for sun but for cover, so I can watch in every direction without giving it away. Lucas is less subtle, but he's big enough to get away with staring.

The spiral pattern on my map matches Main Street exactly. The epicenter is the block between City Hall and the bandstand, which is ground zero for today's events. I flag every trash can, every portable generator, every vendor cart that could conceal a device. Lucas whispers under his breath, a running commentary: "Blue shirt, backpack, possibly armed." "Booth five, gas can under the table." "Guy at the corner keeps circling." I make a mental log of every anomaly, then cross-reference with the fire department's own assignments for the day. Three are off-duty, and one—Morgan—is supposed to be manning the dunk tank for charity. I don't see him anywhere.

We do a slow lap, blending in, but the tension is coiling. Lucas's grip is tight on my hand, not enough to hurt, but enough to communicate urgency. Every time I see a firefighter or cop, I try to read their posture: are they at ease, or are they scanning, too?

Two hours in, the sun is peaking. The floats for the parade are lining up at the edge of the park, high school kids and Cub Scouts sweating through their costumes. The crowd is thickest near the main stage, where the mayor will make a speech before the fireworks. I spot the suspicious man first—a fire department jacket, but old and faded, not standard issue. He moves like he's practiced at not being noticed, hugging the shade of the food trucks, a red plastic gas can swinging low in his left hand.

I don't even have to signal Lucas. He sees it, too. "That's not standard fuel for the generators," he says, sotto voce.

"He's headed east," I say, peeling off and matching the man's pace. I loosen my hand from Lucas's—he hesitates, then gives a nod and keeps a ten-yard shadow.

The man darts behind the kettle corn tent, then ducks down a side street toward the loading dock behind the bakery. I pick up speed, feeling the prick of sweat on my spine. There's no one else back here—just the dumpsters, the reek of fryer oil, and the click of my own shoes on the cracked pavement. I hold my breath, listening.

A shape moves behind the industrial trash bin. I step closer, trying not to look like I'm hunting, just a lost civilian. But the man clocks me, quick and sharp—he pivots, gas can swinging, and I see his face for half a second. Pale, pockmarked, an old burn scar twisting one side of his mouth into a permanent sneer.

He doesn't speak. Just sets the can down and walks past me, hands up in mock surrender. "Just a refill," he says, but his voice is wrong, tinny and dry.

I let him go, but I memorize the lines of his face, the scars, the way he favors his right side. I snap a photo with my phone, discreet, then check the gas can. The cap is off. The inside is coated with a pink residue—accelerant, mixed with something else. Lucas jogs up, breathing heavy.

"Lost him," I say, but Lucas is looking at the can, not me.

"Shit," he says. "That's magnesium. It'll go up even if you're standing in the middle of a fire blanket."

He wipes a palm over his face, smearing sweat and worry. "We need to tell them now."

But before we can move, the PA system squawks to life, feedback shrieking over the crowd. "Main stage, five minutes to presentation!" A wave of sound rolls down the block, the population of Willow Creek surging as everyone converges on the bandstand.

Lucas and I run, not even trying for subtlety now. We cut through the crowd, elbows and apologies, until we hit the main stage perimeter. I scan for the man with the can, but he's vanished.

"We need to split up and search," I say, rushing in the opposite direction to Lucas. For once, he doesn't argue.

Lucas

I SEE SOPHIE, STANDING NEAR THE STAGE, FACE BONE-white. She's motionless, eyes on the scaffolding under the platform. I shoulder through the bodies until I'm at her side. "What did you find?" I say, barely above a whisper.

She doesn't answer. Just grabs my wrist and pulls me under the stage, ducking behind the speaker stacks and duck tape. Inside, it's a maze of crossbeams and sandbags, the air thick with dust and old fireworks smoke.

She points. "There."

Wired to the main supports are two canisters, wrapped in black tape, with wires snaking back to the generator. It's not amateur hour—this is a professional job, the kind of setup you see in news stories that end with a crater.

"They're planning something big," Sophie breathes, close to my ear. I can smell her fear—no cologne, just sweat and the faint tang of metal.

I call it in, my voice steady only because I've trained myself to fake it. I give the exact location, the device description, the potential for casualties. I hear the dispatcher's voice go tight, then the static as the line goes dead.

We crawl out the back, away from the stage, as the first police cruiser pulls up, lights spinning in silent urgency. Uniformed men appear, moving fast but pretending not to panic the crowd. The fire chief—Bennett, of course—arrives in plainclothes, scanning the scene like a wolf checking its flock.

Sophie and I stand in the shadow of the bandstand, watching as the bomb squad goes to work, as the crowd continues to grow, oblivious. Somewhere above us, the mayor starts his speech, voice echoing through the speakers with forced optimism.

I look at Sophie, who's shaking now, but not with fear—with rage.

"We're not done," she says, jaw set. "This was a decoy. The real ignition is still coming."

She's right. I can feel it in the way the air vibrates, in the look on Bennett's face, in the fact that the man with the scar is nowhere to be seen.

But for now, the platform is safe. The bomb is disarmed. The festival continues, the world spinning as if nothing is wrong.

I reach for her hand, and she takes it, tight, anchoring.

We wait for the real fire.

Sophie

We make it home in silence, the kind that isn't awkward or angry but just packed to the brim with everything that didn't explode today. I shed my jacket as soon as the door closes, dropping it on the tile where it lands with a wet slap. Lucas double-checks the deadbolt, then does a slow circuit of the house—lights on, lights off, shades drawn, the whole security drill we invented after the third threat in as many days.

I head straight to the kitchen, but there's no hunger. My

hands buzz, nerves still tripping from the close call. I pace—three steps, pivot, three steps back. I tell myself I'm running the sequence in my head, making sure I didn't miss anything in the crowd, but really, I'm just burning off the static.

Lucas finds me standing by the fridge, eyes locked on nothing. He opens his mouth like he's about to speak, but I cut him off with a shake of my head. I need to move, not talk.

I sweep through the living room, grabbing the notebook from this morning, flipping it to the page with the festival diagram. The circle of potential targets is still there, but now I've drawn a thick black X through the bandstand. Next to it, I jot: "Attempted decoy, 19:32. Disarmed." The rest of the page is blank. We're running out of time.

Lucas settles on the couch, elbows on knees, watching me pace. "They'll try again," he says, voice soft. "But we'll be ready."

I want to believe him, but belief is a luxury we ran out of three fires ago.

I shut the notebook with a snap, stand in front of him, and look at his face for the first time since we left the chaos. He's exhausted. Hair damp, jaw shadowed, eyes sunk deep into their sockets. There's a smear of dirt or soot on his cheek, and the blue of his t-shirt is dark with sweat at the collar.

It hits me: he nearly died today. We both did.

The knowledge lands like a punch, winding me. I take two steps and kneel between his knees, my hands on his thighs, my fingers digging in. I mean to say something, but the words won't come out. Instead, I press my forehead to his knee and let the tremor run through me until I'm steady.

His hand comes to the back of my neck, thumb tracing the ridge of my spine. "I'm okay," he says, barely above a whisper.

I shake my head. "You're not," I say. "None of us are."

He laughs, a raw sound. "You want to fix it?"

I look up. "Yeah," I say. "I do."

He opens his mouth, maybe to make another joke, but I stop him with a kiss, hard and sudden, teeth clacking against his. His hand tightens at my neck, not gentle, not quite rough. I push up onto the couch, straddling his lap, the notebook wedged between us and then falling to the floor with a dull thud.

He grabs my ass, pulls me in, the contact sparking like static. I grind against him, needing friction, needing proof that we're both still alive. My hands find the hem of his shirt, yanking it up, baring his ribs and the bruises that are just starting to blossom purple under his skin. I run my tongue along the edge of the bruise, then bite down, just hard enough to leave a mark.

He hisses, a sound that's half-pain, half-yes-please. His hands are everywhere, kneading my hips, tracing the waistband of my jeans, slipping under my shirt to palm my breasts. He thumbs my nipple through the bra, rolling it until it's hard and sensitive, and I arch into him, fingers twining in his hair.

He tries to shift, tries to flip us, but I push him back, pinning his shoulders to the cushion. "No," I say. "Not tonight."

He blinks, caught off guard, then nods, surrendering. I unbutton his jeans, pulling them down just enough to free his cock, already hard and heavy in my hand. I stroke him, slow at first, watching his face as I do. He grits his teeth, eyes locked on mine, like if he looks away he'll lose his place in the world.

I slide my own jeans off, then straddle him again, my panties damp and sticking to my skin. He runs his hands up my thighs, thumbs brushing the crease where leg meets hip. I reach between us, line him up, then sink down, slow and steady, feeling every inch. The stretch is perfect, the way he fills me grounding in a way that nothing else is.

I ride him, slow at first, building a rhythm, the muscles in my legs burning with the effort. He grips my hips, guiding me, but I set the pace, refusing to cede control. I rake my nails down his chest, leave red trails he'll feel tomorrow. I want to own him.

"Let me be the dangerous one tonight," I whisper into his ear.

He laughs, but it's a broken sound, all need. "Yes, ma'am."

I increase the pace, grinding down, clenching around him. The friction builds, every thrust a reminder that we're not dead yet, that there are still things worth fighting for. His hands move up, pulling my shirt over my head, then reaching behind to unhook my bra. He buries his face in my chest, biting and sucking at the flesh, marking me as his.

I throw my head back, hair falling like a curtain around us. I want to scream, but all that comes out is a gasp, sharp and high. The sensation crests, and I shudder, pulsing around him, my orgasm tearing through me so hard I see black spots. He follows, thrusting up into me, losing rhythm as he empties himself, hands bruising at my waist.

We collapse together, sweat-soaked and breathing hard, the world reduced to the couch and the space between our bodies. I curl into his chest, his arms winding around me like the last sandbag in a flood. We stay like that for a long time, just breathing, letting the adrenaline drain out and the quiet soak in.

Eventually, he kisses the top of my head. "You saved a lot of lives today," he says.

I shake my head, lips pressed to his collarbone. "We did," I say. "But it's not over."

"Nothing ever is," he says. "But I wouldn't want to fight it with anyone else."

I pull the throw blanket from the back of the couch, drape it over both of us. The house is quiet, the world outside holding its breath.

For now, we're safe. For now, we're together.

Tomorrow, the fire starts again.

But tonight, I let myself believe we might win.

15

Flashover

Lucas

At ten fifty-seven, the second day of the festival is holding at DEFCON Two. My shift log says I'm supposed to be patrolling the west barricade, but I'm halfway through a funnel cake and updating Sophie on the number of unaccompanied minors when the world goes sideways.

It starts with a pop—sharp, electronic, a sound that doesn't belong in the symphony of carnival and country covers from the main stage. I'm three steps from the safety tent, clipboard in hand, when the PA cuts out and the first firework of the afternoon detonates right over the crowd. Not a scheduled launch. Not any kind of legal pyrotechnic. This one is pure white phosphor, a bloom of magnesium so bright it ghosts the shadows on the street.

"Move!" I shout, voice already shot from hours of crowd control. I lob the clipboard at the nearest folding chair and muscle past a cluster of senior citizens clustered around a lemonade stand. "Everyone east! Away from the park!"

Most people obey. Most people always do, even when they don't know why. But the edges of the crowd are already bunching up, people spinning in place, phones out, everyone looking for the threat but nobody willing to name it.

I spot Sophie before I see her. She's moving fast, half a head shorter than the panicked civilians, but her elbows are up and she's using them like an expert. There's a woman on her arm—mid-seventies, oxygen tank bouncing in a tartan-plaid stroller—and Sophie's jaw is set in a way I haven't seen since the last time someone tried to break into her apartment.

We lock eyes across the crowd. She mouths, "Stage left," and I nod. She's already clocked the hot zone. We triangulate without another word, me pushing toward the stage, her moving to intercept from the other side.

The smoke is chemical, dense and sticky, rolling off the edge of the stage like dry ice on steroids. I taste the acrid melt of plastic before I see the fire—someone's hit the food truck row, turned the soft-serve trailer into an instant inferno. Flames crawl up the awning, licking at the edge of the adjacent popcorn cart, and the heat punches me in the face like a wall.

People are screaming now. I shove through, planting a hand on the shoulder of a man in an inflatable T-rex costume and spinning him out of the way before he can trample a cluster of kids in matching Little League jerseys. The banner for the corndog contest goes down, taking three chairs with it and nearly clotheslining a city councilwoman. I leap over it, not even slowing.

The safety alarm kicks in, a banshee wail that warps and distorts under the pressure of the crowd's panic. I ignore it, counting the seconds as I break for the stage access ramp. Every fire drill says you clear the perimeter, establish a safe zone, and let the professionals handle it. But the spiral on Sophie's map, the pattern in my head, says otherwise. I know this playbook. It's not about casualties—it's about the message. The panic is the point.

At the edge of the crowd, I spot another fire—smaller, intentional, set in a plastic barrel near the generator that powers the east block of food vendors. That's not a coincidence. I key my radio and shout for backup, but the channel is nothing but static and overlapping shrieks from a dozen other units.

Someone grabs my arm. It's Morgan—off-duty, supposed to be manning the dunk tank, but he's in full gear and sweating through his t-shirt. "It's staged," he yells. "The hydrant's been tampered with. Pressure's garbage."

"Contain the perimeter," I tell him. "I'll handle the ignition point."

He blinks, then nods, vanishing back into the crowd with a speed I'd envy if I weren't so fucking busy.

I make the stage in four bounds, plant a boot on the guard rail, and haul myself up. The curtains are already curling in the heat, and a second fire is running like a rumor along the stage-left rigging. I rip the fire extinguisher from its bracket, thumb the pin, and sweep the base of the flames. The white powder chokes the air, but it blunts the worst of the heat.

That's when I see the shape moving backstage—a tall figure, firefighter jacket but no helmet, moving with purpose. Not a responder. Not any of the guys I know. He's got something in his left hand, and the right is flicking a lighter like a nervous tic. I charge.

He spots me and bolts, heading for the generator, but I'm faster. I catch him by the collar, drag him down, and drive a knee into his ribs. The impact jangles up my leg, but he doesn't scream, doesn't even curse. Just twists, elbows me in the jaw, and slips free. He leaves the canister behind, but I'm too slow to catch him before he vanishes into the crowd, ducking low and weaving like he's done it a hundred times.

The canister is jury-rigged, black tape over the label, but I know the smell—pure accelerant, probably homebrewed. I upend it, empty the contents onto the burning edge of the stage, and hit it with the extinguisher again. It sputters, goes out. For now.

The PA crackles, and the mayor's voice—smarmy, unsteady—blasts out over the panicked square. "Please, everyone, stay calm! Emergency services are en route—"

A second explosion pops, this time at the far end of the park, and the crowd surges like a single organism. For a second, I can't see Sophie, can't see anything but the blur of people and the stutter of blue strobes as the first cop cars arrive.

I leap down from the stage, adrenaline making my vision

narrow and spark. I spot her—still guiding the old woman, but now moving double-time toward the med tent. Her face is a mask, cold and determined, and for a second I wonder if she even needs me at all.

I bull through the crowd, arms wide, shouting orders nobody's listening to. I grab a kid who's about to trip on a dropped cooler and set him upright. I drag a dazed teenager away from the path of a slow-moving ambulance. I don't stop moving. There's no margin for error, not today.

At the med tent, Sophie's already got the old woman seated, checking her pulse, barking instructions at a volunteer EMT who is clearly in over his head. I catch her eye, nod toward the stage. "It was a plant," I say, breath ragged. "Not just the trucks. Somebody hit the main generator, too."

She points at the old woman. "She saw him. Says he was wearing turnout pants, but the patch was wrong."

"Arsonist wants us to see him," I growl. "We're on the guest list."

She grabs my arm, nails digging in. "He doubled back. I saw him cut through the vendor alley. He's heading for the west end."

I curse, break away, and take off in a sprint. The far side of the park is chaos—families huddled behind the beer tent, cops trying to form a human chain, two more fires smoldering in trash bins along the service road. I scan for the jacket, the height, the particular slouch I'd recognize from a lifetime of watching people who don't want to be seen.

There. By the chain-link fence, trying to blend in with the city maintenance crew. He's got a duffel bag now, slung over one shoulder. His eyes lock with mine, and for a split second I see the intent—cold, empty, focused.

I vault the last picnic table, nearly wiping out on spilled soda, and close the distance. He ditches the bag, turns to run, but I cut him off, tackling him into the fence. The metal rattles, and we both hit the dirt. He's strong, but desperate, and I've got the advantage. I drive an elbow into his gut, pin his arms, and wrench the lighter from his hand.

"Game's over," I snarl, breathing fire into his face.

He spits blood, then grins, teeth pink. "You don't get it," he hisses. "It's already started. I'm one of many. And there is more to see today."

I cuff his hands with a zip tie from my belt, then drag him upright. The duffel is heavy—more canisters, a tangle of wires, a roll of blueprints for the park layout. I shoulder it, half-carry him back to the main plaza, and dump him at the feet of the first cop I see.

"Book him for attempted murder," I say. "And get the bomb squad for that bag."

The cop stares, but then nods, calling it in on his radio.

The adrenaline drops out all at once, leaving me hollow and shaking. I lean against the curb, sweat cold on my back, and watch as the festival staff tries to reassert order. There's a kind of beauty in it—people helping strangers, water bottles passed hand to hand, a woman in a Minnie Mouse costume giving CPR to a heat-stroked teenager.

I scan the crowd for Sophie, and this time I find her. She's standing by the med tent, arms crossed, face streaked with sweat and grime. Her hair is wild, her shirt ripped at the shoulder, but her eyes are bright and alive. She raises a hand, and I raise mine back, a silent salute.

Somewhere, the PA is still blaring. Sirens wail in the distance. But for a second, it's just us, two survivors in the ruins of the world's worst party.

I close my eyes, count to ten, and let the pain wash through me.

"There's more to see today." The man's words echo in my mind. There's another bomb, one designed to hit responders; it has to be near the stage.

Under the stage, it's a different planet. The light is syrup-thick and orange, strobing with every flareup above. All the sound from the festival—music, screaming, the hydraulic shriek of a distant siren—melts to a dull, underwater throb. I have to crouch to move, knees and elbows grinding through a soup of old flyers, cigarette butts, and the shredded confetti from last year's parade.

The crawlspace is hotter than the surface; every cubic foot of air jammed with off-gassing plastic and insulation fibers. Sweat soaks my back in seconds, but I ignore the itch, focus on the target: the place where the shadow ducked and didn't come out. I kill my flashlight, counting on the firelight overhead to paint the way.

It takes me less than a minute to find the device. Not because it's expertly hidden, but because it isn't—just stashed behind a plywood brace, wires trailing obvious and ugly, like a rattlesnake daring you to reach. The canister is the size of a milk jug, black tape sealing the edges, and the digital timer blinks bright red in the dark. Ninety-three seconds.

My hands go cold even as the rest of me boils.

I drop to my belly, crabbing closer until my nose is inches from the package. No anti-tamper. No shrapnel layer. Whoever built this wanted fire, not a blast. I see the logic of it in two seconds—burn the stage from underneath, panic the crowd, then trigger the accelerant above for a perfect flashover.

I mutter a curse, then dig the multitool from my belt and pop the canister open. The timer is a cheap kitchen model, wires hot-glued to the back, but the leads are color-coded wrong—deliberately, maybe, or just the work of an enthusiastic amateur. I count the wires: black, blue, and a twisted mess of orange. I know what Sophie's Dad would do—he always said to trust the battery line, never the logic circuit. But I'm not him, and I'm not in the mood to guess.

Eighty seconds.

I run through the last bomb drill I ever took, the way the instructor's hands shook when he said, "The only safe explosive is one you've already disarmed." I lick the sweat from my upper lip and grip the blue wire, the one tied to the battery mount. I follow its path—no secondary, no trick switch—then brace my wrist against the frame and close the jaws of the multitool around it.

Seventy-five. Seventy-four.

I can't breathe, lungs jammed with scorched air, but my hands are stone steady.

I snip the wire, half-expecting the world to go white. Instead, the timer jumps to zero, blinks once, then dies. No drama, no fireworks. Just a sudden, profound quiet, like someone has cut the audio track from the universe.

I sag back, knees giving out, and let my head drop to the filthy carpet. It smells like old beer and gunpowder, but to me it's the best thing I've ever tasted.

A sound above—the stomp of boots, voices shouting. Someone yells, "Clear!" and then the sound of water hitting the stage in a sheet. I haul myself upright and crawl to the edge of the crawlspace, sucking in sweet, smoky air.

From here I can see the field behind the stage, a chaos of cops, city workers, and festival refugees. The fire is mostly out, just white steam and the stink of wet ash. I spot Sophie instantly—she's ditched her jacket, hair wild, cell phone held high as she clicks through photos at speed.

She's not looking at me. She's looking at a man on the far side of the lawn, leaning against a battered service truck. He's bareheaded, face streaked with sweat and soot, one sleeve of his department jacket shoved up. On his forearm is a tattoo—a line of flames, blue and black, with the number "19" inked just above the wrist.

It's the station's badge number. It's our badge number.

My throat closes. I know that arm.

He's older now, but the face is the same—square jaw, a break in the nose, the cocky slouch of a man who thinks he's the only wolf in the yard. I trained him. He was my first ride-along, my shadow, the kid who washed the engines after every run and left a six-pack in the locker room on the last day of probation. I remember his name, but my mind won't say it. My mind can only repeat, "Bennett's."

He's one of Bennett's.

Sophie is taking photos, fast and methodical, her eyes never leaving the man's. He sees her, too. For a heartbeat, their stares lock, and I see a flicker of recognition. He raises his hand—just for a second, just a twitch—but it's enough.

Then he's gone, lost in the mass of first responders.

I crawl out from under the stage, legs heavy, brain buzzing like a hornet's nest. The bomb is still in my hands, wires limp, timer dead, but the shakes are starting. I don't want to let go, but I also want to smash it to pieces and light the whole thing on fire.

Instead, I walk it to the nearest cop, set it at his feet, and mutter, "For evidence." He opens his mouth, but I'm already gone.

Back at the med tent, Sophie is waiting. She hands off her phone to a paramedic, points at the photo of the tattoo, and says, "Run that face." She turns to me, checks my arms, my face, then hugs me so hard I think I might black out. She smells like burnt sugar and adrenaline.

"You got it?" she asks.

"Yeah," I say. "But it's worse than I thought."

She nods, lets go, and for a second we just stand there, two kids lost in the aftermath.

Over her shoulder, I see the man with the tattoo, slipping between two parked fire trucks, blending into the mass of helmets and jackets. He's already looking for his next ignition point.

I squeeze her hand.

"We're not going to stop him, are we," she says.

"Not today," I answer.

But we both know that next time, it'll be personal.

Ash clings to every crease of my skin, packed deep in the webbing between my fingers, ground into the seams of my boots. The food truck fire is a skeleton now, frame warped, nothing left but scorched chrome and a puddle of melted plastic in the gutter. Emergency crews swarm the perimeter, heads bent over tablets, radios spitting out codes I can't process through the fatigue.

My statement to the fire marshal is half memory, half autopilot. I list the sequence: pop, smoke, panic, the suspect in the fire jacket. She scribbles in a tiny notebook, asks me to repeat my badge number, then tells me to stay available for further questions. I nod, but the world is already telescoping to a pinpoint, a single fixed target: the silhouette waiting at the edge of the caution tape.

Sophie's hair is tied up with a red festival bandana, but strands have escaped and hang like live wires, buzzing with leftover adrenaline. Her face is streaked with sweat and soot, and she blinks like she's been staring at the sun for an hour straight. She's clutching her phone with both hands, thumb hovering over the screen, as if letting go will set off a bomb.

She meets my eyes, then closes the distance. Her hand shakes as she shoves the phone at me. "Look."

There are three photos. All of the same man: close-up of the tattoo, then a wider shot, then the man's face, half-turned as he slips through the fire crew. In every frame, the badge number is visible. The last image is blurry, but I can still see the curve of the jaw, the twist of the old scar on his cheek.

I feel my gut pitch sideways.

"It's him," I say.

She nods. "He knew I was watching."

I want to say something reassuring, something strong and clean, but my tongue is glued to the roof of my mouth. All the old training, all the years of drills and lectures about compartmentalizing trauma—they don't mean shit when the threat is someone you once mentored, someone who knows exactly how you think.

Sophie's shoulders are tight, her whole body vibrating with unspent energy. I put a hand on the small of her back, steer her toward my truck parked behind the station house. She doesn't protest, just moves with me, eyes locked on the middle distance like she's still cataloguing every face in the crowd.

Inside the cab, the world goes quiet. I slam the door, kill the engine, and the only sound left is our breathing, ragged and out of sync.

She starts to speak, but I cut her off, pulling her onto my lap, arms wrapped tight around her waist. Her bones are bird-thin under the festival t-shirt, but the strength in her back is all steel cable and wire.

"You scared the hell out of me," I say into the hollow of her neck.

She shivers, but doesn't pull away. "Not as much as you scared me. I saw you go under the stage—I thought—"

"I'm not that easy to torch," I tell her, but my voice is raw, scraped down to the nerve.

She turns in my lap, straddling me, and presses her forehead to mine. There's a gash above her eyebrow, nothing serious, but it's still bleeding slow, a line of red into her hairline. She wipes it away with the heel of her hand, then kisses me hard, like she's trying to push the air back into my lungs.

It's not a gentle kiss. It's all teeth and salt and the desperate knowledge that if either of us had fucked up today, we'd be vapor. She bites my lower lip, not enough to hurt but enough to make me gasp, and then her hands are everywhere—my chest, my ribs, the band of skin just above my belt. Her nails dig in, marking me, and I let her.

I pull her shirt off, careful of the scrape on her shoulder. She does the same to mine, then plants both palms on my chest and grinds down, slow at first, then faster. I want to tell her to take it easy, that there's time, but the lie won't come. We both know there isn't. Not really.

She unzips her jeans, shimmies them down over her hips, then drapes them on the dash like a flag of surrender. Her panties are bright blue, dotted with tiny cartoon flames. She sees me staring, laughs—one short, ragged exhale—and says, "On brand."

She yanks my jeans open, tugs me out, and strokes me until I'm hard and aching, then lowers herself onto me in one smooth, practiced motion. She's soaked, every inch of her slick and hot, and when she starts to move, I lose track of the world for a while.

It's not romantic. There's no time for that, no luxury of

candlelight or clean sheets. It's just skin and sweat and the thud of her heart against mine. Her hands claw at my shoulders, her breath hitches with every thrust, and when she comes, it's a silent thing, a tremor that ripples through her body and leaves her trembling in my arms.

I follow her over, biting her shoulder to muffle the sound. We collapse together, chests heaving, skin slick with sweat and ash.

For a long time, we just sit like that, holding each other in the fading light. The world outside is chaos—sirens, voices, the distant roar of another engine rolling up to the scene. But in here, there's only us.

She kisses my jaw, softer now, and says, "He's coming back, isn't he."

I nod. "Yeah. And he knows we're onto him."

She doesn't look scared. Just resolute. "Let him try."

We clean up as best we can, wiping the ash from our arms, pulling on new clothes from the duffel I keep behind the seat. We watch the last of the emergency crews roll out, then drive home in silence, fingers tangled across the console.

At the house, Sophie checks every lock, every window, then sets her phone on the table and collapses onto the couch. I sit beside her, close but not touching, and we stare at the ceiling for a while.

Finally, she says, "Why do you think he did it?"

I shake my head. "Does it matter? It's not over."

She nods. "Then neither are we."

We fall asleep side by side, still dressed, still alert. I dream of burning buildings and the taste of her mouth, and when I wake up, she's still there, warm and alive.

Tomorrow, we hunt.

Tonight, we heal.

16

Flashover

Lucas

THE MORNING AFTER, I WAKE UP WITH THE TASTE OF HER still on my tongue and my head full of smoke. The sun's not even up yet, but the birds are already at it, drilling holes in the air like they're paid by the decibel. Sophie's hair fans over my bicep, sweat sticking the strands to my skin, and she's managed to take all the covers but none of the pillows. Her leg is looped over my thigh, her breathing the slow, even draw of someone who's learned to steal sleep when she can.

I don't move, not for a while. I just let myself drift in the weird, weightless space between sleep and memory, taking inventory of every inch of skin where she left a bruise, a bite, a line of red that'll turn purple by noon. I can still smell fire on her, under the soap and the ghost of perfume, and it makes me want to curl around her until we both ignite.

My phone chirps, too loud, the screen flaring in the gloom. It's a push alert from the county dispatch, something about a traffic snarl on Route 40. I almost laugh, it's not like anyone in this town is in a hurry to get anywhere.

Sophie mumbles, shifts, and cracks one eye. "Is it the end of the world?"

"Just a fender bender. You can go back to sleep." I brush her hair from her face. There's a healing scab just above her eyebrow, souvenir from the festival, and for a split second, I want to take her in and never let her out again.

But her eyes are awake now, bright and surgical. "You ever just...wish you could freeze this? Before the next disaster?"

"Where would be the fun in that?" I smile and give her a wink.

She lifts her head and stretches until her spine pops. "Good, because I think I figured out who he is."

The air gets tight. "The guy with the badge tattoo?"

She nods, her voice still husky with sleep. "I ran the photo through three facial rec programs. Most gave me garbage, but one, one flagged a match. Caleb Rowe. You know him?"

I suck in a breath. Of course I do. Not personally, but by reputation. "Rowe was a ghost. Did odd jobs at the station, night shifts, off the books. Never made probation. Never made probation. Bennett always said he was just a temp, but I knew he was covering."

"Covering what?" She's propped on her elbow now, every muscle in her body laser-aimed at me.

"He had a record. Juvenile. Sealed, but the rumors were..." I shake my head, remembering the bar gossip, the way the old-timers spat the name like it was cursed. "He never should've had access to the station, let alone gear."

Sophie grabs her phone and brings up the picture. She zooms in on the arm, the flame tattoo warped by muscle and time. "I watched him at the festival. I know he set the charges, then double back. He wanted us to see him. He wanted to be remembered."

I stare at the photo, my stomach twisting. "We need to bring this to Bennett."

She laughs, flat and humorless. "Yeah, let's walk it right to the guy who's been cleaning up Rowe's messes since day one. He'll throw it in the incinerator and say we made it up."

I hate that she's right.

She senses it, reaches out, and rests her palm on my chest, right over the scar I got in the summer of the Grant fire. "We need more. A link. Something he can't destroy."

I watch her face as she works the problem in real time. "Maybe a paper trail. Or a file he forgot to scrub."

She shakes her head. "We checked every digital record. The only thing left is—" She trails off, her eyes distant, then lights up like she's seen a match struck in the dark. "The cabin."

I blink. "The one on Clark?"

She's already sitting up, sheets tangled around her hips. "Dad did a bunch of odd repairs there when he was suspended. He said he was always fixing something, but the cabin was fine. He was hiding evidence, Lucas. I bet my life on it."

She's in motion, out of bed, halfway to the closet before I've even found my boxers. "You want to do this now?"

She turns, already shimmying into yesterday's jeans. "Unless you want to give them another head start."

I should say no. I should say let's eat first, let's plan, let's think about this. But the look on her face—the raw, wild hope, the determination—I can't kill that. Not after everything. And I know her too well, that look, I couldn't stop her if I tried.

"Give me five minutes," I say.

We're out the door in twelve.

The drive to Clark Street is short, but the weight in the car makes it feel longer. Sophie's hands are tight on the wheel, eyes fixed on the ribbon of asphalt ahead, even though she's making every stop sign by muscle memory alone. I watch her profile, the cut of her jaw, the way her lips go white at the corners when she's holding something in.

"Talk to me," I say, keeping my voice gentle.

She doesn't look over. "If I'm wrong, and we drive a crowbar through the cabin's drywall for nothing..."

"If you're wrong, we spackle. And I'll blame it on the pipes."

A smile flickers, gone before it lands. "You're a shit liar, you know that?"

"I know."

We park right in front of the cabin, it's more like a little house, but got called the cabin years ago, and the name stuck. The fake shutters and dead rhododendrons out front show it's been ignored. Nobody's stayed here in ages, but the key's still hidden under the ceramic frog by the porch. Inside, the place smells like dust and lavender sachets.

Sophie moves straight to the kitchen, where the cabinets still look new and every drawer slides smoothly. "Dad fixed these three times," she mutters, scanning for the tell. "He told Aunt Lillian he kept getting measurements wrong, but..."

She pulls out the bottom drawer, then kneels and knocks on the baseboard. The sound is wrong—hollow. I drop to my haunches beside her and run a finger along the edge. There's a screw missing, replaced with a dab of caulk. I dig at it with my nail, and the board pops free.

Behind it, wrapped in freezer bags, is a clump of something that might once have been a USB stick. It's sticky with what I hope is just old glue, but the logo is still visible: a blue flame, same as the department patch.

We stare at it, in mutual awe and terror.

Sophie takes it, holding the evidence like it might bite. "He wanted us to find this."

She stands, brushes dust off her knees, and puts the stick in her pocket. "We need to see what's on it. Now."

I follow her outside. The sky is heavy with cloud, threatening rain.

Before we get in the car, I grab her hand. She pauses, lets me interlace our fingers.

"If this is what you think it is," I say, "you know they won't stop."

She meets my eyes, unblinking. "Neither will I."

We stand there, hands locked, surrounded by the ghosts of everything that's burned, and for the first time since this started, I feel like maybe—just maybe—we're going to win.

THE DRIVE BACK IS PURE AUTOPILOT. I DON'T REMEMBER turning left at the old granary or blowing through two school zones, but somehow we end up on my block, the morning light gray and lusterless. Sophie's hand doesn't leave the stick; she taps it against her thigh the whole ride, like if she stops moving it'll self-destruct.

Inside, I kill the alarm and open every blind in the living room, needing space and light and air. I clear the table with a single swipe—mail, prescription bottles, an old book of fire codes—then set the laptop dead-center. Sophie perches on the edge of the couch, knees pulled up, the USB balanced between two fingers.

"You want to do the honors?" I ask.

She shakes her head, jaw set. "If it's a virus, you can yell at yourself."

I plug it in. The screen blinks, then goes black. For a hot second, I think the drive's nuked the system, but then a grainy blue window pops up, password prompt blinking like an accusation.

I try "Grant." No dice. "Dad." Still nothing.

Sophie leans over, staring at the field. "He always used my birthday, but reversed. Try zero-three, one-two, six-eight."

I type it. The screen goes white, then flickers to a media player. There's one video, labeled "For S.G." A timestamp: eleven years ago. I double-click.

The video's shot in an office, the kind with cheap wood paneling and a trophy case in the background. Her father sits at a desk, the kind of laminate relic that soaks up decades of coffee rings. He looks older than the last time I saw him, more tired, face gone soft around the jowls. His hands are folded, but they keep flexing, like he's trying to wring the fear out through his knuckles.

He takes a breath, looks straight at the camera, and says, "If you're watching this, I failed." The words land so heavy it feels like the whole room sags.

Sophie's breath hitches. She freezes, eyes on the screen, but her hand finds mine on the table and clamps down.

He goes on, voice steadying as he starts his confession. "This department has never run by the book, not really. Sometimes you look the other way for a brother, sometimes you fudge a supply order so the city council doesn't gut your budget. But three years ago, it changed."

He rattles off names, dates, phrases that sound like code: "Operation Phoenix," "Pattern 47," "insurance suppression." He lays out how the fires were used to cull houses ahead of eminent domain claims, how equipment was "lost" on purpose to create slush funds, how every suspicious blaze had a pattern that, if you knew where to look, pointed to a man at the top.

He keeps saying "Bennett." Over and over.

There's a second cut—he's wearing a different shirt, looks even more tired. "They'll say it was an accident. They always do. But if I vanish, or if Sophie gets threatened, that means Bennett knows I got this far."

Sophie's fingers dig into my hand, bone white.

He hesitates, voice going soft. "I'm sorry, kid. I wish I'd

been smarter. I wish I'd left sooner. But you always were the one who saw through the smoke."

At the edge of the frame, a door opens. There's a voice, muffled but sharp. It says, "That's enough for today, Grant." My spine goes cold. I know that voice. It's Bennett, for sure.

The video ends.

For a while, the only sound is the fan on the laptop, whirring like it's about to take off.

I turn to Sophie. She looks hollowed out, but her eyes are diamond-hard. "You okay?"

She shakes her head, once. "Never again."

I want to say something—anything—but there's nothing big enough to fill the hole that video just burned in the room. So I start practical. "We take this to the state fire marshal. Today. Screw the local PD."

She's quiet for a beat. Then: "No."

I blink. "No?"

She stares at the screen, her jaw flexing. "If we go public, they'll hit us first. Bennett's got cops, firefighters, probably half the council on retainer. We need more than just Dad's word. We need a smoking gun."

I try to protest, but she steamrolls me, voice rising. "Rowe is the weapon. He's the only living link. If we don't tie him to the current fires, Bennett just walks away."

I nod, slow. She's right. In a town like this, dead men don't testify.

She wipes her eyes, all business. "Let's see what else is on the drive."

We pull up the files. Most are PDFs—scanned logs, invoices, the kind of digital trail any smart criminal would have burned. But tucked in the last folder is a spreadsheet labeled "Field Work – CR." There's a list of dates, addresses, and a string of coordinates. Each matches a fire in the last ten years.

But the last line is different. Instead of an address, it's labeled "Yard." The coordinates drop in the west end, near the old train yard. There's a note: "Supplies stashed. Backup if things go wrong."

I look at Sophie. She's already grabbed her phone, thumb flying across the screen as she checks the map.

"Caleb's hiding out there," she says. "Or at least his toolbox is."

"We go tonight," I say.

She nods, resolute.

We sit for another minute, letting the video play in the background, Dad's voice looping through the litany of corruption. When it gets to the part where he says, "You always were the one who saw through the smoke," I see Sophie's chin come up, her whole body steeling.

We close the laptop, pocket the USB, and start packing gear—flashlights, gloves, burner phones just in case.

As we leave, I brush my hand over hers again, and this time she holds on, warm and strong.

Maybe this is the part where we finally burn it all down.

For real.

I LAY THE GEAR OUT ON THE TABLE: TWO FLASHLIGHTS, both with fresh batteries; a roll of duct tape, half a box of nitrile gloves; my phone, charged and loaded with the GPS coordinates from the drive. There's also my old fire helmet—cracked, paint peeling at the crest—and a Maglite heavy enough to double as a blackjack. I make a show of checking everything twice, mostly so I don't have to meet her eyes.

Sophie sits on the couch, her knees up, a spiral notebook open in her lap. She's not writing, just doodling, eyes locked on the page but tracking every move I make.

"You sure you want to do this tonight?" I ask, voice as neutral as I can manage.

She snorts, flips the notebook shut. "What, you think

Rowe's going to take a personal day? Might as well catch him before he burns down another middle school."

I like her tough, but I like her safe even more. "You don't have to come."

She stands, crossing the room in three fast steps. "If you say that one more time, I'm going to hit you."

"Just saying—"

She jams a finger into my chest, hard. "I'm not letting you face this alone. Not now."

I let out a long breath. "Fine. But if shit goes sideways, you follow the plan. You run."

She tilts her head, studying me like a bomb she needs to disarm. "You really think I'm the running type?"

I want to say yes, because that's how I want to see her: not as the target, but as the one who survives. But she's right, and we both know it.

The room's too quiet. I drop the helmet on the table, the sound echoing off the walls. "We should go," I say.

But she doesn't move. She just stands there, breathing a little too fast, fists balled at her sides.

"Hey," I say, softer now. "If you're scared, we can wait."

She shakes her head, then steps forward and kisses me. It's not gentle—her mouth is hungry, open, the kind of kiss that says "pay attention, because this could be the last one." I pull her close, hands at her hips, and she pushes me back until my knees hit the counter.

She hops up, legs scissoring around my waist. "If this goes bad," she whispers, her breath hot against my ear, "I don't want my last memory to be fear."

I don't answer. I just crush my mouth to hers, rough and desperate. My hands grip her ass, pull her forward until there's nothing but friction and heat. She tugs my shirt up, fumbles the buttons, and we make out like we're teenagers on a time bomb.

I slide my hand up her shirt, thumb circling the scar on her ribs. She hisses, but doesn't stop me, just pulls me tighter. I shove her jeans down, underwear with them, and she yanks at my belt, almost laughing when it jams on the buckle. She's off-balance, half-naked, but she doesn't care, just pulls me in, her knees bruising my ribs.

I enter her in a single stroke, not even bothering to go slow. She bites my shoulder to stifle the sound, her arms around my neck. We fuck like we're trying to leave fingerprints on each other's bones. The edge of the counter digs into her spine, but she wants it rough, wants the pain to mean something. I set the rhythm, but she matches me, hips rolling, hands fisting in my hair.

It doesn't last long. It can't—not with the adrenaline, not with the way she's looking at me, like I'm the last living thing she'll ever see. We come together, shaking, mouths pressed to each other's skin, sweat pooling in the hollow of her back.

When it's over, I rest my forehead against her sternum, breathing her in, every inhale a promise.

She lets go first, hopping down, tugging her clothes back into place with a nonchalance that almost makes me laugh. She glances at the window. The sky's gone full dark, the streetlamps casting orange halos through the glass.

"We should go," she says, her voice back to business.

I nod, grab the helmet and the gear bag. At the door, she pulls me back, just for a second, and rests her hand at the base of my skull. "If I die tonight, I'm haunting your ass," she says.

"Deal," I say, and kiss her again, softer this time.

We head out, locking the door behind us. The air outside smells like creosote and wet grass, the kind of night that makes you believe anything is possible, even survival. We get in the truck, slam the doors, and look at each other. No words left.

We drive, headlights slicing through the dark, the train yard looming on the horizon like a graveyard of failed escape plans.

If this is how it ends, at least we'll go out together.

And if we're lucky, maybe we'll take the whole goddamn web with us.

17

Blaze of Truth

Sophie

THE TRAIN YARD IS A CONTINENT OF DARKNESS, TWELVE acres of rusted metal and thorn weeds, bounded on three sides by chain-link and on the fourth by the low-slung mass of the chemical plant. The old switch tower has no windows left; every rail car on the lot wears the same uniform—rust, dent, spray paint tags in the colors of a dead gang. Somewhere to the east, a tank leaks sweet, rotgut diesel into the drainage ditch. Every breath tastes like old pennies and disappointment.

We park on the shoulder, kill the lights, and walk in single file along the gravel perimeter. My boots crunch loud in the hush, and Lucas flattens his palm to my back to keep me close, not because he's worried I'll wander, but because he doesn't trust the night not to try and take me.

It's a hundred yards to the main gate, padlocked and chained but sagging so far the fence could be peeled back by a five-year-old. Lucas tests the metal with a fingertip, then wedges the bolt cutters under the weakest link. It snaps with a noise so loud I wince, sure the sound will wake every neighbor in the west end. But nothing stirs. We squeeze through, our shadows slotting into the geometry of the tracks.

"Stay low," he mutters, voice pitched for me alone.

We keep to the gravel path, step between the rails, duck under the shadow of the boxcars. Every one of them is tagged with a different goddamn animal—rat, cat, vulture, two-headed dog. The effect is like walking through a bestiary designed by someone who hated nature.

The coordinates from the drive point to the north end, where the maintenance sheds squat like tumors. Sophie leads, head on a swivel, checking every window, every patch of ground where the grass has been trampled flat. She finds the door she wants: a plywood slab painted orange, warped by weather and time, but not locked.

Inside, it's pitch black. We step into the smell of fuel oil and mold, a dead-quiet dark that presses in with every heartbeat. I keep my hand on the wall, and Lucas slips in behind, using his phone screen as a flashlight, thumb hovering over the camera just in case.

We move slow. There's no electricity, but the floor is a minefield of nails and busted glass. Every step crunches, but it's less the sound than the texture—crunch, squelch, a weird drag like syrup or coagulated blood. I see him point the torch down, the floor has spilled glue or paint on it.

The first room is empty—just racks of broken hoses, a row

of battered lockers, the carcass of a Shop-Vac with its intestines spilling out. But at the back, past a door that's barely hanging on its hinges, we find the cache.

There are crates. Not cardboard, but those thick, military-issue plastic bins, the kind with seals tight enough to keep out plague. Lucas opens the first with a crowbar, the latches stiff and sticky with something that looks like dried resin.

Inside: a buffet of accelerants. Canisters labeled in Sharpie, gallon jugs of denatured alcohol, bottles of acetone, even two brown-glass jars of pure sodium with the warning stickers still intact. The next crate is smaller, but packed with pro-grade fire starter kits: magnesium blocks, windproof lighters, lengths of det cord coiled like dead snakes.

I snap photos with my phone, angling for clean shots of the labels, the serial numbers, the weird custom tools wrapped in oilcloth at the bottom of the bin.

"Jesus," I breathe. "This isn't amateur hour. This is like, government ops."

Lucas nods, silent, then pulls out a third crate. This one's lighter. Inside: hand-drawn maps, thick with red X's. He lays them on the floor, hands gentle despite the tension in his jaw. Every X marks a building—half are municipal, the rest schools, the hospital, the water plant.

"Look," he says, running a finger along the spiral path. It's the same pattern from Dad's journal, from every fire that mattered. The sick geometry of a mind that didn't care about people, just about symmetry.

I snap more photos, hands moving fast, then kneel for a

closer look. "These are dated. All within the next three months."

Lucas scans the shed, eyes adjusting. He finds a calendar tacked to the wall, the days circled in red. "They're going to start soon," he says. "Probably tonight. This is just the warmup."

I grab the maps, folds them, and tucks them into her jacket. "We need to get this to the state fire marshal. It's the only way."

He puts a hand on her shoulder. "We need more. Chain of custody, proof of who's running it. Otherwise, Bennett shreds it before we even get a phone call."

I look up at him, jaw clenched. "You got a better idea?"

He considers, then shakes his head. "First, we call it in. Then we set a trap."

I hesitate, then nod. "I trust you," I say, and I believe it.

Lucas dials a burner number, voice disguised, and reports a suspicious fire hazard at the train yard, then hangs up. "They'll be here in ten minutes, tops."

We move fast, backtracking through the shed, keeping to the shadows. The plan is to beat the responders to the exit, blend into the night, and double back to watch who shows up. But the plan dies halfway down the line of boxcars, when the air splits with the sound of breaking glass.

A bottle arcs in from the dark and smashes against the hood of Lucas's truck. The world lights up in a sheet of orange. For a second, it's beautiful—the way the flames curl around the old car logo, the way the metal glows from the inside. But then the heat hits, and the air turns to liquid fire.

Lucas shoves me down, hard, behind a stack of railroad ties. The wood is old, soaked with oil, but dense enough to give them five seconds of cover. Glass shatters again, a rain of burning gasoline soaking the ground.

"Stay down," he barks, voice gone full command.

I pull my knees up to my chest, fists clenched so hard my nails draw blood. The flames crackle, hungry and fast, the heat makes my eyes water. I can hear other footsteps now, boots on gravel, someone circling for the kill shot.

Lucas peeks up, spots the shadow moving along the line of cars. He lifts the Maglite, ready to blind or brain whoever comes around the corner.

But the attack is less direct. A chunk of metal, what looks like an old brake shoe, jagged and heavy, flies through the air and catches Lucas on the forearm, just above the wrist. The pain is instant, electric. He drops the flashlight, and his arm blooms red.

I move on instinct. I grab a large piece of metal from the ground and hurl it at the attacker's knees. It lands with a solid thud, and the figure yelps, then limps away, cursing in a voice that's familiar but too distorted to ID.

"You're hit," I say, voice shaking as I look at his arm.

Lucas grits his teeth, pressing his good hand to the wound. "It's not deep. Just a gash. We need to get out before this whole place goes up."

The fire is spreading, licking along the soaked rail ties and catching on every dry scrap. The air is a whiteout of smoke, I hold Lucas, the fear beginning to take hold, then music to my ears I hear the sirens, faint but closing fast.

I grab the evidence and shoulder Lucas's weight. We move in a crouch, backs to the flames, eyes locked on the perimeter fence.

When we make it to the breach in the chain-link, Lucas is fading, the blood pooling in his palm. My jacket sleeve is already tacky with it, but I don't let go. Not for a second.

We clear the fence, hit the gravel, and collapse behind the boundary, the world behind us lighting up like a funeral pyre.

The sirens are close now, fire trucks, cop cars, maybe an ambulance. I press my hand to Lucas's wound, tearing strips from my shirt to make a tourniquet.

"Don't die," I whisper, voice raw.

He laughs, shaky but real, and I want to slap him stupid. "Not tonight," he says. "You still owe me a steak dinner."

The sound of first responders fills the air, but for a second, we are invisible. Just two bodies in the dark, stitched together by adrenaline and the knowledge that nobody is coming to save us except each other.

I tuck the maps deeper into my jacket, then lean my head against his shoulder. The smoke stings my eyes, but I don't cry.

I don't have time.

We watch the trucks roll in, lights strobing the night to shreds, and wait for the chaos to find us.

It's only a matter of time. "We need to move, Lucas," I say, trying to haul him up.

We don't make it a hundred feet before Lucas's knees give. He tries to walk it off—he always does—but the blood loss is real, and the edges of his vision are probably starting to burn black. I see it in the way his hands start to tremor, just a little, like he's freezing even though the night air is thick and sticky.

I hook his arm over my shoulders, take the weight. "Rail car," I grunt, and he nods, jaw locked so tight I can hear the teeth grinding. There's one five yards off—old, sun-bleached, door half open, the tag on the side a mess of letters that used to spell EMERGENCY. We stumble over the ballast, boots skidding in the loose rock, and I haul him up the three iron rungs and into the maw of the car.

Inside, it's cold as a crypt. The metal walls sweat condensation, and every sound is a doubled echo, louder and closer than it should be. There's a rank, sweet rot from whatever last used this as a nest, but I barely notice. I get him down, back against the wall, and slide his jacket off.

"Fuck," I say, because the gash is deeper than I thought—a ragged line just above the wrist, blood pulsing in a slow but steady rhythm. It's already soaked through the shirt, hot and sticky on my palm.

Lucas looks down, then up, and there's a glint in his eye that says don't you dare start crying. "I've had worse," he says, voice shredded but steady.

"Bullshit," I mutter, and pull off my own jacket, balling it up and shoving it against the wound. I fish my belt off—black vinyl, cheap, but it's what I have—and loop it tight above the elbow, cinching it until the blood slows.

Lucas watches the whole time, not moving, not even when I jerk the belt an extra notch and the veins pop under the skin. "You're a natural," he says.

I shoot him a look. "You say anything about Florence Nightingale, I will break your other arm."

He grins, then winces. "That's my girl."

The phrase makes something in my chest twist, but I don't let it show. Instead, I put both hands on the makeshift tourniquet and hold, counting in my head, the way Dad taught me. Count to one hundred, let the clot form, pray there's enough left to keep him upright when the time comes.

Outside, the world is all siren and chaos, but in here, it's just the two of us, locked in a metal coffin. I lean in close, forehead to his, and whisper, "I meant what I said, don't you die on me, Lucas Hayes. Not after all this."

He closes his eyes, the lashes dark with sweat and soot. "Wouldn't dare," he says. "Not with you watching."

I PRESS HARDER, AND THE BLOOD OOZES SLOWER. My hands are slick and red, but my mind is calm. I know this drill, better than most. It's the waiting that's hard—the minutes dragging like they're on fire.

His fingers find mine, curling around my wrist. "Hey," he says, softer now. "Remember the night at the reservoir? After the junior prom?"

I almost laugh. "We snuck out the window and rode your brother's bike all the way to the spillway. You tried to impress me by climbing the chain-link, but you ripped your shirt and spent the rest of the night trying not to bleed all over my dress."

He nods, a ghost of a smile. "You made me a bandage from your hair ribbon. Pink. It stained the hell out of the cut."

"You always looked good in pink," I say, and this time I do laugh, short and sharp.

The silence after is full of every word we never said, every chance we almost took and every disaster that brought us back together. I move my hand to his cheek, thumb rough on the stubble. "We get out of this, you owe me a dinner."

"Steak," he says, automatic. "Medium rare."

"You're an animal," I say.

He shrugs, the movement sluggish. "You love it."

He reaches for my hand again, brings it to his lips, kisses the palm with a weird, old-fashioned formality that makes my heart hiccup. His blood is drying on my skin, sticky and dark, but he doesn't seem to care.

"I'm not losing you again," I whisper, voice breaking for the first time all night.

His eyes are wide, pupils blown, but he pulls me in with a gentleness that's at odds with every scar on his body. "You won't," he says. "Not unless you want to."

I lean in, forehead to his, breath mingling in the cold air. "I don't," I say, and mean it so hard it almost hurts.

He kisses me—slow this time, deliberate, a promise written in salt and heat and the taste of copper on his tongue. His hands are still strong, even with the blood loss, and he holds me like I'm the only thing tethering him to the world.

The sirens outside are louder now, bouncing between the cars. We don't move. For a second, we let the world go on without us, just two ghosts in a steel mausoleum, clinging to each other because there's nothing else left.

The kiss deepens, urgent and sweet, and for a moment I'm seventeen again, invincible and stupid and in love with a boy who could never sit still. But then reality comes crashing back—the taste of smoke, the pain in my shoulder, the way the night is about to end in fire and blue lights.

We pull apart, barely. His lips brush my ear. "We have to move," he says, but he doesn't let go.

I nod, and press my mouth to his temple, once. "Just a minute," I say, and we stay there, breathing together, the metal walls echoing our heartbeats.

When the searchlights start to sweep the yard, we get ready.

But for now, for just a moment, we're still alive.

The first responder convoy arrives with the subtlety of a parade—strobes and high beams painting the boxcars blue and white, the engines rumbling so loud it shakes rust from the ceiling. Within sixty seconds, the yard is crawling with bodies—firefighters in full turnout, cops in windbreakers, two EMTs with a stretcher and that look in their eyes like they've already triaged three dead tonight.

I flag them from the doorway, waving both arms. "In here!" I shout, and they charge up the steps, gear clattering. The lead EMT is a woman my age, arms freckled and strong. She takes one look at Lucas's blood-blackened shirt and says, "Pressure, now." I'm already there, hands fused to the wound, but she peels me away and takes over, her touch brisk and surgical.

The other EMT checks his pulse, then threads an IV with the speed of someone who hates blood but loves fixing things. Lucas doesn't react—not once. He keeps his eyes on me, and even with half his shirt gone and his skin sheet-white, there's a faint curl at the edge of his mouth. "Told you I'm hard to kill," he rasps.

The EMT shoots me a side-eye. "Was it a fight?"

I shake my head. "Shrapnel. We got caught near the truck when it went up."

She nods, not buying it but not caring. "We'll need to clean the cut, maybe ten stitches. Can you get him to County yourself or do you want the ride?"

Lucas tries to sit up. "No ambulance," he says, stubborn as ever.

She shrugs, tapes gauze over the arm, and hands me a trauma pad. "Just hold until you can get it looked at. Bleeding should stop, but keep him awake. Guy loses consciousness, call 911. Okay?"

I nod, and Lucas tries to make a joke but his teeth are chattering now, adrenaline cratering. I pull him close, let him lean on me, and wrap what's left of my jacket around his shoulders.

The fire crew swarms the truck, axes and hoses ready, but it's mostly for show. The engine block is a single slab of char; the hood melted to slag. They put it out anyway, white foam billowing over the black skeleton, and one of the younger guys takes a selfie with the wreckage. I watch it all, numb, until the crowd parts for a new arrival.

Bennett.

He's out of uniform, hair perfect, jacket tailored. But he fits here like he was born in the ruins, hands tucked in his pockets, face so blank it's like he pressed pause on whatever emotion he had queued up. He saunters past the engine, surveys the crime scene, and only then acknowledges me—one eyebrow raised, a smile just short of legal.

"Didn't expect to see you here," he says, and his voice carries, even over the pumps and the radios.

I grit my teeth. "Surprised you're working the night shift, Chief."

He glances at Lucas, bandaged and bleeding, then at the scorched shell of the truck. "Looks like you had an exciting evening."

"Nothing compared to your department," I shoot back.

He lets that hang, eyes narrow. "You don't look like your father," he says, quiet. The way he says it, I can't tell if it's a compliment, a threat, or just a fact.

I stare him down, not blinking. "No. But I'm learning."

He shifts his weight, hands still in pockets, and the smile goes from fake to feral. "Careful, Sophie. Sometimes the smoke gets in your head and you forget what you're fighting for."

Behind me, Lucas tries to stand, fails, and the EMT steadies him. "She's got a better memory than you think," he says, and Bennett's gaze flicks over, landing on him like a hawk on a rabbit.

The tension is heavy as the night air, but then the radio on Bennett's belt crackles. He taps the mic, barks a few words, and just like that, he's gone—striding away through the crowd, the king of ashes.

The EMT finishes the wrap, gives Lucas a nod, then looks at me. "You two should get home before the reporters show up."

I thank her, then help Lucas down the stairs. His legs are steadier now, the color coming back, but the hand he puts on my shoulder is all gravity. We limp through the wreckage, ducking the last of the rubberneckers and the yellow tape, and find the back lot where the air is quieter.

For a long minute we just stand there, catching our breath, watching the blue strobes flicker over the field of dead grass and shadows.

"You okay?" I ask, brushing sweat from his brow.

He nods, voice weak but real. "Yeah. Better than last time. You?"

I look back at the yard, the scorched truck, the line of fire tape fluttering in the breeze. I think about the look on Bennett's face, the not-quite-threat, the way he called me out in public like it was just another handshake.

I realize I'm not scared. Not anymore.

"Yeah," I say, and surprise myself by smiling. "I'm good."

Lucas pulls me in, wraps both arms around me, careful of his wound. He holds me tight, and for the first time in years, I feel safe—even with the world on fire.

We hold that pose, two survivors in a wasteland of secrets, until the last siren fades.

"I think this is just the beginning," he says, voice close to my ear.

I nod, jaw set. "Let him come."

We walk away together, arms locked, bleeding and bruised but whole.

I never meant to be my father.

But if that's what it takes to end this—

So be it.

18

Smoke and Mirrors

Sophie

The kitchen table has vanished under an avalanche of evidence. Every square inch is buried in Dad's old logbooks, court exhibits, maps dotted with pins, and two separate laptops —one for the real digging, one for the plausible deniability. I've arranged everything by type and then by chronological significance, so the table looks like the workbench of a conspiracy theorist with OCD. The only food present is the crust of a day-old bagel, now serving as a coaster for my second mug of instant coffee.

Lucas paces a rut from fridge to window to back of my chair, his bare feet slapping the linoleum. The makeshift bandage on his forearm is already flecked with brown, but he won't let me rewrap it. Each time he passes me, he tests the range of motion, wincing a little, then rolling his shoulder as if he can bully the pain into leaving. I can smell his restlessness—

sweat, soap, and the faint coppery tang of blood that's soaked through the sleeve of his old station tee.

He's never been good at idle. I think he'd rather be inside a burning building than left out of the action, even when the action is just me, three highlighters, and a stack of court records from the era when fax machines ruled the earth.

"Can you please stop walking?" I mutter, not looking up from my screen.

He ignores me and keeps pacing. "I feel like a caged animal."

"Good. Then maybe you won't chew through your stitches before they have a chance to clot."

He grunts, pivots, and braces his good hand on the counter. "Did you get through to the forensics guy?"

"Voicemail," I say. "He's not calling back unless I bribe him with gift cards."

Lucas swears, then goes silent. The clock on the microwave ticks over, the only other sound in the house besides the background hum of our combined anxiety.

I scroll through another hundred lines of department expense reports, looking for the pattern. It's always in the numbers, Dad used to say. People lie; paper trails don't. The firehouse had a way of laundering funds through "lost" equipment—boots, hoses, overtime hours for disasters that never got called in. Bennett signed off on all of it, always just inside the margin of plausible deniability.

My phone vibrates, just once, and my chest seizes up. The number isn't saved, but the area code is local. I answer, and there's a second of static before the voice comes through, brittle and exhausted.

"Sophie? It's Meredith Holloway."

It takes me a beat to respond. "How are you? Aren't you supposed to be in the burn unit?" I say, then wince at how harsh it sounds.

She snorts. "They kicked me loose after the skin graft consult. The hospital wifi is so bad I'm writing this on my phone. You got a minute?"

I tuck the phone between my shoulder and chin, hands free for typing. "For you? Always."

Lucas mouths, "Who is it?" and I shoo him away.

Meredith's voice is low, urgent. "You were right about the report fudge at the Clark Street fire. My sources confirmed Bennett ordered the logs scrubbed. But there's more—a pattern. It matches with at least three other fires in the last five years. Same suppression, same insurance play."

I already have the spreadsheet open. "You want to come over and compare notes?"

She hesitates. "I can't. I think someone's been following me. I need to keep it public."

"Diner?" I ask.

"Too obvious. Meet me at Levee Brew in half an hour. Bring the evidence. And bring someone who can watch the door."

I say yes, hang up, and finally look at Lucas. He's waiting, hand flexing around the countertop.

"Trouble?"

I push back from the table, stretching. "We're meeting the reporter at Levee Brew. She's got new proof. Wants a security blanket."

He starts for the door, but I stop him with a hand on his wrist. "You sure you're up for this?"

"Better than staying here," he mutters.

Levee Brew is the kind of coffee shop that's always cold, regardless of the season, and the mismatched tables all wobble unless you find the one with the folded napkin jammed under the leg. Meredith is in the farthest corner, a blanket scarf covering her neck and the bandages on her arms, phone and battered legal pad at the ready.

I clock the crowd as we walk in—two teens with laptops, a couple of retirees in fleece vests, and the barista, who's so absorbed in the espresso machine he doesn't even glance up. Lucas does a slow circle before he sits, just close enough to block the line of sight from the window. He takes his seat with a wince, but hides it behind his mug.

Meredith's hands are steady, but there's a flush in her cheeks that isn't just from the burns. "Thanks for coming," she says.

I hand her a flash drive, the backup from Dad's records. "I brought you the digital. Paper's too easy to torch."

She slides a business card across the table, her nails bitten to the quick. "You're going to need this. They'll believe you before they believe me."

I pick it up. It's heavy-stock, embossed with the logo of the Bureau of Alcohol, Tobacco, Firearms and Explosives. There's a name and a cell number, handwritten in blue Sharpie.

"She's the real deal," Meredith says, voice flat. "If you want this to stick, she's the one who can make it happen. Just... don't say my name."

I nod, pocket the card, then glance at her wrists. The edges of the gauze are tinged pink, the skin under still angry and new.

"You doing okay?" I ask, softer.

She flexes her fingers. "I'll live. Worse things than getting a story right."

The meeting lasts less than ten minutes. We talk in code,

old habit from the years of covering city council scandals. Lucas never lets his guard down, eyes always scanning the door, the windows, the street outside.

As we leave, Meredith catches my sleeve. "He's going to come for you," she whispers, so quiet I almost miss it. "Bennett. He doesn't lose."

I think of the wreckage at the train yard, the way he looked at me, already calculating my odds of survival.

"He hasn't taken me on yet," I say, then turn and go.

Back at the house, the kitchen table is exactly as we left it, except the bandage on Lucas's arm is starting to leak again. He grabs a clean towel and tightens the belt with his teeth, silent.

I call the number. It rings three times before a woman answers, voice clipped and bright: "Special Agent Collins."

I don't give her my real name. "I have evidence of ongoing arson and official corruption in Willow Creek. I want immunity for myself and my witness."

She doesn't even pause. "You have proof?"

"Hard and soft copies. You can vet it yourself. If you want a chain of custody, you'll need to move fast."

There's a click as she puts me on speaker. I hear a second voice in the background, male, bored. "Where can we meet?"

I scan the table, the highlighter stains, the maps, Lucas's knuckles gone white from pain. "Neutral ground. You pick."

"We'll send you a location by text. One hour."

I end the call and jot a quick summary on my notepad, just in case I get turned inside out on the way there. As I write, my fingers drift to the scar on my side—hidden by shirt and jacket, but raised and rough under my touch. I trace the edge, the reminder of the first fire, and breathe in slow until my hands stop shaking.

Lucas watches me. "You nervous?"

"Always," I say.

He nods, as if that's the answer he expected.

My phone vibrates again—a new text, coordinates for a run-down motel by the interstate.

I stand, gather the folders, and toss him the car keys.

"You drive," I say, forcing a smile. "You look less suspicious."

He barks a laugh, then limps after me, the towel bright red against his arm.

We're down to the last match.

If I'm going to burn, I'm taking the whole stack with me.

It's midnight by the time we're ready to start connecting dots. The world outside is a two-bar fire on the thermometer and dead-quiet, but the inside of Lucas's kitchen is a sauna of paper and frustration. The air smells like printer toner, cheap ramen, and the antiseptic tang of his wound.

We've covered the table with enough evidence to indict a small government. Timeline charts and fire reports are spread in neat layers, every page corner tabbed with sticky notes, every photo captioned in ballpoint. In the center, a battered three-ring binder bristles with printouts, and my laptop glows cold and blue at the head of the table, casting both our faces in the color of old bruises.

Lucas is a force of nature when he's locked on a puzzle. He paces back and forth, every so often jabbing a finger at the map, then pivoting to highlight a snippet in the arson logs. His voice is stripped to the essentials—short, sharp, everything clipped as if each syllable costs him. Every so often, he pauses to roll his shoulder, then flexes his bandaged arm like he's checking to see if the pain is still real.

"Here," he says, sliding a sheaf of photos my way. "That's the fire pattern at the old canning plant. Same starter mix as the one at the train yard—accelerant poured in two lines, then crossed at the point of ignition."

I line up the photos, side by side. "And the timing matches. Both set during the night shift change, when there's the least surveillance."

Lucas grins, but it's all teeth. "It's textbook. Except no textbook recommends this unless you want it found."

"Or you want to scare off the next guy who might talk," I say.

He nods, then scans the board again. "How many is that?"

I flip my notebook. "Five arsons, two 'accidents' with bodies that never made it to the coroner."

"Bennett and Rowe at the epicenter of every single one," Lucas mutters, running his thumb along the edge of the table.

I glance at my laptop. The spreadsheet is up—cell after cell highlighted, tracing every suspicious overtime request, every out-of-budget supply run, every insurance claim that got pushed through when nobody was looking.

"Department finances are a disaster," I say. "If you wanted to run a slush fund, this is exactly how you'd do it."

He leans in, arms braced on the table, his gaze so intent it burns. "And your father?"

I flip to the journal. Dad's script is spiky and uneven, but the dates don't lie. Every one of his "suspicions" matches the incidents on our timeline. He even noted the times Bennett was off-grid, always aligning with the worst fires.

Lucas traces a finger down the page. "He saw it. And he tried to stop it."

"He was too good," I say, voice catching. "He kept a record

of everything. He thought... I think he thought if he could just get it all down, someone would listen."

Lucas is silent for a minute, then says, "You did."

I nod, and a weird ache fills my throat. I want to say thank you, but my mouth refuses.

We keep at it, cross-referencing every photo, every log, every ink-stained margin. When we hit the fourth hour, the world outside is solid black, the silence broken only by the slap of sticky notes and the whir of my computer fan.

Then, with no warning, the laptop pings—a soft alert, but loud as a gunshot after so much quiet. The file transfer has finished. Dad's video, downloaded and decrypted, the filename a single word: "Truth."

I freeze, finger hovering over the trackpad.

Lucas stands behind me now, his shadow thrown huge across the wall. "You want me to give you space?" he asks, voice soft for once.

I shake my head. "You don't have to watch this with me."

He pulls his chair next to mine, so close our knees touch. "I'm not going anywhere."

I glance at his hand—resting on the table, knuckles swollen and ringed with old burn scars. I put my hand over his, and he squeezes once, hard.

The room is too bright. I kill the kitchen lights, leaving only the laptop screen. Our faces reflect off the glass—mine pale, Lucas's half in shadow. I double-click the file. The first frame is Dad, alive and moving, eyes red from lack of sleep but burning with purpose.

My hand shakes, just a little. Lucas leans into my shoulder, grounding me.

"Ready?" he asks.

I nod, and click play.

The video is a single, unbroken shot. The camera sits on a shelf, propped at a weird tilt, framing Dad behind a battered metal desk in the firehouse office. Fluorescent lights strobe overhead, making everything look a little sick, a little overexposed. Dad's hair is thinner than I remember, his face sunken at the temples. He's not wearing his uniform. Instead, he's in a Willow Creek softball T-shirt and old cargo pants with a black smudge across the knee.

The timestamp in the corner says it was recorded four days before he died.

He folds his hands in front of him. His wedding ring catches the light, a glint at the end of a trembling finger.

"If you're seeing this," he starts, "it means I didn't make it. Or worse, I'm not allowed to talk anymore." He tries to smile, fails. "I don't know who's watching. Sophie, it's probably you. Maybe I should be sorrier about that, but I'm not."

I hear Lucas's breath beside me, shaky and shallow.

Dad opens a manila folder on the desk, thumbs through a stack of paperwork. "There's something wrong at the top. Been wrong for years, maybe longer than I've been in the job. I tried to keep my nose out of it, but these days it's impossible." He fans the papers, showing each page to the camera—a blurry parade of checks, city memos, handwritten notes that I instantly recognize as his.

"There's a spiral," he says. "I don't mean the pattern in the arsons, although that's part of it. I mean, there's this thing, a system, a process. They burn it down before anyone can fix it. Then they sell off the ashes and call it progress."

He slams a page on the desk, hard enough to echo through the speakers. "Troy Bennett. That's your guy. He's got the city manager, the fire marshal, half the council in his back pocket. The others—" His voice warbles, anger and defeat knotted together. "The others are gone. Retired, vanished, or dead."

Dad sits back. The light catches the gray in his beard, the new lines around his mouth. "I kept records. Every conversation, every weird supply order, every time Bennett showed up somewhere he didn't belong. The blue book in my locker is the master copy. If you're the one who found it—Sophie, I'm sorry. I wanted to keep you out of this. I really did."

He looks down, rubs his forehead, and when he comes up again his eyes are glassy. "There's a chance you'll get hurt, kid. That's what I've been scared of this whole time. But if you let this go, more people will die. I tried to warn them. I tried to make noise. But they're all too scared or too well paid to listen."

His voice goes soft, barely above a whisper. "Don't trust anyone with a badge. Not even your friends. You're smarter than me. You always were. But if you can find someone to watch your back, do it."

He closes the file, breathes deep. "I love you, Sophie. More than anything. I'm proud of you, no matter how this ends."

He reaches for the camera, and for a second the frame fills with the ridges of his fingers, then black.

I stare at the screen, not breathing.

Lucas doesn't say anything, but when I look over, I see the tears running down his face. He blinks, fast, then scrubs his good hand across his eyes, leaving a streak of red from the scabbed knuckles.

"He was a good man," Lucas whispers, voice gone ragged. "He didn't deserve to be—" He cuts off, shakes his head, and looks away.

I pause the video, the image frozen on the last full frame of Dad's face. I close the laptop, quietly, and sink to the floor in front of Lucas. I take his hands in both of mine—his are clammy, cold, still shaking.

"I'm sorry," I say, and it's all I can manage.

He drops his forehead to mine. "I should've seen it," he rasps. "I should've stopped Bennett."

I squeeze his hands tighter. "Nobody could have. Not alone."

We sit like that, in the darkness, until our heartbeats slow down and the air stops tasting like grief.

Finally, Lucas pulls himself together. He kneels, touches my cheek, and says, "We have to move fast. The last spiral date is two days away. If they follow the pattern, they'll go for a target nobody expects."

I nod, already running the logic in my head. "City Hall, probably. Or the water plant."

"Both, if they're smart," he says, but his voice is stronger now.

I get up, move to the window. The street is empty except for the lazy yellow wash of a sodium lamp and the distant wail of a train. My reflection is sharp, eyes too big for my face.

"The fire runs in my blood," I say, softly, tracing the glass. "But I know how to control it."

Behind me, I hear him laugh, a real laugh, small and surprised.

"You're a badass," he says, and I almost believe it.

THAT NIGHT, NEITHER OF US WANTS TO BE ALONE. I SLEEP on top of the covers in Lucas's room, the air conditioner humming a lullaby from the far window. I don't drift off, just watch the slice of streetlight crawl across the ceiling, slow as old honey.

After a while, Lucas comes in, limping and shirtless, his arm bandaged in a fresh white sling. He moves slow, like every muscle hurts, but he still crosses the room to me.

He sits at the edge of the bed and looks at me for a long time. There's no trace of bravado left, just a man held together by adrenaline and duct tape and the hope that the world might get better if we make it through the next forty-eight hours.

"I never asked," he says, "about your scar."

I shrug, lifting my shirt just enough to show the ridged oval on my left side. It's ugly, the color of old copper, but not as big as the memory of it.

He reaches out, slow and careful, and traces it with a finger. The touch is feather-light, but I feel it all the way down. His thumb circles the edge, then flattens over the center, warm and steady.

"You're not broken," he says. "You're forged."

I close my eyes, because if I keep them open, I'll cry. "You sure?"

He leans in, kisses the scar, then kisses my mouth. The taste of him is smoke and sleep and salt.

I pull him down next to me, and for a long time, we just breathe, curled together in the silence.

When I finally sleep, it's deep and dreamless.

When I wake, the world is already burning.

But this time, I'm ready.

19

Code Red

Lucas

THE ALARM SLAMS INTO MY BRAIN AT 12:03 A.M., A FULL-throated siren that jerks me upright and nearly tears the stitches out of my arm. I'd been dreaming about Dad, about the old kitchen with its wood-panel walls and his voice rising over the police scanner, but now the world is nothing but klaxon and red strobe and the immediate, white-hot sizzle of pain.

I swing my legs out of bed and immediately regret it—every muscle is stiff, my forearm pulsing with a sick, wet ache. The makeshift bandage I'd wrapped before crashing for the night is stuck to the wound, fused by dried blood and probably half a roll of paper towel. I peel it off, bite down on the inside of my cheek, and taste copper all the way down to my stomach.

Down the hall, Sophie is already in motion. She barrels into the bedroom, hair wild, sweatshirt on backwards, phone pinched between her shoulder and ear. She clocks me—still sitting, not dressed, not ready—and her eyes go so wide I half-expect the whites to start flashing like the alarm.

"Up, Hayes," she snaps, and the voice isn't hers; it's command, it's muscle memory, it's every late-night drill we ever ran. "You're not dead yet."

I haul myself upright, yanking on my turnout pants with my good hand. She's still on the phone, spitting details at a dispatcher—address, visible flames, possible injuries. I know she'd rather be at the scene already, but she's refusing to leave me behind. I want to snap at her, tell her to go, but the look on her face says she'll break my other arm before she lets me lag.

The ride to the station is a blur of red lights and potholes. Sophie takes the corners at murder speed, engine whining as she floors it down Main. I grip the dash, every bump a jolt through my wrist, but I don't say a word. Not until we pull into the station and see the rest of the crew already suiting up, grim-faced in the sodium glare.

The Chief is waiting at the door, helmet under one arm, clipboard clamped in the other hand. "You good to work?" he asks me, eyes flicking to the bandaged arm.

I nod, jaw clenched. "I can run hose or pump. Whatever you need."

He stares a beat too long, then tosses me the keys to Truck One. "You drive. She rides."

Sophie gives him a look that could strip paint, but says nothing. We sprint to the bay, the radio already blaring with the incident details: "Structure fire at Willow Creek Elementary. Possible arson. All units respond."

There's a lump in my throat that has nothing to do with pain.

The fire truck is a beast, built in an era where bigger was always better, and every lever, every gauge, every wheel is sized for a giant. My hands find their places automatically; I force my fingers to grip, ignoring the way my left one shakes on the wheel. Sophie rides shotgun, headset already on, relaying updates to the rest of the convoy.

"Smoke visible from three blocks out," she barks into the mic. "Evacuation in progress. Repeat: teachers are clearing the building."

In the side mirror, I catch a stutter of blue and white—the first police cruiser, lights cutting a jagged path up the street. Behind us, another engine falls in line, then an ambulance, the whole parade converging on the target with the grace of a well-practiced nightmare.

At the corner of Maple and Main, the world shifts from dark to hell-bright. The east wing of the school is already vomiting smoke, thick and oily, and the air is full of screaming—the high, unsteady pitch of children, layered with the bark of adult orders. I park the truck with a squeal, and Sophie is out before we even stop, sprinting to the main doors with a yellow vest from the cab. I kill the siren, slap the parking brake, and haul myself down to street level.

The scene is chaos. Kids cluster in groups on the lawn, huddled in blankets, eyes shining with animal fear. A line of teachers hustles the stragglers to the far curb, some barefoot, some with faces streaked black. Firefighters from our station, half-dressed and half-awake, drag hoses off the truck and shoulder through the haze toward the main entrance.

I find the incident commander—a captain from Station Three, already sweating through his helmet. "Where do you need us?" I yell.

He jerks his chin at the west side. "Basement mechanical. It's burning hotter than the rest. Suppression units on main; you two take the north hall. Floor plan is taped to the door."

I don't argue. I grab my helmet, clamp it over my ears, and run after Sophie, who's already flanking the building with a length of hose in one arm and a Halligan tool in the other. She's smaller than most of the crew, but tonight she moves like a missile, single-minded and terrifying.

We make the side door in seconds. She kicks it in—literally, I can hear the wood splinter—and the world goes from cold night to steam bath. Smoke billows out in a rolling mass, choking and wet, but I pull my mask on and keep close behind her, counting steps as we move.

Inside, it's a different universe. The fire eats up every sound except its own, a constant low roar punctuated by the crash of falling ceiling tiles and the hiss of pipes venting steam. The tiles on the floor are slick, every surface hot enough to blister. Sophie leads, crouched low, sweeping with the Halligan. I shoulder the hose, bite off a yelp as it tugs the stitches on my arm, and follow.

Halfway down the hall, we hit the first victim—a janitor,

crumpled behind a stack of overturned chairs, breathing but limp. Sophie hauls him up, drags him to the exit, and I hold the door while she rolls him onto the lawn. Then we're back in, searching the next room, and the next. Every step is a punch to my arm, but the adrenaline drowns it out, keeps me upright.

We're in the gym when the ceiling starts to fail. A chunk of plaster slams down, missing my shoulder by inches, and Sophie curses under her breath. "Hurry," she says, voice hoarse from yelling. "This thing's got minutes."

We clear the last room, find it empty except for a fish tank and a shelf of third-grade trophies, now melted into a single, gold blob. I want to laugh, but there's no breath for it. We turn to go, but Sophie hesitates at the door.

"What?" I shout.

She stares at the floor, then points. In the scorched linoleum, right where the fire has burned through the wax, is a symbol. A spiral, black and perfect, cut deep into the tile by some kind of blade.

The pattern from Dad's journal. The one from the train yard. This time, it's finished, a full circle.

Sophie's face goes slack, just for a second. "We need to go," she says, and this time, her voice shakes.

We make it outside, coughing and snot-faced, just as the building's windows blow. The fire leaps into the sky, every orange tongue licking at the night. For a second, all I can do is watch it. The school is lost, but everyone's out. Every single kid, every teacher.

Sophie stands next to me, helmet off, hair pasted to her skull with sweat. She watches the spiral in the dirt, then looks up at me, and I see it in her eyes—the realization, the fear, the way it's all closing in.

"They're not just targeting buildings," she says. "They're sending a message."

I nod, even though I can barely feel my hands.

She breathes in, deep and shaking. "Next one's going to be us."

I don't say it, but I know she's right.

We spend the next hour in triage. I help set up tarps and sort the injured by severity. Sophie floats between the teachers, every few minutes a hand grabbing her shoulder, a voice whispering, "Thank you, thank you, thank you," as if she were the one who saved their kids. Maybe she was. I see the way the teachers look at her, like they know something, like there's a secret in the way she moves. One of them, a woman in a pink bathrobe, hugs Sophie so hard she nearly lifts her off the ground.

A few yards away, the Chief makes a show of pacing the lawn, talking to reporters and barking orders. He glances at me, at my arm, but doesn't say anything. I can tell he's angry, not at us, but at the world. At the spiral.

When the last ambulance pulls out, I collapse on the curb,

boots untied, lungs burning. Sophie sits beside me, arms around her knees.

"Are you going to make it?" she asks, voice raw.

I look at her, and for the first time in years, I don't have a glib answer.

Instead, I rest my head on her shoulder, and let the smoke roll off us in silence.

She's right. The next one is going to be us.

But at least we'll go out together.

We're on our fourth sweep around the perimeter when the adrenaline finally starts to bleed off. The fire's under control but not out—crews from two towns over are rotating through the hot zone, mopping up, rolling hose. The field behind the school is a muddy war zone of tire tracks and half-melted jungle gym. Every time the wind shifts, I get a lungful of burning rubber and whatever polymers go into making playground equipment so indestructible during recess and so damned flammable after midnight.

Sophie walks just ahead of me, flashlight angled low, sweeping for the telltale gleam of accelerant or the shine of broken glass. She moves with a weird, purposeful calm, each step calculated. I want to call her back, tell her to stay put, but I know the look on her face: jaw set, eyes narrow, all the fight compressed into a single, silent beam of willpower.

We're almost at the front of the building when I see it.

The sidewalk leading to the main doors is buckled and stained with soot. In the center, right where every parent and kid would walk in on the first day of school, someone's carved a spiral. Not a spray-paint tag, not a kid's doodle, but a deep, careful incision, each groove deliberate, like someone spent hours working it into the concrete. It's maybe two feet across, perfectly proportioned, the lines getting tighter and tighter until they close in on themselves at the core.

This is no warning. It's a signature.

Sophie stops dead, her boot landing half an inch from the edge of the spiral. Her whole body goes rigid. She kneels down, runs her fingers over the groove, then glances back at me, her face ghost-white under the layer of grime.

"It's complete," she says, voice flat but vibrating at the edges. "Last time, at the train yard, it was just a half circle. This... this is finished."

I step closer, ignoring the way my stitches tug with every stride. "You think it's for you?"

She laughs, a hard, humorless sound. "Not me, specifically. But this—" She gestures at the spiral, then at the burning school behind us. "This is a ritual. A countdown. Whoever's doing this, they're not just burning buildings. They're working toward an end."

I kneel next to her. The symbol looks even more brutal up close. The concrete is chewed away, sharp as broken shell, and the soot has settled in the groove, turning it from gray to black.

"How do you know it's a countdown?" I ask, keeping my voice soft.

She chews her lip, then shakes her head, frustrated. "Patterns. All the fires, all the dates, everything Dad tracked. The spiral always closes, always ends at a center. Whoever left this... they're telling us where it leads."

Her hands shake, just a little, but she presses them flat to the sidewalk, grounding herself. I reach over, lay my palm over hers, and the contact is electric—steadying for both of us.

"We're the center," she says, barely above a whisper.

I feel the hairs rise on my arms, despite the heat coming off the building.

"Not just you," I say, voice firmer than I feel. "Both of us. They want us to see it burn."

She looks up, searching my face, and I see the war going on behind her eyes: fear, rage, the bone-deep need to see this through even if it means getting scorched.

I squeeze her hand. "Let's find what else they left."

She nods, and together we circle the building. At the edge of the playground, I spot a patch of grass that's been torched, the fire burned hot and fast, leaving a ring of dead earth and another spiral—smaller this time, almost invisible. Sophie snaps photos with her phone, cataloging each one, like she's collecting evidence for a trial nobody will ever hold.

Back at the front, the crews are winding down. The air is full of the hiss of cooling metal and the pop of glass as it contracts in the night chill. The school is a ruin, but the sign above the door still reads "Willow Creek Elementary," the letters warped but legible.

We sit on the curb, side by side, letting the tension slowly drain out. Neither of us speaks for a while. The fire in the gym flares, then gutters, casting everything in flickering orange.

Finally, Sophie turns to me. "This ends with us, doesn't it?"

I shrug, then nod. "Yeah. But we end it our way."

She smiles, small and broken, but real. "I like the sound of that."

Behind us, the last window shatters, and the whole building glows like a jack-o'-lantern. The spiral on the sidewalk catches the light, turning it into a shadow that stretches across both our feet.

We sit there a long time, until the sun's not far off and the world smells less like fire and more like the wet, clean promise of a day that hasn't been ruined yet.

When we finally stand, the spiral is still there, a dark memory burned into the concrete.

But so are we.

The cab of Truck One is an island, a capsule sealed against the wail of sirens and the churn of engines. The windshield is streaked with sweat and soot, and every surface smells like a thousand other fires, all layered atop each other until you could believe the world was always burning, and always would be.

I climb into the driver's seat and just sit, arms draped over the wheel, staring straight ahead. My hands tremble on the rubber, knuckles split and aching. For the first time in a year, I have no idea what happens next. I'm used to the illusion of control—even when it's a lie, it's something to hold onto. Tonight, all I've got is a half-healed wound and the sense that every turn in the spiral is one step closer to the flame.

The passenger door creaks, and Sophie slides in, silent. She slams it hard enough to rattle the window, then sits there, head bowed, hands fisted in her lap. Neither of us talks. Outside, the world is an inferno, blue and orange dancing on the wet blacktop, the ruins of the school burning like it's not just wood and drywall but the whole memory of childhood itself.

She leans forward, elbows on her knees, and the edge of her shirt rides up, showing the scar at her ribs. I want to reach out, to touch it, but I don't.

Instead, she says, voice so thin I almost miss it, "I don't want to be alone tonight."

I swallow. My mouth is dry as cardboard. "You're not."

She looks at me, eyes glossy and wild, then scoots over the console and climbs into my lap like we're seventeen again and the whole world is just parking lots and secrets. She doesn't say anything else—just grabs my jacket, pulls it open, and buries her face in my chest. Her shoulders shake. I think she's crying, but when she lifts her head, there are no tears, just raw, undiluted need.

She kisses me, hard enough to bruise. There's nothing gentle about it. It's a collision, lips and teeth and breath gone jagged, a way to remind both of us that we're not dead yet. Her hands claw at my shoulders, nails digging through the canvas, like if she lets go the whole truck might tumble into the fire.

I kiss her back, harder. My hands find her waist, the curve of her spine, the bare skin at the small of her back that's hot even in the freezing cab. We don't talk. The only sound is the syncopated crash of our hearts, the distant scream of a collapsing beam, and the way she gasps when I bite her lower lip.

She breaks first, pulls back just enough to look me in the eye. "Say it," she whispers, desperate. "Tell me you won't let it happen."

I cradle her face, thumb sweeping the soot from her cheek. "You're mine," I say, and my voice cracks, but I mean it. "I'm not letting you burn."

She sags into me, fingers tangled in my hair, breath coming in little gasps against my ear. I hold her, tight as I dare, and for a second, the chaos outside is just noise, and the spiral, the fire, the end of everything—none of it matters except for the weight of her in my arms.

She pulls at my shirt, unbuttons it with hands that are barely steady. I help her, shrug it off, ignore the flash of pain when the fabric snags my bandage. She runs her palms down my chest, traces the line of the new scar, then dips her head and kisses it, soft and slow. I shiver, not from cold, but from the way it feels to be alive, to have someone see every flaw and still want you.

She grinds down, hips rolling, pressing against the fly of my pants. There's no subtlety—she's desperate, and so am I. I fumble with her jeans, get them open, push them down past her knees. She's wearing nothing underneath. Her skin is slick with sweat, thighs shaking as she settles astride me. The cab is too small, the steering wheel digs into my ribs, but I couldn't care less.

She sinks onto me, slow at first, eyes locked on mine. The heat is overwhelming, the friction perfect. I grip her hips, guiding her, letting her take whatever she needs. She sets the pace—hard, relentless, a rhythm that drowns out everything but the two of us.

Her breath comes in ragged bursts. "Don't let go," she pants.

"Never," I promise, and pull her in, holding her so close I can feel the hammer of her pulse through her chest.

The world shrinks to the cab, the taste of her, the pressure building until I can't hold it. She comes first, trembling, teeth clamped on my shoulder to keep from screaming. I follow, hips jerking, the release so intense I see stars behind my eyes.

For a while, we just stay there, forehead to forehead, our sweat mingling, breath fogging up the glass. Her hair is wild, her mascara streaked, and there's a bloodstain on my sleeve where her nails broke skin. We look like hell. But we're alive.

Outside, the school keeps burning. The spiral waits, black and unbreakable, in the concrete.

She leans back, runs a hand through her hair, and lets out a shaky laugh. "We're not done yet, are we?"

I shake my head. "Not until we finish it."

She nods, then kisses me, this time gentle, almost shy. "Good," she whispers.

We stay in the cab, watching the world burn, until dawn comes and the fire finally dies.

And when we walk out together, I know—whatever comes next, it'll be us at the center.

And we won't let go.

20

Firestorm

Sophie

The house is so quiet it might as well be dead, except for the buzz of my phone and the way every clock in the place ticks half a second out of phase. I sit on the couch, staring at nothing, the heat from the school fire still radiating off my skin even though I've showered twice and changed into the oldest, softest shirt I own. My hands won't quit shaking, so I clamp them around a mug of tea gone cold two hours ago and pretend it helps. The only light in the room is the neon-blue bruise of my phone screen, lighting up again with the same message I've listened to five times now.

The voicemail is exactly thirteen seconds long. It starts with a half-second of static, then the voice—measure, professional, the kind of voice that could lull you to sleep if it wasn't a needle pressed into your neck.

"Sophe. I know you have the files. If you want to save what's left of your father's name, meet me where it all began." A brief pause, a wet click of a tongue against teeth. *No police. No one else. You know where."*

He hangs up without waiting for a reply. I do know where. The words play over and over, each time carving the same groove in my brain: meet me where it all began. The childhood home, burned out and abandoned, still on the edge of town like a rotten tooth that won't fall out. Nobody went there if they could help it, not after what happened. Not after Dad.

My thumb hovers over the delete button, then slides away. I play it again.

The sound of the lock rattling nearly stops my heart. I'm up in an instant, mug clattering to the floor, hand groping for the knife I had grabbed earlier. But it's only Lucas, back from wherever they sent him after the last run. He takes the room with a glance—my posture, the way I'm standing too close to the door, the puddle of tea creeping across the tile. His eyes land on me and hold, blue as burning bleach, sharper than I remember.

He doesn't speak until he's close enough to smell the anxiety off me. "You get a call?"

I nod, then shake my head. "Voicemail."

He takes a slow, deliberate breath, like he's trying to draw the poison out of the air. "Bennett?"

"I think so."

He kneels, wipes up the tea with the hem of his sleeve, and sits back on his haunches. "What did he say?"

I recite it, word for word, apart from the location, even though it makes my tongue feel like a strip of sandpaper.

Lucas listens, jaw flexing. "It's a setup."

"Of course it's a setup," I snap. "He's not even trying to hide it."

He looks away, then back, voice low. "You're not going alone."

I want to say yes, I am. I want to say it so loud the windows rattle. Instead, I clutch my arms around my chest and mutter, "I have to."

He stands, shoulders squared. "Bullshit. You're not disposable."

The words sting, because I can see in his face that he believes it. More than that, I think he's afraid he might lose me again. That's not in the plan, but I have to finish this, and it's the only way.

"It's not about me," I say, softer now. "It's about my dad. He's...I need to clear his name."

Lucas shakes his head, pacing. "You want to clear his name, you outsmart Bennett, not walk into his fucking kill box."

"Don't you think I know that?" My voice cracks. "Don't you think I've thought about every possible way this can go wrong?"

He stops, fists clenched. "Then let me help."

THE PLEA IN HIS VOICE IS WORSE THAN A PUNCH. HE STEPS in close, close enough that I can smell the singed edge of his skin, the soap, the wound still healing on his arm. His hands shake too, not from pain, but from wanting to touch me and not knowing if he's allowed.

"Let me help," he says again, so soft I almost don't hear it.

"I can't," I whisper. "Not this time."

He blinks, like the words physically hit him. Then he sets his jaw, grabs his jacket from the back of the chair, and jams his arms through the sleeves. "Fine. You want to walk into the fire alone, you do it. But I'm not letting you lock the door behind you."

The argument is done. I move before he can change his mind—grab my keys, the burner phone, a flashlight, and bolt for the door. He's at my heels, but I fake left and slam the door in his face, thumb the lock, and run. I hear him cursing, pounding the wood, but I'm already gone.

The night outside is cold enough to burn. I get in the car, turn the key, and let the engine idle. My hands are shaking again, this time so bad I can barely work the stick. In the rearview I see Lucas—on the porch, hair wild, watching me go with a look I have never seen before. Not anger. Not even fear. Just pure, undiluted heartbreak.

I look away, put the car in gear, and drive.

The town is dead at this hour, every street empty except for the yellow haze of streetlamps and the occasional, lonely mailbox standing sentry. I pass the fire station, lights off except for the emergency glow in the dormitory windows. I drive past what's left of the diner, the gas station, the used car lot with its garland of faded pennants fluttering in the wind. Every landmark is a memory, every turn a wound that refuses to heal.

As I hit the edge of town, the houses fall away and the fields stretch out, endless and black. The road to the old house is a ribbon of cracked asphalt, barely wider than the car. I kill the headlights for a second, just to see what darkness feels like. It's absolute—thick and suffocating. I flick them back on, relieved and shamed at once.

Dads memory flows through my mind.

"Never trust the easy answers, Soph," he'd say, voice a growl from too much coffee and not enough sleep. "The world's always one match away from going up, but it's never as simple as who lit it."

I drive faster, the lines of the road blurring. Every second that passes, I'm closer to the place I don't want to be, the place Bennett is waiting.

I slow as I near the turnoff. The mailbox is still there, barely upright, name faded to a memory: GRANT. The driveway is overgrown, grass up to the windows, but I know every pothole by heart. I cut the engine a little bit back from the house and walk the rest, careful, silent, flashlight off. If this is a trap, I want to see it coming, and not have focus only where my beam lands.

The house is like it was when I visited it weeks ago, barely a skeleton. The fire stripped it to bones—charred beams and half a roof, the rest caved in and rotting. The yard is wild, a tangle of weeds and brambles, but in the moonlight I see footprints in the dirt. Fresh ones, big, with the chevron print of a standard-issue police boot, or firefighter boot.

I take a breath, try to steady my hands, and step into the ruins. The living room is just a slab of concrete and a few stubborn nails. It still smells like smoke, years later. I pick my way across the ash, every step a whisper.

I hear him before I see him. A click, like a lighter. The scrape of a shoe on stone.

He's waiting in the center of what used to be the kitchen. Hands folded, head bowed, like he's praying. He's wearing his badge, but it's tucked under his coat, almost like he's ashamed.

"Glad you made it," he says, not looking up.

I stop three paces away, close enough to run, far enough not to get hit. "You called?"

He grins, a razor edge. "You always did like a challenge."

I clench my fists, nails digging into my palm. "You going to tell me why?"

He looks up. His face is older, more wrecked than last time I saw him. The lines at his mouth have turned to scars.

His eyes are black. "You think you're the first kid who wanted to torch the old guard? You think your dad was a saint?"

"He was better than you," I snap

He nods, once. "Maybe. But he got burned anyway."

He takes a step toward me, "Walk with me," he says gesturing for me to walk ahead.

"Why?" I ask.

"Because we have much to discuss."

We walk in silence for minutes toward the woods, the clearing is lit by torches—actual torches, jammed into the ground at perfect intervals, casting light among the trees that come into view and the old beaten down barn at the end of the clearing.

Bennett steps inside the barn, I hesitate, I know this is a trap, but I need to finish this.

As I step in I can see movement: a man pacing, measured, no hurry at all.

I creep closer, boots silent on the mossy ground. That's when I see the barrels. Four of them, bright blue plastic, ringed around the perimeter of the room. Each has. a red diamond and a stenciled word: GASOLINE. The smell is heavy, sharp, already fighting with the scent of old ash and wet rot. Someone's planning a show.

I step into the shell of the old barn, my shadow stretching huge across the broken floor. Bennett stands in the center, arms folded, the same look on his face as every review board he ever chaired: calm, patient, just waiting for the evidence to prove him right.

At his left, half in shadow, is the other man—the one from the train yard, the festival, every nightmare since this started. Caleb Rowe. He's lost weight, maybe a few teeth, but the smile is all wolf.

"Welcome home," Bennett says, voice rolling through the barn like he's giving a Sunday sermon.

I keep my hands loose, eyes moving. "If this is your idea of an apology, it's fucked up."

Caleb's smile cracks wider. He shifts his stance, blocking the only obvious exit.

Bennett laughs, but it's all air. "Apologies are for accidents, Sophie. This—" he gestures around us, "—is destiny."

I scan the barrels, the torchlight the distance between us. "You lured me out here for a bonfire?"

He shakes his head, almost sad. "For closure. Your father chased that until it killed him. He couldn't leave well enough alone."

"Because you were laundering half the town's budget through fake arson jobs?" I snap.

He shrugs, as if I've said the sky is blue. "Nobody cares until the bodies pile up. Even then, they only care for a week." He glances at Rowe, a flicker of something passing between them—respect, or maybe fear.

I edge a step to the right, pretending to study the barrel nearest me. The smell is so strong it makes my eyes water. "You could've just left it alone," I say. "Let the truth die with him."

He steps forward, not close enough to touch, but close enough that I see the blue ring under his thumbnail, and a bite mark on his wrist. "You don't get it. Your dad was about to blow the whole thing. He was going to take it state, maybe federal. If he'd lived, half this town would be unemployed."

"Better than dead."

He tips his head, conceding the point. "Maybe. But you'd have lost more than a job. You'd have lost the illusion. The comfort. The idea that things are under control." He gives a little sigh, almost like he's tired. "I never wanted to hurt you,

Sophie. I've known you since before you could ride a bike. But you're too much like him."

There's a pause, thick enough to choke on. Rowe doesn't move, but I can feel his eyes on me, calculating.

Bennett's voice drops, almost a whisper. "You made it easy, following the breadcrumbs. I knew you'd come."

"Because you needed an audience?" I spit.

He smiles again, and this time it's real. "Because it's the only way you learn. You see the fire, you run toward it, every time. Like father, like daughter."

He reaches into his pocket, slow, and pulls out a matchbook. It's the kind they give away at bars—cheap, logo faded. He flicks a match, and the flare is tiny but blinding in the dim light. He holds it up, studies it, then lets the sulfur burn down to his fingers before shaking it out.

"Don't do this," I say, hating the tremor in my voice.

He shrugs again. "It's already done. You just get to decide if you walk away, or if you finish the job your father started."

Another match. This time, he doesn't shake it out. He touches it to the rim of the nearest barrel. The flame crawls up the plastic, slow and hungry, then races down a line of gas-soaked rope I didn't even see until now.

Everything happens at once. Rowe lunges for me, but I'm faster, I kick the barrel with everything I have, sending it rolling into the center of the space. The fire leaps, catches on the old beams and explodes into a bloom of orange.

Bennett stands in the middle, arms wide, lit from below like some fallen angel. "You're the only one who can stop it now," he shouts over the roar.

Rowe tries to grab me, but the heat is already unbearable. I duck, roll, and make for the window. The wood splinters under my weight, but I tumble through and hit the ground, and run.

Behind me, the barn is an inferno. The barrels are popping,

sending jets of blue and white into the sky. For a second, I see Bennett framed in the doorway, arms still wide, fire crawling up his sleeves.

I run until my lungs are glass, until the only sound is the blood in my ears.

At the edge of the clearing, I collapse. The light from the burning barn pulses against the clouds, turning the whole world the color of warning.

I don't know if he meant for me to get out. I don't know if it matters.

But I do know this: some fires you don't put out. You just survive them.

I watch the barn burn, and when I finally stand, I'm stronger than I was before. I move into the wreck of the old house and watch from between the gaps of the broken frame.

But I didn't see the other barrels. Two more in the skeleton of the old house suddenly explode. The floor of the old house is a blackmouth pit now, flame pouring from every surface. The barrels explode one after another, each time shoving a wall of heat against my skin. I duck behind a slab of what used to be the kitchen counter, coughing until my ribs ache.

The fire is so hot it eats the sound. My ears ring with a high whine, the roar of the house collapsing into itself like a dying sun. I make it halfway across the yard before my lungs clamp shut. The air is all chemical, the taste of burning childhood and old gasoline crawling down my throat.

Then I hear it: someone yelling my name, sharp and raw enough to punch through the sirens in my head.

I whip around, just as Lucas barrels into the clearing. He's a wreck—shirt half-burned, blood spattered down his arm, a gun in one hand and his face wild with fear. He sees me and nearly breaks his ankle leaping a burning beam. "SOPHIE!" he howls.

Bennett and Rowe have vanished into the dark. Lucas ignore both, eyes locked on me, and runs straight through the smoke like nothing else matters.

Lucas finds me, he drops to his knees, grabs my face with hands so rough they scrape the dirt off my cheeks. He's shouting but I can't hear the words. His mouth is on my hairline, my ear, my jaw. His fingers jam into my armpits and yank me up so hard my teeth snap together.

"Can you run?" he shouts, voice shredded.

I nod. "I think so."

He doesn't wait, just slams the gun into his belt, grabs my hand, and drags me through the debris. We duck, roll, crawl over broken tile and under timber that spits sparks into my eyes. My boots melt to the floorboards in places. The world narrows to the three feet of air in front of my face and Lucas's hand locked around mine.

A piece of ceiling comes down, nearly takes Lucas's head off. He shoves me sideways, takes the brunt on his shoulder, and doesn't even slow. I see the blood bloom on his shirt, but he's still moving.

We're almost out when my foot snags on a burning plank and I go down, palms first into the ash. I scream—not in fear, but in rage. I will not die in this fucking house, not when I serviced it once already. Lucas drops beside me, hooks his arm under my ribs, and hauls me up. I can smell his sweat, the panic on his skin, the animal need to keep me alive.

We round the last corner and hit the doorframe just as the beams of what was left of the roof give way. The collapse is total, a tidal wave of flame and splinters. For one second, we're trapped, the exit blocked by a wall of burning wood.

Lucas looks at me, wild-eyed. "Jump!" he yells, and I don't think—I just grab his arm, leap, and let the world catch up.

He tackles me through the gap. The fire licks at my back, grabs my hair, but then we're rolling on wet grass, choking and screaming and coughing out the taste of death. The house crashes behind us, a monster finally slayed.

For a long minute we just lay there, limbs tangled, staring up at the boiling black sky. My mouth is full of dirt, my hands full of Lucas's shirt. His chest hitches under my cheek, air tearing in and out, but he doesn't let go.

When I finally look up, his face is so close I can count the flecks of soot in his eyelashes.

He tries to speak. Fails. Tries again.

"You're insane," he rasps, and then his mouth finds mine.

The kiss is not gentle. It's desperate, teeth and tongue and the wild gasping need to be sure the other is real. His hands tangle in my hair, tug me closer, and I taste blood, sweat, fire. I want to crawl inside him and never let the world touch us again.

He pulls back, foreheads smashed together, both of us panting. "Are you hurt?" he asks, searching my face.

"No," I say, and it's true. My shirt is burned, my knees are raw, but I am fine.

"Bennet and Rowe got away," I say softly.

He cradles my jaw, thumb gentle now, tracing the line of my cheek. "Don't you ever do that again," he says. The words are rough but the touch is soft, the softest thing I've ever felt.

I laugh, or maybe sob, because there's no room for pride anymore. "Only if you're there to drag me out."

He stares at me — I'm unsure if it's adrenaline or my desire for him. I grab his shirt, pull him close, and press my lips to his. We break apart, and he smiles, gently brushing the hair from my face.

He kisses my eyelids, gentle, like a benediction. "You did it," he whispers.

"We did," I say, voice gone.

He holds me, tight, as the ruins of my old life burn to the ground.

In the morning, there will be questions. Pain. Maybe even consequences.

But for tonight, there's only us, the heat, the promise of something better.

I lay my head on his chest, close my eyes, and for the first time since this started, I'm not afraid.

Let the world burn.

We survived.

21

Scorched Earth

Sophie

The fire marshal's office has that post-disaster stink of burnt coffee, fluorescent light, and air that's been recycled through the lungs of too many tired men. I sit in the visitor's chair, hands folded in my lap, forearms dusted with fresh scabs and yesterday's smoke. Across the desk, the marshal himself—Reinhold, according to the nameplate and the looming set of his shoulders—taps a pencil against a notepad. There's a digital recorder, too, pointed straight at my face like a tiny, red-eyed accusation.

Lucas stands in the corner, arms crossed, whole body humming with the kind of energy that means he's barely holding back from pacing a trench in the linoleum. He's showered, technically, but there's a line of dried blood at his hairline and the start of a new bruise blooming along his jaw. His shirt is too clean for the hour; he must have borrowed it from the station's lost and found.

The clock on the wall says it's just past dawn, but time here feels dislocated—like the sun might never rise, or it already has and nobody told us.

The interview starts like they always do: date, time, spelling of my name. He offers water, which I take, and the first sip scours my throat raw.

"Walk me through the events of last night," Reinhold says, flipping to a blank page.

I do. I start with the message, the drive to the ruins, the way Bennett set the scene and waited for me in the wreckage. I keep my tone even, no drama, just the facts, the way Dad taught me: evidence first, feelings after.

Reinhold interrupts only to ask for clarification. "You're certain it was Troy Bennett who started the fire?"

"Yes," I say. "He used a matchbook. He told me exactly what he was going to do. Then he did it."

"And you didn't attempt to restrain him?"

I meet his gaze, dead-on. "He had a partner. Caleb Rowe. I was outnumbered. And unarmed."

Lucas shifts, the floor creaking under his boots.

Reinhold scribbles, his pen scratching louder than my heartbeat. "You say you escaped through the barn window. How did you avoid injury?"

"I didn't." I show him my palms, still red and blistered from the fall. "But I was trained to evacuate. My father made sure of it. And my time as a volunteer firefighter helped too."

Reinhold's eyes flick to the bandages, then back to my face. There's no sympathy, just assessment.

"Did Bennett threaten you directly?" he asks.

"Every word out of his mouth was a threat." My own voice is almost gone, smoke-rasped and low, but I won't let it shake. "He told me it was the only way I'd learn. That I was 'too much like my father.'"

Lucas pushes off the wall. "It's true," he says, tone flat and dangerous. "She's not exaggerating. I saw them both. Bennett and Rowe."

Reinhold raises a hand, the gesture neither polite nor dismissive—just a pause, like he's tuning out a static channel. "I'd like to hear from Ms. Grant first."

Lucas clenches his jaw, but steps back.

I finish the story. I describe the explosion of the barrels, the wall of fire, the crawl out over broken beams. I leave out the part where Lucas found me, held me, where we clung to each other like animals under siege. Nobody needs to hear that.

When I'm done, Reinhold shuts off the recorder with a click. He sits for a moment, staring at the heap of papers and evidence bags on his desk. There are photos, too—shiny print-outs of the crime scene, the spiral burned into the floor, the scorched plastic barrels. My house is a black-and-white ghost, stripped of color and dignity.

"Thank you, Ms. Grant," he says, voice softer. "You've been very forthcoming."

He gathers his papers, stacking them with military precision. "I need to make you aware of a counterclaim," he says, almost as an afterthought. "Mr. Bennett's attorney has already contacted my office. He alleges that you initiated the fire. That you staged the event to frame him."

For a second, I can't process the words. It's not surprise—I knew this would happen—but the way he says it, so matter-of-fact, like he's reading a weather report. I grip the edge of my chair, knuckles going white.

Lucas is at my side before I can speak, his palm a furnace on my shoulder. "You have got to be kidding," he snarls, voice a thread away from breaking. "You think she torched her own family home just to—what, ruin Bennett's reputation?"

Reinhold doesn't blink. "It's not my role to decide. My role is to document all statements."

I take a deep breath, letting the accusation settle, fill the air, then burn itself out.

"Of course he'd say that," I say. "He's been covering his own arson for years. If you check the incident logs—my father kept records, detailed ones—you'll see the pattern. Every fire, every suspicious payout, every time Bennett was on shift."

Reinhold flips a sheet, scans it. "We've begun reviewing the archives. But as you know, the burden of proof—"

"Is on me," I finish for him. "Story of my life."

He pushes the recorder and his notes to the center of the desk. "I'll need you to stay available for follow-up. And I would advise you to keep your distance from Mr. Bennett or any of his associates."

"Don't worry," I say. "I don't plan on starting any more fires."

He almost smiles. "Good. You're free to go."

I stand, knees stiff, and for the first time I realize I still have ash on my face. It's worked itself into the lines around my mouth, smeared across my cheekbone. I wipe at it with the back of my hand, but the gesture feels childish, like trying to erase a scar.

Lucas shadows me to the door, not touching but close enough that his heat presses through the space between us. In the hallway, he stops and leans in, voice low.

"You okay?"

I want to say yes. I want to say I don't care what they think. Instead, I let myself sag against the wall, just for a second, and close my eyes.

"I'm tired," I admit. "But I'm not done."

He smiles, the bruised side of his mouth curling up. "Didn't think so."

We head out into the gray light together, neither of us sure what comes next.

THE SIDEWALK IN FRONT OF THE FIRE MARSHAL'S OFFICE IS still slick from the night's drizzle, but already the world is resetting itself. Delivery vans trundle down Main, leaving trails of exhaust and the promise of another ordinary day. The only trace of what happened last night is the faint whiff of smoke lingering in the gutters, and the two of us—me and Lucas—moving slow, like we're afraid the pavement might open up and swallow us whole.

We don't talk. The silence between us is a comfort, but the world outside is anything but. Every window we pass has eyes in it. The hardware store, where Dad used to buy bulk nails and chat with the old guy behind the counter; the bakery, with its gold-lettered door and the first batch of cinnamon rolls stacked in the case. People see us coming and either look away or stare too long, their expressions flicking between curiosity, pity, and something close to contempt.

We round the corner by the library and the hush follows us —conversations stalling out, only to resume in whispers once we're past. I hear my name, the word "arson," and then, distantly: "She's always been like that, you know. Her whole family." There's a laughter at the end, brittle as ice.

Lucas keeps his head up, but his hand hovers near my back, ready to catch me if I stumble. I can see the bruise on his jaw turning a sick yellow, and the way his wrist is wrapped tight in fresh gauze. We look like escapees from a disaster movie, dropped into the middle of perfect suburbia.

At the grocery store, we stop to grab something cold—neither of us has eaten since before the fire. I move for the dairy case, reach in, and catch a reflection in the glass: hair wild, eyes red, streaks of ash still on my neck. Behind me, the cashier, a guy from high school I barely remember, blinks like he's seen a ghost.

"Didn't think you'd come back here," he says, not unkind but not friendly, either.

"I live here," I say, more to myself than to him.

Lucas tosses a bottle of water onto the counter, the thunk louder than necessary. "You got a problem?" he asks, every syllable loaded.

The cashier shrugs. "Town's been talking, that's all."

I want to say I don't care, that I'm used to it, but it sticks in my throat. Instead, I pay, take my change, and walk out into the glare of the morning sun. I can feel eyes tracking us from every angle, people rehearsing the story, deciding where they stand.

Outside, a woman in a pink windbreaker hustles her toddler away from the bench, glancing at us as if we might combust on the spot. Across the street, Mrs. Larsen—my babysitter from when I was six, who used to make the world's worst grilled cheese—crosses to the far curb, not even pretending it's a coincidence.

I grip the bottle so hard it almost bursts. "It's like a contest," I say, "to see who can believe the worst of me the fastest."

Lucas snorts. "Small towns love a villain."

"Then they're going to love what happens next," I say, and though my hands are shaking, the words steady me.

We keep walking, step by step, past the post office, the barbershop, the edge of the park. People watch. People talk. I let them.

Because the more they talk, the more I know I'm still here.

And this time, I'm not backing down.

Lucas's place is a time capsule of his worst habits: stacks of backdated firefighter magazines, laundry piles of uncertain age, and a kitchen counter sticky with forgotten coffee. There's still yellow police tape folded neatly by the front door, as if he's not sure whether to hang it up or burn it in the grill. I let myself in, trailing ash and humiliation, and land at the dining table with the graceless flop of someone whose entire nervous system is in protest mode.

He lingers in the doorway, eyes scanning the street, then double-locks the deadbolt and stands in the entryway, not moving. I can feel him wanting to talk, but neither of us starts.

Finally, he cracks. "You should leave," he says, not looking at me.

I don't answer, so he says it again, voice harder. "You need to get out of town. At least until this blows over."

I snap the plastic on my water bottle, twisting the cap until it nearly strips. "I just spent all night proving I'm not afraid of Bennett or anyone else in this shithole. You think I'm going to hide in a motel for the rest of my life?"

Lucas steps forward, the old fireman's bravado flickering behind his exhaustion. "You don't get it, Sophie. They're not going to stop. Not after what happened last night."

I bite back a laugh. "That's the point, Lucas. They want me gone. They want to scare me into running. But I'm not running this time. I'm not a victim anymore—" I look him dead in the eye— "I'm fireproof now."

He circles the living room, restless, hands on his hips. "You're not made of stone, Soph. I saw you after the call this morning. You looked like you were about to collapse."

I stand up, water bottle in one hand, and follow him. "So what? You want me to just vanish and let them finish the story? Let them say I started the fire, that my dad was a fraud and a coward, that I'm just the next in a line of—" I clamp my jaw shut, afraid my voice will crack on the word.

He reaches for me, then stops himself, palms open and trembling. "It's not just about you. If something happened—if you got hurt—" He swallows, hard. "I couldn't take it. Not again."

The way he says it, all the air gets sucked out of the room.

"I'm not your responsibility," I say, softer now. "I never was."

He looks at me, really looks, and for the first time I see the cracks in his armor. The way his lips tremble, the way his eyes can't quite hold mine.

"Then why can't I stop thinking about you?" he asks, barely above a whisper.

I set the bottle down, slow, like I'm defusing a bomb. "Because you love me," I say, the truth landing between us like a live wire.

He pauses, but doesn't look away. "I don't know how to fix any of this," he says. "I can't protect you from the town, or from Bennett, or from—" He stops, shaking his head. "All I know is, when I saw you walk into that fire, I knew I'd do anything to keep you breathing."

He sits, hands pressed to his eyes, voice muffled. "It's not fair to ask you to stay. It's not fair to ask you to leave, either. But I'm fucking terrified, Sophie. I'm terrified of losing you."

I sit, too, our knees barely touching under the battered Formica. "You don't have to save me," I say. "But you can stand with me, if you want."

He looks up, the wet in his eyes catching the light. "I do," he says, voice steady now. "God, I do."

We don't move, both of us frozen, the house so quiet I can hear my own pulse. Then, suddenly, Lucas gets up, circles the table in two long strides, and pulls me to my feet.

He kisses me, hard. It's not sweet, not the way I remembered. It's desperate, almost angry, like he's trying to pour every ounce of fear and hope and apology into my mouth. I bite back, push him against the fridge, and feel the thud of his heartbeat through my ribs.

His hands are rough on my arms, on my back, on the base of my skull. He smells like old smoke and fresh sweat. My fingers tangle in his shirt, then underneath it, finding skin—hot and alive and scarred from a lifetime of fires he couldn't always win.

When we finally break apart, breathless, our foreheads pressed together, he says, "You're impossible."

I grin, lips swollen. "You love that about me."

He laughs, the tension draining out. "Yeah," he says, "I really do."

We stand there, arms locked, chests heaving, for a long time.

For the first time, I believe we might just make it through.

Not as hero and rescuee.

But as survivors.

Together.

We move around each other in the tight orbit of the house for hours, keeping to opposite corners—me at the window, pretending to read, Lucas in the kitchen cleaning something that never needed cleaning in the first place. There's a charge in the air, an aftershock that's both relief and the uneasy sense of waiting for the next alarm. Every so often our eyes meet, and each time it's like striking flint.

When the sun dips behind the neighbors' roofline and the house cools from oven to tomb, I take my cue. I find him in the living room, standing by the picture window, arms folded across his chest like he's bracing for impact.

I approach from behind, slow and deliberate. My palm finds his back—a gentle touch, but there's nothing accidental about it. I follow the curve of his spine, the hard knots of muscle still jumpy from the day, and rest my cheek between his shoulder blades.

He shudders, and I feel it travel through both of us.

"No more fear," I whisper, the words lost in his shirt.

He turns, and for a long beat, neither of us says anything. There's just the sound of the old fridge kicking on, the creak of his hand as he cups the side of my face.

"Promise?" he asks.

I nod, then guide his fingers to my mouth, pressing a kiss to his knuckles. "Promise."

We move together, slow at first, like we're afraid to spook the moment. I hook my hands into the hem of his shirt, and he lets me lift it over his head, revealing a mess of scars and new bruises. I map the surface, running my nails lightly over the landscape, feeling him twitch and tense at each unfamiliar touch.

He backs me toward the bedroom, steps careful, always watching my face for some hidden pain. When he unbuttons my jeans, he does it one-handed, the other cradling my waist so I don't tip over. When he strips away the last of my shirt, he stops to study the bruises blooming under my collarbone, the place where last night's smoke painted a dark half-moon.

He traces the bruise with his thumb, reverent, almost apologetic. "Does it hurt?"

"Only when I laugh," I say, and then I do.

He laughs, too, and the sound is raw and beautiful. "God, I missed you."

I slide my hands down his back, feeling the shudder return, then pull him in so our hips align, our breath mingles. He presses his forehead to mine and whispers, "Are you sure?"

"Stop asking," I say. "Start doing."

He does. He kisses me, softer than before, letting it build until it's less about claiming and more about belonging. We collapse onto the bed, a tangle of limbs, and for the first time, I don't care how I look or if the window's open or if the whole damn town is talking. His hands are careful with my ribs, but everywhere else he holds nothing back. When he runs his tongue over the scar on my side, I arch into him, hungry for the heat.

There's an urgency, yes, but also a strange new patience—like we're both determined to catalog every inch, every reaction. He doesn't just move inside me; he lingers, cataloging every gasp, every stuttered "yes, there, please." I let him see me—sweat, spit, need, the whole messy truth of what it means to want someone so much it terrifies you.

When he comes, it's with a groan that sounds like surrender. When I come, it's his name I say, over and over, until my throat goes hoarse again.

We stay knotted together, breathless and shaking, for a long time. He buries his nose in my hair, and I listen to his pulse hammer against my cheek.

"You're really not afraid?" he asks, voice small in the dark.

"Not as long as you're here," I say, and mean it.

He laughs again, softer. "God, you're a pain in the ass."

"Fireproof," I remind him.

We fall asleep like that, skin-to-skin, the world for once too small to keep us apart.

And when I wake, sunlight spilling over us, I know: if

there's a next time, if the fire comes for us again, we'll face it the only way we know how.

The sun crawls across the bedroom ceiling in thin, trembling lines, like it's afraid to wake us too soon. I shift under the covers, half tangled around Lucas's thigh, and let the heat from his body anchor me to the moment. For the first time in weeks, I slept without dreaming—no flames in the hallways, no voices in the walls, just the low, steady cadence of his breath against the hollow of my neck.

He wakes before I do, his hand tracing lazy shapes over my hip. I pretend to be asleep for a while longer, soaking in the hush and the comfort, until he plants a kiss on my shoulder and says, "Your hair's on fire."

I open my eyes, and he grins, running his fingers through the static-charged mess. "Seriously," he says. "I might have to call it in."

"Don't you dare," I say, rolling onto my back and stretching until every muscle pops. "Last thing I need is half the crew showing up to see me in your bed."

He laughs, the sound still a little surprised, like he can't quite believe we're both here and alive. "They'd be more interested in the evidence wall you've started in my kitchen."

I sit up, dragging the sheet with me. "It's not a wall, it's a 'visual organization system.'"

He snorts, then climbs out of bed and heads for the bathroom, naked and unashamed. I watch the way his shoulders flex, the fading scars from last year's three-alarm on Clark

Street, the fresh bruise from last night's brawl with a collapsing ceiling. I want to follow, but I make myself wait, savoring the stretch of quiet before the world starts demanding things of us again.

By the time I make it to the kitchen, Lucas has already made coffee and laid out a highlighter-colored battle plan on the table. Every fire in the last six months—dot, circle, cross—connected by red string and his own spiderweb of tactical notes.

"You sleep okay?" he asks, not looking up from the map.

"Better than I have in years," I say, which is only partly a lie. "You?"

He shrugs. "Hard to turn off the alarms. Even harder to wake up and realize you're actually here."

I pour coffee for both of us, then take a seat, pulling my knees up to my chest. "We need a new strategy," I say, scanning the map. "Bennett's playing defense now. He'll be looking to discredit every move we make."

Lucas slides a folder my way, the edges scorched at one corner. "I've been thinking about that. You know the training barn on County Line? It's next up in the spiral. If Rowe's still in town, he'll try to hit it by the weekend."

I flip open the folder. "You think you can predict him?"

He nods, rubbing at his jaw. "He's not as smart as he thinks he is. He follows orders, even if he doesn't get the why. Bennett was the architect. Rowe's just the spark."

I chew this over, tracing a line from our house to the training barn with my finger. "So we let him think he's got the jump. Let him make the first move, then catch him in the act."

Lucas looks at me, approval in his eyes. "Exactly."

We just sit there, the silence filled with the drip of the coffee pot and the faint static of the police scanner Lucas keeps tuned low in the background. It's almost domestic, almost normal, except for the way my hand shakes when I reach for the pen, and the way he watches, always ready to catch me if I drop it.

"I want to clear my name," I say, finally. "But I want to end this more."

Lucas reaches across the table and covers my hand with his, thumb stroking the scar on my wrist. "We will. This time, we're not alone."

I squeeze back, and for a second, the fear falls away.

We spend the morning prepping—photocopying evidence, mapping out entry points, planning backup contingencies for if (when) the fire marshal decides to drop by unannounced. Lucas is relentless in his logic, but leaves the final decisions to me. Every step, every argument, is a negotiation—my caution against his experience, his muscle against my stubborn will.

At noon, the police scanner clicks to life. There's a crackle, then the dispatcher's voice: "Possible 11-79, warehouse fire at Municipal and 7th. Units respond."

I feel the blood leave my face. "Lucas, I put Dad's notebooks in the old records room, I figured they'd be safer there than with us."

Lucas is already up, grabbing his turnout jacket and tossing me mine. "Let's go," he says.

We hit the street running, two steps ahead of the rest of the world. By the time we reach the end of the block, the column of smoke is already visible, black and ugly against the blue of a perfect spring sky.

We don't speak until we're in the truck, engine running, sirens a distant chorus.

"You think it's him?" I ask.

Lucas nods, gaze fixed on the growing plume. "It's always him."

I close my eyes, force myself to breathe. "Then let's catch him."

We floor it, the engine howling, and race toward the fire.

When the warehouse comes into view, there are already half a dozen onlookers, their phones out, faces painted with the lurid delight of tragedy unfolding live. Lucas parks at the edge of the caution tape and we bail out, running for the command tent.

Inside, the new fire chief is a kid I remember from high school—barely old enough to shave, but already more respected than I'll ever be. He clocks us, then nods toward the wall of smoke. "Started in the loading dock, spread fast. No injuries yet, but the whole building's going."

Lucas surveys the scene, then leans in. "Any sign of accelerant?"

The chief's face says yes before he does. "We found traces on the back door. Same stuff as the last few."

I move to the edge of the cordon, scanning for anything—anyone—out of place. There, by the access road, a figure in a dark jacket, hands buried deep in pockets. Watching the flames with an expression that's all calculation.

"Rowe," I say, pointing.

Lucas follows my gaze, jaw set.

"He's not going anywhere," he says.

We stand side by side, watching the warehouse burn. My hand finds his, and this time it's me who interlocks our fingers, squeezing until I'm sure he feels it.

"They'll never believe us until we have him in cuffs," I say.

Lucas shrugs. "So we'll do it. Even if we have to drag him out ourselves."

I watch the smoke, thick and endless, curling against the sun. "You ready?"

He looks at me, eyes bright. "With you? Always."

The camera crews arrive, then. Someone shoves a mic in my face, and for once I don't flinch.

"We're not stopping," I say, voice strong. "Not until the truth is out."

Lucas grins, proud and fierce beside me.

And when the world burns again, we'll be the ones to walk through the flames.

22

Backdraft

Sophie

THE WAREHOUSE IS THREE BLOCKS OF MISERY AND BROKEN glass, the old brick walls weeping black trails where the windows used to be. By the time Lucas and I get there, the worst of the fire is out, but the sky above still pulses with that weird, living orange, like the horizons been infected. The closer we get, the thicker the air, smoke, yes, but also this ugly, metallic taste, the ghost of scorched wires and burning history.

We park by the old loading dock, right up against the cordon tape. The other units are already packing up, most of the firefighters milling around with their helmets off, steam rising from the shoulders of their gear. One guy nods at Lucas, but nobody stops us. I think they all know whose fire this is, and they're grateful to leave it alone.

I duck under the tape, heart in my throat, and head straight fro the side door where the lock has been popped off like a beer cap. My boots crunch in the char, every step sending up little puffs of black dust. Inside, the warehouse is a cathedral of ruin —steel beams glowing with residual heat, the air as thick as wet wool. It's not just the fire that's done the damage; it's the water and the boots and the axes, the total indifference to anything not bolted down.

I go for the back wall, where I know the records room is—or was. The door is a skeleton, hinges warped so bad it doesn't even pretend to close. I push through, breathing shallow, eyes scanning the racks for the one thing that might have survived.

What's left of the records is a black soup, layer upon layer of paper fusing into an unreadable slab. There are melted plastic bins, the kind Dad used to hoard for secure storage, now shrunk to puckered hunks of slag. I see the color-coded labels—yellow for incident reports, blue for evidence, red for pending investigation—all gone now, the rainbow pallete rendered uniform by heat and smoke.

I drop to my knees and start digging, ignoring the way the soot claws at my throat. Lucas catches up, his shadow filling the doorway. "Careful," he says, but I'm already elbow-deep in ash. My gloves do nothing; the stuff seeps through blackening my wrists, my fingertips.

I find the safe—a cheap metal cabinet, the kind Dad thought was uncrackable. The fire's gotten to it, but the lock is still stubborn, warped but clinging ot its last illusion of purpose. I brace my foot against the frame and yank with both hands, the skin of my palms screaming in protest.

It gives with a sick pop. The door swings open, and for a second I hope—God, I hope—but there's nothing inside but a mess of half melted folders and a single, burned-out spiral notebook.

I know it before I even touch it, but I reach in anyway, hands trembling. The cover is half gone, the edge of the coil fused to the metal shelf. I pull, and the pages crumble between my fingers, leaving a smear of black on my thumb.

I sit there, numb, with the ruins of Dad's journal in my lap.

Lucas kneels beside me, one hand heavy and real on my shoulder. He doesn't say anything. He just lets his presence fill the space, a counterweight to the emptiness crawling up my spine.

"You okay?" he asks, after a minute.

I want to say yes, but my mouth won't move. I just stare at the ashes, watching them sift through my hands.

A voice from the hall: "You folks aren't supposed to be in here." It's the fire marshal, a guy with a beard like an oil spill and a clipboard bristling with forms. He doesn't look made, just tired.

"Official business," Lucas says, voice clipped. "We're looking for evidence."

The marshal shrugs, steps inside, and surveys the carnage. "Whatever was here is gone," he says. "Fire burned hot, fast. Looks like an accelerant job. Professional."

He's talking to Lucas, but his eyes keep flicking to me. "Was this your—" He gestures at the notebook, then at my face.

I nod.

He sighs, sympathy brief and clinical. "Sorry. If there's anything left, we'll find it. But between the fire and the water —" He spreads his hands, as if the physics of destruction are somehow a comfort.

Lucas stands and brushes off his knees. "Did you pull any security footage?"

The marshal shakes his head. "Cameras went down first. But we found canisters out back, brand-new, not a drop left. Whoever did this knew the layout. Knew what to hit."

I can't stop staring at the ruined pages. Dad's handwriting is just a memory now, the careful notes reduced to a smear of carbon. For a second, the world tunnels down to that one point, a single black knot in the pit of my stomach.

I don't realize I'm crying until the soot runs in dark streaks down my wrist.

Lucas crouches again, closer this time. He puts both hands on my shoulders, grounding me. "We'll figure it out," he says. "We always do."

I want to believe him, but right now all I can feel is the weight of everything I just lost.

The fire marshal clears his throat. "If you need a moment —" He leaves the room, closing what's left of the door behind him.

We're alone. The heat is gone, but the air is still thick, every breath a fight.

I let the notebook fall, watch it break apart on the floor. Lucas helps me up, his grip steady. He brushes the ash from my face, careful, almost tender.

"Hey," he says, voice low. "You're not alone in this."

I nod, still not trusting my voice. My hands are shaking so bad I have to tuck them into my jacket.

We make our way back out, the noise of the mop-up crews growing louder as we get closer to the exit. Outside, the sunlight is too bright, the world too normal. I blink, trying to adjust.

The evidence is gone. Dad's story, gone. Every trace of what he tried to build—torched, drowned, scrubbed from existence.

For a second, I feel like giving up.

Then, out of nowhere, a memory slams into me—Dad, hunched over his desk, copying something onto a tiny flash drive, then grinning at me like it was a secret only we would ever share.

"Wait," I say, stopping short. "There might be another copy."

Lucas looks at me, hopeful for the first time all day. "Where?"

I think, sifting through the layers of memory, searching for the anchor point. "My mom's house. The jewelry box. If he backed it up, that's where it'd be."

Lucas grins, and the tension in his jaw softens. "Then let's go, we could get there in about four hours if we leave now."

"No, let's leave in the morning, early." I smile, finally feeling some hope.

We leave the scene behind, the taste of ash still clinging to the back of my throat.

Maybe all isn't lost.

Maybe there's still a way to burn this whole story back into the light.

For a long time during the drive to my mother's, the drive is silent, except for the low whine of the defroster fighting to clear the windshield. The world outside is dull and half-frozen, every lawn still rimmed in ash from the warehouse fire. I keep my eyes locked on the road, hands at ten and two, like if I let go for even a second, everything will spin out and we'll end up in a ditch.

Lucas doesn't say anything, just sits there with his chin propped on one bruised knuckle, staring at the blank space where the dashboard clock used to be. At some point, he reaches over and rests a hand on my thigh—no squeeze, no pressure, just a quiet reminder that I'm not alone, and I love him for it.

We pull into my mom's place around noon. She's at work, as always, but the porch light's still on. The house hasn't changed in years: vinyl siding, faded garden flags, the same chipped mailbox that's been threatening to fall for as long as I can remember. I unlock the door, and the smell of dryer sheets and old wood hits me like a memory.

Inside, the place is a hoarder's paradise. Every flat surface is covered in something—family photos, commemorative spoons, the ceramic angel collection that Dad used to call her "heavenly infantry." I head straight for the closet in the master bedroom, barely noticing the dust that puffs up around every step.

The jewelry box is right where I left it, buried behind a pile of winter coats and two deflated yoga balls. It's heavier than it looks: lacquered wood, inlaid with mother-of-pearl, the lock busted from when I tried to force it open as a kid. I set it on the bed and pop the lid. Inside, chaos—tangled gold chains, faux-diamond tennis bracelets, a snarl of cheap plastic beads.

I dig in, fingers moving fast, sorting through the mess with the practiced aggression of someone who's had to look for things her whole life. I can feel Lucas hovering in the doorway, hands shoved in his pockets, eyes locked on my every move.

Necklaces go flying, one after another. A set of earrings drops to the carpet, tiny blue stones scattering. I ignore it all, focused on the bottom layer. That's where the keepsakes are—the real ones. The high school class ring, the bronze pin from Dad's first firehouse, and finally, the charm bracelet.

It's just as I remember it: tarnished silver, the chain kinked where I used to twist it in my fingers during boring math class. But the charm is what matters—a perfect little fire truck, wheels and hose and all, polished to a mirror shine.

I hold it up to the light, and for a second, I can almost see Dad's face the night he gave it to me. He was exhausted, dark circles etched so deep they looked tattooed, but he smiled anyway. "For when you need to remember you're tougher than you think," he'd said.

I snap out of it. Lucas moves in closer, silent but attentive.

"Watch this," I say, and work my fingernail into the undercarriage of the charm. It takes a minute—the thing's tight as a bank vault—but then the clasp pops open, revealing a tiny, silver cylinder no longer than a pencil eraser.

Lucas blinks. "Is that—?"

"USB drive," I say, voice shaking a little. "Dad always thought he was a spy."

Lucas grins, relief visible in the slack of his shoulders. "Smart man."

I thread the chain over my head and lead the way to the kitchen table. I pull my laptop out of my bag and open it up. The drive clicks into the port with a satisfying thunk. A heartbeat later, the folder opens: DAD_ARCHIVE. There are hundreds of files, each labeled with various titles.

Scanned reports, PDF after PDF. Photos—crime scenes, burn patterns, close-ups of chemical residue. And video files, the names cryptic but familiar: "SPIRAL_FINAL," "BENNETT_CALL," "ROWECONFESSION."

I scroll through, hands still shaking. Lucas is so close I can feel the heat from his arm, the way he leans in to see the screen. His shoulder brushes mine, grounding me, steadying my hands.

For a second, we just sit there, staring at the digital mountain Dad built out of paranoia and desperate hope.

I let out a breath I didn't know I'd been holding. "We've got everything."

Lucas doesn't say anything, just pulls me into a sideways hug, his arm heavy and warm across my shoulders. He presses his cheek to the top of my head, and for a moment, the world tilts back into focus.

We drive the two hundred and forty miles back to Lucas's and take everything inside.

"Let's get to work," he says, and I nod, blinking away the sting in my eyes.

We spend the next hour opening files, piecing together the story Dad never got to tell. Every document is a blow—proof of how deep the rot goes, how long Bennett and his crew have been burning this town to keep themselves warm. Each new video is a gut-punch, but with every click, the picture gets clearer.

We're still scrolling when the afternoon light goes gold across the kitchen floor, still glued to the screen, hands intertwined beneath the edge of the table.

This time, nothing's getting lost in the fire.

This time, we're the ones with the matches.

By the time we finish the first pass through the files, my head is a haze of numbers and names, the only constants the words "FIRE REPORT" and the dates, always the dates, the slow spiral of years tightening around my family and this fucked-up town.

Lucas takes over the laptop, scrolling with a focus I haven't seen in months. His jaw ticks every time he finds a duplicate entry, a misplaced decimal, a payment rerouted through the shell accounts that Dad had color-coded in three shades of highlighter. He's relentless, barely pausing for water, his hand never straying far from my own.

I go for the video files. Most are simple: Dad's own face, sleepless and unshaved, reciting summaries of the paperwork in a monotone that's more exhausted than scared. But a few are different. The timestamp jumps, and there's a second figure—sometimes a shadow, sometimes a voice off-camera. I crank the volume, straining for any clue.

The third video is the one that lands the first real hit. Dad's sitting in the kitchen, the old clock ticking in the background, a legal pad in front of him. "If something happens," he says, voice raw, "you need to know that this is bigger than a city scam. They're using the fires to erase people. To bury what they did." He glances off-camera, like he's afraid someone's listening. "Start with the adoption records. That's where it all starts."

I freeze, finger hovering over the trackpad.

Lucas looks up, blinking. "What?"

I rewind, replay. "Start with the adoption records," Dad says again.

Lucas sets down his mug and leans in, so close I can smell the stale coffee on his breath. "You think he means Bennett?"

I shake my head. "No. He's talking about Rowe."

We dig. The DAD_ARCHIVE folder is a rabbit warren, but Dad was nothing if not methodical. I search for "Rowe" and get a single PDF: ADOPTION_FINAL.pdf.

I open it. The first page is a standard intake—Rowe, Caleb Thomas, DOB 1991, placed with Robert Singer, firefighter, Willow Creek VFD. The second page is a newspaper scan, edges yellowed even on the screen. The headline: LOCAL FIREFIGHTER KILLED IN BLAZE, TWO ORPHANED.

I scroll, my gut going cold. The date of death is the night before the fire that killed Dad.

Lucas reads over my shoulder. "No fucking way," he breathes. "They were both there."

I flip through the pages, hands barely steady enough to track the text. There's a police report, witness statements, a photo of a boy, fifteen years old, with big ears and eyes like a kicked dog. I recognize the shape of the face. It's Rowe, years before he became the ghost that's haunted this town.

I keep going, heart pounding. The last page is a redacted

interview. The only clear line is a quote: "He blames the other chief. Says if he'd gotten there faster, his father would still be alive."

I sit back, air wheezing from my lungs.

Lucas is silent for a long moment, then says, "He's not just torching evidence. He's coming for you."

I stare at the screen, all the lines and arrows suddenly forming a noose. "He wants to erase my father," I whisper. "Burn everything that's left. Including me."

Lucas's hand finds mine, squeezing so tight I almost wince. "He's not going to get the chance."

We don't speak for a while, just let the cold truth settle in. This was never just about Bennett, never just a cleanup operation. Rowe is the hammer, but it's my head on the nail.

"We need to warn the fire marshal," I say, voice shaky.

Lucas shakes his head. "We need to trap him. Set the bait and be waiting."

He's right, but I'm scared. Not of Rowe, not even of the fire —of what it means if we fail. Of losing Dad for real, this time.

Lucas reads my mind. "You don't have to do it alone," he says. "I've got you. I always have."

I nod, unsure if I believe it, but grateful for the lie if it is one.

The afternoon fades, the light outside shifting from gold to bruise. On the screen, the old photos of Dad and the reports glow in the half-dark, a reminder that every story leaves something behind.

"Let's finish this," I say, and Lucas nods.

For the first time since the fire, I feel ready.

Let him come.

THE FIREHOUSE AT NIGHT IS A DIFFERENT BEAST—NO chatter, no ringing phones, just the echo of your own footsteps and the knowledge that the next call could snap you out of existence. I like it better this way. Less distraction, more time to think. To feel.

Lucas and I slip in through the side entrance, the one we used to sneak smokes behind when we were barely old enough to drive. The air inside is warm and dry, always a little tinged with ozone and whatever detergent they use to bleach away the human parts of firefighting. We don't bother with the main floor, don't bother pretending we have business here. We just head straight for the locker room, the familiar click of boots on tile grounding me better than any pep talk ever could.

The room is empty, rows of open lockers standing sentinel along the wall. Someone's left their turnout gear on a bench—an invitation or a warning, I can't tell, there's nothing here that we can use. The harsh white light overhead hums like a thousand wasps, casting everything in a stark, surgical glow. My eyes adjust too fast, and the shadows are sharper than I remember.

We don't say much. There's nothing to say. Everything we need is already humming in the air between us, thick and electric. I can feel Lucas's stare at my back as I pull my hair into a loose knot, exposing the ring of ash around my neck. I think about how many times we've been in this exact room, how many times we've orbited each other, never quite colliding.

Tonight, there's no gravity left.

He closes the distance, the heat of his chest radiating through my shirt. His hands find my waist, not tentative, not questioning. He spins me so I'm leaning back against the row of sinks, the porcelain biting cold through my jeans. The silvered mirror behind the faucets gives me a double: my face, jaw set, eyes wide; and his, just over my shoulder, raw and open.

He dips his head, lips grazing my ear. "You don't understand," he says, voice a scrap of sandpaper. "You're everything I ran from—and everything I came back for."

It's not a line. It's a confession.

The tension snaps. I grab the collar of his shirt and pull him in, hard. His mouth crashes into mine, the taste of coffee and adrenaline and the faint burn of whiskey from God-knows-when. He kisses like he fights—unapologetic, hungry, desperate to leave a mark. I answer with my teeth, my nails, my whole body straining for his.

"We shouldn't do this now," I whisper between kisses, "Someone might come in."

"Yeah, I know," he says against my lips as his hand slides under my shirt, palms rough against the curve of my ribs.

He fumbles with the buttons, urgency making him sloppy. I break away just long enough to yank the thing over my head, the static popping in my hair. He does the same, and we stand skin to skin, both of us mapped with old scars and new bruises. His chest is a landscape of stories I've never asked him to tell.

He lifts me onto the edge of the sink, the cold shocking my thighs. I hiss, and he grins, hands gripping my hips so tight I know I'll wear his fingerprints for days. He spreads my legs and steps between, the heat of him a living thing.

Our jeans tangle somewhere around our ankles. He trails kisses down my jaw, along my neck, pausing at the hollow just above my collarbone. He bites, gentle, then harder, like he wants to brand me.

I gasp, threading my fingers through his hair, tugging his head back so I can see him. "Is this what you want?" I ask.

He shakes his head, breathless. "It's what I need."

His fingers hook into my underwear and slide them off, slow at first, then gone. He drops to his knees, kisses the inside of my knee, then higher, letting the anticipation build until I want to scream.

When his mouth finds me, it's fire—hot and perfect, a line of sensation that burns away every doubt. I dig my nails into the back of his neck, feeling the shudder run through him, and I realize how much he needs this, too. We're both running on fumes, both so close to breaking that all we can do is hang on to each other.

He stands, wiping his mouth, and fumbles in the pocket of his discarded jeans. I know what he's looking for, and I beat him to it—grabbing the condom, tearing the wrapper open with my teeth.

He laughs, the sound low and wrecked. "God, I love you," he says, and I freeze, just for a second.

Then I pull him in, wrap my legs around his waist, and guide him inside me.

There's nothing slow about it. He pushes in all at once, the stretch delicious and brutal. I bite his shoulder, smother the cry in his skin. We set a rhythm fast, bodies moving together in time with the pulse of fluorescent lights. The sink creaks beneath us, the mirror fogs with our breath.

He lifts me, carrying me to the shower stall, where the tile is slick and the air is full of leftover steam. He pins me against the wall, hands under my ass, lifting me with a strength I'd forgotten he had. Water beads down from a leaky showerhead, mixing with the sweat on our bodies.

We fuck like we're trying to exorcise something. Every thrust is a promise, a challenge, a dare not to give up before the end. His hand is between us, thumb working circles that send me over the edge. I clench around him, legs shaking, and he follows, shuddering, face buried in my neck.

For a while, we stay tangled together, hearts racing, breath ragged. The world outside the locker room could be burning, and I wouldn't care.

He sets me down, tucks a damp strand of hair behind my ear, and kisses me slow. "You good?" he asks, voice back to normal, but thc question is real.

"Yeah," I say. "Better than."

He leans against the wall, pulling me into his lap. We sit there, backs to the tile, letting the heat of each other chase away the cold. For the first time all day, the fear is gone, replaced by something like hope.

"We can do this, right?" I ask, voice small.

He nods. "We already are."

I rest my head on his shoulder, eyes closed, breathing him in.

Tomorrow will be hell. There's no guarantee we survive it.

23

Kindled Rage

Sophie

The halls of justice have a smell: disinfectant overlaid on old sweat, cheap coffee, and the paper rot of decades-old files left to fossilize in offsite storage. I walk straight through the entryway of the county courthouse, the sound of my boots ricocheting off every polished inch of marble and glass. There's a metal detector, but the guard clocks the evidence bag slung under my arm and waves me through without a word. Everyone here knows why people show up with folders and that look in their eyes. Nobody expects you to smile.

I cut a line to the DA's office. The glass door has the name SANDRA LEE, DISTRICT ATTORNEY in big, law-firm block letters. I push through, the hinge squeal sharp as a scalpel.

The receptionist is new, young, in that way where you can

still see the pastels under the business suit. She blinks up at me from her computer. "Can I help—?"

"I'm here for Lee," I say, and drop the sealed envelope and flash drive onto her blotter. She doesn't touch them.

"Do you have an appointment?"

"Tell her Sophie Grant has the final piece." I look her in the eye. "She'll want to hear this. Now."

She hesitates, then hits a button on her desk phone and mutters into the receiver. There's a brief back-and-forth. I hear my name in a clipped whisper, then a low, "Send her in."

The double doors to Lee's private office are engineered to close with an intimidating hush. I shoulder through, and for a second, the world shrinks to the windowless walls and the hard geometry of a single metal desk. DA Lee is already standing behind it, arms folded, as if bracing herself for a confession or a gunshot.

She's taller than I expected, with silver-threaded hair in a perfect twist and a mouth that never quite reaches a smile. Her eyes are the color of an x-ray: nothing but bone and intent.

"Ms. Grant," she says, as if we're already in the middle of a trial.

"Ms. Lee." I hand her the envelope and the drive.

She weighs them in her hand, then lays them on the desk

with exaggerated care. "What's in here that couldn't wait for a phone call?"

"Proof. Pattern, motive, method. The arson is organized, not random. And your suspect is protected by every badge in this town."

She doesn't sit. Neither do I.

"Walk me through it," Lee says.

I take a breath and slide the journal pages across the metal. "My father's notes. Handwriting matches, dated and annotated. He documented the first fire, the payoffs, the falsified insurance claims. Every instance Bennett shows up, there's a payout—sometimes to city officials, sometimes to the firefighter's relief fund. All laundered."

She flips through, fast. "He had a grudge. That won't hold in court."

I nod, expecting this. "That's why I brought more." I plug the USB into her desktop, open the folder labeled DAD_ARCHIVE. My fingers don't shake, not until I double-click the first video.

On the screen, Dad's face. Worn thin, bristling with anger but tired—so tired it makes my teeth ache to watch. He spells it out, point by point: Bennett's involvement, the spiral pattern, the names. The dates.

Lee watches, face unreadable. "Is this admissible?" she says, eyes never leaving the feed.

"Every file has a timecode, location stamp. Most are from the firehouse or our kitchen. I have the originals, and copies offsite."

She absorbs this, then pulls up a spreadsheet. The numbers on the screen match the ones in Dad's hand. She cross-references, flicking from file to file, her hands getting faster, more precise. For a second, she forgets I'm in the room.

"Okay," she says finally, voice thinner. "Suppose I believe this. Suppose I take it upstairs. Bennett's not just a department head, he's the city council's pet. He has connections from here to Chicago. You understand what you're walking into?"

"I do," I say. My jaw clicks as I say it—it's the only way to keep from grinding my teeth to dust.

She stands, pacing behind the desk, eyes darting between me and the whiteboard on her wall: CASES IN REVIEW. There's Bennett's name, not at the top, but too close for comfort.

"You want me to subpoena him," she says, more statement than question.

"I want you to burn him down," I say. "The way he did to every witness. Every family he ruined. Mine included."

The silence stretches. I count my pulse in my wrist, white-knuckled around the back of the guest chair I refuse to sit in.

Lee circles, then softens—just a fraction. "Why now?"

"Because if you don't, someone else will." I think of Lucas, of the way he looked at me after the last fire, hands shaking with the urge to fix what couldn't be fixed. "I'm not the only one with nothing left to lose."

Lee leans in, bracing her palms on the cold metal. "You realize he'll go scorched earth. There are going to be consequences, Ms. Grant. For you, your friends, anyone who ever tried to help you."

"Good," I say, and this time the tremor is in my voice, not my hands. "Then he'll know how it feels."

She draws herself upright, all authority now. "I'll file the paperwork within the hour. You'll need to make a formal statement to internal affairs. And I want you to turn over every piece of evidence, physical and digital. If you hold back, I won't be able to protect you."

I nod. "You'll get everything. Including the backup drives and the chain of custody logs."

She actually looks impressed, but only for a microsecond. "One more thing," Lee says, voice low. "Stay close to home. Don't talk to the press. And if you see Bennett before we do, don't engage. Not even a little."

I smile, but there's no humor in it. "I can do that."

"Good. My assistant will take your statement."

I turn to go. At the threshold, Lee calls after me, "Ms. Grant—"

I stop.

"Your father was a good man. He didn't deserve any of this."

I swallow, hard. "I know."

The door closes behind me with the same surgical hush. Out in the hall, my knees almost give. I lean against the wall, eyes shut, counting backwards from ten until my breathing evens out.

The receptionist waits, pen poised. I sign the visitor's log and hand over the backup drives. She gives me a look—not quite pity, but not just formality, either.

I step into the lobby, a sudden weight gone from my chest. My phone vibrates, two quick pulses.

It's from Lucas.

Delivered to State Fire Marshal. All received. Heading back to you.

I text back: Good. Stay safe.

I don't expect an answer. I don't need one.

There's work to do, but for the first time in months, I feel like I've done my part.

Let them come. I'm not running.

Not this time.

Lucas

Yesterday I went to the local fire marshal, today, I will take the next step. I keep my head down and drive straight to the state fire marshal's office, two counties over, with the evidence case buckled into the passenger seat like a newborn. The further I get from Willow Creek, the lighter my chest feels, as if the stink of all those burned secrets can't cross the city limits.

At the front desk, I give my name, flash the department ID, and say I'm here on urgent business. The receptionist, an older woman with hair like a weather map in March, clocks the fireproof satchel and the look on my face and just nods me through. No paperwork, no handoff, just a direct line down the corridor to the glass-walled office with the STATE FIRE MARSHAL stenciled in government-issue Helvetica.

Marshal O'Brien is old school. Fifty-something, trim in a way that says he still runs five miles a day. His face is the color of sun-baked concrete, and his handshake is calloused and brief. He waves me to a seat, but I stand anyway, setting the evidence case on the edge of his desk like a bomb I need him to defuse.

He opens it, methodical, and starts flipping through the folders—incident reports, insurance forms, a couple of heat-damaged notebooks. He doesn't say a word, just makes a note here and there with a brass fountain pen. When he gets to the drive, he holds it up to the light, squinting at the label: "GRANT—PERSONAL."

"Walk me through it," O'Brien says, voice like a ground-up road.

I keep it short. "This is a pattern case, sir. Years of arson-for-profit, covered by two or more local officials. Main actors are Bennett—chief now, was deputy before—and Rowe, career fire-fighter. All the red flags are there: missing gear, bogus overtime, shopped-around insurance claims."

He clicks the pen twice. "You got dates?"

I slide a printed timeline across the desk, every entry under-lined and annotated. "Correlates with every major payout and suspicious suppression report in the last ten years. You'll see that in Grant's logs. He tracked everything."

O'Brien flips through. "Grant was a hell of a paper trail guy," he mutters. "Died in a structure fire, right?"

I nod. "Ten years ago. Official story is 'misadventure.' But if you watch the footage on the drive, you'll see he was about to go public with the records."

O'Brien's face doesn't change, but his hand pauses on the pen for half a second. He slides the drive into his laptop, keys in a password, and opens a video file. My gut goes tight watching Grant's face on the monitor—drawn, exhausted, but still talking like every word counts double. O'Brien doesn't look away, not even to blink. When the video ends, he scrolls through another half-dozen folders, then leans back in his chair, steepling his fingers.

"You understand what happens next," he says. "If this holds up, it's going to eat the whole department from the inside."

I let that hang. "That's why I'm here, not at the district."

He taps the case, then drums his fingers against the desk. "You think Bennett knows you're in the wind?"

"He knows," I say. "But he doesn't know about the backup. Or that we had help on the inside." I stop myself, careful. I don't mention Sophie by name. I just say, "There's a civilian in the line of fire. She's not safe until he's inside a cell."

O'Brien doesn't ask for details. He just scribbles a name on a yellow pad, tears off the sheet, and hands it to me. "Take this to the state police. If you see anything—anything—out of order, you call the number at the bottom. Direct line, no hold music."

I pocket the number, feeling the first flicker of relief in weeks.

O'Brien stands, shakes my hand again. "You did the right thing, Hayes. Lot of guys would've let it go."

I don't know what to say, so I just nod and walk out. The hallway is brighter, somehow. Lighter.

On my way back to the truck, I swing by the gas station for a black coffee and a moment to breathe. There's a stack of local papers by the door, headline already three inches tall: LOCAL WOMAN UNCOVERS DECADE OF CORRUPTION. I almost laugh.

Out the window, I spot a couple of townies in the café, hunched over their plates, looking up at me like they're seeing a ghost in the daylight. One of them lifts his mug in salute.

I raise my own, return the nod, and head for home.

Maybe this time, the right people will get burned.

Sophie

I almost don't notice it at first. The porch is a mess, as usual—yellowed flyers underfoot, mud tracked in an arc from last night's rain, the neighbor's dog's teeth marks on the bottom of the screen door. But there's a smell, an acrid twist on top of the morning air: melted plastic, bitter and faintly sweet, a scent you only forget if you never grew up around fire.

I nudge the culprit with my boot. It's a toy horse, or what's left of one—a warped mess of pink and white plastic, mane fused into a crusted ridge, one back leg burned away entirely. Even half-melted, I know it. The horse from my bedroom shelf, the only thing I managed to save the night everything else went up.

My hands shake as I pick it up, soot blackening my palm. It's a calling card. I know it, and whoever left it knows I know.

My stomach goes cold, and suddenly the air outside the house feels five degrees colder.

I turn, scanning the street. A minivan idles at the corner, waiting for the light. Across the street, the kid in apartment 2B stares down from his window, face slack with curiosity, or maybe fear. I watch him until he disappears, then walk back inside, lock the door, and double-check it for good measure.

In the kitchen, I set the horse on the table, wipe the soot off my hands with a dish towel, then scrub them again just to get rid of the taste. The laptop is still open from last night, Dad's files stacked in neat columns across the desktop. For a second, I just stare at the horse, letting the memory play out: hiding it in my backpack at eight years old because I couldn't stand to lose it, clutching it to my chest while Dad carried me through the smoke.

The new threat arrives as an email, subject line BLINDFIRE. No text in the body, just an attachment: a cellphone pic of my porch, the horse visible in the corner, timestamped to fifteen minutes before I got home.

Underneath, a single line: One match left. One last name to burn.

I stare at the words until my vision goes blurry.

When Lucas gets in, he's still wearing his work shirt, collar damp from sweat or rain, or maybe the pressure of holding it together all day. He clocks the horse immediately, his face going hard.

"Rowe?" he asks.

"Who else?" I pick it up, show him the photo on my screen. "He's taunting us. The only thing left for him to burn is me."

Lucas says nothing. He just takes the horse from my hand, turns it over, then tosses it in the sink. "We're leaving," he says, already in motion. "Now."

I follow him to the living room, anger sparking through the fear. "We can't just run. That's what he wants. He's watching."

Lucas spins, eyes bright and sharp. "It's not running. It's strategic retreat. You know damn well the safest place is somewhere he can't get to you. You're too close to the case—he knows that, Soph. He knows how to get in your head."

I clench my fists, trying to keep the tremor out of my voice. "If I stop working, he wins. If I hide, he erases Dad for real this time."

Lucas sets his jaw, but there's a crack in it now—a hairline fracture that shows how scared he actually is. "You can work from anywhere. Take the evidence. Take the backups. We'll go to my family's cabin, like we planned. You can keep building the case, and I can keep you safe."

For a second, I want to scream. I want to say something that will break through the stubborn line of his shoulders and get him to see what it feels like to be prey, to be hunted by a memory that won't die. But instead, I just breathe. Slow. Measured.

"Fine," I say, voice low. "But I'm not shutting down. I'm not changing my name. I'm not giving up the fight."

Lucas nods, relief flickering behind the anger. "Good. But you do what I say, when I say it. No more solo runs, no more late-night walks. Deal?"

"Deal," I say, though I know it's a lie the second it leaves my mouth.

We pack in silence. I take only the essentials—laptop, charger, journal, three changes of clothes, the external hard drive with every file and video. Lucas packs his own bag, methodical and quiet. He moves like a soldier, every motion practiced, every snap of a zipper or click of a latch a reminder of what's at stake.

I glance back at the kitchen table as we leave. The horse is gone, but the shape of it lingers in the soot on the Formica.

I close the door behind us, not looking back.

This time, if something burns, I'll be ready to put it out.

The cabin, or safehouse as Lucas has referred to it, is a box of poured concrete and paranoia, parked two miles up an unpaved road with only the buzz of mosquitoes and the wind in the pine needles for company. Whoever built it didn't care about comfort—there are no family photos, no books, not even a TV, just the bare minimum of what you need to stay alive and off the map. The front door is reinforced steel with a double deadbolt; every window has a crosshatch of chicken wire embedded in the glass, less to keep people out than to slow them down once they decide to come through. There's a single bedroom, a narrow galley kitchen, and a main room with a table made of honest-to-God wood so solid I wonder if it's been repurposed from a felled telegraph pole.

We bring in everything we'll need in one trip, neither of us saying much until the door's locked behind us and we've drawn the blackout shades tight. Lucas checks the perimeter, then sets up a charging station by the back wall. I go straight for the table, dumping the laptop, Dad's journal, and the day's worth of maps onto the surface.

I lay out the evidence in neat rows, not because I'm organized but because it's the only way to make the chaos manageable. Lucas hovers, his hands twitching to help but not knowing where to start.

"Here," I say, pulling a chair for him. "Let's run the timeline again. There's something about the spiral—something I missed."

He sits, shoulders hunched, eyes gone narrow and focused. "You're sure it's not just a scare tactic?"

I shake my head, flipping to a page in the journal where Dad had copied the symbol a dozen times, always tighter, always closing the circle with a different date inside. "Every time Rowe leaves a spiral, there's a fire within twenty-four hours. Sometimes closer. The last three matched up with anniversaries. Not just of the original fire, but of people tied to the investigation. Survivors, or witnesses."

Lucas runs a fingertip along the edge of the map. "So he's escalating."

"Not just that," I say, thinking out loud. "He's refining the pattern. Making it more efficient. More...personal."

A pause. Then Lucas, very quietly: "You think he's going to target you directly."

"He already is," I say, not bothering to soften it. "And if he follows Dad's math, the next strike is tonight. Maybe tomorrow."

Lucas's hand clamps over mine, and I let the weight of it hold me steady. "We set a trap," he says. "Leak a fake address to Bennett, let Rowe try and light it up, and catch him in the act."

"He won't go for it unless it's bait he can't refuse," I say, brain already running through the permutations. "What if we leak that I'm meeting the DA with the originals? That I've got nowhere else to go?"

Lucas grins, a flash of teeth. "He's already watching us. If we make it obvious, he'll come running."

I boot up the laptop, fingers flying through a decoy email, carbon copying the right people, dropping breadcrumbs straight to the inboxes I know Rowe can't resist. Lucas queues up the security cameras—motion sensors on every tree, a silent alarm tied to the burner phone in his pocket.

We spend an hour in silence, making sure every angle is covered, every possible entry mapped. I see the gears turning in Lucas's head, his firefighter's brain plotting airflow, burn paths, worst-case scenarios. He sketches diagrams on the back of a takeout menu, then tears them up and starts over when he's not satisfied. I catch him glancing at me, maybe to make sure I'm still here, maybe to remind himself he's not alone in this.

It feels like the longest night of my life, but when the work is done, we're left with nothing but the thump of our own hearts and the steady tick of the kitchen clock.

I stand, stretch, and roll the tension from my shoulders. "You want first watch, or should I?"

He shakes his head. "We'll stay up. Together."

For a while, we sit, side by side, the hush between us dense enough to muffle even our thoughts. I want to say something, to break the spell, but everything feels too big or too small for words.

So when I touch his hand, it's not for comfort—it's for grounding. He looks at me, blue eyes tired but still hungry, and in that second, I know what I want more than anything is to be seen, to be wanted, to be more than just the sum of my ghosts.

I find the scarf at the bottom of my go-bag, a piece of black silk from my mother's closet that I've never worn in public. I hold it out to him, wordless, and watch the understanding ripple across his face.

"My turn to trust you," I say, and he closes his eyes, lets me knot the silk around his head, covering everything from eyebrows to cheekbones. He could slip it off in an instant, but he doesn't.

I guide him to the bed, push him down so he lands with a

bounce that surprises even him. He laughs, the first honest sound I've heard from him in hours.

I straddle his hips, slow and deliberate, pressing my palms to his chest. His heart is a fist, hammering the cage of his ribs. He tries to reach for me but I pin his wrists to the mattress, holding him there, just on the edge.

"You're safe," I tell him, and it's a promise, not a command.

He breathes in, lets it go shaky.

I lean in, lips grazing the scar along his collarbone, then down the seam of his pec, each kiss slow and hot as a match. His hands flex, wanting to move, but he doesn't break the hold. When I let him go, it's to guide his palms to my hips, then up under my shirt, skin to skin.

He tilts his head, blind to the world but mapped perfectly to me, every movement an act of surrender. I let him touch, let him find the curve of my waist, the edge of my ribs, the ridge of the old burn that's always made me pull away. This time, I press his hand to it, hold it there, daring him to look away, but he doesn't.

I sink down, slow at first, taking my time. He groans, the sound muffled by the pillow, and I ride the edge, building the friction until I'm raw and greedy for release. His hands roam, gripping, guiding, but never taking control. I set the pace, relentless and patient, until the world narrows to just the two of us, bodies locked in a standoff with the rest of the universe.

I come first, shuddering hard enough to see stars behind my

eyelids. He holds me through it, then lets go, following with a pulse that nearly buckles my knees.

After, I untie the scarf, watch him blink up at me, face slack with wonder.

"You're insane," he says, but there's nothing but awe in his voice.

"You like it," I shoot back, and he just grins, dragging me down until we're forehead to forehead, breathing the same air.

We lie there, tangled, sweat drying on our skin, the threat of tomorrow kept at bay by the thickness of the walls and the certainty that for once, just this once, we're exactly where we're supposed to be.

Outside, the night is black and bottomless. But inside, there's light. Not much, but enough.

We fall asleep that way, limbs locked, hearts syncopated, waiting for the next match to strike.

Let them try.

We're ready to burn them all down.

24

Smoke Trail

Sophie

THE SAFE HOUSE IS A CONCRETE SLAB WITH THE insulation value of a cardboard box, but at least the coffee is real and the walls are thick enough to muffle the outside. We sit across from each other at the kitchen table, arms braced like boxers at the bell.

Lucas's eyes are rimmed in red. He hasn't slept, or maybe he just hasn't let go of the night before. His hand is steady on the mug, but every now and then the fingers twitch. I watch the flex of tendon, the little betrayals that say he's ready to spring. The laptop is open, screensaver a slow blue pulse, and behind it the police scanner hisses with static.

We don't talk much. The plan doesn't require words, just timing, precision, and the absolute trust that comes from being the only two left who care whether the truth gets out. It's almost like being married, if your vows are written in accelerant and blood.

I dial the public tip line from a burner. The phone vibrates in my palm like a live animal. On the third ring, a tired-sounding woman picks up, her voice pitched high and professional: "State Arson Hotline, please state the nature of your report."

I inhale, slow and deep, like Dad used to before a critical call. "There's something you missed," I say, pitching my voice an octave lower, the accent just off enough to pass for out-of-town. "That fire in Willow Creek? They're reopening the investigation. The fire marshal's office is sitting on evidence—they're pulling all the records tonight."

A pause. "Do you have a name, Ma'am?"

"No," I say, and hang up. I kill the phone, yank out the battery, and toss it into the ceramic trash with the rest of our day's work. Lucas watches, says nothing, but I can feel the approval, a current between us.

He tunes the police scanner to local traffic, then to state. We listen, ears bent to the frequencies where real news gets made. There's nothing at first—just routine calls, a report of a coyote hit on County Line, a traffic stop gone sideways. Then, at 7:42 p.m., the tone changes.

"All units, be advised—possible break-in at fire marshal's annex, County storage. Suspect vehicle dark sedan, no plate. Surveillance offline, requesting backup."

Lucas sits up straight, all the exhaustion gone, replaced by a brittle charge. He points to the wall clock. "He'll want to move fast—thirty minutes, tops, before they gridlock the area. If Rowe's going in, it's now."

He's right, of course. Rowe isn't the type to linger. He's an opportunist, a man who sets fires not for the joy, but for the story that comes after. The cleanup. The cover-up. The only thing he loves more than burning it down is not getting caught.

We wait, the scanner our only heartbeat. I run logistics in my head—if I were Rowe, I'd come in the back, neutralize the alarm, avoid cameras. Go straight for the archive room, snag the files, then vanish. No signature, no trace. But everyone leaves something.

An hour later, the call comes through. The annex was hit, files ransacked, but nothing stolen. The suspect was gone before police arrived, but they found a print. "Partial thumb on the steel cabinet, looks recent. Running through the system now."

I grin, despite myself. "He couldn't help it. Had to make sure he got the right files."

Lucas shakes his head, but his mouth curls up at the edge. "They'll run it through the database. If we're lucky, it'll pop in twenty-four hours."

"If we're lucky," I echo.

That night, sleep is an experiment. I manage maybe two hours, most of it spent listening for a car that never comes, the other half tracing the cracks in the ceiling and wondering if the universe is just fucking with us for fun. At five, I give up. I go to the kitchen, make coffee, and count the seconds until Lucas joins me, his hair sticking up and his face washed with the kind of resolve you only get from knowing the target is finally in the crosshairs.

He pours coffee, checks the laptop, refreshes his email. There's a notification from the fire marshal's office, flagged urgent. He clicks it, and the message jumps to the foreground:

"Thumbprint match. Caleb Rowe. APB issued."

I don't say anything, just stare at the screen as the facts click into place. After months of chasing ghosts, we finally have a body to hang it all on.

Lucas lets out a breath that's almost a laugh. "It's enough for a warrant."

The relief is tidal. I feel it roll through me, head to heel, washing out the old panic, replacing it with a dangerous kind of hope.

I turn to him, my voice steadier than I expected. "They'll move on him tonight, right?"

He nods, eyes shining. "He'll run, but not far. Not now that he knows we've got him."

I want to punch something, or shout, or maybe just sit and

watch the sun come up for once without wondering which side of the glass I'll be on by lunch.

But I settle for this: I pour two mugs, hand him one, and let our hands linger, just a second longer than before.

"We did it," I say, and this time, it's not a lie.

The war isn't over. But the tide just turned.

And I'm not afraid of the fire anymore.

THE AIR OUTSIDE THE GARAGE IS THIN AND MEAN, BITING through my coat as we slip under the police tape. There's no crowd—just four patrol units idling in the gutter, their light bars strobing dull blue, and a cluster of cops hunched against the cold. Their faces are drawn, set in the way of men and women who know they're only here to fill out the paperwork after the real show's already left town.

Lucas slows as we approach the door. For all his intensity, he's careful not to draw the wrong kind of attention. He nods at the nearest officer—one he recognizes from a few calls before everything got ugly—and the guy lifts the tape, wordless. That's all the permission we need.

Inside, it's a tomb. Concrete block walls, no windows, the only light a strip of LED lanterns clipped to a pipe overhead. The smell is fresh singe: ozone, burnt plastic, and the ghost of whatever lived and died here before Rowe took up residence.

There's chaos everywhere, but not the kind that comes from a struggle. It's deliberate, curated. A cot is overturned, blanket flung to one side like it got up and left on its own. A duffel bag gapes open, half its contents scattered on the floor: a change of clothes, an old phone, the corner of a Ziploc bag marked with evidence tape. On the makeshift table—a plywood slab on cinder blocks—a coffee cup steams in a ring of its own sweat.

Lucas circles the room, hands curled into fists. He barely glances at the coffee or the mess. His eyes are on the far wall, where something black and glossy scorches the gray surface.

A spiral. Bigger than before, burned deep into the cinder block with what must have been a blowtorch. The pattern is perfect, the center so clean it's almost white.

Lucas goes very still, then rears back and slams his fist into the wall beside it. The sound echoes, sharp and mean, and for a second every cop outside stops talking.

"He fucking knew," he says, voice ragged. "He's always one step ahead."

I want to tell him it's not his fault, that nobody could have predicted Rowe would torch his own safe house and vanish before the raid. But that's not what he needs. I walk to the table, pick up the coffee cup, and hold it out. The heat bites my fingers.

"He left in a hurry," I say. "Look at the bag. Look at the way he tried to cover his tracks, but not really. He wanted us to see the spiral."

Lucas turns, not meeting my eyes. "He wants you to know he's not done."

"No," I say. "He wants us to think he's still in control. But he's running scared, Lucas. He's making mistakes."

He shakes his head, all the frustration and failure boiling just under the surface. "I promised I'd end this. I promised you'd be safe."

I set the cup down, step close, and put a hand on his arm. His muscles are like cable, but they soften at my touch. "You haven't failed anyone," I say. "You got him out of his hole. You got the warrant. He's desperate now, and that's when people slip up."

He exhales, the anger draining off his face, replaced by something brittle but real. "We're so close. I just—" He stops, shakes it off. "I can't let him hurt you. Not again."

I want to tell him I'm not afraid, but that's not true and never has been. What matters is that we're here, still moving, still breathing, still the only people in this town willing to see the thing through to the end.

I squeeze his arm, then let go. "Next time he shows, we'll be waiting."

Lucas nods, jaw set, the blue in his eyes fierce as ever. "Together?"

"Together," I say, and mean it.

We step back into the cold, leaving the spiral burning in our wake.

THE KITCHEN IS A WAR ROOM: FIRE MAPS DRAPED OVER every inch of Formica, highlighters scattered in a bruised rainbow, a whiteboard propped on a chair because the wall won't hold thumbtacks. Lucas stands at the window, backlit by the late sun, body tense in a way that says he's thinking three steps ahead but not liking where the path leads. I sit at the table, cross-legged, tracing the spiral pattern with my finger, over and over, until the heat of friction leaves a ghost on my skin.

We're both silent, too tired for argument and too wired for sleep. I grab a Sharpie and start marking, connecting the sequence of fires: the first on South Pine, then the train yard, then the warehouse, then the ruin of my own house. The lines tighten, each one a pass through the center, until I see it—a curve, subtle at first, but unmistakable once you know where to look.

"He's not just running," I say, Sharpie squeaking as I draw the arc. "He's circling back."

Lucas turns, the muscles in his forearm flickering under the skin as he crosses to the table. "To what?"

I jab the marker into the spot dead center of the spiral.

"Here," I say. "The old elementary school. Willow Creek Academy. It's been shuttered for years, but the building's still standing."

Lucas's jaw flexes. "You're sure?"

"As sure as I can be without walking into the match myself." I close my eyes, try to remember the layout. Two wings, basement gym, the old boiler room that always smelled like hot pennies. "It's perfect for him. Far enough from the main drag to buy time. Plenty of accelerant left in the walls—books, insulation, God knows what in the janitor's closet."

He leans in, the tension in his shoulders visible even under the flannel. "We need to get there before he does."

"He'll wait for night. He always waits for night."

Lucas runs both hands through his hair, wild and frustrated. "We're so close. If he pulls this, he'll bring the whole block down."

I tap the map, the marker leaving a black dot that bleeds through the paper. "Then we catch him before he lights the fuse."

He looks at me, and for a second, the hard exterior cracks. "You ever think we'd get this far?"

I think of all the days I wanted to quit, all the mornings I woke up convinced I was fighting a battle already lost. I think of Dad, of the way he'd grin after a big win but always keep his shoes by the door, ready for the next fire.

"Yeah," I say. "I did."

We run the scenarios for an hour, maybe two. I lose track of time, the world narrowing to just the two of us and the fevered lines of the spiral, tightening and tightening until there's nowhere left to go but the center.

At some point, I realize Lucas hasn't moved in ten minutes. He sits across from me, head bowed, hands folded, the way a kid might wait for judgment. His whole body is humming, but he's trapped by something he can't name.

I reach across the table, cover his hands with mine. "You okay?"

He doesn't look up. "I keep thinking if I'd been faster—if I'd trusted you sooner—maybe we'd have stopped him already."

"Stop," I say. "We're here. That's what matters."

He lifts his head, and for a moment he's so open it hurts to look at him. "I don't know how to turn it off," he says, voice low. "The fear. The guilt."

"Then don't," I say. "Just... let it be what it is. But don't let it eat you."

He tries to laugh, but it's a choked sound. "Easy for you to say."

I shake my head, a smile fighting through the fatigue. "You think I'm not terrified?"

He's silent, but the look in his eyes is answer enough.

I stand, move to his side, and tug him up by the wrist. He follows, slow, like he's not sure if he's allowed to touch me, or if the world will end if he does. I guide him down the hall, past the barricade of our hastily packed go-bags, straight to the bathroom.

The light is harsh, but the air is warmer here. I twist the shower to full blast, steam roaring in seconds. Lucas just stands there, blinking through the mist, until I step in fully clothed and pull him in with me.

Water pounds us, soaking his flannel, plastering my shirt to my chest. I yank at his buttons, pop them one by one, each snap louder than the spray. He shivers—not from cold, but from the shock of someone else taking charge for once. I press him against the tile, kiss him hard, and feel the tension drain from his body, replaced by something hotter, wilder.

He grabs my waist, hauls me up, and our mouths collide again, teeth and tongue and the taste of water and relief. My hands fumble with his belt, then the fly, and when I finally get him free, he's already hard, desperate.

I hook my legs around his hips, the friction of soaked denim making every movement electric. He lifts me like I weigh nothing, slams me back against the wall, and fucks me with a violence that's all apology and all promise at once.

The water scalds our skin, washes away the salt and the ash and the residue of fear. I dig my nails into his shoulder, ride the rhythm, let him pour everything he can't say into my body. We move together, fast and rough, the sound of our bodies lost in the roar of the water.

I come first, a flash of light behind my eyes, clenching around him until he swears and follows, hips jerking, head buried in my neck. He doesn't let go, even when it's over. He just holds me, breath ragged, water dripping off his nose and chin.

We strip out of the sodden clothes, dry off with a towel that smells like motel sheets, and climb into the bed, still naked, still wet. He curls around me, arms banded tight, and for the first time I believe he might actually sleep.

Tomorrow, we hunt the center of the spiral. Tomorrow, we catch Rowe, or die trying.

But tonight, the world is just a bed, a pair of bodies, and the faint, persistent echo of hope.

I close my eyes and let it carry me, for once, all the way to morning.

25

Ignite

Lucas

The call goes out at dawn: possible explosives, Willow Creek Elementary, all units respond. My first thought is that Rowe wouldn't use a school, not with his whole righteous-fireman complex. But when the dispatcher repeats it—same address, urgency ratcheted up—I know he's snapped, or maybe the spiral has finally closed.

We suit up at the station. The air tastes like caffeine and unbrushed teeth, every man and woman here vibrating with the bad-joke energy of people who expect to be blown up before breakfast. I check my turnout gear three times, feeling for any sign of defect. Every snap, every Velcro strip, is suddenly the thing that's going to save me or fail when I need it most.

Captain eyes me, nods once, and shoves a handheld radio into my palm. "You know this building better than anyone,

Hayes. You take point with Squad One. I want a sweep of the north and east entrances. If it looks like a real device, we back out and let the bomb boys play hero."

"Copy that," I say, keeping my voice level. I catch the rest of his meaning—if it's a decoy, or if there's a chance, we go in.

We load out. The rig's engine is a shotgun blast in the quiet neighborhood. I can't hear my own thoughts over the sound, which is good, because all my thoughts are wrong.

I don't see Sophie until we pull up to the scene, but I know she's coming. She's like gravity; even when I want her on the other side of the planet, she's already at my elbow.

The school looms like a mausoleum. It's been empty for years, but the brick is still clean, the playground still chained off with polite yellow banners. There's a strange, almost holy silence as we approach—no birds, no wind, not even the traffic from Main Street. Just the scrape of boots and the jangle of gear, echoing off the empty glass.

The first squad fans out around the perimeter, eyes up, hands tight on radios. I take two new recruits, both barely out of academy, and we circle around to the north entrance.

That's where I see the first sign: a length of PVC pipe, capped and duct-taped, jammed in the doorway. Not professional, but not amateur either. The cap is wired, and from here I can see the thread of blue wire running up the frame and into the gap above the door.

I signal the others to hang back, then inch forward, heart

climbing up my throat. I squat, study the device, careful not to cast a shadow on the pressure plate. The wiring is a mess, but there's a logic to it. The tripwire is the real trigger—open the door, you complete the circuit, and whatever's in that pipe becomes the last thing you ever see.

"Squad One, this is Hayes. We've got confirmed device, north entrance. Recommend perimeter at fifty yards. Repeat: fifty yards."

The reply is instant, Captain's voice clipped and military: "Acknowledged, Hayes. Pull back and coordinate with EOD. No heroics."

But as I step away, I spot something on the roof—movement, a figure perched on the edge of the old music room like a vulture. Black windbreaker, jeans, a ball cap pulled low. Even without the binoculars, I'd know that stance anywhere.

Rowe.

He's holding a phone, arm outstretched, the lens pointed right at the front lawn. He's livestreaming. If the bastard's put this much effort into his sendoff, he's not going to let anyone get in the way.

"Squad One, be advised. Suspect is on the roof. Repeat, roof. North corner, over the music wing. Livestreaming on a cell."

Captain's voice goes harder. "Hold positions. No one approaches until bomb is clear. I want eyes on him at all times."

I step back, breathless, watching the man above me. He's pacing the edge now, talking into the phone, his voice lost in the morning hush.

And that's when Sophie barrels onto the scene, screeching her old sedan to a halt on the sidewalk, almost sideswiping an ambulance that's waiting in the cold. She's in civilian clothes—jeans, battered jacket, hair wild—but her hands are full of paper.

She makes for the command post, ducking under the caution tape, voice already raised. "You can't wait for bomb squad, Captain. If Rowe's up there, he's got a failsafe. He's not going to let them get close."

Captain, already strung tight, turns the full force of his scowl on her. "Ms. Grant, this is a controlled scene. I can't—"

She cuts him off, flipping the pages in front of him. "Listen to me, okay? Dad documented a dozen of Rowe's designs. He always sets up a main charge, but there's a manual ignition somewhere inside. If you wait, you lose the chance to defuse it. He wants the show."

The Captain's nostrils flare. "Bomb squad is five minutes out—"

"And the school blows in four," Sophie says, voice flat. "He's a narcissist. He times everything to the minute."

There's a pause. Every eye in the circle shifts from the Captain to the roof, to the bomb, to me, and back to Sophie.

She steps in, voice lowering. "Give me a shot, please. You know my father—he would've wanted it this way."

Captain's jaw ticks, but he nods at me. "You go with her, Hayes. No one else crosses that threshold. You get two minutes inside, then you pull out, or I drag you out myself."

I nod, and that's it—I'm committed, and so is she.

We duck under the tape, outpacing the first responders who are already pulling back to the new safe radius. I catch up to her as she flips through the notebook, eyes scanning the chicken-scratch diagrams and annotated spirals.

"Have you actually done this before?" I hiss, low enough that only she hears.

She shrugs. "Dad let me wire the Christmas tree once. Does that count?"

I snort, despite myself. "You're out of your mind."

She looks up, and for a second I see the old Sophie—the one who ran toward fires, not away. "Are you scared?"

"Only of you," I say, and it's not entirely a joke.

We slow as we approach the side entrance, careful not to disturb the tripwire or set off any secondary charges. The building's cold up close, the brick sweating with night condensation. My gloves stick to the metal of the door handle as I edge it open, one millimeter at a time.

Inside, it's black as pitch. The only light comes from the frosted glass at the far end of the corridor, diffused into a blue haze. The air stinks of fertilizer and wet chalk dust. Every sound we make echoes forever.

Sophie moves ahead of me, hunched over the pages, muttering numbers and wire colors to herself. She's in her element now, weirdly calm, the storm in her eyes focused into a single, sharp point.

We reach the first junction, a tangle of wires snaking along the ceiling and into a utility closet. She gestures for me to cover her, then kneels and flips the lock with a hairpin from her pocket. The closet opens, revealing a nest of wires, batteries, and what looks like a hacked smoke detector acting as the main timer.

I can see right away that it's a two-part system: one electrical, one chemical. Rowe must have spent weeks rigging this, using whatever scraps he could scrounge from the supply rooms. The smell of sulfur is overpowering.

Sophie stabs a finger at the pages. "Look—see the twist at the end of the blue? Dad always said blue is the decoy. It'll loop you into thinking it's safe, but that's just to stall until the main goes off."

She traces the yellow wire to a set of batteries duct-taped to the wall. "If I can break the circuit here, we might have a chance to—"

A click above us. I freeze. Sophie does too.

From the vents overhead, a voice, amplified but scratchy: "You shouldn't be in there, Lucas. This is for me and the chief and the ghosts. Not for the tourists."

Rowe.

Sophie snaps her eyes up. "He's patched in through the intercom."

"I know," I say. "He's probably watching us right now."

I look around—there, above the door, a tiny glass lens. The old security camera. He must have jimmied the feed and hooked it to his cell.

I glance at my watch. Ninety seconds left.

I drop to one knee beside Sophie. "Tell me what to do."

She works the wires, hands steady, voice a whisper. "Cut the yellow, then the green. If you do blue first, it'll spike the current and pop the charge."

"On three," I say.

She nods.

I count, and on three I slice through the yellow with my multitool. Nothing happens. My vision tunnels. I cut the green. Still nothing.

We both exhale, then Sophie dives for the red, the last in the cluster, and yanks it clean out of the terminal.

Silence.

Then, from the hallway, a slow clap, amplified and sarcastic: "Bravo," Rowe says. "But you missed the real party. Try the gymnasium."

Sophie grabs the radio from my belt. "Captain, this is Grant. Secondary device likely in the gym, west wing. Tell EOD to focus there."

The Captain's voice is sharp. "Acknowledged. Hayes, get her out of there. Now."

I pull Sophie close, and for a second we just stand there, shaking, alive.

Sophie

We don't wait for backup. The bomb squad is still staging, half a block away, and the police have cordoned off the street, but we're inside before anyone thinks to stop us. Lucas takes the lead this time, flashlight angled low, boots barely making a sound on the ancient linoleum. I follow, notebook clutched tight, my thumb working the edge of the pages until it's raw.

The school's interior is a time capsule of elementary trauma: trophy cases crusted with dead bugs, motivational posters curling off the walls, lockers with peeling stickers from kids whose names are now on LinkedIn or gravestones. Dust floats in the beams of our lights, thick enough to eat the sound, and every step forward is a step into the world's creepiest museum.

The smell hits halfway to the gym—a synthetic sweetness overlaying the rot of old lunchboxes and mildew. Fertilizer bomb, probably, or some chemical cousin. Rowe is nothing if not thematic; he likes his work to be memorable.

Lucas checks each classroom as we pass. He's methodical, almost tender, like he's afraid to disturb the ghosts. The only thing out of place is the silence—no wind, no wildlife, just the hush of a building that knows it's doomed.

We reach the gym entrance. The double doors are painted with a cartoon bulldog mascot, its snarl half-obscured by a slur of black spray paint. I step closer, squinting at the jamb. There, at knee height, a thin rectangle of pressure pad, the wire barely visible as it snakes into the crack between the doors.

Lucas doesn't touch it. He leans close, studying the line with a practiced eye. "He's got a pad under the threshold," he whispers. "Opens more than a quarter inch, triggers the relay."

I nod, flipping the notebook to a page marked with a sticky note and a circle in red pen. Dad's handwriting—always blocky, always too much pressure on the downstrokes.

I scan the diagram, following the logic. This isn't just a bomb; it's a system. There are backups, redundancies, an obsession with making sure the building doesn't just burn but annihilates itself.

"He must have spent months on this," I say, voice shaking.

Lucas glances at me, blue eyes sharp even in the dark. "You see a way to kill it?"

I trace the wires with my eyes, matching the setup to Dad's notes. "It's a modified cross-trigger," I say, thinking out loud. "If you cut power to the main, it trips a backup. If you try to move the doors, it completes the circuit."

Lucas grunts. "So what's the workaround?"

I study the diagram, the real thing, the options collapsing around me. "You have to bypass the relay," I say. "Access the wiring from behind, without moving the doors."

He looks down the hall, then up—searching for a vent, a crawl space, anything.

"There," I point. Above the entry, a ceiling vent barely big enough for my hips.

Lucas boosts me up without argument. His hands grip my thighs, then my calves, steady as iron rebar. I clamber into the duct, notebook wedged in my waistband, headlamp switched to its lowest setting.

The metal is cold, but my palms are sweating. I elbow-crawl forward, feeling every rib of the vent rattle under my weight. The air is worse here—thick with the ghost of gym socks and something chemical that makes my teeth ache.

I pause at a junction, peer down through the slats. I have a perfect view of the doors, the wires, and the mess of electronics glued to the far wall. I take out the notebook, page through with shaking fingers, looking for the right sequence.

Below me, Lucas's voice, barely more than a rumble: "Talk to me, Soph."

I take a breath, steady my hand. "It's here. He's got the timer set, but the actual trigger is a backup relay on the west wall. If I can reach it, I can short the system without tripping the main charge."

I slide forward, knees catching on every screw and seam. The ductwork vibrates with my pulse. I reach the end, where a section of vent has already been unscrewed and set aside—Rowe's handiwork. He wants someone to see this, to get close enough to admire the craft.

I peer through the gap. The device is uglier up close—old car batteries, sticks of fertilizer taped together, a tangle of wires that look like the inside of a dead animal.

I whisper down, "I need the pliers."

Lucas's arm reaches up, a shadow in the beam. I reach down, grab the tool, and almost drop it. My hands won't quit shaking.

I use the pliers to peel back the duct tape, exposing the relay. It's exactly like Dad's diagram, down to the color of the wires. I feel a weird, awful pride at how well he taught me this.

I brace my knees, stretch as far as I can, and clip the blue wire—first, just like in the notes.

For a second, nothing happens. My whole world shrinks to the point where the pliers meet the wire, and I wonder if maybe I was wrong, maybe Dad was wrong, maybe this is the last thing I'll ever do.

Then the relay clicks. A soft, almost polite noise.

I drop the pliers, back up fast, nearly slamming my head on the duct ceiling. "It's good," I shout. "The relay's dead. We have maybe sixty seconds before the backup timer cycles and resets the circuit."

Lucas doesn't wait for instructions. He runs for the doors, slides a crowbar under the seam, and pries them just wide enough for me to squirm out of the vent and drop onto the gym floor.

I hit the floor running, the impact knocking the air from my lungs.

Together, we make for the far wall, where the rest of the bomb waits.

There's a digital readout—forty-two seconds, and dropping.

I rip the notebook open, thumb to the next page.

"Green, then white," I say, my voice barely audible.

Lucas grabs the wires, hesitates. "You sure?"

I look up at him, and he sees that I'm not—but it doesn't matter.

"Do it," I say.

He does.

The timer goes dead. Just like that.

For a long second, neither of us moves. Then Lucas lets out a whoop, a sound so primal and unguarded it actually echoes in the gym.

I slide to the floor, knees giving out, and press my face to the cold wood, breathing in the sweat and varnish and memory.

Lucas sits beside me, back to the wall, eyes squeezed shut in relief.

After a minute, he turns, brushes the hair from my eyes, and says, "Remind me never to piss you off."

I laugh, and it sounds like sobbing, but I don't care.

Above us, the gym lights flicker, then come to life, harsh and white and perfectly normal.

We're safe.

For now.

We kill the lights and leave the gym, blinking into the sunrise and a wall of noise: cop cars, fire trucks, at least two news vans already spewing out wires and flustered interns. The moment we cross the threshold, someone yells my name—probably a dispatcher, but it sounds like the voice of God, or maybe Dad, or maybe the universe just admitting I've finally gotten its attention.

They corral us behind an ambulance, medics shoving bottles of water and emergency blankets at us like we're kids at a track meet. I don't remember sitting down, but suddenly I'm there, knees up, hands folded, the notebook pressed so hard to my chest I think I've bruised a rib.

Lucas stands a few feet away, jaw clenched, hands shoved so deep in his pockets I wonder if he's holding himself together by force of habit alone. Every so often, he looks over at me—just a flick of the eyes, quick enough to miss if you're not watching for it.

Reporters swarm in like sharks at a drop of blood. They want a quote, a name, a face for the morning feed. I'm not ready for it, but I do what I've always done: I square my shoulders, tilt my chin, and talk. I give them the facts—step by step, no drama, just what happened and why. My voice sounds wrong to me, too loud, too certain, like I've been playing this part my whole life.

Somewhere in the flurry, Lucas's name comes up. They call him a hero, or maybe they call me one, or maybe it's both of us, tangled together in the same old story. He doesn't react, just stands there, silent and solid, letting the spotlight tilt my way for once.

When the noise ebbs, and the last camera is packed up, he comes over, crouches beside me, and says, "You did good."

He touches my knee—just a quick squeeze, not for show—and I almost lose it. Not from fear, not from the crash, but from the way he looks at me, like I'm the only thing left that matters.

"You okay?" he asks.

"Yeah," I say. "Just...tired."

He grins, all teeth and exhaustion. "I'll carry you, if you want."

I snort, the laugh sharp and real. "Not a chance. I'm fireproof, remember?"

He stands, offers me a hand. I take it, and the world tilts back into place.

We spend the next hour filling out statements, answering questions for the state boys who show up late and act like they've been running the show all along. There's a moment where it feels like it might turn on us—some suit with a badge starts asking why we went in without authorization, why I have a copy of a dead man's bomb manual, why anyone should believe two burned-out local misfits over the official narrative.

I start to panic, just a little, but Lucas steps in, voice calm and measured. He lays it out for them—how we followed the chain of evidence, how every decision was made by the book, how he was ready to take full responsibility if it meant saving lives. The way he talks, even I start to believe it. The state boys take their notes, nod, and eventually leave us alone.

I watch him, the way he fills out a report, the way he signs his name with that slow, deliberate drag of the pen. I think about what it would be like to just...stop, to let someone else take over for a while. It's terrifying, and beautiful, and I'm not sure I deserve it.

But when he looks up and catches me staring, he winks. Like it's a secret just between us.

They let us back inside to do a final walkthrough. The building is empty, the bomb squad having triple-checked every inch and left chalk marks on every cleared wire. The gym smells like sweat and ozone, the echoes of our near-death still bouncing off the rafters.

We're supposed to be collecting evidence, or maybe just decompressing, but neither of us says a word. We stand at center court, under the faded Bulldogs logo, and breathe.

The silence is different now—not the tense, waiting kind, but the heavy, satisfied kind. Like after a storm, when the air is scrubbed clean and every leaf is exactly where it's supposed to be.

I break it first. "We're not done," I say. "Rowe's still out there."

Lucas nods, slow. "We'll get him."

I shake my head. "No. There's one more fire. One more spiral. I can feel it."

He steps closer, close enough that I can feel the heat rolling off him, even through the chill of the gym.

"You trust me?" he asks, voice low.

"I wouldn't be alive if I didn't," I say, and this time, I mean it.

He puts his hands on my shoulders, then slides them down, slow, to my waist. The touch is electric, the kind of charge that makes my skin tighten and my heart hammer in my throat.

I don't think. I just move—step into him, crash our mouths together, all teeth and tongue and the taste of smoke still lingering on his lips.

He groans, low and rough, and pushes me back, gentle but insistent, until I hit the gym wall. My hands are already on his shirt, tugging it free, fingers clawing at the fabric until I get to skin.

He lifts me, easy, so my legs wrap around his hips. The wall is cold against my back, the contrast making every inch of him feel like a furnace.

We kiss like we're starving. There's no patience, no pretense, just raw need.

His hands are everywhere—under my shirt, in my hair, sliding up my thighs. When he finds the line of my underwear, he pauses, looks at me, gives me a chance to say no.

I don't.

He pushes the fabric aside, finds me wet and ready, and slides two fingers in, slow at first, then faster as I gasp against his mouth. I rock into him, greedy, shameless. Every thrust is a promise, every pulse a declaration.

He unzips his jeans, frees himself, and pushes in, the stretch sharp and perfect.

We move together, hard and desperate, the sound of our bodies echoing off the empty gym. I bite his shoulder to keep from screaming, dig my nails into his back to hold on.

He fucks me like it's the last thing he'll ever do. I let him. I want to be ruined by him.

When I come, it's like nothing I've ever felt—violent, blinding, a wave that knocks all the words from my head. He follows, hips jerking, mouth buried in my neck.

We stay like that, pressed together, catching our breath.

Eventually, he sets me down, careful, and we sink to the floor, backs against the wall, bodies tangled.

He strokes my hair, soft, and says, "You're impossible."

I grin, eyes closed. "You love that about me."

He laughs, and the sound is everything.

For a long time, we don't move. The world is just this gym, this man, this feeling.

Then, finally, I open my eyes. There's something in the air —a new tension, a new promise.

I look at him, serious now. "One more," I say. "We have to finish it."

He nods, pulls me close, and whispers, "Together."

We walk out of the school side by side, the sun blinding and the world too bright, but for the first time, I feel ready to face it.

Whatever happens next—Rowe, the fire, the spiral—I know we'll meet it head on.

And we'll win.

Or burn trying.

Also by Laci Mae Wyld

Vow of Redemption

Haunted by a debt he never wanted, former Navy SEAL Lieutenant Mason Phillips is thrust back into a world of shadows and danger when a ghost from his past calls for help. Emelio Zentarra, the arms dealer who once saved Mason's life, has been brutally murdered, leaving his daughter Yelana as the unexpected heir to a treacherous empire.

Yelana harbors resentment towards Mason, blaming him for her brother's sacrifice years ago. Their initial animosity ignites a spark of undeniable attraction as they navigate a web of deceit and peril within the Zentarra Organization. With enemies closing in and betrayal lurking at every turn, Mason and Yelana must confront their shared past and uncertain future.

As danger escalates and trust becomes a scarce commodity, Mason grapples with his true motives while Yelana faces a heart-wrenching choice between loyalty to her family legacy or embracing a love that could either save her or shatter everything she holds dear.

In a world where loyalties are tested and love comes at a cost, will they find redemption in each other's arms or will the shadows of their past consume them both?

Beneath These Ruined Walls: Whispers in the Highlands

In a quest for solace, Fi MacPherson's journey to the Scottish Highlands leads her to the haunting ruins of Sutherland Castle. A chance encounter with a Highland warrior, who fades into thin air before her eyes, initially seems like a mere illusion.

Yet, as his presence lingers in her dreams and his touch ignites a fire within her, Fi is thrust into a realm where time blurs and souls entwine across centuries.

As Fi unravels the entangled memories of Isla—a woman torn between two brothers in a bygone era—she realizes that she is destined to relive their tragic tale over and over. Lachlan, the loyal and fierce warrior, and Hamish, his jealous and vengeful brother, are forever linked with her fate.

I Do...Hate You

In the heart of a city ruled by crime, survival means embracing the darkness within.

Meli Vasquez, a fierce and clever young woman, has long been confined to a life of servitude within the walls of a notorious crime family's stronghold. When the ruthless and feared Corbin Argyros, known as "The Executor " for his lethal efficiency, unexpectedly claims her as his bride to fulfill an ancient family decree, Meli is thrust into a world of opulence, danger, and power beyond her wildest dreams.

To Corbin, Meli's defiance is an intriguing challenge, her sharp wit a valuable asset. But to Meli, he is nothing more than a monstrous captor with haunted eyes and hands that stoke a dangerous fire within her. Their fiery clashes soon give way to forbidden passion, blurring the lines between loathing and longing.

In Corbin's brutal world, where compassion is weakness and love is a liability, Meli and Corbin realize that their unlikely partnership may be their most potent weapon yet. As betrayals mount, they must stand together against all who seek to tear them apart.

Content Warning: Contains explicit language and sexual scenes, including light choking, oral sex, manual stimulation, sexual violence, murder, kidnapping, torture, physical and sexual abuse, and themes of parental death.

Mark Me

35-year-old Mica Greer harbors a talent for intricate designs and a shield against emotional entanglements. But when Nyah Summers, with her haunting past and hidden pain, walks into his life, the flames of change flicker to life.

In a bold stand against Nyah's abusive past, Mica's defiance sets off a spark that neither of them can ignore. Drawn together by shared scars and unspoken desires, their connection deepens as they navigate the shadows of their histories.

Offering Nyah refuge within his sanctuary and a role in his creative world, Mica finds himself unraveling the layers of his own defenses. As their bond intensifies from friendship to something more, they must confront the looming threat of Nyah's vindictive ex-lover.

Experience a tale where redemption emerges from chaos, and the brightest flames are forged from the depths of darkness.

Good Girl To Goddess: Dancing with Desire

Cast aside on her birthday for not fitting in a mold, Elara James sheds her timid skin and overnight becomes a bold enchantress. Guided by her loyal confidante, she swaps modest clothing for daring outfits and quiet behavior for a fearless, take-no-prisoners attitude.

For six months, Elara indulges in fleeting affairs and casual flings, vowing to avoid emotional entanglements to protect her heart. One golden rule guides her nights: never stay until dawn.

Then enters Ryker Davis—confident, commanding, and undeniably captivating. In the heat of passion, he awakens her submission to his every whim. But beyond the bedroom, he reveals a tenderness that challenges the barriers guarding her heart.

As her former lover seeks reconciliation and her closest friend leaves town, Elara faces her deepest fears alone. Will she embrace the vulnerability that comes with true desire, or retreat into the safety of emotional distance?

Betrayal of Blood

In a whirlwind of betrayal, Sarsha Mitchell's once-promising future implodes when she catches her fiancé, James, entangled with her very own sister. Reeling from the heartbreak, Sarsha takes flight, leaving the shards of her shattered dreams behind. With her picture-perfect life in ruins, she seeks solace on an impromptu getaway to their abandoned honeymoon destination with her loyal confidante, Jess.

From the sun-kissed shores of Perth to the dazzling allure of the Gold Coast, Sarsha attempts to outrun her anguish amidst carefree escapades and electrifying nights out. Just as the shadows of her past threaten to engulf her present, a chance encounter at a club propels Sarsha into an unexpected charade with a mysterious stranger named Riley.

As sparks ignite between Sarsha and Riley during their fabricated romance, healing begins to seep into her wounded soul. However, upon their return to Melbourne, old wounds are ripped open anew as James refuses to relinquish his hold on her heart while envious desires stir chaos within her own family.

Supported by Riley's unwavering presence and unwavering gallantry, Sarsha finds the courage to confront the toxicity suffusing her familial bonds. Yet just as hope blossoms for a brighter tomorrow, a cruel act of revenge orchestrated by James and Megan threatens to shatter everything they hold dear.

In a race against time and treachery, Sarsha stands vigil by Riley's bedside, clinging to hope amidst the turmoil. Together, they uncover the depths of deceit woven by those she once trusted most. With Riley's love paving the way towards redemption and renewal, Sarsha severs the ties that bind her to darkness and steps boldly into a future brimming with promise.

www.ingramcontent.com/pod-product-compliance
Lightning Source LLC
LaVergne TN
LVHW050916080826
845145LV00001B/104

* 9 7 8 1 7 6 4 5 1 6 9 1 4 *